It's 1925 in Los Angeles, and motor patrol officer Del Randolph keeps making one mistake after another. Struggling to keep his job with the Los Angeles Police Department, Del is also lonely and heartbroken after his last lover left him.

But then he meets Ev, a gentle but cynical invert, and has his heart stolen again. Del knows he's no great catch—he isn't smart or particularly handsome or rich—but he's determined to show Ev how much he loves him.

Unfortunately, his misguided attempts at winning Ev's affections might end up destroying their relationship instead. Del joins a hapless gang of bootleggers to try to make some money but quickly winds up in trouble. Soon he's in debt, breaking the law, and lying to Ev about all of it.

My Baby Chased Away the Blues

R.A. Thorn

A NineStar Press Publication

Published by NineStar Press
P.O. Box 91792,
Albuquerque, New Mexico, 87199 USA.
www.ninestarpress.com

My Baby Chased Away the Blues

Printed in the USA
First Edition
July, 2019

Print ISBN: 978-1-950412-97-6

Also available in eBook, ISBN: 978-1-950412-96-9

Warning: This book contains sexually explicit content, which may only be suitable for mature readers, racism, homophobia, mentions of domestic violence, police violence, and forced sex.

To MJ and Gabi

Chapter One

DEL POINTED AT the double white line running down the center of the road. "See that?" he said to the motorist he had stopped. "You need to stay on the right side of those lines, Mr...?"

"Hollister. My name is Ernie Hollister. I own a bakery on Thomas Street—that's where I'm headed now, in fact, and I'm going to be late. All I did was stray slightly—very slightly—to the side of that line." An indignant flush covered Hollister's cheeks as he glared at Del through the open window of his car.

Del strove to keep his tone polite, wishing Hollister would keep his voice down at the very least. "You were all the way over in the other lane, sir. And you missed that stop sign back at the last crossroads."

Hollister spluttered. "I did no such thing, officer. More to the point, this traffic situation has gotten completely out of hand. Two years ago, we didn't have any lines on the road. A year ago, it was a single line. Now it's a double one. Where is this all going to end? Doesn't the government of Los Angeles trust a grown man to drive an automobile?"

"Thousands of people die in accidents every year, sir. We need to make the roads as safe as possible."

"I was in no danger of causing an accident. It's four in the morning— no one else is on the road."

"I was on the road," Del pointed out. "And you never know when another car might appear, or a pedestrian, or a streetcar."

"There is such a thing as being overzealous in the pursuit of duty," Hollister said, growing more heated. "Interfering with law-abiding citizens and tagging them for no good reason—why aren't you out catching bootleggers or raiding a speakeasy? There's enough of them in this town to keep the whole passel of you busy."

Del looked away from Hollister's outraged expression, focusing on the traffic tag and trying to keep his hand steady as he wrote the information. He couldn't afford to have citizens making complaints to Captain Gardner about him.

"I'm a traffic patrolman, sir. My job is to enforce the laws." He handed the tag to Mr. Hollister, who snatched it from him, almost tearing the paper.

"Mark my words, officer, you will hear the full measure of my displeasure. I shall speak to your captain this afternoon."

So much for being polite. But being rude to Hollister would only make it worse, so he said, "Yes, sir," and waited for Hollister to drive away in a huff before returning to his motorcycle and heading back to the police station. His shift was almost over, and he still needed to write up his report.

The streets of Lincoln Heights were pretty deserted in the early hours of the morning, but there were always those like Mr. Hollister who thought obeying traffic laws was a choice rather than a requirement, and it was his duty to deal with them. But he did hope Hollister wouldn't follow through on his threat. His appointment to the motor patrol had come about mainly through luck. Carl Hutton was supposed to get the position, but his mother had fallen ill, and Carl had taken time off to look after her. Captain Gardner promoted Del instead, elevating him from his previous duties of walking a beat and directing traffic at an intersection. Now he got to ride a motorcycle, which he loved, and his pay had been raised too. But Carl's mother had passed away two weeks ago, and now Carl was back on the force. Any slip up on Del's part and Carl would be there to take his place.

At the station, Del parked his motorcycle and headed inside to write his report and change out of his uniform. As he came around the corner of the building, he ran right into Tom Kirkpatrick.

"Well, if it isn't Mr. Minus," Kirkpatrick said, a smirk twisting his mouth. Kirkpatrick worked on the morals squad and had several years' seniority over Del, although he was still a harness bull, not a detective.

"I told you not to call me that," Del mumbled, avoiding Kirkpatrick's eyes and wishing yet again he had never acquired the stupid nickname.

It had all started when Chief August Vollmer came down from the Berkeley Police Department the year before. A bunch of the reformers in town who thought the police were too cozy with the politicians at City Hall asked Vollmer to reform the department and weed out some of the corruption. Vollmer gave a big speech about how policemen should be drawn from the best of the nation's manhood and how the department should operate on a professional basis. Officers needed to be appointed based on their qualifications, not because some commissioner owed them a favor, he'd said. Vollmer made all of the cops, Del included, take a whole bunch of intelligence tests. The Army Alpha to start with, followed by psychological tests, and even a test where you had to write an essay. Del had made it through the seventh grade, but he had never been able to write a decent essay to save his life.

Harry Mackenzie sneaked a look at everyone's scores and told Del he'd gotten a "C-minus" on the Army Alpha. Del wasn't sure if that was true or not—Mackenzie could be a real shit when he wanted to be—but he knew he hadn't scored an "A" either. Luckily, Vollmer gave up when it became clear the mayor and his cronies at City Hall didn't intend to surrender their influence over the police. Vollmer went back to his high-hat college cops that he recruited from the university in Berkeley, and the LAPD settled back into its usual rhythms of bribery and payoffs before anybody could fire Del for not having enough smarts. He thought the whole thing was bunk—he didn't need to have gone to college to know when someone blew through a stop sign.

But Mackenzie blabbed about the scores to Kirkpatrick, and Kirkpatrick took to calling Del "Mr. Minus." Del knew he wasn't smart. Only last week Lieutenant Miller called him into his office to reprimand him for a number of misspellings in Del's reports and ordered Del to improve his handwriting because he couldn't read a "damn word of his chicken scratch." In fact, it would be best if Del typed his reports, Miller had decided. Del had attempted the typewriter yesterday and dreaded his next encounter. It took him a good minute to type most words, as he had to hunt for every letter, plus the paper got stuck and ended up all crumpled when he finally managed to yank it free.

He was trying his best—he'd spent all winter studying traffic laws until he could recite them backward and forward in order to qualify for the motor patrol. When he got the promotion, he figured Kirkpatrick would stop with the nickname, but it appeared it was going to stick with him his whole career. He didn't get people like Kirkpatrick, always trying to run a fellow down. Del had never done anything to him except be born a few years later. Sure, the veterans gave all the rookies in the department a hard time, and he shouldn't give a damn what Kirkpatrick called him, but the nickname hit a sore spot.

"Don't call you that?" Kirkpatrick laughed. "I can call you whatever I want, Randolph."

William Brooks, another cop on the morals squad, strolled over and slapped Kirkpatrick on the shoulder. "Ah, leave the kid alone, Tommy. Let's go write our report. The missus said she'd cook sausages this morning. Don't know about you, but I'm starving."

Kirkpatrick snorted, but he turned to go inside. Del would have liked to avoid their company, but he couldn't very well hang around on the front steps, so he followed a pace or two behind. Brooks and Kirkpatrick started bickering about a bet they had going over whether Dazzy Vance would pitch a no-hitter in his next game with the Brooklyn Robins, but Sergeant Friedman, stationed at the front desk, motioned for them to be quiet.

"What the hell, Friedman?" Kirkpatrick said. "You think the bums in the drunk tank are gonna complain?"

"You know who walked in here not ten minutes ago?" Friedman replied, his voice hushed. "Dick Lucas. His car's parked down the block."

That silenced Kirkpatrick, and Del swallowed, looking uneasily down the hallway.

"The Gray Wolf's enforcer, huh?" Brooks said. "Damn—does he have business with Captain Gardner?"

"I guess so. Captain's been here all night—word is there was some trouble with the Italians."

"Crawford wouldn't take too kindly to any infringements on his territory, that's for sure."

Kirkpatrick nodded. "Yeah, those wops should know better than to try and take over any of the legging from the Gray Wolf."

Del, still hovering behind them, experienced a sick thrill at the idea of meeting anyone connected with Charlie Crawford. Crawford, known to many as "the Gray Wolf," controlled the vice trade in the city.

"This might be a good opportunity to introduce ourselves to Lucas," Brooks mused. "Let him know that if he ever needs the right men for a job, we're available."

Del sidled off in the opposite direction from Captain Gardner's office. Maybe Brooks would consider trying to get the attention of the Gray Wolf of Spring Street, but he sure as heck wasn't about to risk it. Certainly not with Dick Lucas. That guy walked around the downtown police station in broad daylight with a Thompson submachine gun slung over his shoulder, bold as brass. He'd brush Del away like an irritating fly.

The typewriter went about as well as Del had expected, and the sun was rising by the time he finally left. He squinted against its brilliance as he took the streetcar home. Maybe soon the lieutenant would give him a few more day shifts. Night shifts weren't as bad in the summer, but he still wouldn't mind going to sleep when it was dark instead of having to block the light in his bedroom as best he could. Then there were all the daily noises of his apartment building to contend with—kids shouting, people talking and listening to the radio, water pipes clanking, and alligators barking.

He had chosen his apartment based on the attractive price, which had seemed low considering the spacious rooms, private telephone, and full electricity. Only after he'd moved in had he discovered it was near the alligator farm located across from Lincoln Park. The gators' raspy, throaty bellows sounded day and night. There had to be hundreds of alligators there, and if a couple of them got going, it sure made a racket. At least he was on the second floor. Mrs. Howser down the street had found an alligator in her backyard one morning, and every time the rains got heavy, a couple of the gators escaped the fences around their ponds and relocated to the park to the delight of the kids and terror of their parents.

But moving seemed a lot of effort, and he could endure loud alligators in exchange for the telephone and lower rent. Even with his higher salary, the bills seemed to pile up, and he always had to send money to his father every month. Aunt Sophie might be willing to let her brother live with them, but some extra cash made it easier. His father's bad leg meant he wasn't able to work anymore, and he depended on Del to help.

His last lover, Lawrence, sure had hated Del's apartment, though. Lawrence hadn't liked a lot of things, including the green and yellow chintz armchair Del now sat in while undoing the laces on his boots and then pulling them off. Personally, Del thought the colors were a cheerful combination, and it had been on sale. But after he'd wrestled the thing up the stairs, Lawrence had made him cover it with a sheet.

"Those are appalling colors, Del," he'd said. "What were you thinking? It's going to give me a headache looking at it."

"I thought you would like it," Del had mumbled. "You were saying as how I didn't have any comfortable chairs here, and you wanted somewhere nice to sit and listen to the radio." At the time, he had only had the four hard-backed chairs around the kitchen table.

"I didn't mean you should run and buy the reject from the upholsterer's bargain bin," Lawrence had replied.

Of course, nothing Del did was ever good enough for Lawrence. He'd ended up leaving Del for a rich stockbroker who had a fancy car and could take him on vacations in Florida.

It was the story of his life, really. No matter how hard he tried, he always came up short.

ONE BOWL OF Post Toasties later, he climbed into bed, hoping the alligators were in a good mood today. Either they were or he was too tired to be disturbed because when he woke, it was midafternoon. He wasn't working that night, so he lay in bed awhile before rousing and scrounging some more substantial food in the kitchen. He was finishing his fried eggs when the phone rang.

"Del Randolph here," he answered.

"Hey, Del; it's Glen."

"Oh, hey, pal. Somethin' the matter?"

"What, a guy can't call up a friend now? I want to know how things are with you."

Del could hear the ringing of more phones in the background and figured Glen must be at the office.

"Everything is Jake."

"That so? Then what are you planning on doing this evening? I want it on the level too."

Del twisted the phone cord around his finger. "I don't know. Hadn't thought about it yet."

Glen sighed. "You're still in a funk, aren't you? Dammit, you have to get over that lousy kid. It's been what—three months now?"

"Lawrence wasn't lousy. Things just didn't work out."

"He was lousy. Using you like that—and you letting him do it."

"I didn't."

A frustrated noise from Glen. "Look, we aren't going to have this argument again. I'm calling to say you should go out tonight. Have some fun. Don't sit stewing in your apartment."

"I guess." He rubbed a hand over his unshaven jaw. "Will you come along?"

"Can't. It's crazy here today. Yesterday the sheriff raided that actor Willard Louis's mansion and found a couple thousand bucks worth of liquor. I'm supposed to go interview one of his former costars and see if I can uncover some more dirt."

Glen worked as a reporter for the *Los Angeles Examiner* and kept odd hours. It wasn't often they managed to have the same night off.

"Guess the cold water men must have been making a fuss to send the sheriff after a Hollywood star, huh?" Del hesitated. "I don't know. If you can't make it, maybe I'll stay in."

"No. Go out. You tried the Elephant's Ear yet? It's a dive, but I heard a pretty bouquet of pansies is there almost every night."

He told Glen he would go, mostly to get Glen off his back, but that evening found him putting on his nicest suit and splashing on some extra Aqua Velva when he finished shaving. Glen was right—he couldn't mope around over Lawrence forever.

GLEN HAD GIVEN him the instructions for finding the speakeasy and the password to get in the door. Located in the rear rooms of a drab and cramped tailor's shop with a phalanx of mannequins in front of the door, the Elephant's Ear proved to be a dive indeed.

A motley array of wobbly tables and chairs cluttered the space while cigarette smoke and the scent of fried oysters thickened the air. The proprietor was too cheap for a live pianist, relying on an old player piano instead that was creaking its way through out-of-tune rags that had been popular before the war. Still, when Del ordered his drink it tasted like the real McCoy, not the doctored swill they'd had to put up with since the Great Drought began.

The joint wasn't too crowded yet. A large party occupied a table in the corner, loud and boisterous, one of the girls already spiffled, her movements sloppy as she hung onto the arm of her beau. Two men were at another table, bent over a game of cards. A third table definitely had some of the pansies Glen had promised, but Del didn't like the looks of them—too brassy, the carmine on their lips too red, their eyes too bright and sharp.

He'd almost decided to leave because he'd never find someone who could compare to Lawrence in a place like this, when the door opened, and a young man stepped into the room.

Del knew in a second he was a fairy with his plucked eyebrows, manicured nails, and the sway in his hips. He wore slim trousers with a gray vest over a green shirt. A lamé coat, covered in brocade roses and really too heavy for a June night, hung from his shoulders, complemented by a copper-colored turban hat. The clothes treaded the line between legal and illegal, the coat and hat clearly feminine, the rest more masculine—although nothing about this enchanting stranger could really be called masculine.

Unlike the fairies sitting at the table, he had a natural grace, captured in the curve of his neck and tilt of his shoulders. If the others were bright and flashy, he was elegant and sweet. In the dim light, he stood out like— well, like one of the electric windows at Bullock's department store on Broadway. Del had read a similar description of the romantic interest in a story in the *Saturday Evening Post*, but had never expected to have such a person wander into his own life.

As Del stared, entranced, the fairy's expression...*softened*. When he first walked in, his mouth had been set, his eyes flickering over the room, assessing its occupants, one shoulder half-turned to the door, ready to vanish back into the summer night. But now he sighed, a small frown line appearing between his brows, his eyes almost wistful for a moment as he gathered his coat close about his throat. Weary, he looked, and gentle. Then he pivoted, coat flying open again as he released it, preparing to leave.

Del was on his feet before he was quite aware of it.

"Hey," he said, gaining this enchanting vision's side in a few breathless strides, catching him just as his hand landed on the doorknob.

Hazel eyes snapped over to meet his. The softness had disappeared, replaced by a calculating wariness.

Del cleared his throat. "Can I buy you a drink?"

An appraising look in reply, eyes traveling down and back up his body. And then a smile. Not gentle, no, that was gone, but sultry and practiced.

"Since you're offering, mister, sure. I'll have a highball."

"Call me Del," he said, daring to put his hand on the fairy's arm to guide him toward the table. "Watch out for the chair—the one leg's shorter than the rest."

"Oh, thanks." He sat down, shrugged off his coat, and fished out a cigarette.

Del fumbled for a light. "What can I call you?" he asked when it became apparent the information was not going to be volunteered.

After allowing Del to light his cigarette, he took a drag and then murmured, "My name's Ev."

Del repeated it with a smile and ordered Ev his highball.

"This is my first time here," Del said after a minute.

"It isn't much, is it?" Ev wrinkled his nose. "You'd think they could at least wipe off the tables. And open a damn window."

"I'm glad I came here, though. I mean, now that I've met you and all," he hurried to explain.

"I knew what you meant. You need better lines than that if you want to surprise—or amuse—me." Ev stubbed out his cigarette and sipped his drink.

Ev's dismissive reply to the compliment, which Del had meant sincerely, took him aback, so he tried another avenue of conversation. "Been in town long?"

"About five years, I guess." Ev's eyes roamed the room, bored.

"I've been here for eight. My family moved out during the war so my father could work at one of the shipyards. Where are you from?"

"Texas."

"Oh, yeah, I noticed your accent a little. You like it here?"

Ev crossed his legs, frowning. "What's with all the questions?"

"Sorry." Del smoothed his hands over his trousers. "I only wanted to know a little bit more about you. You can ask me anything too, if you want." Although he hoped Ev wouldn't inquire about his line of work. It was better to ease up to that, once it was clear he wasn't trying to trap Ev and haul him in for lewd vagrancy.

Ev finished off his drink and then waved a hand at Del. "I've got all the answers I need right here. And my answer is yes, in case you were wondering."

"Your answer?"

Ev frowned again. "You do want to come back to my place, right?"

"I—of course," Del stuttered. A flare of heat went through him at the thought of getting to curl his hands around Ev's slim hips and kiss the smooth skin on his shoulders.

"There you go then. Get me another drink, will you? I want to get completely zozzled tonight."

WHEN THEY LEFT the Elephant's Ear, Ev said that his apartment was only about a twenty-minute walk away, over by the river. Del offered to get a cab, but Ev declared he wanted to enjoy the night air.

"Besides, if I don't sober up a little, we won't get to do much," he added, slipping a hand under Del's jacket and tugging on his vest. "That would be a shame, wouldn't it?"

Del agreed it would be, his voice rough, and Ev laughed. So they walked, and Del grabbed Ev's arm every time it looked like Ev was going to wander off the curb.

"You're sweet, aren't you?" Ev said the third time it happened. "I've gotten myself a real live gentleman."

His steps paused, and Del halted, hand still on Ev's elbow.

"It's nice," Ev said softly, and for a moment, gentle fingers touched Del's.

Then Ev was walking again, pulling away from Del's grip. "But don't be *too* nice. I like it pretty hard and fast. I can take whatever you want to dish out."

Del hurried after him, caught between arousal and regret that Ev's gentleness had been covered again, giving him only the briefest of glimpses.

Ev's apartment building sat on a little side street that ran perpendicular to the riverbanks. It looked as though the neighborhood had gone to seed in the last few years, the former houses converted into flats and apartments. Ev unlocked the door to his rooms after a little fumbling, jiggling the knob when it jammed.

"Oh good, Camilo isn't home," he said when a dark room greeted them. "That means I don't have to be too quiet. Of course, the neighbors will probably make a fuss. They sure got upset the other night when I had a fellow over."

An irrational surge of jealousy at the thought of Ev with another man made him grab Ev's wrist, pulling him against his body. Ev was maybe an inch shorter than him, and he stared up into Del's face, running his tongue over his bottom lip. Del lifted the wrist he had grabbed and pressed a kiss there, soothing.

"First things first," Ev whispered and went to a cabinet, rummaging around and pulling out a wine bottle. It looked like pretty cheap foot juice, and it tasted like it too, when Ev had poured each of them a tumbler full, clinking the mismatched glasses together.

"Thought you were trying to sober up," Del said, and Ev shrugged, pouring himself another glass and spilling some on the table.

"Finish yours too," he demanded after draining the second glass, and Del swigged his last mouthful, grimacing, and then followed Ev into his bedroom.

Ev turned on the gas lamp—no electricity in this place yet. It cast a weak sphere of light over the immediate surroundings. They consisted of a vanity, cluttered with cosmetics, paste jewelry, and a curling iron; a chair, piled with a mound of colorful scarves; a dresser with a broken leg, propped up on a stack of magazines; and the bed, narrow and covered in a thin blanket. The room spoke as eloquently of Ev's financial situation as the cheap wine and shabby building.

Del couldn't have cared less. All his attention was fixed on Ev, who was kicking off his shoes and unbuttoning his shirt. When Ev shoved down his trousers, Del's heart played a quick game of Double Dutch because silk stockings encased Ev's legs, and he wore a peach-colored step-in hanging from lacy straps on his shoulders.

Ev sat down on the bed and tugged the stockings carefully back into place. "Pretty, aren't they?"

"Gorgeous," Del assured him, a catch in his voice, and Ev glanced up at him, a pleased flush spreading over his cheeks.

"You can touch, you know."

That was all the permission Del needed. His shoes joined Ev's in a pile on the floor. Gently, he pushed Ev farther up the bed so he could kneel on the mattress and smooth his hands up Ev's legs. The silk snagged on his calluses, but when he reached the bare skin at the top of Ev's thighs, the roughness made Ev visibly shiver and spread his legs a little wider. Ev sucked in a breath and held it as Del finally fit his palm over Ev's cock through his step-ins. Ev pushed up his hips, and then let them drop again, making a moue of disappointment when Del moved his hand, sliding it over the hollow of Ev's stomach and then stretching out his fingers across Ev's chest, grazing one of his nipples that peeked above the lacy top.

"Catch me, if I let you have all the fun," Ev complained, tugging at Del's collar. "Take it off." He started pulling at a button but couldn't get it undone thanks to the angle and the alcohol in his system.

"Here, I got it." Del popped the button and followed with the rest, all down the line. The shirt came off, and he pulled his undershirt over his head, tossing it onto the foot of the bed.

"That's what I wanted," Ev said, happy now, sitting up to feel the muscles in Del's arms and shoulders. He slipped his arms around Del then and brought their faces close together. Del kissed him, and Ev's mouth softened against his. He cupped Ev's ass in his hands, squeezing, and Ev wriggled, mumbling out some variation of "hell, yes," against his lips.

"What else have you got for me?" Ev asked when they broke apart. He pulled on the fly of Del's trousers, humming appreciatively when he got it open far enough to reach in and take out Del's cock. "You're already so worked up," he added, trailing his knuckles along the underside and up to the wet head.

"I want you real bad," Del agreed, leaning forward so Ev tipped backward onto the mattress again.

Ev giggled, wrapping his legs around Del's thighs. "I can see that."

It brought his cock against Ev's, and it felt like heaven to roll his hips and think about how good it was going to be when he got inside Ev and fucked him.

Ev was making impatient noises and trying to get his garters and stockings off. Del caught his hands.

"Hey, take it easy. You don't want to ruin your pretty things."

Ev panted for a second, tense, and then relaxed. He stretched out his legs. "Go on, then."

So Del carefully rolled each stocking down Ev's legs and gave his foot a little squeeze at the end. Fingers shaking a little, he reached in between Ev's thighs to unbutton the step-in and push it aside, showing Ev's cock curving up toward his stomach.

"There's some lotion on the table, there," Ev said. For some reason, he had hidden his eyes under his arm.

Del reached for the bottle and poured a dollop into his hand. "You all right?"

"Yes." Ev took his arm away, revealing a defiant expression, and dug his toes into Del's leg. "Getting sick of waiting—ah—ahhh."

Del stroked Ev's cock again, pulling more gasps out of Ev. Then he pushed Ev's thighs wider with one hand and reached down with the other to slide a finger inside him.

By the time he had loosened Ev up, they were both getting sweaty. Ev had his eyes shut, forehead wrinkling every time Del pumped his fingers. He moaned when Del pulled them out entirely and lifted Ev's legs, settling them against his shoulders.

Del shut his eyes too as he entered Ev, opening them only when he was fully inside to press a kiss on the inside of Ev's knee and wait for him to relax. Then he kept his thrusts shallow and fast until Ev went boneless and arched into it. Pausing, he gave Ev's cock some more attention, Ev screwing up his eyes and jabbing a heel into Del's back.

But when Del pulled out and let his legs fall, Ev's eyes opened, wide and confused.

"Come up here for me," Del said, grabbing his arm and tugging.

Ev nodded, catching on. They rearranged themselves, Ev straddling Del, who sat against the bedstead for support. He'd pushed his trousers down, but didn't want to take the time to untangle them from his legs. He got his cock back inside Ev, and they moved together, the bed springs creaking. Del gripped Ev's hips, grunting with effort, Ev's cock sticky against his stomach.

He'd been expecting Ev to be loud, given his earlier comment, but he wasn't, often completely silent except for his heavy breaths panted against Del's ear. He did make the sweetest moan when he finally came, though, pulsing into Del's fist and then sagging against his chest. Del kissed his sweaty temple and lifted him, his cock slipping out of Ev's body. Ev sat back a little, watching as Del jerked himself to completion.

For a moment, Ev seemed to waver, leaning toward Del again, as though he were going to curl against Del's chest, all tired and warm. But no—Ev pulled away and climbed off the bed, slipping into a pale green kimono and going to fetch a cloth to clean up the mess.

He hoped Ev wasn't going to kick him out. He didn't want to leave—wanted to stay, to spend as much time in Ev's company as he could. And when Ev didn't say anything upon his return from the kitchen with a wet cloth, he took the initiative to put his shorts and undershirt back on and slide beneath the covers. Still no comment from Ev, who was standing in front of his dresser, as though undecided about something. Then, his movements stiff, he let the kimono fall to the ground, pooling around his feet, took a cotton nightgown out of a drawer, and pulled it over his head. The off-white fabric hung loosely around his hips, straining a little against his chest, and Del's breath caught at how the lace looked, running across his shoulder blades.

Still silent, Ev climbed into bed again. The two of them had to cram together to fit. Del shifted onto his side to give them more room, and their knees knocked together. He couldn't help reaching out to pet Ev's hip and feel the soft fabric, warmed with his body heat. Ev turned his face into the pillow, and for a moment, Del could see that gentle, soft grace in him again that he had noticed when Ev first came in the door at the Elephant's Ear.

But then Ev said, "Turn the lamp off, will you?" and after Del had stretched out an arm to reach it, leaving them in darkness, the mood between them changed. Ev turned to his other side, his back to Del. He could have slipped an arm around him, but something in Ev's posture and his silence suggested that would be unwelcome, and so Del could only lie there, trying to breathe quietly, because Lawrence had always complained he couldn't sleep with Del's snoring and snuffling, hoping that maybe Ev would let him kiss him again come the morning.

More than anything, he wanted to try and bring that softness back to Ev. What had happened to Ev in the past to drive it into hiding, appearing only for brief, unguarded moments, he didn't know. He imagined it would be quite wonderful to have Ev speak gently to him and perhaps smile tenderly, pleased to have him there.

Chapter Two

HE WOKE TO a cool breeze drifting over his face and the smell of burned toast. Blinking his eyes open, he found himself staring at Ev's bedside table and the issue of *Vogue* that lay upon it. Curtains fluttered in an open window above. He rolled onto his back and discovered Ev lounging next to him in his kimono, nibbling around the charred sections on a piece of toast, and staring at him.

"Morning," Del said as he sat up and leaned over for a kiss. This seemed natural, still half-asleep as he was, giving Ev good-morning kisses the only proper course of action.

Ev's hand in the middle of his chest stopped him.

"We did enough of that last night. There's coffee in the kitchen if you want a cup. Bathroom is down the hall. You know the way out."

Del opened his mouth, brought into unpleasant alertness by this cold reception. But he paused, unsure of what to say. Granted, Ev hadn't spent the night cuddling in his arms—as he would have preferred—but Ev had certainly been a willing and enthusiastic participant in the evening's earlier activities. To reject even a small kiss...

After a few moments of silence, in which Ev ignored him in favor of picking over the remains of his toast, he finally got out of the bed. Ev had piled up all his clothes in a messy lump on the chair. He dressed slowly, glancing at Ev to see if there was any change in his demeanor, but Ev remained aloof, tugging his kimono closer around his chest and transferring his attention from the toast to *Vogue*.

Del didn't know what to say to break the silence, but he had a sinking feeling that once he left the bedroom, he would not regain admittance easily.

At last he stammered, "I'll see you later then?"

But Ev only hummed noncommittally and turned a page.

Swallowing a reluctant sigh, he opened the bedroom door and let it fall closed behind him. In the kitchen, Del discovered another man frying some eggs. He had darker skin and an accent blurred his words when he spoke. Del was somewhat taken aback that Ev was living with a foreigner, but then, he'd already figured out that Ev probably couldn't afford to rent in a better neighborhood.

"There is still coffee in the pot," the man said and nodded at a blue mug placed beside it. "I'm Camilo," he added, smiling. "A lovely morning, isn't it?"

"I'm Del." He would like to think Ev had left the mug there for him, but perhaps Camilo had put it out.

Camilo did not seem surprised at Del's presence. When he saw Del glancing at Ev's bedroom door, he laughed. "Everett will not be out until noon at the earliest. He is sleeping again, very likely."

"Oh." Del sipped his coffee, mulling over the fact that Ev's full name was Everett.

"I've lived here several months now, so I know he does not like early mornings," Camilo continued, flipping his eggs onto a plate. "I emigrated from the Philippines last year. My boarding house was terrible—all night it was music and such disgraceful food—and so my darling José introduced me to Ev, who needed someone to share the rent."

Del nodded. Camilo seemed a friendly sort, but he really wanted to be talking to Ev. And not just talking—he wanted Ev's attention, affection, and interest. He wanted to see his pretty hazel eyes again and kiss him and make him smile. Unfortunately, though, he couldn't remain in Ev's kitchen all day waiting for him to emerge from the bedroom. Grimacing, he drained his coffee mug. "Guess I'll head out."

Camilo waved, and after a last glance at Ev's bedroom, Del left the apartment. Ev's window didn't face the street, and so he turned toward home, rubbing at the stubble on his chin. Come to think of it, maybe the reason Ev had ignored him that morning was because he'd made no effort to compliment Ev or tell him how perfect he'd been the night before. He was no smooth-talker, but he could have made more of an effort instead of gawping at Ev like a fool.

The idea that maybe he'd missed his chance with Ev made him restless and frustrated. Back at his apartment, after a shave and some breakfast, he collected his laundry and hauled it three blocks over to Mrs. Huang and then headed over to Glen's, seeing as it was a Sunday and Glen usually didn't go into the office that day. He needed to talk to *someone* about Ev or he'd burst.

Glen had moved into a bungalow last autumn and ever since seemed to spend half his life engaged in trying to fix broken things. He was working on the door of the garden shed when Del arrived and let himself in the side gate. His dog, Greta, came bounding over, barking, and Del crouched down to tousle her ears.

"Hand me that wrench, will you?" Glen grunted as he drew near, and Del fished in the toolbox for it.

"What's wrong this time?" he asked.

"This blamed handle won't latch right. But damned if I can figure out how it *should* work." Glen stopped talking in favor of breathing heavily and trying to contort himself to see the underside of the handle. Finally he gave it a good whack with the wrench and sat back, scowling.

Del chuckled and picked up a stick to throw for Greta.

"I'd like to see you try fixing it," Glen said sourly. "Anyway, enough of this. I've got some root beer in the icebox. Let's have a couple, and you can tell me how last night went."

"His name is Ev," Del said as soon as they were settled in Glen's kitchen, root beer in hand, Greta placated with a milk bone for the loss of her stick.

"Oh, so you *did* go out. Didn't I say you'd find someone at that joint?"

"But you should have been there when Ev walked in. He was like—like a blooming lily in a field of weeds." Usually he couldn't think of such poetic sentiments, but Ev inspired him.

Glen snorted. "That pretty, huh?"

"Beautiful," Del corrected.

"And how did the rest of the night go?"

He twisted the bottle in his hands, willing his face not to turn red. "Pretty swell."

Glen smirked and leaned back in his chair.

"I'm gonna go back to the Elephant's Ear soon as I can, and maybe Ev will be there again. If he isn't... Do you think turning up at his door would be regular? Or do you think he'd get mad?"

Glen's chair clumped back onto the floor. "Hold on—what's all this about seeing him again? You got your fun."

"Yeah, but Ev is... Ev is... I, well, I want to see him again, that's all."

Glen frowned. "Now look here, Del. I told you to go out so you could forget about Lawrence, not fall into the whole mess all over again."

He shook his head. "I want to see Ev again," he repeated.

"You get attached too damn easily. Besides, if you're so keen on him, why are you here in my kitchen instead of in bed with him still?"

Del hesitated. "He didn't want me to stay this morning," he admitted.

"So this is just you, then, throwing yourself at another punk who's going to hurt you."

"Ev is different."

"You've known him for less than twenty-four hours. How the devil can you be sure?"

How could he explain to Glen the softness he had glimpsed and that called to him? It reminded him of a small, starving animal desperate for someone to shelter it, to give it affection and nourish it. He suspected that Ev willingly showed that side of himself to only a very, very small group of people. He wanted to be counted among their number. But such thoughts would sound absurd if he voiced them.

"Since I don't know him, then it's all the more reason for me to spend time with him," he concluded. Let Glen try to contest that piece of logic!

Glen sighed and rubbed his forehead. "Just...be careful."

"I will. If Ev tells me to get lost, I'll go, and I won't pine over him. I promise."

"You better not." Glen gave him a long look and then stood up, going into the other room and returning with a magazine. "*Outdoor Life* came in the mail today. We've got to get up to Big Tujunga Creek for some fishing soon."

Del nodded vaguely, his mind still on Ev. But if he said any more on the subject, Glen would only berate him for being stupid and giving his heart away too easily. So he forced his attention to the magazine. "Anything good in the advertisements?"

"These Heddon reels look mighty tempting," Glen said, flipping through the pages. "And there's something called Nostealum hooks. The ad says they stop the fish from skinning off your hook—imagine that."

He grabbed the magazine from Glen to see for himself. He was well acquainted with fish and their wily habits and would gladly accept any help he could find, although the price seemed a bit steep for what was, in the end, a little piece of metal.

DEL LIKED FISHING, and Glen was mad about it, along with camping and climbing and anything else that gave him an excuse to get into the mountains or a forest. But although talking about flies and casting distracted Del, it didn't take his mind completely away from Ev.

He had to work that night, but the very next chance he got he went back to the Elephant's Ear. One of the mannequins in the tailor shop had acquired a fedora set at a rakish angle, the souvenir of a drunk customer, perhaps, but other than that, it was the same dingy, cheap dive as before. Del's suit was freshly pressed, and he took a seat where he could watch the door. He nursed his drink, waiting and waiting, but Ev never showed. Finally he had to give up and go home. His next night off, it was the same story.

Both times—and every day as well—he thought about going to Ev's apartment and knocking on the door. He turned the idea over in his mind once again as he cruised along the midnight streets about a week and a half after meeting Ev. Ev's failure to appear at the Elephant's Ear didn't necessarily mean he would refuse to see Del again. After all, they had never agreed on a place to meet, and Ev hadn't liked the Elephant's Ear much. But if he went to Ev's apartment, and Ev refused him to his face, it would all be over without having properly gotten started.

Of course, he couldn't ignore Ev's cold greeting the morning after they slept together. But Camilo had said Ev didn't like waking up early. Probably he had just been in a crabby mood given the hour. If he really hadn't liked Del, he wouldn't have hauled him off to his bed a mere hour after meeting him, would he? Besides, at the time Del had been too groggy and tongue-tied to properly express his feelings.

He was turning the question of what to do over in his mind for the umpteenth time when he arrived for work on Thursday night and wasn't really paying attention beyond exchanging greetings with the other men when Brooks grabbed him by the shoulder and yanked him to a halt.

"Hey, Randolph, listen up when someone calls your name."

"Sorry. I didn't hear you."

"No kidding. Anyway, come with me. A raid's going down at that hall on Sichel Street where those Reds set up shop a few weeks ago. Captain wants a few more hands on deck."

He'd never been on a raid before, although it was the standard practice when any union or communist agitators came into town. Anyone who was too slow to make an escape during a raid got arrested and were either floated over the county line or ended up in jail. Some of the cops took great pleasure in roughing up the prisoners before hauling them to court on vagrancy charges.

He obeyed Brooks's summons, piling into a squad car with Brooks, Kirkpatrick, and Carl Hutton. Del bit back a groan when he saw Carl, who gave him a friendly smile and frowned when Kirkpatrick called Del "Mr. Minus." Even though Del had taken the position on the motor patrol that should have been his, Carl was never anything but genial. That was the problem with Carl—he was such a decent fellow that Del couldn't resent him for being so much more skilled at the job. Carl had scored an "A" on the Army Alpha, earned the praise of the Chief for his marksmanship, and helped make an arrest in a high-profile robbery case. Carl could probably type a mile a minute.

Del kept his mouth shut and stared out the window, willing Brooks to drive faster.

By the time they made it to Sichel Street, most of the excitement was over. A line of sullen men and women were sitting on the curb, watched over by two cops with nightsticks. A broken chair and glass from a smashed window littered the lawn, and several officers were dumping papers into an oilcan and burning them. One of the Reds was still putting up a fight, yelling at an officer carrying out a bundle of paper, but a sergeant slammed his fist into the man's stomach and then wrestled him onto the ground. Another sergeant kicked the man in the ribs.

Del looked away. He knew the police's job was to scare the Reds bad enough that they decided Los Angeles was too dangerous a place to set up shop. But that man hadn't been hurting anyone, and he couldn't understand how a bunch of leaflets and circulars could cause that much harm in the first place. Of course, he wasn't too clear on what it was the Reds wanted anyway. He remembered his seventh-grade teacher warning them about the dangers of the French commune where you were always at risk of having your head cut off and women would have sex with anybody, not just their husbands. That probably hadn't been the best way to warn a bunch of boys off of socialism, but anyway, Del imagined the Reds wanted something like that. But he could be wrong. After all, for the longest time he'd thought a "Wobbly" referred to a drunk person and not a member of the Industrial Workers of the World. All he knew for sure was that his father always voted Republican, and so he did too.

Brooks and Kirkpatrick had disappeared inside the building, and Hutton was helping corral the interested bystanders off to one side of the street. Absent any specific orders, Del went over to the line of prisoners on the curb. One of them had a bad cut over his left eye, blood dripping down his face and onto his collar. He was trying to staunch it with his shirtsleeve. The man sitting next to him started to lean over to help, but then shot a nervous glance at the two sergeants watching them and stopped.

"It all right if I treat that fellow's wound?" Del asked one of the sergeants.

The sergeant grunted an affirmative. "Guess we don't want him bleeding all over the paddy wagon."

Del crouched down in front of one of the women, who gave him a nasty glare. "Ma'am, I'm sorry to ask, but would you be willing to lend me that scarf you're wearing? I doubt anybody here has any medical supplies."

Her glare wavered, and she unwound the white-and-blue-patterned silk from around her neck, handing it to him.

Del got it tied around the man's head. "You all right or do you need a doctor?" he asked.

"I'll manage," he said. "I've taken worse from you bulls and come out standing."

"Shoulda learned your lesson," one of the sergeants said, thumping his nightstick in his palm. "Maybe we went too easy on you this time."

"None of that talk now, sergeant." A lieutenant joined them—Lieutenant Cutter from the downtown station, if Del remembered correctly. Cutter had come to ask Del about some stolen cars once and given him a description of the missing vehicles in case he saw one on his patrols. "Not that the papers would take their side, but we can keep things civil."

"You call this civil?" the woman whose scarf had been pressed into service demanded, gesturing at the broken furnishings and windows.

"For enemies of our nation? Yes. You can hardly call yourselves citizens when you're plotting the overthrow of the rightful government."

"There's nothing right about it," the woman retorted. "It's been bought and paid for by the trusts and the owners who turn it to their own ends."

"It's a shame that after the president grants you women the right to vote, you choose to urge decent, hardworking folks to strike against our institutions," Cutter said, glaring down at her.

"We fought for the vote—long and hard—no one granted us anything. And we'll fight for the closed shop too, for unions that protect those hardworking folks you mention."

Del had been following the exchange between the woman and Lieutenant Cutter, wondering where some people found the passion to keep pressing forward in the face of so much hostility. He was quite taken aback when the woman turned to him and demanded what he thought of the matter.

"After all, it was policemen just like yourself who struggled so courageously in Boston six years ago for the right to form a union," she said. "And Coolidge goes and calls on the state militia, when you were the ones protecting the public and deserved fair treatment. But I suppose you voted for him for President anyway?"

Del cleared his throat. He remembered the Boston police strike, sure. His parents had thought it an awful thing, the police abandoning their duty to protect the public by going on strike and leaving the city open to looters and criminals. He couldn't say what he'd do in a similar situation.

"Oh, but I'm forgetting," the woman continued before Del could think of an answer. "You're all dirty cops in this city. You've got the gangs and the gamblers lining your pockets. You don't care about making an honest living."

"That's enough from you," Lieutenant Cutter said, his voice sharp. "Let's get these prisoners into the wagons and send them to cool their heels in the cells for a few hours."

"I'm glad you helped that man," Carl said to Del in a low voice as they walked back to the squad car once the prisoners had been removed and the onlookers started drifting away. "I'm afraid I'd lumped you in with Kirkpatrick and that lot who think their fists can solve any problem."

Del hated the thought of being connected with Kirkpatrick in any way. "I'm not going to stand by while someone's bleeding, even if they are a Red."

"That's right. Between you and me, I think it's disgraceful what's happened in this department since Chief Vollmer left. Of course, we can't very well allow radical elements to have free rein, but you can hardly call that scene back there professional."

"That's so," Del allowed, shooting a nervous look over his shoulder to make sure Kirkpatrick wasn't within hearing distance.

"Speaking of professional matters, I'd like to take some courses in criminology," Carl added. "Criminal psychology is a fascinating subject, don't you think?"

"Yes," Del said, as he didn't know what else he could say. He'd heard some detectives talking about hereditary defects and glandular dysfunctions as contributors to criminal behavior one day and hadn't understood two words out of three.

Carl talked on, cheerfully oblivious. "If you decide you'd like to take a class as well, let me know. We could study together."

"Er, thanks." Del had no intention of taking a class and wished Carl would drop the subject. He'd never been good with books. In his experience, school meant long, dull periods punctuated by agonizing moments when the teacher asked him a question, and he had to admit he didn't know the answer with the eyes of all the other students staring at him.

He was thankful to return to the station and get back on his motorcycle, escaping Kirkpatrick and Carl both.

It worried him a little, what Ev would think when he found out Del wasn't too smart. But he needed to find a way to see Ev again in the first place before getting tied in knots about that. Obviously Ev wasn't going back to the Elephant's Ear, and Del could spend months trying to track him down in cabarets and speakeasies. There was nothing for it but to go to Ev's apartment and hope he could convince Ev to give him another chance.

ON SUNDAY, FIVE minutes after noon, he arrived at Ev's door, a bouquet of daisies in hand. The roses had been too expensive or he would have gotten those instead. He knocked, hoping Ev was home.

A few seconds later, the door jerked open, and Ev stuck his head out. He blinked when he saw Del. "Why are you here?"

Del shuffled his feet and held out the daisies.

Ev stared at them, as though they were an incomprehensible artifact from an ancient civilization.

"They're for you," Del clarified.

"Oh for the love of—I *know* that." Ev grabbed the daisies and gestured for Del to come inside. He stuffed the daisies into a glass jar that had been sitting above the sink and slammed it on the table. "There. Now why the hell are you bringing me flowers?"

"I thought you might like them," Del replied meekly, gesturing at the offending daisies. "You might want to add some water or they'll wilt. They're fresh cut, but I'm not sure how long—"

"Yes, yes," Ev interrupted, seizing the jar and adding the water with an irritated glare in Del's direction. "Are you satisfied now?"

Del nodded, scratching the back of his neck. Perhaps if they had been roses, Ev wouldn't have been so angry. "I, uh, wanted to ask if you'd like to go out for the afternoon. We could head down to the beach. It's a lovely day."

The same uncomprehending expression came over Ev's face. Then he narrowed his eyes and sauntered over. He put his hands on Del's arms, sliding them over his biceps to his shoulders. Reaching up, he tugged off Del's hat.

"Or we could do other things," he whispered, leaning in for a kiss.

And so they ended up back in Ev's bed instead.

Del wasn't complaining, mind. Of course, he'd have liked to spend more time petting and kissing Ev, but Ev seemed to want him *now* and made no bones about it, fingering himself open and slick while Del was still shucking off his trousers. He turned Ev over on his stomach, so he could at least lie close against him, kissing and sucking on the back of Ev's neck, one hand gripping Ev's right wrist tight, pinning it to the mattress while he thrust.

"You're heavy," Ev said, turning his face to the side, eyes shut.

Del stuttered to a stop. "Sorry, I can—"

"No, it's all right." Ev pushed back against him, slotting them together again. "I was only saying."

He wished Ev would say his name in that soft, gentle voice instead. But Ev stayed quiet again, breathing deeply, only the occasional small noise escaping him when Del's thrusts hit the right place.

"Can I come inside?" he asked when he knew he wouldn't be able to hold back much longer.

Ev nodded, tugging against the hold Del had on his wrist. When he let go, though, Ev captured his hand, wrapping their fingers together.

Oh.

He came with a long, drawn-out shudder, squeezing his other arm tight around Ev's chest.

When he had recovered his breath somewhat, he disengaged his fingers from Ev's, a little cramped from the pressure of Ev's grip. Ev turned onto his side, reaching for himself, but Del curled around him and replaced Ev's hand with his own. Ev came on a little hiccupped moan. Del cradled him through the trembling aftershocks, closing his own eyes and smelling Ev's hair, smiling. He reached down to pull the sheet over them when Ev didn't immediately move.

"Now would you like to go to the beach?" Del asked when Ev finally stirred and started to extricate himself from Del's arms.

Ev froze for a second and then rolled away, propping himself on one elbow so he could face Del. "I—" He ran a hand through his hair, which was already sticking up in all directions. "For God's sake, I don't even know anything about you, Del."

"What do you want to know?" he asked, smiling at Ev who made the loveliest picture just then, the tousled sheet low on his hips, the clear daylight slanting across his shoulders.

"What do you do, for starters? Or your last name."

Del only knew Ev's last name was "Sharples" because he'd seen it on an envelope the last time he'd been here. Still, it was somewhat embarrassing to think they had never even gotten so far as to properly introduce themselves.

"My last name is Randolph—full name is Delbert Michael Randolph."

"Delbert?" Ev repeated, raising an eyebrow.

"I prefer 'Del.'" He hesitated. There were other reasons why he hadn't immediately shared more about himself with Ev. "I'm a...cop."

Ev shut his eyes and shook his head. "I have the worst luck. The worst."

"I'd never turn you in, Ev. You can't believe I would."

"No—you'd have done it the first night if that had been your plan. Or asked me for money the next morning in return for keeping quiet." Ev took a deep breath. "Still. It's just one more reason why all of this is a bad idea."

"Don't say that," Del pleaded, reaching for him, but Ev slipped away and climbed from the bed. He grabbed his shirt and started getting dressed. "Ev—give this a chance. I want to get to know you, to spend time with you."

"No." Ev gave him a stony look. "I've been here before, and it always ends the same way. We've both gotten what we wanted. And maybe in a month or so, I wouldn't say no to fucking you again. Although I'd be a fool to keep getting involved with a cop. But anyway, that's it. I'm not going to become your damned lover."

Del scrambled to his feet. "Please, Ev, don't make up your mind so fast. I think we could be happy together. You just have to—"

Ev crossed his arms over his chest. "I don't have to do anything. Now get dressed and get out. I have other things to do today, none of which involve you."

"Ev—"

"*Now.*"

And so Del hopped around getting dressed while Ev stared at him disapprovingly. Ev slammed the door shut on him too, leaving him on the doorstep with all his promises and arguments unsaid.

He was reeling a little from Ev's sudden hostility, and he had to sit down on the curb after he'd only made it a few blocks away, too stunned to figure out when the next streetcar would be by. It had been so wonderful—Ev eager to make love again, Ev wanting to hold his hand, Ev staying in his arms for a bit afterward. He'd been sure Ev would want to spend the whole day with him—to spend many days with him. And then it had crumbled apart in the space of a few minutes.

Chapter Three

"WHY ARE YOU so fixated on this kid, anyway?" Glen asked.

"Not a kid," Del replied. "Ev's got to be in his twenties, same as me."

"Fine, but the question still stands."

Del considered, shifting into a lower gear as they chugged up a hill. Glen had called him the evening after that horrible morning at Ev's and asked if he wanted to go for a fishing trip the next weekend. Del had hoped he'd be spending the weekend with Ev, but he hadn't hit upon any brilliant ideas for overcoming Ev's reluctance, so he agreed. They took Glen's car, a battered 1918 Oldsmobile whose electric starter kept misbehaving. Del drove, as he enjoyed it, and Glen preferred watching the scenery—or grilling Del about his love affairs.

"He's beautiful—I told you that. And there's this...gentleness about him sometimes. He hides it away, but I've seen it. I want to coax it out of him again, to show him it's all right to be that way with me."

A beat of silence, and then Glen cleared his throat. "Well that's damned sentimental, even for you. I didn't realize you were so far gone already."

"It's not like before."

"Isn't it?" Glen frowned. "You were exactly like this with Lawrence too. Fawning over him, infatuated, and then it turned out the bastard was cheating on you."

The memories always stung, and his voice was harsh as he said, "Yeah, well, Ev hasn't even agreed to see me again, so there's no danger of that happening, is there?"

Another pause. Greta poked her wet nose against his ear. Although she could easily have stuck her head out the car in the back seat, she preferred a front row view.

"But you're still hurting," Glen finally said. "All I'm saying is you should let it go. If this Ev doesn't want to be with you, then it's his loss, but you have to snuff out that torch you're carrying."

"But I think he might really want to be with me. He was so sweet in bed—I know he liked it—but he assumed all I wanted was a quick fuck or two. If I can convince him I want more, then maybe he'd allow himself to want more too."

Glen let a disbelieving silence fill the air between then.

Del blew out a frustrated breath. "Why am I listening to you for advice on romance anyway? You don't care about it, after all."

Before Glen could reply, Greta clambered over the seat and took up residence in Glen's lap, nose to the wind, ears streaming behind her.

"Oof—you're heavy, baby," Glen muttered, but he put his arms around her, anchoring her in the car. Then he gave a small, resigned shrug. "You're right; I guess I'm not one to talk about love."

"Sorry," Del muttered. "I didn't mean to throw it in your face."

"Nah, don't worry about it. Besides, it's the truth. I'm still seeing Lillian off and on, but I met a pansy named Charlie the other weekend at a drag ball, and he let me take him home. We've been together twice since then, although he's got a wife and a kid, so I can't see him as much as I'd like. But I don't expect either of them to last past the summer."

"But you won't ever try to make them last."

"Why should I? I'm not interested in any kind of commitment. Besides, it's old-fashioned. Even if a couple does get married, it only takes a trip to Reno and you have a divorce in fifteen minutes. This is the modern age."

"But you still get attached. I know you do. Lillian—you care about her."

Glen snorted. "Lillian is stringing along three of us, far as I can tell. And the only reason Lillian's stuck with me this long is because I can give her all the gossip about the movie stars, thanks to my working for the *Examiner*."

Del sighed inwardly. Glen would never admit to the possibility that he might want to be with someone for more than a few months or that he would ever fall in love. They might as well move on to another area of dissatisfaction in Glen's life. "You complain about working at the paper, but it gives you a topic of conversation with girls. I never know what to say to them. Remember when I tried going with Ella Bennet, when I worked at that hotel? I never managed to say more than three words at a time when I was with her."

"But you know I hate it—grubbing around in the private details of people's lives. Yesterday they had me in divorce court again—this time it was that actress Claire Anderson—can't think of the names of any of her pictures offhand. Anyway, she's married to a rich automobile agent over in Hollywood named Harry. She showed up in court with a black eye yesterday. Judge Gates didn't even give her a chance to say Harry gave it to her, just put a restraining order on both of them. Harry's claiming that she's lying, of course, and accusing her of bringing home other men to sleep with and indulging in affairs with naval officers. Having to sit there and listen to it all..." Glen scrubbed a hand through his hair, sighing.

"And your boss won't put you on other stories if you ask?"

"It's because my dad was a clerk for Judge Gates, and I was always there visiting as a kid. I know everyone around the courthouse and can get good tips and interviews. And people want to know about the scandalous lives of starlets, you know that."

"You aren't going to move, are you?" he asked because Glen had floated this idea before, of starting fresh in another city.

"Nah—it would be chancy, counting on getting a job somewhere else. And what if I couldn't sell my place for enough to take care of the mortgage? Anyway, I've lived here my whole life. I'd miss it if I left."

"Even if you went somewhere you could fish every day?"

"Sure, I'd like that, but—hell, we're city boys, you and me. We can manage it on weekend trips out here, but can you imagine me roping cattle or becoming a forest ranger?"

"I wouldn't want you to leave anyway," he said, and Glen smiled. "You could go work for the *Daily News*, though. They won't print any sensational stuff."

"Yeah, but they're hurting for dough, or so I heard. Probably they'll fold pretty soon. That's what happens when you can't run headlines about sex and crime."

"Well, anyway, this is why you don't have any call to be ragging me about Ev," he concluded, peering anxiously out the windshield at the hood—had that been a whiff of smoke he'd smelled just now?

"All right, you've made your point." Glen ruffled Greta's ears. "But—well, I say it as shouldn't, but you've got a good job now. Leaving aside the issue of whether Ev will ever love you or not, it might be time to find a girl and get married."

Del didn't respond immediately. It was true that a distant part of him—the part that remembered Sunday School and a slim volume his mother had handed him entitled *Manhood: The Facts of Life*—experienced some disquiet whenever he thought too long about his choice of lovers. According to that pamphlet, words like "abnormal" and "degenerate" floated around men who chose to fulfill their sexual urges in ways that didn't result in children. Del wasn't too sure that diagnosis described the situation, though. He wasn't like those university types who talked philosophy and then did it the twentieth-century way with each other. He'd never suck another man's dick, and he sure wouldn't ask Ev to do something so low either. With his graceful, womanly essence, Ev deserved to be treated right, not like a prostitute you picked up for a night.

Ev's feminine nature was why Del was attracted to him. It was like when he was a teenager and found himself captivated by Roger Ormsby, who had been known round the neighborhood as a fruiter and regularly went to pansy balls. Roger could give someone like Julian Eltinge a run for his money when it came to transforming himself into a woman. Del had seen Eltinge's vaudeville show once and had been completely convinced the person on stage was a woman and not a man. But Roger had a feminine spirit, unlike Eltinge, who hunted and played football when he wasn't acting. Ev had that same feminine spirit and so it wasn't unnatural that Del should be attracted to him.

But at the rate things were going, Ev seemed unlikely to even give him the time of day let alone allow Del to get closer to him. If he couldn't turn things around, Ev would sail out of his life without ever having properly been in it.

"I don't care about getting married," he said at last. "And I want Ev. Not... not..."

"Yeah. Hell, you know I understand, pal."

"I know."

"But don't hang all your hopes on Ev, you hear me? You can't force him to love you."

"I only want a chance with him." If Ev would give him a chance, then he would be sure not to make a mess of things, like he had with Lawrence.

Glen changed the subject, commenting on the invigorating smell of the mountain air and how he couldn't wait to eat some fresh-caught trout for supper that night. Del transferred his attention to the radiator, which was showing hopeful signs of making it up the last hill without overheating. The road, which by this point had become the remnants of an old logging road, was rutted and rocky, and in a rainstorm, it would be nigh impassable.

THEY WENT TO their usual spot—a stand of oak trees, far enough apart they could drive easily between the trunks, about a quarter mile from the river. Del brought the flivver to a halt, Glen and Greta two eager bundles of enthusiasm in the passenger seat. The mountains always succeeded in transforming Glen from a jaded newspaperman into an overgrown boy. If he'd been a dog, Glen would have been in the same state as Greta—tail wagging madly, rushing around barking up trees and sniffing everything. Del was relieved to see him happy. He hadn't meant to make Glen think about all the problems in his life.

Glen went to open the door, but when he yanked on the handle, it wouldn't open. "Dammit, the door is stuck, Del. I *know*, Greta—calm down, girl, we'll get out in a second."

Del let Greta thunder out on his side, and then went around to see if he could open Glen's door from the outside. It took a few tries, but finally the handle surrendered.

"I need to get that fixed," Glen said. "And don't think I didn't see you worrying over the engine overheating on the way here."

"Let's put some grease on the door when we get home," he suggested, bending down to untie some of their gear from the running board.

They set up their auto tent first, stretching the awning over the top of the flivver so they didn't have to mess with the poles, and then unfolding the two cots underneath.

"And now to hunt down our supper!" Glen exclaimed, pulling their tackle boxes, creels, and boots from where they had been stashed in the back and making a jumbled pile on the ground. "You head upstream, and I'll go down."

Del sat on the ground to switch his shoes for the boots and roll his trousers above the knee. "Think the fish will be biting today?"

"The wind's in the south, but it's a calm breeze." Glen took a deep breath. "Smells hot, a regular summer afternoon. I think they'll be biting for sure. We'll make a howling success of it and have a real fry-up tonight."

Del took this pronouncement with a grain of salt. Glen, bless him, almost never managed to catch anything. Repeated failures had never managed to dull his zeal, however. Del was the better fisherman of the two of them, although he still sometimes got his line tangled in the willows and often spent the hours fruitlessly wandering up and down the bank, waiting for a bite.

As humble devotees of Izaak Walton, as Glen liked to refer to them, they spent the weeks in between fishing trips studying technique, dressing their lines with deer fat on Glen's lawn, and doing all they could to prepare for their next sortie against the aquatic denizens. So maybe this time they really would have better luck.

As he waded through the shallows, looking for a likely spot, he wondered what Ev would make of all this. He didn't imagine Ev would be too keen on camping. But maybe Ev would surprise him. Either way, Del wanted to know—to know this and more besides, all the details of Ev's personality that he had only glimpsed hints of so far.

Back at the campsite several hours later, Del triumphantly displayed the three trout in his creel, and Glen exhibited the one small trout he had caught with as much pride as though it was twice that size and multiplied by ten.

"Greta kept splashing about and scaring the fish," Glen admitted. "Should have tied her to a tree back here."

Despite this threat, Glen would never have the heart to do so and withstand Greta's pleading whines.

Catching the fish was one thing—cooking it was something else entirely, and on this score, Del fell as equally short as Glen. They got the little Kampkook stove going without too much trouble, but their four fine trout ended up charred on one side and underdone on the other. Not to mention the difficulty of picking out all the little bones. They opened a can of beans to supplement it, and if Del had wistful thoughts of hamburger and potatoes, he could hardly mention it when Glen kept raving about the fish, although he did allow that next time they would have to try harder not to burn most of it.

"Can't understand it," Glen said through a mouthful. "I remember my mother frying fish on our wood-burning stove. You'd think it wouldn't be as hard as all that." He took a deep breath and pointed at the sky. "But never mind—look over yonder, and I bet that bright star is a planet, just coming up over the horizon."

Del made an admiring noise and let a drooling Greta lick his plate clean. He also made it into his cot before Glen, which meant he was able to get Greta curled on his feet before Glen could do anything about it. Sure, it meant he couldn't really move for the rest of the night, but Greta kept his feet warm, while Glen was left to grumble about how the one steady woman in his life wasn't faithful.

Chapter Four

DEL EASED HIS motorcycle to a stop at the back of the police station, stifling a yawn and looking forward to going home and getting some rest. He and Glen had stayed by the river until well into yesterday afternoon, and Del barely made it back in time for his shift. He'd just dismounted when the beam of headlights rippled over the wall, and the paddy wagon pulled into the alley. It rumbled to a stop in front of him. Brooks was behind the wheel, and Kirkpatrick sat next to him.

"Hey, fellows," Del said, gathering his courage and walking over. He couldn't let Kirkpatrick scare him off all the time. "What'd you pull tonight?"

"The usual," Kirkpatrick replied, jumping down from the passenger seat while Brooks turned off the engine. He was either too tired or too disinterested in ribbing Del, for he continued, "Arrested some drunks disturbing the peace and a gal running a beer flat, although her customers skedaddled before we could nab them." He circled round to the back of the wagon as he talked and started unlocking the doors. "Oh, and Kelley trapped a fairy at the Crown Jewel. They're having a busy night at Central, so we brought 'em all here."

He flung the doors open, and Del found himself face-to-face with Ev. At first, all he could do was stare. Ev had gotten his hair marcelled since the last time Del had seen him. The blond waves framed his face, accenting his high cheekbones, painted with a touch of rouge. He wore a paisley shirt and had colored his lips a light pink. Del would bet his whole week's pay that a pair of silk stockings and ribbon garters clung to him underneath his trousers.

Del took a closer look at Ev's expression and found it was about as far from pleasure as it could get. He swallowed and held out a hand, momentarily oblivious to the presence of his fellow policemen and the assorted prisoners.

Ev scorned his hand and jumped to the ground unaided. He straightened his jacket and smoothed down his hair. Del could have been a lamppost for all the attention Ev paid him.

Kirkpatrick and Brooks started herding the little crowd of prisoners into the station, and after a moment Del recovered his wits and trailed along behind them. He really shouldn't talk to Ev here of all places. It would be obvious they knew each other. But he couldn't let Ev be ushered into a cell with no communication whatsoever. He finally got a chance to draw him to one side while Brooks tried to get the lady with the beer flat to give him her name and age and other details.

"What the heck were you doing in the Crown Jewel?" he whispered. "Didn't you know the owner tips off the cops?"

Ev's jaw twitched. "Guess that passed me by. Don't have your sort of connections, do I?"

"What does that have to do with anything?" he demanded, wishing Ev would at least look at him.

"It means you're a damn cop, and I told you I didn't want any more to do with you."

He gripped Ev's elbow, angling his body closer. "Don't be like this, Ev, please. I care about you. I don't want to see you in jail."

Ev jerked away, giving him a suspicious glance. "You're taking me for a buggy ride. The only thing fellows like you care about is getting some. Well, you got yours. So leave me alone."

"That's not true. I—"

"Hey, you—the pansy—get over here," Brooks called. Ev stepped forward, crossing his arms over his chest and lifting his chin in the air as Brooks started filling out the arrest form.

"The fag would probably suck your dick if you took him to the toilet," Kirkpatrick said to Del.

Del flushed, hating that Kirkpatrick could say such coarse things about Ev.

Kirkpatrick snorted and shook his head. "Come on, Randolph. I know you have a taste for sissy boys."

"Not in the *station*." And he'd never treat Ev so cheaply.

"Have it your way." Kirkpatrick shrugged. "You should sign up for Kelley's squad. Then you get the fuck and the credit for bringing in the little cocksuckers. Better than writing traffic tags."

Kirkpatrick went over to help Brooks move the prisoners to the cells, saving Del from doing something rash like introducing his fist to Kirkpatrick's nose, a sure way to let slip that his feelings for Ev went deeper than a simple physical release. He stared after Ev for a moment and then went to attend to his paperwork, frowning. Thrilling stuff to put in his report too—three speeding tags and a warning for an odd bird whose headlights were out but who claimed he could see just fine by the light of the moon. Del had told him that maybe he could, but the car that might ram into him around the next curve sure as heck couldn't.

When Del finished his battle with the typewriter—a draw in this case—he thought about trying to see Ev again, but figured Ev would only ignore him. He didn't fancy making a spectacle of himself in front of the other prisoners. Still, he lingered in the hallway for a few minutes before sighing and heading for the streetcar stop.

WHEN DEL REACHED his apartment, he shaved and put on a fresh shirt and bowtie. His bed sat there tempting him, but sleep would have to wait. Ev would be arraigned that morning at the courthouse. Del needed to be there, to know what sentence Ev received and to serve as a friendly face in an otherwise hostile or indifferent crowd. So he drank an extra cup of coffee to chase away the fatigue, scarfed a bowl of Post Toasties, and then called Glen to ask if he could borrow his car. The last thing Ev would want after court would be to struggle through the crowds on the streetcar and walk home. Glen agreed, although he added in a few comments about Del being a fool when he came 'round to pick Del up at eight. Del dropped him off at his office and then continued to the courthouse. The city was building a fancy new Hall of Justice, but it wouldn't be finished until next year. The old courtroom could hardly handle the crowds. Since the oil boom a few years back, it seemed like everybody in the world wanted to move to Los Angeles, and Prohibition brought a lot of those people to the courts. Not that the police department was keen on enforcing the Volstead Act, but you couldn't do absolutely nothing either. Even New York City arrested its share of leggers.

Sitting in the courtroom on the hard wooden bench, he watched the lawyers and the judge and various detectives working their way briskly through the night's arrests. If he had a detective badge or was pals with the district attorney, maybe he could have made the charges against Ev disappear. But he didn't have that kind of clout. Being on the motor patrol was a step up from standing in the street directing traffic, but a large gulf still separated him from the likes of a detective.

When Ev was finally brought in, Del sat up straighter and tried to catch his eye. Ev looked rumpled and tired, and he held himself stiffly, shying away from the bailiff's hand on his arm. At some point he'd washed off his makeup, leaving his face pale, the shadows plain under his eyes. He spotted Del, and surprise flickered over his face. Then he frowned and turned away, staring at a spot on the wall.

To Del's surprise, the charge against Ev was "disorderly conduct" as opposed to the more serious "lewd vagrancy" offense. The judge, sounding bored, fined Ev twenty dollars and moved on to the next case. Ev was taken off to fill out the requisite paperwork and pay his fine, and Del, pushing through the crowd in the hallway, managed to catch him when he emerged onto the courthouse steps a while later.

Ev squinted against the bright sun and heaved a sigh. "Guess I'll ask you the same old question—why are you here?"

"'Cause I was worried about you." He reached toward Ev before thinking better of it and shoved his hands into his pockets instead.

"Risky for you to be seen with me here."

Del waved a hand at the passersby. "None of them knows what you did—'disorderly conduct' could be anything. And how did you get off so lightly?"

"I cut the detective who pinched me in on the gravy."

"He didn't make you...*do* anything, did he?" Del asked, remembering Kirkpatrick's comment.

Ev snorted. "Nah. He only wanted money. Luckily I'd just got paid and had enough cabbage on me. Guess I'll have to take out a loan to cover the fine. They'll print my name in the papers, I suppose, but it isn't as though I have a reputation to ruin."

Del shadowed Ev as they walked along the street. "Can I give you a lift home? My car's parked just over there."

Ev hesitated. "If you're offering, I'd appreciate it. But I'm not inviting you in, got it? I've had enough of cops for one day."

"That's not why I asked."

"But you're thinking about it. You want to sleep with me again, don't you?" He narrowed his eyes at Del over the hood of the car.

Del drew in a breath, trying not to sound too exasperated. "Well, sure. But it's not the *only* reason I do things, Ev. Gee, what kind of shiftless fellows have you been with?"

"A many and varied assortment," Ev said as he climbed into the passenger seat. "None of them with your bullheaded persistence, though."

"Not quite the sweet talk I'm looking for, but I'll take it," he replied, starting the engine.

Ev snorted again and slouched in the seat, shutting his eyes. "Wake me when we get there, all right? I'm beat."

Ev dozed off a few moments later, and Del drove in silence, trying to shift gears as quietly as possible. But Ev still woke before they arrived at his apartment, starting from sleep abruptly and then relaxing when he remembered where he was. He let his hand dangle out the window, cupping his fingers to let the wind blow through them.

"Camilo will be furious at me for not having my rent money. Again."

"Where are you working?"

"A hotel downtown—Calenders. I have the lovely job of emptying the automatic dishwasher in the kitchen. A real treat, I tell you—trying to work fast and not drop plates or get burned 'cause the water gets so hot. But it was the only job I could rustle up."

Del pulled to a stop in front of Ev's apartment. "If you were with me, you wouldn't have to do stuff like that."

"What, you'll pay my rent? Buy me groceries? Make me your punk?" Ev rolled his eyes. "I'm not a kid anymore. Besides, you don't have the dough to make me that kind of offer."

It was true. Sending money to his father, the rent, groceries, payments on some loans he'd taken to buy a radio and the few pieces of furniture in his apartment—he was lucky to have two dimes to rub together by the end of the month.

"Can I at least see you again?"

Ev was about to open the door, but he paused.

"Please?"

"You'll show up whether I say you can or not, won't you?"

Del shrugged and rubbed his thumb along the steering wheel. "If you really don't want me to, I'll leave you alone," he made himself say.

Ev sighed and slumped back against the seat for a moment. "Fine. Saturday afternoon, you can come over."

He grinned, elated. "You won't regret it. I promise."

"I don't trust your promises." Ev went to open the handle and then frowned, giving the door a shove.

"Oh, hell, the door must be stuck again. Hold on." He scrambled out, calling the flivver a few impolite names in his head.

He tugged and tugged to no avail. At last Ev said, "Never mind. I'll climb out on your side."

"You know," he continued when he'd clambered free, "if you're going to offer someone a ride, you should make sure they can get out of the car as well as in."

Shamefaced, Del nodded. There he'd been, going on about taking care of Ev when he couldn't even afford his own car. If only he could buy a new model, painted a bright color with shiny leather seats.

"Well don't look like the world's going to end." Ev surveyed him for a moment and then yawned. "See you Saturday, I guess. If you show up."

"I will," Del hastened to assure him. "We'll go someplace swell, I promise."

Ev gave him a very doubtful look and turned to go inside, waving a hand at Del's "good-bye" but not turning around.

He got back into the car and then sat there awhile, thinking. He'd have to plan out Saturday carefully in order to make sure Ev had a good time and would want to go out with him again. A jolly outing, a real nice dinner somewhere, and maybe he could manage a present for Ev too. He could always skimp on groceries this month if necessary. He hadn't realized until too late that he wasn't giving Lawrence the sorts of things he wanted, and he didn't want to make the same mistake with Ev.

"THE CAR DOOR got stuck again," he informed Glen when he returned the flivver that evening after snatching a few hours of sleep. It was almost seven, but Glen was still stuck at the office, hunched over his typewriter and trying to finish an article for the morning edition. Del was sitting on the other side of the desk, legs tucked under the chair so he didn't accidentally trip any of the other reporters bustling around the room.

Glen grunted, hammering on the keys. "Haven't had a chance to fix it. How'd things go with your kitten? He okay?"

"No jail time—just a fine. And he agreed to a date with me on Saturday." Del flushed with pleasure at the memory.

Glen paused, raising his eyebrows. "Yeah? That's good, then." He sounded cautious, though, and was probably restraining himself from warning Del again about throwing his heart away too easily.

Glen's protectiveness irked him a little, but it made him happy too. Before he became friends with Glen, he'd never had a real pal looking out for him. Kids in the neighborhood or at school had included him in games at recess or trips to the soda fountain, but he'd never had a true best friend. But Glen knew most everything about him, and he knew most everything about Glen. He knew about the sister in New Hampshire that Glen never spoke with anymore, on account of how she and her husband hadn't helped with the medical bills or anything when their father had been sick and dying. He knew how Glen still missed his parents and visited their graves every other Sunday, regular as clockwork. He'd gone with Glen when he adopted Greta from the pound when she was a little puppy. And he still remembered clear as crystal the day when Glen had decided to try fishing and asked Del to go with him, smiling and excited, and Del had felt an answering leap of happiness that Glen wanted to include him in the adventure.

At any rate, Glen didn't pursue the subject of Ev, leaning back in his chair with a tired sigh. "I didn't get to sleep until two last night. My own fault—I met a girl and took her to supper, and then we ended up dancing at a gin joint."

"Another new girl? What happened to Lillian?"

Glen shrugged. "It's over with Lillian. And don't make that face at me, pal. When there are so many sweet gals in the world, what's a fellow to do? Not to mention all the pretty boys," he added in a quieter voice, although no one was listening to their conversation.

If Glen wasn't going to rag him about Ev, though, Del wouldn't nag him about finding someone steady. "As long as you're happy, I guess," he said and changed the subject to ask Glen his opinion on hats and whether he thought Del would look better in a straw boater or a linen cap.

"The boater, definitely," Glen opined. "Saw some on sale at The Broadway for under two bucks." He glanced at the clock on the wall. "My article isn't going to write itself, though—I better get cracking."

But before Del left, Glen grabbed his arm. "I hope you have a grand time Saturday, pal. Let me know how it goes, okay?"

Del promised he would, saying a silent prayer that he'd have good news to report.

Chapter Five

A SMALL CAFÉ sat on the corner of the street where Ev lived, and Del paused in front of its window on Saturday morning, peering critically at his reflection. The new straw boater hat he'd bought yesterday was on straight, and he hadn't nicked himself shaving. He patted his jacket pocket, making sure the slender package for Ev was indeed there. Taking a deep breath, he proceeded up the street to Ev's apartment building, with the peeling green paint on all the windows' trim.

Camilo answered the door when he knocked, still in his robe despite it being eleven o'clock in the morning. He grinned when he saw Del. "Come in, please. Ev is still in his room. Usually he only takes this much time to get ready when he is going out on the town in the evening."

That was a good sign. If Ev didn't care, he wouldn't be putting so much effort into this. "Late night?" he asked, gesturing at Camilo's attire.

Camilo nodded. "Saturdays, I do not get dressed if I can help it."

Ev appeared, jerking open his door and peering at Camilo. "What have you been saying to him?" he demanded.

Camilo held up his hands. "Nothing, nothing."

Ev gave him an admonishing frown and turned his attention to Del. Del had been drinking in the sight of Ev in a vest and the light green shirt he'd worn before, this time with the sleeves rolled up to his elbows. Ev wore a cap, but a few pieces of hair curled around his ears. It was men's clothing, yet with a delicate, elegant touch.

"So, you're here," he said to Del.

Del nodded, wondering if he could risk a kiss but deciding he'd better wait for a more opportune moment.

Ev cleared his throat. "I'll just get my jacket."

"Do not bring him back too early," Camilo said to Del. "And buy that poor boy something to eat," he added in an undertone. "All week, he ate only toast and tinned soup."

"I've got that covered," Del said and then, as Ev reappeared, "I thought we could head over to Venice for starters and ride one of the rollercoasters on the pier."

"An amusement park? What am I, twelve?" But Ev was smiling as he said it.

"Do you mind taking the trolley?" Del asked as they walked down the steps.

"Oh, haven't fixed your car?"

"It's not my car," he admitted. "It belongs to a friend. Hey, you been getting any more trouble from the cops?"

"Nah. I've been lying low as it were. No money to go to a cabaret even if I wanted."

"Next time we go out, you should do your hair the way it was the other night. You sure looked swell."

"The next time? Confident, aren't you."

"I'm gonna try my best to convince you to stay with me."

Ev glanced his way. "I've never been with anyone who didn't disappoint me in the long run. I'm not expecting you to be any different."

Bitterness filled Ev's words, and Del frowned. "I'm going to prove to you it doesn't always have to be that way."

After a moment, Ev relaxed a little, the hint of a smile tugging at his mouth.

A BRISK BREEZE blew in from the ocean when they arrived on the pier, and Del jammed his hat down on his head to make sure it didn't blow off. "Let's get something to eat first," he suggested, mindful of Camilo's words.

"It's not lunchtime yet, but I guess I am kind of hungry," Ev admitted, already turning toward the smell of fried food.

They got frankfurters, with a pickle and root beer soda. Leaning on the railing, they watched the crowd stream by as they ate.

"My brothers would love this place," Ev said. "All we had for fun back home was a muddy swimming hole."

"In Texas, right?"

"Yes. But I shouldn't spend time fretting about my brothers." After swallowing his mouthful, he added, "They sure didn't like me much. My parents didn't either. As you can imagine, they didn't exactly approve of me." He scowled, crumpling the remains of the paper wrapping in his hand.

Del stared at his remaining pickle, not sure what to say. "Sorry. They sound like a rotten bunch."

"Yes." Ev drained his root beer. "What about you? You have any family in town?"

Del shook his head. "My dad lives back in Kansas with my aunt now. My mother died a few years back from pneumonia, and I don't have any brothers or sisters."

"I'm sorry about your mother."

"Thanks. I miss her. Although if she knew what I've been doing..."

"By 'doing' do you mean me?" Ev asked, expression innocent but with a smirk lurking behind it.

Del blushed. "Well...yes. But hey, that's enough family history to be getting on with right?" he finished awkwardly. "Let's go have some fun."

For all his earlier indifference, it turned out Ev was quite enthusiastic about going on the rides. He dragged Del onto the Giant Dipper, yelling loudly as the cars hurtled over the track and around curves while Del hung onto the bar and grimly tried not to lose his lunch.

"Oh, there's that new one—the Flying Circus," Ev said when they disembarked, pointing at a tall tower with cars shaped like airplanes extending from the top on the end of long, metal arms. The planes were currently circling the tower, high in the air, and swooping up and down. Del swallowed, took a look at Ev's eager expression, and marched toward it resolutely.

"I'll just sit down for a second," he gasped when their feet were on good, solid ground once again.

"Are you all right?" Ev asked, concerned.

"Yeah, yeah—it was a little high up, that's all," Del assured him, mopping at his face with his handkerchief.

Ev made him drink some ginger ale to settle his stomach and then tugged him over to the Pig Slide. "Let's play—it's the pig who has to go down the slide on this one, not you."

So he paid the five cents, and they watched as the gate at the top of the slide opened and a little pig trotted out. Forced onto the slide by lack of room and the pushing of another pig from behind, it slid down, squealing.

Ev laughed. "That was a loud one. Oh—a fun house—are you up for that?"

"Sure thing. Anything you want."

"I don't want you to throw up on me. But you're sweet to let me pick." Ev smiled at him. Every time he was on the receiving end of one of Ev's smiles, it felt like a victory.

"As long as we don't go on anything that spins," Del said as they entered the fun house's dark interior.

To get farther inside, you had to wend your way past a bunch of tilting barrels. Air jets in the floor blew upward, and all the girls kept their hands tight on their skirts, laughing.

"Wish you were in a skirt," he said in a low voice to Ev, who blushed.

"I don't wear dresses much," he replied. "It's an awful risk. I couldn't wear one *here*, that's for sure. Which reminds me..." He gave Del a nervous glance. "I'm sorry I didn't get more made up for you. I didn't know where we were going, and it's not always a good thing to...to look like that."

Del squeezed his shoulder. "Hey, I didn't mean it that way."

Ev paused at the entrance to the mirror maze, letting other people push past him. "I wanted to look prettier," he said wistfully, keeping his voice low so only Del could hear him. "I have this honey of a scarf—lavender with blue tassels—and I wanted to wear it. I thought you would like it."

"You can wear it for me when we're alone sometime." He kept himself from reaching for Ev's hand only with difficulty. "Hell, if it was up to me, I'd stroll right into that new El Capitan theatre with you on my arm, decked out in diamonds and a fur coat."

Ev shook his head, but he shot Del a grateful look. "I don't like diamonds."

"No? Why not?"

"Too common—every starlet wears them."

"You look better in green anyway."

"Emeralds, then. Get me an emerald necklace and a big ring to wear on my finger and make everyone jealous."

Emeralds were out of Del's league, and he knew Ev was just wishing out loud. Still—maybe someday he'd be able to grant that wish.

Ev did coax him into going down a slide at the end of the fun house. Not that Del needed much coaxing because it gave him a chance to put his arms around Ev and be close to him with no one the wiser. Then they tried the shooting gallery, at which they both failed spectacularly, and finally ended with ice cream cones at the Chocolate Garden.

"Let's head back into town for a real meal," he said afterward.

"We just ate," Ev pointed out, laughing and licking ice cream off his fingers.

"This didn't count—wouldn't you like a juicy steak? Or some grilled fish?"

"Well…" Ev hesitated. "Are you sure—we've already spent a lot here and—"

"It's fine." Del steered him toward the streetcars. "I've got plenty. Don't worry about it."

HE'D MADE RESERVATIONS at the Barrenburg, although in truth he felt a little nervous going into the place. It wasn't the fanciest restaurant in Los Angeles by a long shot, but it was swankier than the diners and delis he usually frequented. They should probably both be wearing fancier suits, for starters, but they couldn't very well have gone running around Venice Pier in a coat and tails. Besides, Del didn't own a fancier suit than the one he was wearing, and he was pretty sure Ev didn't have a closet full of ritzy togs either.

Ev was looking footsore by the time they got to the restaurant, what with walking around the pier and then covering a fair number of city blocks thanks to having to take the Red Car line. If Del had an automobile, they could have been here in minutes, but instead they were both wind-blown, faces flushed from the sun. It didn't help that just as they drew near to the restaurant, a Duesenberg Model A pulled up in front. A well-dressed man stepped out and hurried round to the passenger side, opening the door for a lady.

Ev wasn't paying any attention to the couple or the car, though, gaping at the restaurant instead. "We're going here?" he asked.

"Sure are." Del smiled at his amazement.

"No fellow's ever taken me to a place like this before."

"Then you haven't been with the right sort." In truth, he really couldn't afford a dinner here, but if worse came to worst, Glen would lend him some money, and it was already worth it for Ev's surprised and pleased expression.

They walked in at the same time as the man and woman. Del held the door for them and then hastened to join Ev in front of the hostess. Beyond her shoulder, he could see crowded tables and hear the clink of cutlery and muted hum of conversation.

The hostess's eyes slid right past Del and Ev, landing on the man and woman. "Mr. and Mrs. Reilly, how good to see you here."

"Yes, hello," Mr. Reilly said. "I know I didn't call ahead, but I was sure you'd be able to find us a table. As I told Mary here, your restaurant has always provided the best service."

Del shifted from one foot to the other, irritated and nervous. Ev had arrived in front of the hostess first, but she was treating them as though they were invisible. He coughed. "Excuse me, ma'am, but I have a reservation for two under the name 'Randolph.'"

The hostess turned a cool gaze on him, and her eyes flicked to her book. A moment of hesitation and then, "I'm sorry, sir, but I don't have you listed. You must have made a mistake."

"I didn't," he protested. "I rang the restaurant this morning."

She gave him a condescending smile. "Are you sure you have the correct place, sir? I imagine you mixed-up the names with an establishment less...exclusive than ours." Her eyes raked down Del's suit.

He flushed, unsure of how to respond. He was painfully aware of Ev at his side, a spectator to his embarrassment, and of Mr. and Mrs. Reilly, who wore expressions of tolerant amusement. He didn't want to cause a scene—it seemed as though that would solidify their low opinion of him— but he didn't know how to combat the hostess's icy disdain.

Then Ev stepped forward. "You think I don't know what your game is, lady?" he demanded, glaring at the hostess. "You're claiming we don't have a reservation so you can give them a seat." He pointed at the other couple.

The hostess's smile grew more strained. "You're mistaken."

Ev was undeterred. "You think because we're not dressed as nice as them, because we didn't pull up in an expensive car, that you can treat us like this? Del's money is just as good as his."

"Sir," the hostess said, angry now in her turn. "Your friend does not have a reservation, and as Mr. Reilly arrived before you—"

"Bullshit."

A gasp from Mrs. Reilly.

"That is no language to use in front of ladies, sir!" Mr. Reilly said. "I shall summon the manager if you do not remove yourself this instant."

Ev grabbed Del's arm. "Let's scram. These skunks aren't worth our time."

Del let Ev drag him outside. "I'm sorry. I should have—"

Ev rounded on him. "Don't you dare apologize. None of that was your fault."

He nodded, grateful but still ashamed.

"We don't need to go somewhere fancy to have a good meal," Ev continued. "So don't worry about it." He fumbled for Del's hand and gave it a quick squeeze. "Don't worry about it."

He tried to recover some of his wits, which had been cast into disarray the moment the hostess told him she had no record of his reservation. "We could go to... um..."

"I know a spot," Ev said, intervening once again, and he tugged gently on Del's arm, steering him down the sidewalk.

They ended up at a diner called Pete's Place, two servings of the blue plate special on the table in front of them. The food wasn't bad, but still, the blue plate special! He had wanted to treat Ev to a real gourmet meal. Ev might say it was all right, but he must still be disappointed. Del had promised him a swell time only to find themselves eating overdone ham in a grubby diner. And his opinion of Del, not high in the first place, must have dropped considerably. Del had let those people tread all over him.

Ev kept up a constant stream of chatter about a moving picture he had seen, the fun they had on the pier, and other random topics. He tried to pay attention, but he couldn't stop thinking about the scene at the restaurant and how he'd fallen all to pieces.

"Hey," Ev finally said, giving his shoe a kick under the table. Del blinked at him. "When we're done eating, let's head back to my place." He lowered his voice. "Spend the evening in bed."

That roused him from his glum thoughts, but he shook his head. "Not tonight."

Surprise and then hurt flickered over Ev's face. He hastened to explain. "I'd like to—sure, I'd like to. I'd like to make love to you for hours and hours. But then you'll be back to thinking that's all I want from you. Let's save it for next time—if you'll let me have a next time."

Ev frowned. "You sure are a hard man to figure out. You treated me all day—don't you want something in return?"

"I was with you. That's all I wanted."

Ev went quiet and wrapped his hands around his coffee mug, lowering his eyes.

"And I'm sorry again about the restaurant." He reached into his jacket pocket and took out the little package that had been hiding there all day. "Maybe this will make up for it."

"I told you not to worry about that," Ev said, but he took the package and, after an uncertain glance at Del, ripped into the paper. When he opened the box, he sucked in a breath, and then slowly took out the necklace. Del had visited four shops before finding the right one. It had brass flowers interspersed with circles of glass colored a cloudy, minty green.

"Oh," Ev said, holding it in his hands and fingering one of the glass orbs. Then he recollected himself and dropped it down into his lap, under the table where no one else could see.

"It's not much, but I… well, I thought you'd look pretty in it."

"It's lovely." Ev smiled. "I'd put it on right now if I could."

"You can wear it for me later—maybe with that kimono of yours."

Ev's smile turned sultry. "And nothing on underneath?"

Del swallowed.

Ev leaned across the table, his voice almost a whisper. "I'll sit in your lap, let you lift me up with those big hands of yours and settle me on your cock."

Del stared at him, dumbstruck, and Ev leaned back, laughing, even though he was blushing a little at saying such a thing.

"Guess I better give you a next time, huh?" Ev said.

He heaved in a breath. "Really? You will?"

Ev nodded. Del couldn't stop smiling then, even when the waitress gave him a suspicious look when he settled the check, as though she couldn't imagine anyone being so thrilled over the blue plate special.

Later that night, though, sitting in his apartment, a concert program playing softly on the radio, he wondered how long his good luck would last. Maybe Ev would be happy with him for a little while, but eventually things like Del's lack of a car would become more than minor annoyances. Cheap flowers and jewelry would lose their charm. And if he managed to embarrass himself again, like today at the restaurant, well, pretty soon Ev would start to wonder why the heck he was staying with him. After all, he'd thought things were going well with Lawrence too, but then Lawrence had found someone richer and smarter and better looking. Del knew it wasn't hard to find someone who outclassed him in all three areas.

There wasn't much he could do about the last two, but maybe he could find a way to rake in a bit more money. Leastways enough to give Ev roses and maybe even buy a car so they wouldn't have to walk everywhere.

Chapter Six

WHEN IT CAME to traffic regulations, Del believed in enforcing the law to the letter. Thousands of people died every year from preventable auto accidents. A city wouldn't be able to function if people drove any way they wanted, snarling traffic and making the streets impassable. But there were plenty of useless and stupid laws out there too. Take Prohibition. Even if every cop wanted to enforce it, the task would be impossible. It was like trying to scoop water out of a sinking boat using a bucket with a hole in it. There were a few cops who clung to the straight and narrow, but they often ended up with the worst shifts or stuck in dead-end positions. It had been different with Chief Vollmer—even if he recognized the futility of the law, he encouraged his men to follow it. But now Chief Heath was in charge, and he was Charlie Crawford's man. Crawford, who kept an iron fist around the vice trade, expected the police to look the other way beyond the occasional raid for appearance's sake.

So Del felt only a minor qualm of conscience when the next night he drove over to a little side street, narrow and full of potholes, whose neglected nature made it appealing to certain parties. Technically, he was supposed to be patrolling over on Griffin Avenue, but he took the chance no one would crash into a lamppost for an hour and he could make it back to a Gamewell callbox in time for his next scheduled check-in to the station.

It was past two o'clock, time enough for the little boats to have made their way to shore and offloaded their cargoes of whisky, tequila, and Scotch from the rumrunners sailing between Canada and Mexico. Del waited, his pulse thumping in his ears. To be honest, he was awful nervous. He'd never tried to get a bribe from a legger before. But after racking his brains all day, he hadn't been able to think of any other quick way to make some money. And since it seemed like most of the city was profiting off bootleg gin, it was only fair that he have the opportunity too. Sure, he'd never want his dad to know, and his mother was probably rolling over in her grave, but it was for a good cause. Once he'd won Ev's heart, he'd go right back to the straight and narrow.

After about fifteen minutes of anxious waiting, a pair of headlights brought the shadows to life. A truck lumbered by the alley. Del started his motorcycle, flipped on his own headlight, and sped out of the alley onto the truck's tail. As soon as the truck turned onto a wider street, he accelerated and zoomed alongside it.

"Hey! Pull over!" he shouted to the driver. "This is the police!" He pulled out his whistle and blew a long, shrill note.

The driver obeyed, coming to a stop by a filling station closed for the night. Del parked his motorcycle and jumped off, turning on his flashlight. For a moment his legs didn't want to obey him, images of coming face-to-face with a gun barrel when he looked in the flivver's window popping into his mind. Gathering his courage, he stepped closer and shined his flashlight into the truck. The driver blinked, squinting as he rolled down his window.

"Is that you, Del?" the driver inquired. "I can't see worth a damn when you shine that in my eyes." He squinted, tugging his greasy checked cap further over his forehead.

"Harrison?" Del heaved in a relieved breath and lowered his flashlight a little, revealing Harrison's narrow visage with his big nose and bigger ears, jutting out on either side of his cap. Harrison had been wearing the same cap the first time Del met him over a year ago when he hauled Harrison's drunk ass out of the gutter. Since then, it seemed Del had often been on hand when Harrison got himself arrested for a variety of minor infractions. It figured Harrison would be involved in a bit of legging on the side.

"Fancy meeting you here," Del said. "Who's the friend?"

"This is Jasper. I'm, uh, looking after him for his mother."

"He looks kind of old to need a nanny."

Jasper glared at Del "Why'd you stop us, officer?" he demanded.

"Speeding," Del replied as he stepped back from the window and let his eyes wander over the bed of the truck and its cargo, currently covered with a tarp. "And you should show more respect to an officer of the law."

Harrison's gaze followed Del's, and he shifted in his seat.

"We weren't speeding. Ten fucking miles an hour is not speeding," Jasper said, also looking antsy.

Del shook his head, his confidence building. He could handle crooks like this with no trouble. "That's not going to fly, boys. If I say you were speeding, you were speeding." He pointed at the tarp. "I think maybe I better have a look at your cargo—see what you were so anxious to get to its destination."

Harrison's lip twitched. He tapped his fingers on the steering wheel. "Cut to the chase, Del. How much do you want?"

Del raised his eyebrows. "Trying to bribe an officer of the law?"

Jasper's hand drifted toward the holster he almost certainly had on under his jacket, but Harrison grabbed his wrist. "No call for that, kid. Me and Del are buddies. Ain't that right, Del?"

"Guess maybe you could call us that."

Harrison grinned and reached into his pocket, pulling out a wad of cash. "That's right. Now be a sport, Del, and let's make a deal. Between friends."

He looked at the money and glanced down the street. It was empty except for them. "To look the other way when it comes to both the booze I know you have under that tarp *and* your reckless driving—that'll cost you a pretty penny."

Harrison counted off a thick stack of bills. "Knew you were a reasonable fella. How's that look?"

It looked swell and whatever remaining misgivings Del had vanished in the rush of victory. "You have a pleasant night, boys," he said, touching his cap with a finger and reaching out to grasp the wad of cash.

Harrison didn't drive away immediately, though. "Our boss is always on the lookout for fellows who want to make an honest living helping the good citizens of this city survive the Drought."

"What's the big idea?" Jasper hissed.

Harrison hushed him. "Del and I are pals, and the Lord intended us to be generous. It says so in the proverbs—if you give to others it will make you richer."

"Not if it means him taking part of our cut," Jasper argued.

"If you're interested in more than just small potatoes," Harrison said, ignoring Jasper and nodding at the money clutched in Del's fist, "go to a restaurant called the Temple of Ra and tell them I sent you. Ask to speak to Mr. Orville Barrett. Me and Jasper call him the Pharaoh, but he doesn't like to be addressed as such. He thinks nicknames are bad manners."

"Mr. Barrett is real particular about manners," Jasper added, scowling.

Del frowned. "The Temple of Ra? Never heard of it. Wait—are you saying you're not in with Crawford and his gang?"

Harrison shook his head. "With them, guys like me don't see nothin' but crumbs. But now there's a new game in town."

"Why do you call him a fool name like the Pharaoh?"

"Because he's wild about Egypt. He's got all these queer artifacts from tombs in his house, and he fancies himself an archaeologist, like that Carter fellow who found King Tut."

Del rubbed his nose. "Doesn't seem like he could challenge Crawford and his cronies. They've got this town locked down tight."

"Maybe, maybe not. The Pharaoh's awful smart. Ain't that right, Jasper?"

Jasper grunted a sour confirmation. "He's always talkin' about middle kingdoms and sun gods and Nubians, whoever they were."

"See? You don't pick up that stuff on the street." Harrison leaned out the window, waving his finger to enunciate his points. "You know the score here, Del. We've got Charlie Crawford, the Gray Wolf as he's called, running practically every bar, brothel, and gambling racket in town. He's got Mayor Cryer in his pocket. Crawford's fixer Kent Parrot is managing things behind the scenes. They just got Cryer reelected in May, and he's put that Captain Heath in charge of the police."

"Of course I know that. Half the squad are on the take."

"Then you also know that unless you've got their blessing, you'll never amount to nothin' in this town. I bet nobody has offered you any opportunities, and you've been a cop for a good while now."

It was the truth. He didn't have the guts to directly approach anyone in the City Hall Gang, as Crawford's operation was known, and no one had offered him a piece of the pie. "Still don't see how this Barrett fellow can do anything about it. If he makes a move, Crawford will swat him back down."

"Ah, but that's where having smarts comes in handy. The Pharaoh's not gonna challenge them directly. Not until we're ready. Sure, it might take a while, but if you get in now, imagine what the rewards will be when we hit the top." Harrison gunned the engine. "Think about it. You could end up a rich man, pal."

Del watched as they drove away and then walked slowly back to his motorcycle. A sense of discontent inspired by Harrison's words had diminished his satisfaction at the money in his hand. It was true what Harrison had said. All the big payouts went to the brass or the officers on the vice squads who got paid off by the gambling rackets, brothels, and purveyors of speakeasies and pool halls to turn a blind eye to their establishments. Maybe in a couple of years he'd have moved up the ranks or made the right friends to be able to take home a big payday, but right now he was like a dog under the table begging for scraps.

If he had a chance to make even more money—why, for one, he'd be able to buy himself a new suit and maybe the next time he took Ev to a place like the Barrenburg they wouldn't be laughed out into the street. He could buy a Duesenberg Model A too, if he wanted. And if what Harrison said was true, maybe he could even offer to look after Ev in a more substantial way. If Ev got in trouble again, he could bail him out. He could make sure Ev didn't have to worry about the rent or having enough money for groceries.

It would be risky to throw in with a rival of the Gray Wolf, of course. Crawford wouldn't take too kindly to anyone trespassing on his turf. But a fellow had to take chances sometimes.

THE NEXT AFTERNOON, he rang Glen at his office. "Got a few free minutes later?" he asked. "I need to talk to you about something."

"Sure, I can make time," Glen said over the sound of someone shouting in the background and another telephone ringing.

"It'll just take a few minutes. Meet me at the diner round the block from your office in an hour."

Glen was waiting for him when he arrived, two bottles of pop already on the table, wet with condensation.

"So what's so important it couldn't wait?" Glen asked. "You're all right, aren't you? Didn't your date go well?"

"Fact of the matter is, we had ourselves a swell time down at Venice Pier," he reported, perhaps a touch smugly, given how much Glen had doubted his prospects in regards to Ev.

"That so, huh? Then what's got you bothered?"

"I want to know all you can tell me about a legger named Orville Barrett."

"Never heard of him," Glen said after thinking for a moment. He narrowed his eyes. "Why do you want to know? Has Crawford got his sights on him? I thought Crawford and Parrot were occupied with the Italians trying to stage that take-over last month."

"Far as I know the Gray Wolf hasn't made a move against him."

"Then why…" Glen paused. "Dammit, Del, don't tell me you're thinking of joining some upstart leggers."

"Why not? There aren't any opportunities for me as things stand, and I need the money."

"Why? Because eventually Crawford and Parrot will take notice, and they'll plug him and every one of his associates."

"But what if this Barrett fellow can challenge them? They can't stay on top forever, and if I'm part of the outfit that takes them down…"

"That's a mighty big 'if.'"

Del finished his pop in a big gulp and leveled a determined stare at Glen.

Glen shook his head. "You sure can act a fool. When I first met you, and you were working as a bellboy at that hotel—remember?"

Del scowled. "Can we skip that story today?"

Glen grinned and kept going. "I saw you trying to stuff all of those lady's suitcases into the trunk of a car. Of course, they wouldn't fit, but you weren't giving up, just kept slamming the lid, and then one of 'em breaks open and all her corsets went flying onto the street, and—"

"You don't need to give me the details. I was there."

Glen subsided with a final snicker. "I thought to myself, 'now there's a kid who doesn't know when to give up a bad job.' And I wasn't wrong." He leaned over the table. "You could land yourself in a world of trouble doing this, pal."

"I know it's risky. But I need some more money."

"I can loan you some dough if you—"

"No, I need more than a loan."

"Why?" Glen studied him intently. "I didn't realize you were so hard up."

Del didn't answer, knowing what Glen's response would be. But Glen figured it out anyway.

"This is about Ev, isn't it?" he demanded. "What, is he complaining about you not taking him fancy places? You don't need another person like that in your life, Del."

"Ev isn't complaining. But he'll be thinking it soon enough. And what else have I got to offer, huh?"

Glen's eyes softened. "Hey, I know I tease you sometimes, but you shouldn't be so down on yourself. You have plenty to offer."

Del shrugged, unconvinced.

Sighing, Glen clinked his soda bottle against Del's. "I'm not trying to tell you how to live your life, but I don't want to hear they pulled your dead body out of a ditch somewhere."

"What's so dangerous about it? Probably every other person in this city is making bathtub gin."

"There's a big difference between that and infringing on the Gray Wolf's territory. We're talking joining up with real crooks here, Del. You don't have the temperament to live a life of crime."

He gave Glen an angry stare. "I'm not a child. I'm tough, and I'm not afraid of a fight."

Glen held up his hands. "That's not what I meant, but—" He stopped and sighed. "Just, please think it over carefully before you do anything you might regret."

GLEN WAS WRONG. He wasn't doing this on a whim, and he was trying to be as careful as he could. Admittedly, Harrison served as a dubious reference at best. He needed to see Barrett himself and draw his own conclusions. So the next afternoon before his shift started, Del went to find the Temple of Ra. The name sounded far too exotic for the dingy building he located sandwiched between a laundry and a furniture store. He stood on the other side of the street for a few minutes under the awning of a barber shop, smoking a cigarette to calm his nerves. At this hour of the day, there weren't many people interested in a meal, and he didn't see anyone go in or out of the restaurant.

Finally after twenty minutes of dithering, he crossed the street and opened the door. The inside was a bit disappointing. A cluster of tables stood in the center of the room, with some more alongside the windows. Salt and pepper shakers shaped like pyramids stood on the tables and a few lotus flowers had been painted on the walls. Del stared for a moment at the large scarab beetle someone had thought would make a good flower pot, although it held only a few battered daylilies at the moment. The Temple of Ra did not have any of the bronze sphinxes or a gold-plated sarcophagus like Del had been imagining.

He had just picked up one of the pyramid salt shakers when the door in the back that led to the kitchen swung open. A man in a gray pinstripe suit stuck his head out. He had a heavy brow and a flat nose.

"You want dinner or something, kid?" he grunted. "Go find some other place. That door shoulda still been locked."

Del quickly set the salt shaker back down and cleared his throat. "I'm here to see Mr. Barrett. Jimmy Harrison sent me."

The man gave him a long look. "Did he? And why'd he do that?"

"I think he figured you needed some friends on the force," he replied, trying to sound confident.

The man's face grew a bit more unfriendly. "A cop, huh? Wait there." He drew his head inside, and the door swung shut.

Del waited, fidgeting. If the man returned and pulled a gun, he would dive to the right and take cover behind the podium that held the menus and reservation book. He could probably make it outside from there. That scarab vase might prove to be a handy projectile—

The kitchen door swung open again, and he tensed to spring for cover.

But Barrett's man just grunted, "The boss will see you," with disapproval clear in every syllable. He jerked his head, indicating Del should follow him. Del threaded his way through the tables and gave the man a nervous grin but only received a harder glare in return.

The kitchen was—well, he would be careful to never eat anything at this restaurant. But the kitchen was obviously not the main concern, for a flight of stairs led down to the basement, and Mr. Barrett's hired gun pointed down them. Del obeyed the wordless order, ducking his head to avoid hitting it on the low ceiling. The skin between his shoulder blades prickled, and he kept expecting to feel the muzzle of a revolver digging into his back. But the guy only followed him down, breathing heavily. At the bottom, he turned to the right and entered a large, dimly lit room.

It was mostly empty except for a table in one corner and a bar stretching along one wall. Two bare bulbs hung from the ceiling, and the floor was unfinished concrete. The bar itself was impressive, though, the gleaming wood supported by bronze-plated statues of Horus and Osiris— whose names Del knew only because he had eagerly followed the news of Carter's discovery of King Tut's tomb back in twenty-two along with the rest of America. Orville Barrett clearly deserved the nickname Harrison had given to him. A few shot glasses lined the bar, along with a half-empty bottle of whisky.

At the bar sat a man and a woman. The man reminded Del of the fellow in the Gillette razor advertisements. He had dark hair slicked back from a widow's peak and a carefully trimmed mustache, the rest of his jaw smooth. His clothes wouldn't have been out of place in a seaside resort—a white linen suit, a pale blue shirt, and a yellow necktie striped with dark orange. That must be Orville Barrett. The woman wore thick gold bangles on her wrists that clinked together as she lifted a long cigarette holder to her mouth and inhaled, blowing out the smoke and surveying Del.

"He looks *awfully* nervous," she observed to the man in a thick, raspy voice that seemed incongruous with her slight figure. "What's your name, sweetie pie?"

"Delbert Randolph, ma'am," he replied, blushing when she laughed.

"So polite. Your mamma must have raised you right. Most coppers don't know how to act around a lady, with their meaty paws and coarse language. I can tell you're different."

"That doesn't mean anything, Hazel." The man who had followed Del down moved behind the bar and picked up a glass to polish. "You can't take every word Jimmy says for the truth. For all we know, he sent us a snitch for Crawford."

Barrett chuckled and drew a handkerchief out of his pocket, dabbing his forehead. "Come now, Mr. Fletcher—don't be jealous."

"Jealous!" Fletcher scowled. "I'm not jealous. But you can't trust a man like Jimmy. He bet on the Red Sox to beat the Philly Athletics the other day. That's evidence of a mental imbalance right there."

"Not everyone has your smarts," Hazel said, giving Fletcher a smile. "You won me ten bucks at the dog track the other day after all."

Fletcher preened, polishing the glass he was holding with a flourish.

Barrett turned to Del. "There's no use debating the matter among ourselves. Let's ask the man himself—Mr. Randolph, are you working for Crawford?"

"No, sir. I'm not the sort of man who'd be a snitch."

Barrett smiled. "That's very good, very good. Integrity—an upright moral character—the qualities a real man should have."

"But darling, we're not looking for *integrity*," Hazel pointed out. "We are lawbreakers, after all."

"Ah, but you know what they say—'honor amongst thieves,'" Barrett replied. He looked at Del again. "Perhaps it would set our minds at ease if we knew your motivations, Mr. Randolph."

"Well, sir, I guess I'd mostly like to make some money. There's someone I'd like to impress, and I can't do it on a patrolman's salary."

"Ah, of course, young love!" Barrett smiled again. "An understandable desire, Mr. Randolph. I myself do not undertake this venture solely for the base motives of greed and covetousness. Rather, I do it to raise the funds for my masterpiece, my magnum opus, if you will."

Del blinked. "Your what, sir?"

"An epic film that will bring the wonders of the verdant Nile and the majesty of the pharaohs to the American public." Barrett opened his arms, face alight with enthusiasm. "Picture it, Mr. Randolph—thousands of extras, lavish costumes, real camels and elephants. Vilma Bánky as Queen Hatshepsut. I have not settled on a male lead yet, but I could imagine Valentino or even Douglas Fairbanks as suitable options. I myself will do a small cameo—perhaps the captain of the guard or a wise soothsayer. I don't profess to be a great actor, but I imagine I should have an undeniable presence on screen."

"I'll have a part too," Hazel said, giving Barrett a pointed stare.

"Of course you will, my dear. You will be the ingénue of the silver screen." He gave Del a benevolent smile. "I'm sure we can fit you in too, Mr. Randolph. Perhaps as the driver of a camel?"

"Oh, uh, you don't have to worry about giving me a part."

"Nonsense, nonsense. I met with a producer at Metro-Goldwyn last week, and he expressed the utmost interest in the project. All I need is the necessary capital."

"What's your job anyway, Randolph?" Fletcher asked. "You a traffic cop or something?"

"I'm a motor patrol officer," Del replied with some dignity.

"Oh, you have one of the new motorcycles, then?" Hazel said, sounding intrigued, and Del nodded.

"I can let your cargoes through without a fuss when I'm out on patrol," he said to Barrett. "I can also get word to you about raids or other stuff I hear about in the station."

"See, Fletcher—an asset to our organization."

"Guess he might be useful." Fletcher sighed and leaned his hands on the bar. "You play bridge?"

"Bridge?" Del frowned. Was this a joke? Some sort of test? "Can't say I do."

Fletcher sighed again, resigned.

Hazel tutted. "I do wish you'd stop harping about bridge, Fletcher. It's positively ridiculous in a man your age. It's not as though you're attending bridge nights at the city club or hosting luncheons for the young marrieds in the neighborhood."

Fletcher's brow furrowed. "It's a swell game—just because you never learned it—"

"Because it's boring and dull," Hazel shot back.

Barrett intervened before Fletcher could reply. "Now, now then, let's not argue. Ah—I know—you have not perused the fashions in this morning's rotogravure, my dear. Some lovely new styles, I shouldn't wonder." He chuckled nervously and stuffed a newspaper into Hazel's hands. She sniffed but took it and after a moment allowed Fletcher to lean over and look at the picture section.

Domestic harmony restored, Barrett relaxed and motioned for Del to come closer. Taking out his wallet, he gave Del a wink and handed him a five-dollar bill.

"Here's an advance payment for you, Mr. Randolph. A taste of what's to come."

"Thank you, sir." It wasn't a *lot* of money, but he couldn't expect that when he hadn't proved his worth yet. Besides, those fancy statues holding up the bar suggested that Barrett had quite a bit of dough.

"There'll be more where that came from," Barrett continued. "I have grand plans, Mr. Randolph, grand plans. Like a pharaoh of old building one of the great pyramids, we will start with a few stones and by the end have an awe-inspiring monument that will dazzle all who come near."

DEL EMERGED FROM the Temple a short while later and realized that although he had entered intending only to judge Barrett and whether he could take on Crawford, he seemed to have ended up joining Barrett's gang. How simple it had been—and Barrett sure was different from a common crook. That motion picture sounded grand. There was a lot of money to be made in the pictures too, after all. He took another step forward and then spotted Harrison's truck parked across the street, its owner leaning against it. Harrison tugged at his cap and smirked at Del.

"That thing belongs in the rubbish bin," Del said, leveling an accusing finger at Harrison's cap as he walked over.

Harrison squawked indignantly. "There ain't no call to be insulting me. Not when I did you a favor."

"Guess I do have to thank you for that. I thought Barrett would be more suspicious of me, but he asked me to join right away."

"That's 'cause he trusts my judgment," Harrison boasted. "Come with me, and I'll buy you a drink to celebrate the rise in your fortunes."

"There's a bar back there," Del pointed out, jerking his thumb at the Temple.

"No, thank you!" Harrison shuddered. "You can't ever relax around that Hazel. She'll skewer you with those blue eyes of hers and put you to work, and if you dare complain, she'll lay into you with language that would make a sailor blush."

"She seemed pretty nice to me."

"Guess she has no taste—sweet-talking an oaf like you and taking a dislike to a gentleman like me."

"Hey!"

Harrison chuckled. "Just joking, pal. Now come on, I'll take you to a nice joint I know of a few blocks from here."

Del wavered, but finally accepted. He did owe Harrison for letting him in on this operation. He couldn't be rude to him now.

Of course, Harrison's definition of "nice" proved to be the cold storage room of a butcher's shop, in among ham hocks and sides of beef. The butcher had hit upon a pretty novel hiding place for the booze too. He reached an arm into one of the dead pigs hanging from the ceiling and pulled out a dark bottle, poured two glasses, and then stuck the bottle back in the pig carcass.

"Foolproof," Harrison said. "No way a Prohi will stick his hand in there."

The booze had quite a kick to it, but it wasn't the worst coffin varnish Del had ever tasted. Leastways, it wasn't distilled from industrial-grade alcohol. That stuff would kill you or turn you crazy after a glass or two.

He and Harrison settled down on a couple of chairs in a warmer section of the shop. They could hear the chatter of the customers behind the door. Harrison took a big swallow and then tipped his chair back against the wall.

"Figured I should give you the goods on the Pharaoh, now you're one of the gang. Can't let a friend wander around in the dark."

"That's mighty decent of you." After a couple swallows, Del was beginning to regard even Harrison's greasy cap with a forgiving, friendly sentiment.

"You're the one who never roughed me up when I got arrested, and you even brought me a cup of coffee that one time." Harrison sniffed nostalgically. "Anyway, the Temple is the headquarters for this outfit, but the Pharaoh has a grand mansion out on the south side."

"The Temple seemed kind of...bare. You really run it as a speakeasy?"

"Oh, not yet. The boss wants to fix it up all fancy first."

"Then where were you taking that alcohol you had the other night?"

"That was for an acquaintance of the Pharaoh, a fellow who deals in antiques. Payment for some kind of rare doodad the boss wanted—a canoptic or canoptet jar or some such. Fletcher said the boss told him Egyptians stuck the brains and liver and whatnot of the people they turned into mummies in the jar. Brrrr—gave me the shivers that did."

"So, it's a pretty small operation? You, Jasper, Miss Hazel, Fletcher—"

"Fletcher!" Harrison snorted. "Thinks he's the bee's knees 'cause he guards the boss and follows him around everywhere. But he's a big enough sonofabitch that I don't like to argue the point."

"He didn't seem too happy to see me."

"He's just jealous and worried someone will steal his place next to the Pharaoh." Harrison clinked his glass against Del's. "Stick with me, pal, and we'll show him. The boss will have us running the place in no time."

Harrison's cap might have assumed a more pleasing aspect, but Del hadn't drunk enough to believe Barrett would hand the reins to him and Harrison. "Still doesn't seem like enough to challenge Crawford," he said, suffering a renewed pang of doubt.

But Harrison grinned and put an arm around Del's shoulders. He smelled strongly of motor oil and fried fish. "The Gray Wolf started just the same as us. No reason we can't do what he did with equal success."

Del imagined the feel of two hundred—no five hundred bucks in his hand. Matching Harrison's grin, he drained his glass. Maybe this would be the year his fortunes turned around. A way to make it rich, plus a person worth loving in Ev.

Chapter Seven

WHEN DEL'S SHIFT ended early the next morning, and he had written his report—earning a reprimand from a clerk coming on duty, who informed Del he was putting it in the wrong file—the prospect of going home to his usual bowl of cereal and a cold bed didn't sound too appealing. Emerging from the station, he eyed the garage that held his motorcycle. Hollister was the lieutenant on duty that morning, and he was a good egg.

He went back inside the station and tapped on the lieutenant's door.

Hollister gave him an inquiring eyebrow.

"I think I might need to take my motorcycle over to a mechanic's this morning, sir."

"We have our own mechanic," Hollister pointed out. "And do you know how many times I've heard that excuse?"

"Well..." Del cleared his throat. "Cut a guy a break?"

"Who's the girl?" Hollister asked, sighing and pulling out a form.

Del grinned. "Thanks, sir. I owe you one. I'll have it back by noon."

He drove over the Broadway bridge, the water shimmering in the rising sun, and over to Ev's apartment. No florist shops opened at such an early hour, of course, and after contemplating a cluster of dandelions growing in the dirt by the side of the street, he decided they were probably better off where they were than clutched in his sweaty fist. The smell of bacon frying permeated the hallway inside the building, but it wasn't coming from Ev's kitchen, for it took ten minutes of knocking and made his knuckles sore before the door jerked open, revealing a bleary and scowling Ev.

"What the *hell*, Delbert?" he growled.

Undeterred, Del grinned. "Thought you might like to go for a ride on my motorcycle."

Ev stared at him. "At six o'clock in the fucking morning?"

He shrugged. "Well, I work nights, you know."

Ev kept staring and then his gaze drifted lower. He swallowed. "You're wearing boots. Knee-high boots. And—and kind of tight trousers."

"Like 'em?" Del asked, lifting one foot. He'd shed his uniform coat and hat, but had kept on the rest of it.

"God*dammit*." Ev turned away. "Give me five minutes."

Fifteen minutes later, Ev was sitting behind him, arms around his waist as they sped down the street. Well, perhaps not *sped* exactly.

"Are you going the *speed limit*?" Ev asked incredulously.

"I'm a patrolman. I enforce traffic laws."

"The entire point of a motorcycle," Ev began and then cut off with a yelp when Del took a corner a little too sharply, and they tipped precariously to one side.

Del kept to the speed limit as they wended their way outside of the city, following one of the wide, empty streets that led to a planned subdivision that hadn't been built yet, only little flags standing in the open fields. The city changed so fast. It seemed every week a new building went up downtown, speculators cleared a street of houses to make room for oil wells, or an entire neighborhood sprouted in the suburbs.

Ev finally stopped complaining about Del's inability to go fast down an empty street with no one in sight in favor of draping himself over Del's back and bestowing kisses on the back of his neck and his ears. Del suffered through this delicious torment as long as possible before he brought his motorcycle to a stop and cut the engine.

"Cutting our trip short?" Ev said in a very smug tone.

"I can't concentrate on the road with you doing that," he replied, shifting on the seat.

Ev pressed his face in Del's collar. "You're the one who wouldn't let me the other night. For all I know, you're going to take me back and leave me sitting on the stoop, cold and lonely again."

"I didn't mean it that way. Were you really lonely the other night?" It seemed too good to be true, that Ev would have been pining for him.

And sure enough, Ev raised his head and laughed. "Hardly. I could have gone out and found another fellow if I had wanted."

At Del's dejected silence, though, Ev said awkwardly, "I didn't. I haven't been seeing anyone else since you've been around."

"Don't," he pleaded. "Don't be with anyone but me."

Ev didn't answer, and after a moment, Del started the engine again and turned around, heading back the way they had come. But when they arrived at Ev's apartment, Ev grabbed his wrist and dragged him up and into his bedroom. Ev took a deep breath, his shoulders lifting and falling, and when he turned around, he was smiling again. Not the gentle smile Del liked best, but a smile nonetheless.

"Give me a kiss," Ev said.

Del did as requested, and the soft, wet sounds they made and the brush of their tongues chased off the last hesitancy between them. Ev rubbed a hand over the front of his trousers, and Del drew a shaky breath. Shoving him back lightly, Ev stepped away and kicked off his shoes, and then crawled onto his bed, fingers busy with the buttons on his shirt.

Del started to come to him, but Ev said, "Wait, don't move—let me look at you for a minute."

Del stood still, trying not to fidget. He caught a glimpse of himself in the mirror on the wall and spared a moment to be thankful Ev was so attracted to him. He'd always thought his ears were too big and his nose too small. But Ev looked at him like he couldn't imagine anyone better.

Ev had gotten his shirt off and his trousers hung low on his waist, revealing a strip of pink cotton. Propping himself up on one elbow, Ev moved the other between his legs, rubbing himself through his trousers, eyes still fixed on Del.

Christ—Ev was going to kill him. He took a step forward.

"*Wait,*" Ev said again, eyes bright with amusement. He stopped, not sure what to do with his hands, a flush creeping up his neck as Ev continued to work himself, shoving his trousers further down and sticking his hand in the cotton bloomers he wore under them.

"Have you been with many boys like me?" Ev asked, tilting his head to one side.

"Yeah. But you're..." *Special. Better.* "I never wanted any of them so bad as you."

Ev arched his back a little as he jerked his hand faster. "What about girls? Have you been with a woman?"

Ev was asking these questions now, when Del could hardly think past his desire? He managed to stammer an answer. "A few."

Ev stroked himself about a minute longer, eyes closed, but the curve of his lips revealing that he knew exactly what this was doing to Del.

"Please," he said at last. "*Ev.*"

Ev's eyes opened, his mouth lifting in a triumphant smile. His movements still managed to be graceful as he slid off the bed, despite the trousers halfway down his thighs. Ev pressed up against him, warm and sudden, and whispered, "Do me with the boots still on."

Del gulped a breath, grabbing Ev's ass in his hands and hitching him closer. They kissed again. Del was far too hot, and he reluctantly let go of Ev to unbutton his shirt. Ev seized the moment to slip out of his trousers, leaving him in just his bloomers, socks, and garters.

"No stockings," Del said, slightly disappointed not to find Ev's legs in the pale pink silk he'd been wearing the first night they met.

"You barely gave me a chance to get dressed, barging in here at such an unholy hour of the morning. Next time I'll wear them," he promised.

Laying his hands on Ev's shoulders, Del pushed gently, backing him up toward the wall and giving him another kiss. When Ev's back collided with the wall, he broke off the kiss, ignoring Ev's disappointed groan, and coaxed him into turning around. Then he pressed up close so his cock was right against Ev's ass, and he reached down to take up where Ev had left off.

A pleased sigh rumbled in Ev's chest, and he leaned his right arm against the wall, resting his head against it and pushing his ass back a little. Del made an approving noise and rolled his hips, hand gently but steadily working up and down Ev's cock. They moved like that awhile, and Del rested his cheek in Ev's soft hair before bending down to kiss and lick and suck the base of his neck. Ev shuddered.

He tucked his head in the crook of Ev's neck, breathing in the scent of his skin. He was starting to sweat and wanted to strip all their clothes off and get Ev stretched on the bed under him. But this was good too, wrapped around Ev and drawing half-stifled groans out of him with every twist of his wrist.

Ev's muscles locked up a few seconds later, and he gritted his teeth, come splattering on Del's fingers. He tipped back into Del's arms afterward on a long sigh.

"Give me a minute," he murmured, "and I'll..." He patted Del's thigh clumsily.

"No hurry. I like looking at you like this."

Ev's cheekbones were flushed, a sweet smile curving his mouth, and his eyelashes dark where they fanned against his skin.

Finally Ev turned, flopping against Del's chest and putting his arms around his neck. "I'm such a fool."

"For staying with me?" he asked, trying not to let Ev's words hurt. "I know you could do better than me, but—"

"You're a fool too," Ev interrupted.

Del smoothed a tentative hand over Ev's hair, not sure what Ev meant, but glad he didn't pull away when he bent to kiss him.

HIS STOMACH GROWLING with hunger roused Del a few hours later. He lifted his head from the pillow, stretching out one leg and hitting his foot against the metal rungs at the end of Ev's bed. The room was hot, the cheap curtain doing little against the sunshine that lurked behind it. The clock on Ev's dresser proclaimed it ten in the morning. His stomach rumbled again.

He tapped Ev's shoulder. "You awake?"

Ev lifted a bleary head. "Maybe. What time is it?"

"Ten."

"Damn. I have to be at work in two hours."

He needed to get the motorcycle back to the station, but he hated to leave Ev so soon. "We should eat something."

"Mmmm, food sounds heavenly. You dragged me out of here before I could eat this morning, and then I got...distracted." Ev sat up. "I don't think there's much besides some stale bread and tinned stuff in the kitchen, though. The milkman refuses to deliver until we pay our bill, and Camilo is as hard up as I am."

"We'll go out, then. How is that little diner down on the corner? Any good?"

"Wonderful doughnuts. And lots and lots of coffee."

They washed their faces, and Ev spent a long time fussing with his hair, applying a touch of lip pomade, and then pushing Del away when he tried to kiss it off, but finally they made it out the door and walked down the street to the diner. Soon a plate of doughnuts and two mugs of coffee sat in front of them.

Ev split one of the doughnuts in two, dipped it into his coffee for a few seconds, and then took a big bite, humming appreciatively. Del followed suit, and as he chewed, thought about telling Ev that he'd joined up with Barrett and entered the bootlegging business. But doing so would mean admitting how hard up for money he was, not to mention how desperate he was to keep Ev with him.

The waitress seemed to know Ev because she came back over to refill their coffee, and they chatted about the latest news from Hollywood and whether Valentino's upcoming film would restore his popularity. They both seemed to think Valentino was the handsomest man to ever walk the planet.

Del let them talk, content to sit at Ev's side and listen. He'd wait to tell Ev about the bootlegging.

"Give me a ride to work, will you, darling?" Ev asked him once they'd finished.

"Sure thing," Del agreed, pleased at the pet name. "Give me another kiss?"

"*One* more," Ev promised, and accordingly, when they got to Calenders, he took Del into the alleyway, but gave him three kisses instead of one before disappearing into the side door with the promise they could spend Del's next night off together.

THE FOLLOWING AFTERNOON, Harrison showed up at Del's apartment. Del had been shaving, and he toweled off the last bits of foamy lather as he answered the door.

"Why are you here?" he demanded.

Harrison glanced over his shoulder into the apartment. "Fine place, pal. Sure is better than my digs. I'm sharing a room with Jasper at a boarding house where the landlady makes watery goulash and charges an arm and a leg."

Del sighed and stepped aside to let Harrison pass. His neighbor Mrs. Johnson was lingering in front of her door, so they couldn't very well have a conversation in the hallway.

Harrison flopped down in the yellow and green chintz armchair and poked at the fabric. "Can't say much for your taste in chairs though."

Boy, if even Harrison thought the chair was bad, maybe he really should get rid of the thing. "Harrison—"

"Yeah, yeah." Harrison waved a hand. "I'm here to enlist your help in a little project. Me and Jasper are buying some booze off a couple Mexicans tonight over in Boyle Heights, near that fancy Jewish church on Breed Street. Now, I figure you can come zooming up, yelling that the police are on their way and brandishing your gun. The spics will be so scared they'll take off, and we'll get the booze for free."

"Will that work?" he asked, dubious.

"Sure it will. I've pulled stunts like it before."

Another problem occurred to Del. "But I don't even patrol in that area."

"So get moved over there. Gosh, pal, can't you handle something simple like that?"

"Sure I can," he retorted.

"Swell!" Harrison popped to his feet. "I figure we'll meet them around one, so you should make your grand entrance about fifteen minutes later. We'll be in back of a printer's shop—the only one near that church."

"All right," Del replied, still uncertain, but he couldn't very well turn down his first opportunity to demonstrate to Barrett that he could be useful to their organization.

"And hey, later this week, me and my girl are going to a new black and tan down on—"

"No," Del cut in before he could continue, "I don't think I can make it."

"But they've got a jazz band and—"

"Sorry—got plans already." It wasn't strictly true, but if he did get to spend the evening with Ev, he certainly didn't want to do it in the company of Harrison. Not that Harrison hadn't been awful decent to him, giving him this chance with Barrett. But Harrison was still...Harrison.

Harrison slouched into the hall, giving him a hurt look as he passed, which Del ignored. He shut the door after him and leaned against it. He'd have to find some way to get the lieutenant to move his patrol area. Otherwise, he'd have to abandon what he was supposed to be doing and ride over there and hope nobody got wise.

Accordingly, when he arrived at the station, he went straight to see Lieutenant Miller. "What is it, Randolph?" the lieutenant asked when he knocked on his door.

"About the patrols tonight, sir. Any chance I could switch with Patterson?"

Miller frowned. "Why?"

"A change of scene?"

Miller scratched a note on a pad of paper. "I suppose you're looking to make a big catch?"

Del shuffled his feet and shrugged.

"Guess you can change for tonight, Randolph," Miller allowed. "You've been stuck on the slow streets for a few months, huh? I'll clear it with the captain. But don't tackle anything you can't handle. You see a whisky six barreling down the road, you get to a call box and send for backup. Understand?"

"Yes, sir. Thank you, sir," he said and escaped before Miller could ask him any more questions. As he put on his uniform in the locker room, he ran over Harrison's instructions again. He sure hoped none of these leggers turned out to be trigger happy.

But Harrison had said he'd seen tricks like this work before, Del reminded himself. He had about two hours until he was supposed to be at the rendezvous. He'd better try and catch a few speeders so he would have plenty to put into his report and no one enquired too closely into what he'd been doing with his time.

HE LOCATED THE printer's shop after some searching. A few minutes after one, he drove toward the alley behind it, loosening his gun in its holster. Maybe he should check out the lay of the land first. He'd look pretty stupid if he went charging into that alley and no one was even there. Accordingly, he stopped his motorcycle about a hundred yards away and walked as quietly as he could to the mouth of the alley, peering around the corner.

Sure enough, there were two cars parked at the far end. He recognized Harrison's rusty truck. It was pretty dark, but the occasional gleam of a flashlight allowed him to count at least six people. Leaving out Harrison and Jasper, that still left four men, which seemed kind of a lot to be spooked by a lone policeman. Swallowing to try and moisten his dry mouth, he turned back to his motorcycle. If anybody did start shooting, he could always scram back the way he came. It would be hard to hit a moving target in the dark alley.

He started his engine and then revved it and shot down the street. He took the corner fast. The alley wasn't paved, and he immediately skidded on the gravel. His headlight threw the scene into sharp relief. All of the men were turning his way. There was a shout.

"This is the police!" he cried out. "Keep your hands where I can see them."

Somebody shouted again, and then there was a loud bang. Del had never been shot at before, but he knew the sound of a gun. Terror blazed through his body, followed by sharp relief that he hadn't been hit, followed by a renewed surge of fear because he was drawing closer to the group, and instead of running, all four of them were leveling revolvers and shotguns at him. He couldn't see what Harrison and Jasper were doing, but whatever it was, it sure wasn't helping.

No way could he fire a gun while driving. He had to get out of here fast. He started to spin his motorcycle around and then realized the alley was too narrow. He was going to run into the wall. Yanking at the handlebars, he tried to compensate, but it was too much. Overbalancing, he slammed right into the ground.

A jarring shock and then a searing pain in his left leg and hip followed as the weight of the motorcycle landed on them. A few seconds later, the world stopped spinning, and he found himself sprawled on the ground, face smashed into the dirt. The engine died, and silence fell.

"Fuck," he breathed out through gritted teeth and managed to roll onto his back. Then there was the ping of metal striking metal, and he realized bullets were still headed his way.

"Fuck!" he yelped and despite his leg screaming protests, he scrambled up and over his motorcycle and flattened himself behind the meager cover it provided. He peered cautiously over the top. What he saw did nothing to reassure him.

It was a little hard to tell what was going on, given that everyone had dropped their flashlights at the first shot, but the ambient light from the headlights of Harrison's truck provided some illumination. The four fellas who were supposed to have hightailed it for the hills were instead crouched behind their car, firing at him and keeping Harrison and Jasper pinned down as well. Actually, he couldn't even *see* Harrison, but Jasper occasionally raised his head over the hood of Harrison's truck and fired a wild shot that went nowhere near the target. Del fumbled for his own revolver, hands shaking. He had almost gotten it out of the holster when another shot pinged off the motorcycle fender in front of him, sparks painfully bright in the dark. He dropped flat again, covering his head with his hands.

The sudden roar of an engine sounded. Del lifted his head. Harrison and Jasper had leaped into the truck, Harrison reversing with a squeal of tires. They barreled forward, clipping the other car, and—they were going to leave him here!

"Hey, wait!" he shouted, leaping to his feet as the truck sped past him. He took off after it, the pain in his leg a distant throb easily ignored in the face of his anger and the danger of being left here at the mercy of four gunmen.

The truck slowed down a little.

"Get in!" Harrison screamed out his window, making wild motions with his arm.

They wanted him to jump into the bed of the truck. What did Harrison think he was, an acrobat?

More gunshots sounded. The truck veered to the left. Del tried to force himself to run faster. Harrison shouted something unintelligible.

Then Del's fingers closed on the tailgate. It wasn't pretty, but he managed to haul himself up and tumble over the side. He landed hard on his left leg again and for a few seconds could only make muted grunts of pain until the worst of it passed. Then he just lay there, staring up at the night sky, jounced and jostled until finally Harrison screeched to a stop on the side of the street. The engine cut off. Everyone remained still for a moment.

"Well, shit," Harrison said at last, his voice filtering through his open window.

That summed it up pretty well.

Del struggled to his knees with a groan and then climbed down to the ground. He limped to Harrison's window. "We have to go back there."

"What?" Harrison's face was pale in the light of the streetlamp overhead. "Not on your life!"

"I can't just leave my motorcycle lying there." He took a deep breath. "They're long gone for sure anyway."

"Yeah, gone along with all the goods we were supposed to get," Jasper put in. He glared at Del. "You fucked the whole thing up."

Del spluttered at this injustice. "That's not how it went down at all."

Jasper made a move to get out of the car, his face dark with anger, probably wanting to pop Del one. Harrison threw out a hand to stop him.

"Things didn't go exactly to plan," he admitted, and winced as both Del and Jasper snorted incredulously. "But instead of arguing—although I'll have you know, Del, that I was *going* to come to your assistance, only my gun jammed—"

"Like hell," Del began, but Harrison overrode him, his voice high and nervous.

"We have bigger problems right now. Primarily the fact that we're supposed to have twenty cases of rum and instead we have nothing."

"And you paid them the money for it," Jasper added. "So we don't have that either."

Hadn't the whole plan been to interrupt *before* Harrison gave them the money?

"They wouldn't let us even look at the booze unless we paid them first," Harrison muttered, sulky at being called out. "I was going to take it back."

Del groaned and rubbed a hand over his face.

"Don't suppose you have some rum hidden in your closet?" Harrison asked him.

Del shook his head. What horrible luck to have his very first job go so far south. "Will we have to tell Barrett what happened?"

"Weelll," Harrison drawled, considering. "Maybe not *exactly* what happened. We'll say more guys were there than we expected and claim they overpowered us." He frowned. "Maybe I should let Jasper have a go at you after all, Del. A black eye would make it more believable."

"Hell no!" He took a step back. "Let him hit *you* if you're so keen on it."

"I'll hit both of you," Jasper snapped.

"Hey," Harrison said. "I'm the one got us this gig. You want to be back schlepping crates for the railroad?"

Jasper subsided into a belligerent silence.

It took a bit of yelling, but Del managed to get Harrison to drive him back to the alley to get his motorcycle. He had to ride in the tail bed again, and although his leg didn't seem seriously injured, it didn't thank him for rattling it around on a hard metal surface either.

Unfortunately, as they drew nearer to the alleyway, it became apparent that Del's fellow cops had arrived to check out the disturbance. Probably a nervous resident in one of the apartments in the vicinity had heard the gunshots and called the police. Harrison pulled onto a side street out of sight of the two patrol cars parked by the alley. Del clambered out of the truck bed again, rubbing his leg.

"The trolley stops here," Harrison said out his window. "I won't be getting any closer to all those cops, no siree."

Del gave a sour grunt. He supposed he couldn't blame Harrison.

"Sure, if it were any other situation, we'd be there with you," Harrison hastened to add. "All for one and one for all! Ain't that right, Jasper?"

"I don't know what the fuck you're talking about," Jasper replied.

Harrison clucked his tongue. "Have you ever read a book? One damn book?" He shook his head. "I can see I need to attend to your education."

"I liked it fine when you attended to my education by introducing me to that gal Ramona. She was a swell dame."

Harrison slapped him on the side of the head. "Cretin!"

Del sighed and walked away, leaving them to it. All he really wanted to do was go home to bed and forget this disaster of a night had ever occurred.

When he approached the alley, he recognized one of the patrolmen and called out to him. "Hey, Owings!"

Owings squinted at him. "Is that you, Randolph?"

"Yeah." Del cleared his throat. "Is there a motorcycle in there?"

"Is it yours? Hell, Randolph, what happened? We got a call about gunshots being fired."

He wiped his sweaty palms along his pants. "I was on patrol, and I saw some leggers down that alley, loading up some crates of liquor."

"And you were dumb and thought you'd take them all on yourself," Owings finished. "Damn, kid. You're lucky you didn't get killed."

"I crashed the bike, and they were shooting at me, so I ran." He didn't have to fake the embarrassment in his voice. "I was trying to find a call box, but then I figured enough time had passed that they had probably left, so I came back to get my bike."

"Your lieutenant is going to give you a real good tongue lashing, you know," Owings said.

Miller wasn't on duty anymore, but Lieutenant Ellis called Del a number of unflattering names when he gave his shame-faced report. Luckily his motorcycle wasn't too badly damaged. Ellis made him type out a triplicate set of reports, which took forever because he kept spelling things wrong band was even slower on the typewriter than usual thanks to his hands trembling in the aftermath of the whole fiasco.

What really bothered him though was that nothing had come out of the evening except a wrecked motorcycle, the chastisements of his lieutenant, a painful leg, and the unpleasant experience of being used as target practice. When Harrison showed up and told him the plan, he had been hoping he might see some money at the end of it. But his pockets were as empty as when the evening had started.

He'd blown a lot of cash taking Ev to Venice Pier the other weekend, and his regular payday wasn't until next week. Which left him with...not a lot of options. Probably Ev wanted to go out to a cabaret, with music and dancing. But Del didn't want to take him to some low-class joy parlor, and he wasn't sure he could afford a nicer venue. Stabbing his finger down on the typewriter keys, he directed a few bitter thoughts in Harrison's direction. Being a bootlegger sure wasn't living up to his expectations so far.

Chapter Eight

HIS DATE WITH Ev was set for the next day. Since Ev didn't have a telephone, he went to Calenders and waited until Ev had a break to talk to him. Ev took him 'round the side of the building, lighting a cigarette and rolling his shoulders. "My back hurts from lugging all those dishes. I'm going to quit one of these days, soon as I get a little money saved."

"I'd help you out."

Ev scoffed. "I don't need you to take care of me."

"But you're still going out with me tomorrow, right?" At Ev's nod, he continued, "I came by to see if you wanted to go on a picnic."

He waited nervously for Ev's reaction. He'd had the idea when he woke that morning. He could make a lunch for them, so that wouldn't cost much, and he'd asked Glen if he could borrow his car again so they could drive to Sunland.

"A picnic?" Ev sounded surprised. "I guess I wouldn't mind it."

He didn't sound particularly enthused, and Del wilted a little. "We don't have to. It was a dumb idea."

"No—no let's." Ev's voice softened, and he put his hand on Del's arm. "I haven't been on a Sunday drive in ages."

He studied Ev's face and, deciding Ev really did mean what he said, nodded. "I'll pick you up around ten, then."

"Okay. Hey, is your leg all right? You're limping."

"Oh, it's nothing," he said quickly. "Just a little accident with my motorcycle the other night." He'd sound a complete fool if he told Ev what had really happened.

THE FOLLOWING DAY they took the county road along the Verdugo hills, bouncing over the washboard ruts and kicking up a dust cloud.

"You're sticking to the speed limit, aren't you?" Ev said. "If you'd go a little faster, we'd have more of a breeze. It's starting to get hot."

Del kept his hand steady on the accelerator. "You never know what might come hopping out of the bushes—rabbits, chickens, deer. Not to mention it's easy to skid off course on the gravel."

Ev pouted and slouched down in his seat, pulling his cap over his eyes. "Wake me up should we arrive a week from now then."

Del's stomach was growling by the time they reached Sunland, and he drove straight to Monte Vista Park. They found an empty picnic table under one of the big oak trees, and Del set down the basket. He'd made his baloney and pickle sandwiches and added some hard-boiled eggs too. He'd also brought several fudge squares—crisp on the edges and chewy in the middle—and a thermos of lemonade.

"Did you make these?" Ev asked, discovering the fudge squares as he poked around the basket.

"Nope, my neighbor across the hall made them. I helped fix her cabinet door, and she gave me them as a thank you." He batted Ev's hand away. "But those are dessert. Don't ruin your appetite."

Ev unwrapped his sandwich from the wax paper and took a bite of it instead. "Not bad," he said after chewing for a moment.

"It's my dad's recipe. Took one to work with him every day for forty-one years." Del gestured at their surroundings. "So, this worth driving out here for?"

Ev looked around the oak grove. "I like the city. Growing up on a farm stuck in the back end of nowhere, I got blamed sick of dirt and grass and mesquite trees. But it's pretty here. And the company isn't half-bad."

He tried and failed to hide a pleased smile. "Looks like we're losing our solitary quiet, though."

A family was walking over to a nearby picnic table, the mother shaking out a red-and-white-checked tablecloth while the father held a baby and gripped the hand of their little boy to keep him close. Del gave them a nod, and the man nodded back, giving him a weary smile.

"That's all right." Ev sighed. "Her hat makes me green with envy, though. Such a darling lilac color for the straw, with the little daisies sewn along the brim. I'd take a photograph of her there, in that patch of sun, seeing as how I couldn't be wearing it myself."

"You like photography?"

"I *think* I do. Never got the chance to try it. I wanted a camera so bad growing up, but my father barely made enough farming cotton to pay the rent on the land, never mind buying expensive presents for us youngsters."

"Not even a Brownie?"

"No. Besides, they wouldn't have given it to me, even if they'd wanted to spend a dollar or two. They'd have thought it a waste."

Del didn't know what he could say to that, so he pushed the plate of fudge squares toward him, and Ev took one, although he didn't eat it right away. Ev didn't often open up about himself, and Del hoped he'd keep talking a bit more.

Sure enough, Ev continued after a moment, "The one magazine my mother always got in the mail was *McCall's*. The pictures would be so pretty. Usually of ladies wearing the most fashionable things and looking soft and dreamy. I'd spend hours hiding behind the woodshed looking at those pictures. I thought that even if I could never wear clothes like that myself, I'd like to at least create beautiful portraits." Ev stared at his fudge square for a few more seconds and then broke it in two and stuffed half in his mouth.

"I'm sorry you've never been able to have a camera. But you are beautiful, you know."

Ev swallowed, his eyes bright. "Don't say such things. How can I be pretty stuck in old brown shoes and this dull gray cap?" He looked over at the woman again and then sighed and ate the rest of his fudge square.

"Why don't you come over to my place after this, and you can get dressed up in whatever you want. No one will bother us there."

Ev hesitated. "I suppose that might be nice."

Del smiled. "Yeah? Good."

Ev gave him a puzzled glance. "I don't get you," he said again.

"I don't think there's much to get about me. I'm not anybody special," he replied, much as he would have liked to have been someone of quality for Ev's sake.

"You took me on a picnic," Ev said, as though that explained everything.

He scratched the side of his nose, not sure what Ev was getting at.

"I've never been with anybody like you," Ev added.

He wondered if this was a good thing or not. "What do you mean?"

Ev didn't respond right away. When he did speak, his voice was quiet, and Del had to lean closer to hear. "All the other men I've had any kind of relationship with have been...well, you were right the other day when you called them shiftless fellows of no account. They all broke the law in one way or another, for starters. Beyond the obvious, I mean. One fellow stole cars and even robbed a few stores, another ran illegal betting on horse races, and the worst was a collector for a loan shark. He was a mean sonofabitch."

Del's stomach clenched. "He hit you?"

"Sometimes."

"You tell me who he is, and I'll give him a taste of his own medicine."

"No." Ev put a hand on his arm for a second before withdrawing. "You're not like that, and I don't want to make you like them. I mean, heck, you're a cop—and I never thought I'd be glad about that fact, but it's kind of nice. To be with someone who actually protects and looks out for people. Not every cop does, but you do. You're on the right side of the law. Well, at least in most respects—some laws I want you to keep on breaking."

A sinking feeling overtook Del as Ev spoke. He suspected that while Ev was obviously all right with him committing sodomy on a regular basis, throwing in with a bunch of leggers who wanted to claim a piece of the vice trade might be a different matter.

"Nowadays, people think gangsters are hot stuff," Ev continued, unaware of the effect his words were having. "They make movies about them, and get a thrill reading about their exploits. But there's a lot of bad stuff too—hurting people—killing them. And at the end of the day, it's not honest work. What kind of future is there in it? One day it comes back to get you. That's what I think anyway."

He paused, as though expecting Del to have an opinion on this, but Del couldn't have spoken. So Ev kept talking.

"I'm so tired of all that mess. I know I'm always breaking the law, that when I try to look pretty, people think it's a sign of a deluded brain or some such. I can never be respectable. But is it wrong to want to be treated with a little dignity?"

Del shook his head, throat tight.

"With those other fellows, I could never have that. But maybe—" Ev paused, his voice catching. "Maybe with *you...*"

Del stared down at the picnic table, clenching his hands in his lap.

"Sorry," Ev said into the silence. "I suppose you must think I'm dumb to get involved with guys like that. Guess you'd prefer someone sweeter, more innocent—not someone who's been tossed around so much. I can't be that pleasant to be around. I don't know why you—"

"Ev." His voice returned, and he reached over for Ev's hand, touching his fingers before drawing back. "That's not true."

Ev didn't say anything, but he smiled, and Del's heart constricted in his chest.

"You're quiet," Ev observed as they walked back to the car a while later.

In truth, Del felt thrown to pieces over what Ev had revealed. "Sorry. Just, uh, wondering if you really do want to come over to my place after this."

"I do."

"It's nothing special, so don't get your hopes up."

"I didn't expect you to live in a mansion, Del."

Ev sounded amused, as though such a thought was beyond the realm of possibility. Which he supposed it was. "I haven't got much, I guess."

"I didn't mean it like that. But you're not a film star, are you?"

No, he was a motor patrol officer who'd probably never get promoted past his current position and whose only chance at making something more of himself might ruin everything with Ev.

"You really are looking blue," Ev observed when they had gotten into the car. "Maybe I should give you a kiss to cheer you up."

"Here?" he said, startled out of his funk.

"No one else is around besides that family, and we're parked facing away from them." Ev crawled over the seat toward him and knocked aside Del's hat. One kiss became two and then three, all of them chocolate flavored thanks to the fudge squares.

Ev ran his hands appreciatively down Del's chest, but Del caught them as Ev's fingers slipped past his stomach.

"Hey. We can't take this so far here."

"Oh, fuck them." But Ev moved over to his side of the seat. "You look better though."

It wasn't possible not to be cheered up by kisses from Ev. With an effort, he pushed his worries into the very back of his mind, deciding he would deal with them later. He didn't want Ev to think that he was unhappy being with him.

It turned out something else came along to ruin the day anyway because approximately halfway between Sunland and Los Angeles, the flivver broke down. It chose a spot with no tree in sight, only scrubby little bushes that didn't provide much shade. While Del fiddled with the engine, Ev had to wait in the car, which grew progressively hotter under the sun. At last he got out and came to see how Del was faring, mopping at his brow with his handkerchief.

"First the car door gets stuck and now this." Ev groaned, sagging against the side and catching himself on the open hood. "It's hotter than the Sahara out here."

"Sorry, I'm trying to get it fixed." He'd gotten grease smeared all over his nice trousers too.

"And no one around for miles. We'd have done better to stay within shouting distance of a mechanic, the way this old bus behaves."

"I said I was sorry. I didn't know this would happen." He took a deep breath, staring down into the recalcitrant engine.

"Don't get mad at me—I was only pointing out the facts," Ev muttered. He got back inside the car, slamming the door.

Del managed to get the engine started again about fifteen minutes later. Ev stayed silent as they drove, staring out his window. Del kneaded his hands on the steering wheel.

"I didn't mean to snap at you," he finally said. "And I'm sorry it's so hot. I have cold soda pop in my icebox at home."

But Ev shook his head. "I think I want to go back to my apartment. I'm tired, and this heat gave me a headache. I'll come to your place another time."

"If that's what you want."

"I just said so, didn't I?"

Del kept quiet, trying not to let his disappointment show, although it was probably a futile effort. When he pulled to a stop in front of Ev's apartment, he couldn't bring himself to ask when they could see each other again for fear Ev would give a flippant reply and brush him off.

A sigh from Ev made him turn to face him. "Look, I don't mean to cut our day short. But I really am tired."

"It's fine."

"Stop by and see me your next night off? We can go out. I'll wear something nice."

"I'd like that," he managed.

Ev hesitated a moment and then got out of the car, giving Del a wave before going inside.

BACK IN HIS empty, quiet apartment, Del slowly washed the breakfast dishes he'd been too excited to bother with that morning. He wished Ev was there, and yet he was also a little relieved he wasn't. If Ev had been there, he'd be sure to notice something was wrong and pester him about it. What would Ev do if he found out about the bootlegging?

He'd be furious Del hadn't told him, disappointed Del wasn't living up to his ideals, and would probably turn his back on him without another thought.

And yet...if Del had owned a nice, new car they wouldn't have broken down on the side of the road, and Ev wouldn't have been upset about it. If Del had more than a few dimes in his wallet, he could have taken Ev somewhere with good food in elegant surroundings instead of feeding him baloney sandwiches wrapped in wax paper.

Heaving a sigh, he stared at the remaining two fudge squares, still sitting on the plate Mrs. Johnson had brought over. He ate one, and then the other as there was no point in saving it anymore. It would be stale by the time he saw Ev again. Then he washed the plate, dried it, and went down the hallway to knock on her door.

"Good evening, ma'am," he said when she opened it. The smell of boiled Brussel sprouts and the sound of the radio wafted out. He thought it was a boxing fight and hid a smile. Mrs. Johnson didn't like to admit she listened to prize fights, but he'd overheard her speak knowledgeably on the likes of Benjamin Leonard and the St. Paul Thunderbolt with Mrs. Pomeroy who lived in an apartment on the bottom floor.

"Did you eat all those fudge squares already, Delbert?" she said, smiling. "Why I thought I'd made enough to keep you a few days at least."

"They're too delicious to last, ma'am. And I shared some with a friend."

"Oh?" Mrs. Johnson's head rose, like a lion scenting its prey. "A friend you say? Does she live in the neighborhood?"

"It's not like you're thinking," he said hastily.

"Is it that newspaperman friend of yours?" A note of disapproval entered her voice. Glen often brought Greta when he came to visit, and Mrs. Johnson did not care for "the barking and muddy paw prints in the hall" as she always informed Del afterward.

"Not Glen, no."

"And I hope it wasn't that man who was here the other day. I didn't like to say anything, but he had a most peculiar appearance. Such an awful hat! Was he a Fuller Brush salesman? I've found them to be the most persistent busybodies imaginable—always coming 'round with their demonstrations, as though I didn't know how to use a mop or a broom myself. I tell them that I have a police officer living across the hall, and they'd best skedaddle and stop knocking on my door."

Del wondered if Harrison would be pleased or offended to learn he had been mistaken for a traveling salesman.

"Anyway, you can't fool me with your 'friend' nonsense, Delbert. Although I imagine your young lady will be baking you fudge squares soon enough herself." Mrs. Johnson took her plate and disappeared back into her apartment with a wink, leaving Del to sigh to himself on the landing.

HE WAS STANDING in the bathroom, brushing his teeth before bed and contemplating his reflection gloomily when the shrill sound of the telephone rattled the air. He hurried into the other room, snatching up the receiver.

"Hello?" He ran his hand over his mouth, wiping away toothpaste remnants.

Harrison's cheerful tones rang out over the line. "How's the weather?"

"Oh, it's you." He slouched against the wall. Not Ev, then.

"Don't sound so thrilled, pal. I'm calling to inquire if you have any interest in attending a prizefight tonight. I've got a betting pool going, and I have some inside information that'll guarantee you favorable odds. Then after we could go tip a few at a swell little speak."

"Thanks, but I'm too tired tonight. Maybe another time."

Harrison protested, but he resisted and finally managed to hang up before Harrison could embark on a detailed recounting of all the times he'd won money at prizefights and how it was guaranteed to happen this time too. He hated to think what Ev's opinion of Harrison would be.

He was buttoning his pajama top when the phone rang again.

"Hello?"

"Hey, pal, it's me."

"Hi, Glen." Del groaned inwardly. He knew what Glen was going to ask.

"What was that this afternoon?" Glen demanded. "Just dropping my car off on the sidewalk and stuffing my keys through the letterbox without even coming in to say hello?"

"Sorry," he muttered.

Glen snorted. "I know why you didn't come inside. I was hoping you'd made a smart decision about that matter we talked over the other day, but I guess not."

When Del didn't answer, Glen made a frustrated noise. "Dammit, Del. How dumb are you? No, wait—don't answer that. I'm coming 'round there to talk some sense into you, so stay put."

"But I was going to bed—I'm in my pajamas."

No reply. He groaned again and hung up before the operator could ask him to get off the party line.

He was waiting in his robe and slippers, frowning pointedly at the clock when Glen and Greta came through the door. Of course, Greta demanded ear rubs and gave Del's face a quick bath with her tongue, which ruined the effect of his frown somewhat. Glen had smuggled a bottle in his coat pocket, and he mixed some gin and tonics before sitting down in one of the kitchen chairs across the table from Del. Greta immediately took the chintz armchair.

"Tell me I misheard you on the phone," Glen said without preamble.

"I didn't say anything on the phone."

"You know what I mean. I can't believe this—joining a gang of upstart leggers. What the hell are you thinking?"

Del folded his arms across his chest. "I explained it all to you the other day. I need more money, and this is my chance to make it."

"You're more likely to end up plugged by one of Crawford's thugs."

Scrubbing a hand through his hair, Del leaned his head back. It had been a long day, and he didn't have the wherewithal to deal with Glen right now on top of it. "Look, I know the risks."

Glen pinched the bridge of his nose. "What are they like then, these leggers?"

"There's the leader of the group, a fellow by the name of Orville Barrett. He's real smart. Crazy about ancient Egypt—the pharaohs and all that stuff. He's planning to make a motion picture on the subject and even said I could have a bit part."

Glen frowned. "What the devil does any of that have to do with legging?"

"Well, it proves he's got brains, knowing so much about history and digging in tombs and hieroglyphics and such. So he can figure out how to take on Crawford without putting us in too much danger."

Glen looked skeptical. "I don't see the connection myself. That's like saying you want your English literature professor to run all your cat houses."

"Why wouldn't that work?" Del asked after thinking a moment. "They'd know about poetry and romance and such."

"Good Lord," Glen muttered. "Who else is there?"

"Barrett's girl Hazel, and a bloke by the name of Fletcher who seems to be the boss's bodyguard. And then there's Harrison and Jasper. I owe Harrison for bringing me in on the operation. I'd arrested him a few times, and I guess since I never roughed him up, he figured I would be a regular guy to have along."

"So how much booze are you moving? You been in on any of the drops yet?"

He thought back to the disaster in the alleyway. "Not as such, no."

Glen grunted. "I don't know about this, Del."

"I never asked your opinion, did I?"

"Yes, you did—you came to me asking if I knew anything about Barrett. So of course I'm gonna check up on you when you tell me straight out you're joining a gang."

The word "gang" sat uneasily in Del's stomach. God, he couldn't tell Glen about what Ev had said, or Glen would never let up. It wasn't that he didn't appreciate Glen looking out for him, but he was mature enough now to be making his own choices. When he'd met Glen seven years ago, he'd only been nineteen. He'd never forget how Glen had taken him under his wing, showing him all the best spots in town where pansies grew and encouraging him to apply to the force. But if he always followed Glen's advice, he'd have given up on Ev after that first night together.

He couldn't lie to Ev forever, though. He'd never be able to keep up the pretenses, for one, and it would be a rotten thing to do. But if he kept quiet a little longer, then hopefully he would be able to save a good supply of cash. Then when he did tell Ev and begged for his forgiveness, there would be ample reasons for Ev to stay with him. Otherwise—well, if he told Ev now, Ev would never stick around with him.

Decision made, he stayed stoic in the face of Glen's admonishments and finally Glen called it a night and went home with Greta.

IT WAS A very pleasant surprise the next morning to receive a call from Ev. "I popped 'round to a friend who has a telephone," Ev explained and then hesitated before asking, "When's your next night off?"

"Thursday."

Another pause.

"I don't want to wait that long to see you," Ev admitted, sounding embarrassed.

"Really?"

"Yes, really." Ev huffed a laugh that dissolved into static over the line. "You have time to see me when I get off my shift this evening around seven?"

"It would have to be quick. I need to be at work later."

"That's all right. Come to Calenders, and you can walk me to my trolley stop."

Del arrived much too early and hung around the front doors of the hotel until Ev emerged. Since they were in the midst of a busy street, he had to content himself with squeezing Ev's shoulder.

"Hey. Here I am."

"I can see that." Ev tried unsuccessfully to hide his smile. He nodded at a grocer across the street. "I have to pick up a few things—come with me?"

Del leaned against the counter while Ev bought eggs, a can of coffee, and three oranges. Ev carefully counted the money from a selection of loose change, a little frown line in between his eyebrows.

"That detective isn't still shaking you down for cash, is he?" Del asked in a low voice as they walked out.

Ev gave him a level stare. "I can pay for my groceries."

"I know. But..." He floundered, uncertain what he could say without offending Ev.

"He isn't," Ev said, relenting. "I've been steering clear of any place where I might get caught. But I'm late getting paid—my boss keeps saying he'll have it the next day, and then he doesn't—plus I had to pay a doctor's bill from a few months ago when I had a bad cough."

"You're better now?"

Ev smiled and touched his arm. "Yes. Don't worry—I'm not going to keel over in the street."

They took what proved to be a winding detour to Ev's streetcar stop, made longer when Ev kept slowing his steps and dawdling to look in shop windows.

"You want to go out on Thursday then? You said that's your next night off, right?" Ev asked, examining a display of dental creams in the window of a drugstore, although why he should find dental cream so fascinating, Del didn't know.

"*Of course* I do."

Ev laughed. "Well, I pretty much figured you'd say yes. Come pick me up around nine? I know a place where no one will give us any funny business."

"Sounds swell."

Ev kept staring at the dental cream. Did he have a toothache? Concerned, Del was about to ask, when Ev spoke again. "I'm sorry to have made you come all the way down here just to walk around the street with me. It was silly of me to call."

"But I wanted to see you. It made me real happy that you called."

"I guess I'm kind of falling for you," Ev confessed, directing the words to a tube of Colgate, but then turning to face Del with an almost defiant expression on his face.

For his part, Del couldn't find any words to reply.

"Don't look like that," Ev said, expression softening, his voice rough. "I'm not such a great catch, you know."

This blatantly false statement brought Del's voice back. "That's not true. You're...everything I could ever want."

Ev's blush deepened, and he moved away from the window, walking again.

Del stumbled after him. "Why'd you have to say it in the street, though? I can't kiss you here."

"Ah." Ev rubbed the back of his neck. "Sorry. Thursday night—you can kiss me all you want."

"I'll hold you to that," he vowed.

Chapter Nine

WITH RENEWED PURPOSE and determined to show Ev a good time on Thursday, Del headed to the Temple the next day. Maybe he hadn't pulled any big jobs for Barrett yet, but surely the Pharaoh could advance him some cash. Hazel was playing hostess to the nonexistent customers in the restaurant. She gave Del a cool-eyed stare.

"How you doin', sugar?" she said.

"Can't complain, I guess." He wasn't about to discuss his actual mood with Hazel. "Can I go through?"

She stared at him for a few seconds and then jerked her head toward the kitchen. "Sure. Jimmy's here too," she added and then went back to her perusal of sewing patterns in *The Delineator*.

The kitchen was as empty and grimy as on Del's last visit. Downstairs, he found Mr. Barrett, Harrison, and Fletcher clustered together in front of the bar. As Del drew closer, he saw they were all staring at a large painting hanging on the wall.

"Del!" Harrison said, catching sight of him first. "What brings you to the neighborhood?"

"Just seeing if Mr. Barrett has any jobs that need doing," he replied, deciding it was best not to ask for some money right off the bat.

"What superb timing, Mr. Randolph," Barrett said, seizing his arm and drawing him closer. He gestured at the painting. "We've only now finished hanging it. What do you think?"

Del blinked at it. It was massive, for one, about six feet by four feet and surrounded by an ornate gilt frame. The scene was definitely from ancient Egypt with some fellow—presumably a pharaoh—sitting next to a woman in a scanty outfit, surrounded by slaves waving palm fronds, with a pyramid in the background. Del squinted at the pharaoh again, leaning closer.

"Wait, is that—?"

"Myself, yes." Barrett tucked his thumbs in his suspenders and bestowed a fond smile on the painting. "I appear as Ramses the Second here, and that's Hazel by my side as Cleopatra. Of course, they weren't alive at the same time in reality, but truth can be stretched in the name of fine art."

Del may not have attended a fancy art conservatory, never mind ever setting foot in an actual art museum, but he was pretty sure this did not qualify as fine art.

"My cousin painted it," Harrison added.

"It sure is something." He cleared his throat. "I like the, uh, camel there in the background."

"I feel it adds a great deal to the atmosphere of the Temple," Barret said. "Another attraction for revelers to our modest establishment. Of course, I had to use most of the cash I had on hand to pay for it, but we'll make up the difference in no time."

Del blinked again, hoping he'd misheard. "You did what, sir?"

"I know I promised you your cut, Mr. Randolph, but I'm sure you can see that we need to invest in our future. I want the Temple to reflect a glamorous and refined sensibility. It can't be another low-class dive. We want to attract customers with plenty of money to spend."

"That's true, I suppose," he said slowly.

Barrett patted his shoulder. "I promise you'll get paid double next time."

"Yeah, but—" Del stopped as Fletcher loomed over Barrett's shoulder, glaring. "I—I guess that's fine."

"The boss does this sometimes," Harrison said to Del as they let themselves out the back door and climbed the stairs from the areaway into the street. "A couple months ago, he bought the headdress Theda Bara wore in *Cleopatra* for Hazel, and it cost a pretty penny."

"I suppose you didn't see any money that time, either?"

"Well, no, but two weeks later he gave us our due—well, minus a bit 'cause of needing to make a payment on the loan he used to buy the Temple. But still a very substantial sum. Don't worry, pal, there'll be plenty of smackers filling your wallet pretty soon."

Del remained silent, chewing over this latest setback.

Harrison lowered his voice. "Oh, and if the boss asks you anything about the *Amanda Lee*, tell him it didn't show up where it was supposed to."

"The *Amanda Lee*?"

Harrison glanced over his shoulder, confirming they were alone. "It's a schooner Jasper and I were supposed to hijack and make off with the liquor it was carrying. We caught up to it okay—a friend of mine in Santa Cruz tipped me off on where she'd be—and we even got the jump on the sailors. But the seas were pretty rough and when we were transferring the cargo, it kind of...slipped."

"Slipped?"

"Fell in the ocean." Harrison sighed. "Sank right down to the bottom. And then one of the sailors got loose, and we had to hightail it out of there before he gutted us on a Marlin spike. Lucky both of us can swim."

Del privately said his thanks that he hadn't been along with Harrison on that particular mission. But damn, he'd been counting on getting some extra money. Now he wouldn't have the money to buy roses for Ev like he had wanted.

ON THURSDAY NIGHT, he put on his good suit and the nicest pair of cufflinks he owned. Absent the money for roses, the best he could manage was a small bouquet of carnations.

Ev opened the door when he knocked, and Del stopped and stared for a moment. Ev looked so stunning. He'd put finger waves in his hair again, and even added a few kiss curls on his forehead. His plucked eyebrows arched in slender, graceful lines over his eyes. Rouge brought out his cheekbones. He could tell the material of Ev's evening suit was on the cheap side, but the black jacket molded to Ev's shoulders and waist so smoothly. Ev had left off the collar on his shirt and wasn't wearing a bow tie. Instead, the necklace Del had given him nestled at his throat. Ev had added a pin with two green stones in one of his lapels, matching the green glass in the necklace. He carried his lamé coat over one arm.

"You're absolutely—" Del had to stop and clear his throat, his voice had come out so croaky. "Gorgeous," he finished.

Ev blushed and took the carnations, fiddling with the stems. Then he put an arm around Del's neck, drawing closer. "Give me a kiss too?"

Del obliged.

"I'll just put these in some water," Ev said, a bit breathless.

"Where's Camilo?" Del asked, following him into the kitchen.

"He's over at José's, helping with a rent party. Camilo thinks we should host one, but I don't want a bunch of strangers tromping about the apartment, getting drunk and ruining the carpets." Ev stuck the carnations into a milk bottle and set them on the table. "They deserve a porcelain vase, but I'm fresh out of those."

The cabaret Ev directed him to was a black and tan on the borders of Chinatown. A sign painted on the wall proclaimed it the Admiral's Blues. Nothing blue about the inside, though. There were white men and Italians cozied up to Oriental girls and Negroes, and a few Chinamen with white women. In short, with all the other boundaries being crossed, no one was going to care about fairies either. Sure enough, as soon as they were by the bar, ordering drinks, another fairy, as made-up as Ev but nowhere near as beautiful, came over and took Ev's arm.

"Ev, I didn't expect to see you here tonight," he said, giving Ev a little hug. Then he turned his gaze on Del. "Is this your current fling?"

Del bristled at being referred to as a mere "fling," and Ev must have caught his expression for he wrapped an arm around Del's waist and said, "We're exclusive, Asta."

"Ev, you should have told me," Asta protested, and he gave Del a sharper, more suspicious stare. "I'd no idea you were going with someone new."

"I don't need your approval for everyone I meet," Ev said, sounding irritated.

Asta transferred his attention to Ev. "Is that so, honey? You sure you aren't making a mistake like the last time?"

Ev rolled his eyes. "Del, this is my friend Asta Taylor."

Asta held out his hand, and Del kissed it. "A pleasure."

Asta raised his eyebrows. "Oh, he has manners."

"See—I'm not completely hopeless when it comes to men. Have a drink with us," Ev continued. "We'll snag a table if we can. Del, get us all some mint juleps, will you?"

The air in the cabaret was smoky and hot. Del was sweating by the time he located Ev and Asta at a table near the dance floor. He set down the drinks and took a seat by Ev, sliding an arm around his shoulders. He'd noticed a couple of fellows giving Ev interested looks, and he wanted to set them straight.

Ev and Asta chatted about various acquaintances of theirs whom Del didn't know. Sometimes Ev would give him a clue, such as "she's a waitress in a restaurant I worked in when I first moved to Los Angeles" or "he got arrested in a big raid at the Palace Baths and only just got out of jail." Del let his attention wander, enjoying the music and Ev's presence at his side.

After a bit, Ev excused himself to go to the powder room, leaving Del with Asta. He shifted in his chair, hoping Ev returned quickly. In some respects, Asta reminded him of how Ev acted when they first met—so hard and defensive. But he couldn't quite imagine Asta ever being as gentle as he was learning Ev could be.

"So," Asta said, "do I need to get someone to throw you out—and I can, a lot of people here owe me favors—or are you serious about treating Ev right? Because that boy has terrible luck when it comes to lovers. The last one abandoned him, and the one before that knocked him around, and the one before *that* cheated on him."

Ev had already confessed as much, but it still made him sick hearing it.

He leaned across the table and looked Asta in the eyes. "I'd never hurt him like that." Not being entirely truthful with Ev about the bootlegging was not at all the same as beating him or two-timing him.

Asta nodded slowly. "Guess I'll let you stay for now. Still, you're a cop. Probably a dirty cop, but the principle stands."

"How did you know I'm a cop?"

Asta shrugged. "You develop an eye for that sort of thing. Well, some of us do. Ev, poor baby, obviously didn't look past your more obvious assets."

"I'd never turn him in."

Asta gave him a cool look and then fished in a pocket for a cigarette and fit it into a holder. He crossed his legs, leaning back in the chair as he breathed in the smoke and let it out in a thin stream. Ev returned as he did, settling back at Del's side.

"Did you two get along?"

"Splendidly," Asta said, downing the rest of his drink. "I'm off to peruse tonight's offerings. Behave yourselves, and Ev, stay out of trouble."

Ev watched Asta leave with a frown and then tucked his hand in the crook of Del's elbow. "Asta was the first friend I made when I came to Los Angeles. I half-thought he would throw you into the street, but since you're still here, I want to introduce you to some of my other sisters."

"Are they going to give me the third-degree too?"

"Would it be so terrible if they did?"

Del thought a moment. "I guess not. It's nice to know you have friends looking out for you."

Ev smiled. "They're awfully protective. Probably because I was such a bunny when I first came here and haven't...well, haven't always made the best choices when it comes to men." He petted Del's arm. "You're the exception, of course."

First Ev introduced him to Princess Nellie, who was one of the few fairies there fully clothed as a woman, in a beaded dress and French heels.

"Ev, really—*another* one?" Nellie said in a lilting voice, pursing her mouth in disapproval.

"I know, I swore after Felix that I was done with love, but then Del appeared, and he wouldn't let me give up on it." It was such a romantic sentiment, so at odds with Ev's usual standoffish and flippant behavior, that Del couldn't help staring at him incredulously.

Ev noticed and blushed, but he didn't take it back.

"So sweet," Nellie declared. "Although I do think you'll be missing out on a lot of fun when the ships come in. I might have to revoke your card in our society."

He gave Ev a questioning look.

Letting go of his arm, Ev took out his cigarette case from his jacket pocket and opened it. Tucked in the back under a clip was a piece of green paper, which Ev handed to him. Del unfolded it. An ink drawing of a bouquet of pansies decorated one corner and swirling letters proclaimed "The American Pansy Society." Beneath that was written, "This is to certify Miss Everett Sharples as a member of the American Pansy Society, forthwith entitled to all benefits and responsibilities included therein."

"Nellie drew those up for some of us," Ev explained. "Isn't it a scream?"

Nellie waved a finger at Ev. "And those responsibilities include keeping a lookout for likely trade for your sisters."

"Don't worry—just because I'm seeing Del doesn't mean I won't notice other men, Nellie. I won't slack off on my duties."

"Oy," Del protested, and Nellie and Ev both laughed.

"Get me another drink, darling, and then I'll introduce you to Philip," Ev said. "He's the piano player in the band."

Del obeyed, floored by Ev calling him "darling" too on top of everything. Ev soon had his cocktail in hand—a Tuxedo #2, which Del ordered because of the dash of absinthe. The color green always made him think of Ev.

"Nellie's been trying so hard to find a good doctor," Ev said as they wandered toward where the band was playing. "She's had all sorts of nervous ailments, and if she could really be a woman—have the body of a woman, I mean—she thinks it would help. We've heard of doctors in Germany who will do surgeries—castration and things with the glands."

"Glands?"

"You know, the liquid nerves—I forget the other name for it. They've done experiments with putting animal glands in humans, and it's helped with all sorts of psychological problems. And I suppose if you can do it with animals you could put glands from a woman into a man."

"Maybe that's how the lie detector the police up in Berkeley invented works. Or was it the crook's heartbeat? I think they tested it with kissing too. Some of the detectives here were trying it out last year."

"The kissing?" Ev asked, smiling.

He huffed a laugh. "No—on criminals. The kissing was to see if women or men were more emotional."

"Well, anyway, I don't understand the science of glands, but maybe it could really make a difference for Nellie. Not that it matters much. There are no doctors here who would consider it—no one we've heard of, anyway."

"Do you feel the same way?"

"Wanting a woman's body?" Ev paused, considering. "I've never— that is, I often thought my life would be easier if I had been born a woman. I know my nature doesn't match my sex. I have feminine impulses and desires. But I've never wanted to try any medical procedures. Although I am thankful I don't ever have much facial hair. I couldn't grow a decent beard even if I wanted. But it's different for Nellie. Oh, there are men who pass as women—with longer hair, skirts, and some makeup, so as you can't tell the difference. But for Nellie that isn't enough."

At that moment, the band finished their current song, and Ev waved to Philip, the piano player, who jumped up from the bench and trotted over to them while the other musicians were taking a moment to rest and have a drink or two.

"Ev, it's been ages," Philip said, wrapping Ev in a hug. "You look so gorgeous tonight."

"Going out on the town with Del—'course I had to look my best," Ev said, and Philip turned toward him with wide eyes.

"You're who Ev was calling the other morning," he exclaimed. "He came 'round begging to use my telephone. I'd never seen him in such a state, absolutely dying to talk to you."

And Ev didn't deny it, only smiled and leaned against Del's shoulder. He had never seen Ev like this—so happy and relaxed, so playful without any of the bitterness or defensiveness that often underlay his words. He knew part of it was being here in a place where Ev felt comfortable, in the presence of his friends. But a small, hopeful part of him thought that perhaps he had something to do with it too. Wasn't Ev proudly showing him off to his friends, after all?

Not that he understood why Ev was so proud. He couldn't think of anything he'd done that would make Ev feel that way.

"Is that a bruise?" Ev said suddenly, leaning closer to Philip and peering at his cheek.

"I got in a bit of a scrap last night," Philip admitted, putting a seemingly self-conscious hand to his face. Sure enough, Del could make out a bruise that he'd tried to cover with some face powder, and a thin cut on his chin.

Ev tugged his hand away. "What happened? Was it those rotten kids again? I heard one of their gang cleaned out Viola's apartment when he brought the kid back for a fuck—so stupid—he should know better."

"Nah, it wasn't them. I keep clear of that neighborhood ever since last fall. No, I had picked up a real sweetheart of a sailor, and we were leaving this cabaret with some of his pals when a bunch of seamen from another ship walked past. I guess they had some rivalry going because everyone started whaling on each other, and I got caught in the crossfire. Worst of it was, my lover got so knocked about that his pals had to take him back to their ship to patch him up. So I never got to have my fun."

Ev made a sympathetic noise and caught Del's hand in his own. "I don't have to worry about that with Del. No fighting, no gangs, none of it. You remember when I was with Michael, and he'd always be carrying that knife around and taking me to those awful opium dens?"

"'Course I remember—thought you'd end up with that knife in your ribs."

"Del's on the right side of the law. An actual cop, if you can believe it."

Philip chewed on his lip and gave Del a solemn look. "Bein' a cop don't mean he isn't neck deep in that sort of stuff. Makes it almost more likely, actually."

"Del would never," Ev said with complete confidence. "Would you?" He turned appealing eyes on Del.

"Of course not," he said, hating himself.

A smile wreathed Philip's face. "You'll both have to come 'round for supper one night. Bring the Princess and Asta too, and of course, any of your friends are welcome, Del, especially if they put on a good show in the bedroom."

The band leader started yelling in Philip's direction, and he winced. "Oops, better get back to work. Don't be a stranger, Ev."

He hopped back onto the piano stool, and the band broke into an energetic rendition of "Old Yazoo."

"Want to dance?" Del asked.

"Let's wait for a slow song. This drink's going straight to my head."

They located two vacant chairs, and Ev took out a cigarette, giving one to Del too. "The three of them—Camilo, too—I don't know what would have happened to me if they hadn't been here."

Del lit their cigarettes, watching as Ev sucked in a lungful and shut his eyes, leaning his elbow on the table so he could prop his head on his hand. Ev continued, "Coming here, I had no money, didn't know a soul. I caught on pretty quick that I could make some dough in the public toilets in Pershing Square. That's where I met Asta—he taught me a few cocksucking tricks."

Del hid a grimace, hating the thought of Ev with other men, even as it brought an uncomfortably arousing image to mind. "You know I'd never expect you to do anything like that," he felt compelled to say.

"I know." Ev's eyes opened a fraction. "I'd do it if you wanted though."

He tugged on his collar, and Ev smirked.

"Anyway, Asta let me stay with him for a bit until I could get my feet under me and introduced me to Nellie and Philip. Nellie showed me how to do my face and took me down to Bullock's to buy my first stockings and garters. Lord, I almost died of fright, but Nellie passed it off so smoothly, saying it was for his wife. As if the salesgirl gave a damn." Ev snorted. "I know that now, but at the time I was dead certain she could see right through us.

"They told me to stay away from Fred—he was the fellow who stole cars and cheated on me. But I didn't listen. I was so fucking dumb. After I left Fred, Asta introduced me to Michael. I think Asta still feels responsible for what happened—that's why he's so protective."

"Michael was the guy who hit you?" he asked carefully.

Ev nodded. "Asta didn't know he was like that—it only started after I'd been with Michael a while. One night when it got...real bad, my neighbor broke down the door to come help me."

"I'm glad someone was there," he said, wishing he and Ev had met each other straight off when Ev arrived in the city.

"None of them liked Felix, either, and he ended up in prison after promising me he would clean up his act. Well, I guess Philip didn't mind him much but that was only because Felix had dimples when he smiled, and Philip loses his head over things like that."

Ev heaved a gusty sigh. "But they've been there for me—making me tea when I needed a good cry, letting me share a bed when I didn't have a place to stay, inviting me to parties and helping me learn how to curl my hair. So I'm glad they liked you."

"I'll have to introduce you to my friend Glen."

"You will?" Ev looked startled but pleased.

"Of course. I've already talked his ear off about you."

Ev didn't seem to know what to do with this information, so he busied himself with stubbing out his cigarette and straightening his cuffs.

Smiling, Del held out his hand. "It's a slow song now."

"You're right." Ev placed his hand in Del's and let him lead him onto the dance floor.

The languid notes meant he could hold Ev close and look into his pretty eyes.

I've joined a bootlegging gang. I know it's not what you want, but it will be worth it. I swear.

The unsaid words weighed him down, and he sighed.

"You're tired, huh?" Ev said, noticing. "Let's call it quits for the night. We could go back to your place, if you want."

Del straightened. He mustn't let Ev notice something was wrong. "My place?"

"You're not too tired for taking the rest of our evening to bed, are you?"

He shook his head, and Ev laughed.

They were heading toward the door when a man walked through it, dressed in evening wear, his hair rumpled, steps weaving unsteadily as though he was drunk. Del grabbed Ev's elbow and steered him over to a dimly lit corner, keeping their faces turned away.

"What is it?" Ev asked, glancing back at the stranger.

"Don't look at him." He jerked Ev back around. "I'm not sure, but I think I recognize his face from the Central station. He might be on the morals squad or an undercover operative. We can slip out once he's farther inside."

They waited until the man was at the bar getting a drink and then made a quick exit. "Guess your job has more benefits than getting to ride a motorcycle," Ev said. "Still—they catch you with me, it isn't going to reflect so nicely on you."

Del shrugged, uneasy but not wanting to upset Ev or make him think that he would abandon him at the first sign of trouble. "You're not a kid, so it isn't like they'll arrest me for corrupting you. You know how it is—most of the guys who get sent to the clink for sodomy got caught with some punk. Nah, they'd care more about you."

"Because I'm unnatural," Ev said in a brittle voice.

The streetlights weren't too bright in this part of town—the city hadn't gotten around to switching them from gas to electric yet—but he could make out Ev's expression, enough to see the pain in it.

"Hey, come on," he said, moving to put an arm around Ev's shoulders and guide him forward. "Let's go home."

Ev took a deep breath, forcing a smile onto his face. "Yes. It's been such a lovely evening—I don't want it to end."

THEY RETURNED TO Del's apartment, climbing the stairs side-by-side, Ev's warmth seeping into him whenever they brushed together. They were almost to his door when Mrs. Johnson's opened, and she stepped into the hallway, a paper bag of garbage in her hand. All of them stopped, frozen for a moment.

"Good evening, Delbert," Mrs. Johnson said, and then her gaze returned to Ev.

"This is my friend Ev." He put a hand on Ev's elbow, then let it drop.

Ev's hands had gone instinctively to his throat to hide the necklace. Luckily it was dim in the hall, and his rouged cheeks could be blamed on a brisk walk, but the curls in his hair were evident.

"I'm in the theatre," he said.

Mrs. Johnson's face cleared. "Oh, the theatre. I'd no idea you had friends in show business, Delbert."

"Yes, I, uh, have them. That is, I have Ev. I mean, as the only friend I know in the theatre." Ev stepped on his foot, and he shut his mouth.

"One of my cousins performed in vaudeville once," Mrs. Johnson said. "What did she sing, now? Was it 'After the Ball'?"

"We're back from the evening show," he interjected quickly. "You're doing well?"

"Oh, my back gives me awful trouble, you know. And the price of milk has been terrible these last weeks. How are we supposed to keep body and soul together when simple necessities empty our pockets?" She sighed and then turned to Ev again. "I imagine you're trying to break into the moving pictures, aren't you?"

"The thought had crossed my mind," Ev replied, fluttering a hand. "The stage isn't what it used to be, is it?"

"That's so true," Mrs. Johnson agreed. "I've heard that Warner Brothers is absolutely the best place to try."

"Why I'll give them a go, then, if you recommend it."

Del edged toward his door. "We won't keep you," he said. Mrs. Johnson could easily spend half an hour chatting once she got going.

"Stop by for some tea or coffee one day, then," she said. "Delbert, you could take a look at my leaking faucet."

"I will," he promised. "You haven't had any more trouble with your cabinet?"

"Oh, no, it's been working like a dream. Delbert helped me fix it," she confided to Ev. "Our landlord takes forever to send a handyman, although since our telephones were installed last year, it *is* easier to get a hold of him. Before you almost had to camp out on his stoop if you wanted anything."

"It was nice to meet you," Ev said, and he followed Del into the apartment while Mrs. Johnson proceeded down the hallway.

"People are very forgiving of actors," Ev commented as they removed their jackets. "It's practically assumed that anyone connected with the stage will act outrageously."

"It was quick thinking on your part, though."

"Well, I'm good at that—coming up with lies."

He didn't like the mocking anger in Ev's tone, so he wrapped him in a hug until Ev barked a little laugh and relaxed.

This was the first time Ev had been in his apartment, and he looked around with open curiosity. Del shoved his hands in his pockets, wishing he had known in advance that Ev would want to come back here. He could at least have taken out the rubbish and dusted a bit.

"Where did you get that?" Ev asked, pointing at the chintz armchair.

"At a yard sale. I suppose you don't like the color."

"Well...it's pretty awful. Were you tipsy when you bought it?"

"Everyone runs down that chair. I'm gonna keep the thing just to be contrary."

Ev made an amused noise and then swished over to him, looping his arms around Del's neck. Del slid his own arms around Ev's waist.

"So, are you going to fuck me now?" Ev asked.

Del squeezed him tighter. Ev's forthrightness about sex always gave him a thrill. "You want that?"

Ev made his eyes wide and wet his lips with his tongue, nodding. Del was pretty sure the babyish attitude was a put on, but it was still cute.

"Did you wear something pretty for me?"

"Uh huh. You'll like it."

"Let's go see then."

At first, Ev kept up the coquettish mannerisms, pretending to smile shyly as he slid off his jacket, and peeking up at Del through lowered eyelashes while he unbuttoned his shirt. He turned away before Del could see what was under it, and he kept his back to Del as he shimmied out of his trousers, revealing a pair of pink silk drawers, an inch of lace at the bottom brushing his knees. Then he dropped the shirt too. A camisole hung off his shoulders by thin straps, swaying and fluttering as he moved.

Ev crawled on the bed without looking at him, plumping up the pillow and laying his head on it with a sigh, his eyes shut. He smoothed his fingers down the camisole, bunching the fabric against his stomach for a moment in a loose fist and then letting go and curling his knees toward his chest. When he opened his eyes, all of the earlier playfulness was gone, leaving a clear, fragile sweetness in its place. Ev looked so delicate that Del was almost afraid to touch him. But then Ev smiled and held out a hand to him.

When Lawrence left him for someone else, it had hurt, but Del hadn't been surprised. He knew he would never be more than a second-best choice for anyone, easy to throw aside when someone better came along. But for a moment, looking at Ev's gentle smile, such thoughts didn't trouble him. Ev's smile promised a love that would never scorn his faults but rather shelter him against the hardness of the world.

"What?" Ev asked in a soft voice, seeing something of Del's thoughts in his expression as Del lay down next to him.

Del cupped Ev's face in his palm, rubbing his thumb along his cheekbone. "I love you."

Several emotions flickered through Ev's eyes faster than Del could identify them. All that remained at the end was desire, the fleeting moment of gentleness gone. Trying to keep it there for more than a few seconds seemed almost impossible.

Ev grabbed Del's hand and sucked two of his fingers into his mouth, swirling his tongue around them to coat them with spit.

"Hold your horses," Del said. "I'm not undressing you so fast." With his free hand, he traced the outline of Ev's hip and leg, slippery with silk. Then he pulled his other hand from Ev's mouth and swept both of them up his chest, rubbing his nipples until they stood out against the thin fabric. The wet fingers of his one hand turned the material dark, and Ev moaned when he pinched the damp silk against his nipple.

Del slipped the straps off his shoulders and bent down to trail kisses over the skin where they had rested. He had gotten as far as taking off his shoes and stripping down to his undershirt when Ev had been undressing earlier, but now he sat back on his knees and worked his trousers open far enough to pull out his cock.

"Come sit on my lap a second," he said, and Ev obeyed, straddling his thighs. Del got a grip on his ass, and Ev grabbed onto his shoulders. They both watched, breaths growing shakier, as Del moved his hips, sending his cock sliding against the silk, the tip leaving a trail of damp spots on Ev's camisole.

"Oh, fuck." Ev searched out his mouth, wanting kisses. He carded his fingers through Del's hair, grip almost turning painful as their kisses grew deeper.

Del finally broke off with a gasp. Hell, he didn't want to come yet. "Now get on your stomach."

"You don't want my mouth?" Ev said, acting surprised.

The thought made his hips jerk reflexively, but God—"I'm not going to treat you like a whore," he said, his voice rough.

Ev hovered his fingers next to Del's cock, which throbbed at the promised touch. "What if I wanted it though?"

Del gritted his teeth. "I—Ev—"

"Such a honey." Ev kissed his forehead. "We'll leave it for another time. On my stomach, right?" He slid off Del's lap and stretched out.

This was what he had wanted—to see the lingerie clinging to Ev's ass. He settled in between Ev's thighs. Ev wasn't fat, but he wasn't skin and bone either, and the curve of his bottom looked nice and plump.

When Del slid a finger between his cheeks and pressed the silk against his entrance, Ev made a startled sound and then groaned, spreading his legs wider. Del got his finger wet with spit and returned it, pushing inside a little, the silk making it easier to finger Ev open.

"That's dirty," Ev said, his voice muffled by the pillow.

"It's getting you stiff." Del reached under him to confirm his words, and Ev squirmed.

It was making him harder too, and it wasn't long before he was pulling off the drawers, baring Ev's ass. More spit, slowly easing Ev open with his fingers, the nighttime noises of the city playing like a phonograph in the background—a barking dog, the distant sound of a train whistle.

Ev finally whispered, "All right. Go on—please."

He tugged Ev up onto his knees, and the camisole slid down, bunching under Ev's armpits. Del stroked himself a few times, teasing out precome and getting the head as wet as he could, and then pushed inside, pausing when Ev tensed.

"Wait—just—" Ev panted quietly for a few moments and then relaxed a little, burying his head in his folded arms, nodding for Del to continue.

As usual, Ev didn't make much noise while Del fucked him, but Del judged his enjoyment by the way the tension uncoiled from his muscles, until he was almost limp under him, Del's grip on his hips the only thing keeping them up off the mattress.

"Right there," Ev did say at one point, his words tight with pleasure. "And go faster."

So he did, sweating by now, losing himself in the rough slide of their bodies.

When Ev worked a trembling hand down to stroke his cock, it didn't take him long to come. Del choked down a shout as Ev tightened even further around him and then drove in harder for the last few thrusts.

He stayed in Ev for a little while after, pressing his hot face to Ev's back.

"Your stubble is scratchy," Ev complained, but he didn't shove Del away, although he did wrinkle his nose when Del finally pulled out and his come trickled down Ev's thigh.

Del fetched a warm cloth, Ev already dozing off by the time he returned. Del cleaned him up and tucked the sheets around him. Ev murmured sleepily when he kissed his forehead but didn't open his eyes. By the time Del had changed into his pajamas, Ev was fast asleep. Del spooned him, sleep dogging his heels too. But he couldn't quite relax, thinking about the evening, about how happy Ev had been to introduce him to his friends, about all that he wasn't saying, and how he might have already ruined everything.

Chapter Ten

IN THE MORNING he was treated to the sight of Ev sitting at the kitchen table in only his underthings and one of Del's shirts while Del fried some eggs and sausage for them.

"I hope you don't want me to cook," Ev had said, coming up behind Del as he brewed a pot of coffee and resting his chin on his shoulder. "I burn everything."

"I can manage breakfast," Del said, turning to give him a good-morning kiss. "I've spent quite a bit of time as a bachelor, you know. Had to learn to cook a few things."

Ev accepted the kiss but didn't offer anything more, retreating to the table and immersing himself in the cup of coffee Del handed him. Del shot surreptitious glances his way. In the morning light, Ev's sweetness the night before seemed a dream. His hand, reaching out to Del, the look in his eyes that had made Del tell him that he loved him—Ev had buried them again, and he didn't know how to bring them back.

"I know my hair is a rat's nest," Ev said, catching his glance but misinterpreting it. "I'll have to attack it with a comb. And you're going to lend me one of your coats and a hat. I'm not walking down the street in my evening attire. Think if we had a little Oldsmobile Speedster. Then we could skip the streetcar. Wouldn't that be jolly, zipping along the road?"

"Yeah." He stared down at the sausages popping in the oil.

"How I dread work this afternoon," Ev continued, sliding down in his chair. "I wish I could hand in my notice—throw it in their faces. Lord, I need to find some other job. But I hate the idea of working in a factory, shut up all day and going deaf from the machines."

He thought of his father and his lame leg, broken and tired from his work in the mills and shipyards. "You can't work in a factory." He never wanted to see Ev end up like that.

"What else is there? If only I'd been able to get more of an education. But I can't manage to save a dime it seems." Ev sat up again and propped his chin on his hand. "I suppose I shouldn't spend so much on clothes. I should stay in instead of going out. But then it will be like I never left the farm, so what's the use of that?"

I'll look after you. I'll give you everything you want. How he wanted to say those words to Ev.

"Don't you start burning the breakfast now," Ev said, and he came back to himself with a start to see that the sausages were starting to edge from brown to black. He took them off the stove and dished them onto their two plates, added the eggs, and brought the plates to the table.

"So tell me a funny story," Ev said around a mouthful. "You must have seen some queer things as a cop."

"There was the time I ran into a guy driving an ostrich hitched to a buggy," he offered, after a moment of reflection.

"Tell it to Sweeney!"

"I swear it's true. I don't know where he got the fool idea, and the bird didn't look too happy about it either. Apparently he owned a bunch of exotic animals to show to tourists and was trying to drum up a bit of publicity. He drummed up a tag instead."

"So strict." Ev hid a laugh behind his hand.

"He'd have caused an accident—everyone sticking their heads out of the windows of their cars gaping at him."

"Yes, I know how much you care about the traffic laws."

He gave Ev a suspicious look, certain he was being made fun of, but Ev gave him innocent eyes. Del huffed. "Now this one didn't happen to me but to two cops named Claxton and Gibbs in Glendale. I heard about it the other day. Someone's billy goat escaped, and it's out in the street, blocking traffic. So they pull up and try to catch it, which takes them a good ten minutes with a lot of sweating and swearing. Finally they get it in the car, and Gibbs makes Claxton sit in the back with it. Then the goat starts making a fuss, butts Claxton in the head, and when Gibbs pulls over to try and help, it escapes out the door. It got a write-up in the *Times*, and I heard their lieutenant gave them each a framed copy."

Ev laughed again. "You all should start a menagerie."

After breakfast they both washed, and Del found a spare coat and hat for Ev. Thankfully, Mrs. Johnson wasn't loitering in the hall, waiting to give more advice about the moving pictures, and they made it onto the street without incident

"Well, thanks for a lovely time, darling," Ev said. "It was jolly."

"Oh—y-yeah," he stuttered, throat closing on the question of when Ev wanted to see him again. But he needn't have worried, for Ev gave him the answer.

"Drop by some evening this week—maybe Camilo will be around, and we'll have something decent to eat in the house." He stared at Del, apparently expecting him to go inside. "I can find my way to the streetcar on my own."

"Right." Del turned away, stopping at the door and looking back at Ev. But he was already walking down the block and never turned to offer a last wave.

THE FOLLOWING AFTERNOON he got a call from Harrison, saying that they were pulling a job that evening and asking if Del could swing by to give them a hand.

He hesitated, recalling Ev's confident assertions to his friends that Del couldn't possibly be involved in any illegal activities.

"You still there, Del?" Harrison asked.

"Uh, yeah. I'm here."

"We're countin' on your help with this, pal."

"I..."

"Oh, and the Pharaoh said to tell you he's got that back pay he promised you. Come over to the Temple and you can pick it up, and I'll give you the details on the job."

Del's grip on the earpiece tightened, and then he sighed, letting his head tip forward to rest against the wall.

"Okay, I'll be right there. I have to get to work in two hours, so let's make it quick."

When he arrived at the Temple, he was met with the strange sight of two horses tied in the alley and a great quantity of burlap sacking piled next to them. He sidled past to the stairwell, thankful he was on the motor patrol instead of the downtown mounted patrol. His motorcycle needed maintenance, but it required far less care and feeding than a horse. There was talk of transferring the department's remaining horses to the parks department, but so far the mounted patrol remained stationed at Central, patrolling an area of downtown, primarily catching parking violations.

"What's with the horses?" he asked when Harrison let him inside.

"They're for the boss's movie," Harrison said.

Barrett straightened from where he was perusing a set of diagrams with Fletcher. "Good afternoon, Delbert. I see you noticed our two new additions outside. It's come to my attention that procuring a sufficient amount of camels for the larger set pieces could be difficult, but Fletcher hit upon the genius idea of using horses instead—disguised, of course."

"Disguised?"

"We make some humps for them out of burlap sacking," Fletcher explained. "Maybe wrap up their tails. If we film 'em from the back, no one will know the difference."

Del tried to picture this and found he couldn't. But they did some amazing tricks in the movies with makeup and models, so maybe turning horses into camels wasn't so farfetched. He looked over at Hazel, who was glaring at the needle she was trying to thread while Jasper attacked a piece of sacking with a pair of shears.

He better get down to business before they tried to rope him into it too. "I can't stay long, Mr. Barrett, but Harrison said they're pulling a job tonight and need my help."

"Meet us behind the Dunrite Deli on Keith and Baldwin around eleven thirty," Harrison told him. "One of Jasper's relatives is settin' us up with some booze—at a discount too."

"Okay." He hesitated, then said, "Uh, Mr. Barrett, Harrison mentioned you had some money for me."

"So I do, so I do." Barrett took out his wallet and handed Del five dollars.

"Is that all?" He'd been expecting a bit more than that, to be honest.

Barrett clapped him on the back. "All I can spare at the moment, I'm afraid. But our plans are proceeding apace—we'll get the Temple open for business soon, and when I have a contract in hand with Metro-Goldwyn we can begin selecting shooting locations."

"It'll be pretty swell, huh?" Harrison said grinning, and Del agreed, although he sure wished it would all happen sooner rather than later.

AT A LITTLE past eleven he drove his motorcycle to the alley behind the Dunrite Diner. Two cars were parked there, one of them Harrison's truck. Harrison popped around the side as Del swung off his motorcycle.

"Del, you're here. Come and meet Mr. Dunnell. He's Jasper's uncle and is a religious fellow—connections with the church and all that. Got himself a permit to buy sacramental wine, and he's passing some along to us on the understanding we'll pay the bill later."

Mr. Dunnell did not look like Del's idea of a religious fellow, with a fedora pulled low over his forehead and several thick gold rings on his fingers. But he shook Del's hand heartily.

"I thought my nephew was lying when he said they had a cop working with them now," Dunnell said.

Jasper had told his uncle about him? Del glanced over at Jasper, who crossed his arms over his chest and looked away with a grunt.

Dunnell laid his arm over Jasper's shoulders. "Maybe this outfit you joined is really going to amount to somethin', huh?" He chuckled and clapped his hands. "Get the rest of the wine loaded, boys, and take a bottle for yourselves."

They transferred the last of the crates to Harrison's truck. Dunnell shook Del's hand again, gave Jasper a brief lecture over the girl he'd brought to the family dinner last week, who apparently had met with the disapproval of Jasper's female relatives, and drove off with a last wave.

"What were you thinkin', takin' Pearl to meet your family?" Harrison asked Jasper. "She ain't the kind of girl you want your parents to see you with, for Christ's sake."

"They'll have to get used to it when I marry her," Jasper said with a glower.

"Marry!" Harrison hooted. "Are you out of your mind?"

"She told me she loves me."

"And you believed her? Haven't I taught you better than that? You can't believe a thing women like her say. She's only doin' it to get you to spend more money on her."

"She means it," Jasper contradicted. "I can tell."

Harrison tutted. "She works in a dance hall. She's had a lot of practice with sweet talk like that for ten cents a dance."

"This is different."

Harrison turned to Del. "Help me talk some sense in him."

He opened his mouth to offer what advice he could when the sound of an engine interrupted him. All three of them turned and watched in horrified silence as a police car pulled to a stop in front of the alley.

It's because Harrison is here, Del thought numbly as two officers got out of the car. *I think it's impossible for anything to go right when he's around.*

There was no time to escape. He could only do one thing. Pulling out his badge, he stepped forward. "It's all right; I'm with the police."

The officers stopped. "You from the East side?" one asked.

"Yep. Delbert Randolph. I'm on the motor patrol." Out of the corner of his eye, he saw Harrison surreptitiously kicking the bottle of wine Mr. Dunnell had given them behind a garbage can.

"I'm Walter Karpink. This is Johnny Carpenter. What are you doing over on this side of the river?"

Del tried to keep his voice steady. "I followed a drunk motorist over the bridge and when I was writing the tag, these two men approached me saying they'd noticed some suspicious activity over here."

"Oh?" Karpink looked at Harrison and Jasper.

Jasper gave the cops a smile that looked more like a grimace. Harrison nodded vigorously. "My mate and I were visiting my aunt, you see. We all went to the Angelus Temple earlier in the evening and heard one of Mrs. McPherson's sermons. Boy, you ever been to one of those, officers? It sure was something else, I'll tell you. My aunt got overwhelmed with all the excitement. She's awful prone to nervous prostration, you see. So we had to get her home and make sure she was all right. I gave her some tea I got from a Chinese herbalist. You ever tried that, officers? It sure did the trick, and—"

"Yes, yes, thank you, sir," Karpink said, finally managing to interrupt.

"The leggers ran off when we got here," Del put in. "They'd been loading up this truck with some contraband wine."

Karpink and Carpenter walked closer, shining their flashlights into the bed of the truck and the crates stacked there. "Looks like quite the haul. Thanks, Randolph—we'll take it from here."

"Of course. You need these two to stick around and give a statement?" Del asked, gesturing at Harrison and Jasper.

"No, that won't be necessary," Karpink said hastily, obviously envisioning the sort of statement Harrison was likely to give. "Unless they can give a description of the leggers," he added reluctantly.

"Sorry, officer," Harrison said. "We didn't see much in the dark."

"There you are, then," Karpink said, relieved.

Del wheeled his motorcycle onto the street, followed by Harrison and Jasper. Harrison gave a low whistle. "Lucky I don't have the flivver registered in my name or we might be feeling some heat in a few days."

"Now we're out the wine *and* your truck," Jasper said, scowling.

"We can get a new one easy. You're the one who's so good at picking locks, remember? But we'd have been headed for the Big House if it weren't for Del." Harrison grinned at him. "You sure handled those cops fine. What would we have done if you hadn't been there?"

"I owe you one," Jasper added, his tone only slightly grudging.

"It was nothing," Del said, taken aback but pleased.

By the next morning, though, he was feeling pretty blue again. Another opportunity to turn a real profit with the legging had failed. All he'd gotten was a measly five dollars, nowhere near enough to impress Ev with an expensive present or treat.

He spent the day wracking his brains trying to think of something he could do for Ev that didn't cost much money—something to keep Ev interested in him until his financial situation improved. It wasn't until that evening that an idea occurred to him. He was helping a lady fix her flat tire at the time, and she must have wondered why he started grinning halfway through the job.

The only drawback to his plan was that it required asking Glen's help. Del hadn't seen Glen for a bit—he knew Glen was still sore at him for joining Barrett's gang. But he went 'round to Glen's bungalow the next afternoon. Glen had caught a summer cold and so was home with his feet up on the couch.

"You sound awful," Del told him as Glen croaked a greeting.

"It's because I've been staying late at the office working on the evening edition this past week, and then they always want me in court first thing in the morning. It runs a fellow ragged, chasing down divorcees and starlets and cuckolded husbands. What I wouldn't give for a quiet day by the river with only the fish and Greta for company." Glen lay back down with a groan, gesturing weakly toward the kitchen and telling Del he could help himself to anything he wanted.

He got himself an orangeade and boiled some water to make tea for Glen.

"So what brings you by?" Glen asked once Del had handed him a cup liberally sweetened with honey and settled into the armchair.

"I need a favor."

Glen coughed and dabbed his nose with his handkerchief. "Shoulda known you weren't concerned about my health."

"That's not true—I'm real sorry you're under the weather. Only I didn't know before coming over, so it wasn't the reason I did."

Glen snorted, coughed again, and gulped some tea. "Hell, pal, don't try to reason your way through this stuff. Now come on and tell me what you need."

Del frowned, but returned to his original subject. "It's like this—I want to do something special for Ev. And I was remembering that Ev said when he was younger he fancied photography. But he never got the chance to try it. I know you have photographers who work for the paper, and I wondered if you knew any of them well enough that you might ask if they'd mind showing Ev their camera—maybe let him try taking a picture with it too."

"Teddy and I are pals, sure. He'd probably be willing—I can ask him next week."

"Yeah? Thanks a bunch."

Glen took another sip of tea. "So, you gonna introduce me to Ev soon?"

"Of course. He let me meet some of his friends the other day."

"Oh? What does he do, by the way?"

"He's a dishwasher at that hotel downtown—Calenders."

"Is he from California?"

"No, Texas, but he's been living here for a few years."

"Well, you better introduce us soon so I can give him my stamp of approval." Glen was half-teasing, but serious as well.

"You're always lookin' out for me, huh?" Del said, smiling. Guess both he and Ev had some pretty swell friends.

IN AN IDEAL world, Del would have been able to talk to Ev every day. As it was, he hadn't expected to get the chance before the weekend, but on Thursday morning, the phone rang.

"I didn't wake you up, did I?" Ev asked when he answered.

"No," he lied, swallowing a yawn and rubbing his shin where he'd run into the bedstead in his haste to get to the phone.

"It's only that I have to get to work soon—I stopped at a pay phone on my way. I wanted to ask if—well, to ask when you might be able to come over for dinner."

Ev sounded nervous, as though he actually thought Del might refuse.

"I don't have a free night until Sunday," he told Ev, regretful. "Would that be okay?"

"Sunday is grand." A pause. "You can spend the night too."

"I wish I had a night off sooner. You could come over for an afternoon before then—Saturday, say?"

"I can't. I've picked up some extra work at the Western Soap and Chemical Company, and my first shift is Saturday."

Del frowned. "Factory work? But—"

"I'm hard up, all right? You know that. And packaging soap flakes is better than some things."

"If you need money, I could—"

"I have some pride too, you know."

"I didn't mean..." He fell silent, abashed.

Ev's sigh crackled over the line. "Look, we'll plan on Sunday, all right? Six o'clock."

"Okay." He leaned closer to the mouthpiece. "I love you."

A long pause. "See you Sunday, Del."

HE FRETTED FOR the next three days, worried Ev would stay angry at him. It hadn't been his intention to imply Ev wasn't capable of taking care of himself. But he also wished Ev would depend on him a bit more.

So when he arrived at Ev's apartment, carrying a fresh shirt, socks, and his shaving supplies in a small bag, his nerves were on the wire, not sure in what mood he would find Ev. But Ev answered the door with a smile. His hair was curled, and he was actually wearing a day dress with an apron. The delicious smell of something cooking wafted from the kitchen.

"Camilo is making pork *humba* for us," Ev said.

"And *biko* for dessert," Camilo added as Del stepped in the door. Camilo was wearing an apron over a day dress too.

Ev smoothed his hands down the skirt. "Camilo found the dresses for us, and Nellie—you remember her—sewed the aprons. Aren't they dear, with the little pockets?"

"Maybe I should get an apron myself. I'm always spilling stuff in the kitchen."

Ev and Camilo both giggled. "Maybe in a more manly color," Ev said.

They sat him down at the table, and Ev brought him a glass of lemonade, then fluttered around the kitchen until Camilo set him to washing some of the dishes.

"How did things go yesterday with the new job?" Del asked him.

Ev shrugged one shoulder. "I had to get up horribly early, and it was boring and made my back ache. But what can you do? At least we'll be able to manage rent this month."

"I told you I could work extra shifts at the restaurant," Camilo said.

"Don't start that again." Ev frowned, setting a plate down with an annoyed thump. "You already work more hours than I do."

"José offered—"

"And I'm not going to accept money from your man, Camilo. What do you take me for?"

Del frowned. Did Ev's acquaintances think Del was shirking on his obligations to Ev?

"I offered to give you some money," he reminded Ev. "This José fellow had no call to be saying such things."

"Do you think I asked him to?" Ev demanded with a glare. "Camilo was probably talking too much, as usual—"

"Oh, blame it on *me*," Camilo muttered.

"All of you need to stop complaining about my working there," Ev concluded. "I'm not a baby. I don't need to be coddled."

In Del's opinion, Ev deserved to be coddled and spoiled, but he held his silence, knowing he'd be pushing his luck if he contradicted Ev.

The atmosphere in the kitchen remained frosty for a few minutes, but finally Ev sighed and leaned into Camilo, who patted his cheek and fussed with Ev's curls before asking him to set the table, as supper was almost done.

The *humba* proved to be a pork stew with a sweet flavor, a recipe Camilo's family often made in the Philippines, as he told Del once they were all seated.

"How do you like the States so far?" Del asked him.

"It is both good and bad," Camilo replied. "I miss my family and friends back home, and it is hard to find any well-paid work here because of my color. Employers only want us as servants or bell boys or out in the fields picking crops."

"What about one of the fishing boats or working down at the docks?" he suggested.

Camilo shivered. "I am staying far away from boats and fish. The first night I arrived here, I was staying at a hotel with one of the men who emigrated with me. But someone took his money that night, and so he could not pay for the room. They told him he must go to the canneries up in Alaska to work off the debt. The company, of course, charges him for board and food, and so he owes even more money when he gets back and has to go again."

Del grimaced. "That's a rotten scam."

"Besides, you can't suggest that Camilo should do rough work down on the docks," Ev chided. "It would ruin his hands and figure."

Camilo exchanged a smile with Ev. "There are good things too. I could not dress like this back home or invite men to my bedroom. Even the girls here are very wild, going out with men and letting them pet and neck. Nice girls are not like that back home."

"Although it is not so good here either much of the time," Ev added, and then said to Del, "Nellie came 'round yesterday. She'd been roughed up by the cops the other night."

"I wish I could talk to those cops, whoever they were, and tell them to stop hurting you."

"God, don't even think about that," Ev said, alarmed. "Sure, maybe they don't care if you're fucking us—half of them have done it too. But they wouldn't like it if you stood up for us. They'd turn on you too."

"Anyway," Camilo said firmly, "I am surviving in the States. I think that is all most of us can manage. And I have José now too, although he is off to some place farther north tomorrow to try and get work in the fields." Camilo pursed his mouth, narrowing his eyes and poking moodily at his stew.

"But they're taking his cousin's truck, not the railroad," Ev reminded him. "Fewer chances to run into punks that way."

Camilo huffed. "On the railcars or not, some pretty little thing will turn up, and José will not keep his promise to me."

Del had seen a few tramps with the boys they picked up in railcars. He'd never been much interested in trying anything with a punk—they all wanted money, and he'd rather have a fairy or a girl. But women were in short supply on the road, so a lot of men who'd never touch a fairy made do with a boy.

Ev was continuing to try and appease Camilo, when a loud, frantic knocking sounded on the door, and a second later, Ev's friend Philip burst into the apartment.

"What is it?" Ev asked, starting up from his chair.

"Oh God, Ev, it's simply awful," Philip exclaimed, chest heaving as though he'd run straight from the streetcar stop. "I've only just found out what's happened to Asta."

Ev paled. "Asta? Is he hurt?"

"No, but—" Philip took a deep breath, steadying himself with a hand on the wall. "He got arrested in the Palace Baths last night."

"Last night?" Ev exclaimed. "But that's hours ago now."

"No one else we know was there at the time, and he's been in jail since, so the news didn't get out. But my niece was at the courthouse this afternoon because that fool husband of hers got himself into a fight at a cabaret last night, and of course she recognized Asta right away. She said he was charged with lewd vagrancy and sentenced to six months in jail."

"Jail?" Ev repeated blankly. Camilo made an outraged noise and got up to usher Philip to a chair. He sat down heavily, shoulders slumping.

"It's beastly, and the worst is that they're sending him up to the state prison by San Francisco because the new county jail isn't finished yet and the one down in Santa Ana is too crowded."

Ev put a hand to his mouth. "Sending Asta to San Quentin? But that—God knows what might happen to him in there. That can't be."

"I'd heard they're shuffling prisoners around a lot until the Hall of Justice gets done," Del said. He hesitated a moment and then went to Ev and put a hand on his shoulder.

Ev looked at him, face tight with anxiety. "I have to see Asta before they take him away. There's his things, and oh Lord, what about Sam?"

"Sam?" Del asked.

"Asta's dog." Ev chewed on his lip, brow creased with worry. "Asta's been sleeping with some fellow named Rex these past weeks in his rooms over on Ninth Street. I have to go right away to get Sam or who knows what Rex might do. Philip, see if you can't get a message to Asta somehow. Tell him I'll look after everything and that he doesn't need to worry about Sam."

Phillip nodded. "Right-o."

"I will go to the butcher and get some bones," Camilo said. "I'm sure the little dog will be hungry."

"But Sam isn't exactly little," Ev said, groping distractedly for the ties to his apron. "I don't know how we'll hide him from the landlord. You know Mrs. Miraglia reports everything she sees to him."

"Glen has a backyard," Del said. "I bet he'd be willing to look after Sam."

"Really? But for six months…"

"I think it would be all right, but at least he'd take him for a bit until you get something else worked out."

"If he can, it would be a load off my mind. I suppose we can ask at any rate. I'll change into something more suitable, and then we'll go." Ev glanced at the table and their half-finished meal. "I'm so sorry, Camilo, and after you spent all the time cooking this."

Camilo brushed it away. "It is no matter. I can heat it up again for us later. Of course we must help Asta."

"And I'm sorry to drag you into this," Ev said a few minutes later as he and Del walked to the nearest Yellow Line stop. His agitated steps hit the pavement in rapid bursts, and he kept pulling ahead of Del, who quickened his own pace to keep up.

"You don't have to apologize. Besides, Glen's always saying Greta needs company. Does Sam get along with other dogs?"

"I hope so. Honestly, I feel so shaken by this, I can hardly think. Of course, we all know it can happen—I've been nabbed myself, after all— but the state penitentiary seems so much worse. How will I ever visit Asta way up there?"

Ev's voice was tight and strained in his distress. Del glanced at him, worried. "You'll be able to write, though," he said, trying to think of something comforting to say.

"Yes—yes, I'll do it every week," Ev said, but the words trembled, and a tear slid down his nose.

"Hey, it'll be okay." He reached out and pulled Ev to a stop for a moment. "Try and calm down."

Ev stilled, but he balled his hands into fists. "He's my dearest friend. It makes me so—so damn angry, Del, that he can get arrested like this. That we're treated like criminals when we've done nothing to deserve it."

Ev's voice was rising, drawing looks from passersby. Del put his hands on Ev's shoulders, standing in front of him to block him from view.

It took a few minutes, and Ev had to wipe away a few more tears, but at last he took a shuddering breath and relaxed a little.

"Better?" Del asked, and Ev nodded.

"Thank you."

Del gave his shoulders a last squeeze and then led the way to the streetcar.

When they reached the rooms Asta had been staying at with Rex, it was getting on past eight. The rooms were tagged on the back of a café, and a light was on behind the curtain. Ev knocked, and a minute later the door opened.

"Are you Rex?" Ev asked the man standing there, who looked half-drunk, his shirt untucked and suspenders hanging down.

"Who's askin'?"

"I'm a friend of Asta's. I heard he was staying here."

"Yeah, but he's not here now. I don't know where in the hell he is."

"He's been arrested at the Palace Baths," Ev explained. "They're sending him to San Quentin for six months."

Rex's face darkened. "He's been off fucking behind my back, is that it?"

Ev's jaw tensed. "I'm here to get Asta's things—and Sam. You'd better have been feeding him."

"That damn dog—shedding over everything," Rex's eyes narrowed into a squint. "That cocksucker wasn't worth it, I tell you, and now I find out he's been running around. He gets out, I'm going to find him and teach him a goddamn lesson. No fairy is gonna make a fool out of me, you hear?"

"If you try and lay a finger on Asta, I'll make you regret it," Ev shot back.

Rex swung his fist toward Ev, who ducked, and Del grabbed Rex's arm, yanking him to a halt. "Hey, pal, simmer down. We don't want a fight."

"Let me go, you fucking—" Rex tried to pull away, but Del crowded in on him, slamming him against the door frame.

"Shit," Rex whined, rubbing his head. "Come and get the dog, then."

Del let him go with another shove, and Rex stumbled into the room, back to a bottle of gin, leaving the door open.

"Sam?" Ev called, stepping over the threshold. A bark from farther inside.

"He's in the bedroom," Rex mumbled, slumping into a chair.

They picked their way across the floor in the dim light and opened the bedroom door. A veritable mountain of dog greeted them, slobbering all over Ev's hands.

"Damn, you weren't kidding when you said he wasn't little," Del said, staggering a bit as Sam pressed against his legs. "Is he a Saint Bernard?"

"Yes. Asta got him as a puppy. It's all right, boy. We're getting you out of here," Ev added, ruffling Sam's ears and then looking around helplessly for some sort of leash.

In the end, they had to knot two of Asta's scarves together and tie them onto Sam's collar. Ev collected a box of clothes, a bottle of perfume, and a pair of shoes. He'd have taken more, but Rex came and hovered in the doorway, shooting wary looks at Del, but still yelling at Ev if he started to pack some of the more expensive items, such as a table lamp with a red shade.

"I'll call the cops, you try to steal anything," Rex threatened.

If Del had brought his badge along, he'd be tempted to shove it in this guy's face, despite the risks.

"You just want to pawn it later," Ev said, throwing Rex a disgusted look. "I'm not going to push it, though," he added to Del in an undertone. "I can't prove it's Asta's, and I don't want a fight."

"I might take prison over living with a fellow like that," Del said after they left. He carried the box, and Ev held Sam's leash.

"I'm sure Asta was only with him because he needed a place to stay. He's been out of work for a few weeks and not picking up much on the side." Ev stopped as they came to an intersection. "But now we have to get home somehow—we can't take Sam on the streetcar."

"Let's find a telephone, and I'll give Glen a call, see if he can come pick us up, and ask about Sam while I'm at it."

They found a soda fountain with a telephone booth in the back, and Ev waited outside with Sam and the box full of Asta's clothes while Del put in a nickel and rang up Glen.

"A Saint Bernard?" Glen asked as Del explained the situation.

"That's right. See, his owner is a friend of Ev's, but he got arrested and is getting sent to prison for a couple months. We've got nowhere to keep a dog that big, and I thought maybe Greta could use some company." He held his breath, waiting for Glen's response.

"This friend got picked up by the morals squad, huh?" Glen clicked his tongue in sympathy. "'Course I can take the dog. Give me a minute to put on my shoes and a hat, and I'll come get you."

He reported the good news to Ev, who sagged with relief.

"Glen should get here in fifteen minutes or so. You want a soda or something while we wait?"

Ev shook his head. "No, my nerves are shot all to pieces. I'm not hungry." He sat down on the curb, and Sam stretched out next to him. Del crouched down, petting Sam's head. Sam put a massive paw on his arm, and Del obediently transferred his attention to Sam's stomach.

"Asta didn't tell me Rex was like that," Ev said in a low voice after a few minutes. "I didn't know. If only I'd asked—Asta could have stayed with me. I wouldn't give a damn if I had to sleep on the floor. Asta's done as much for me, and now he's going to prison, and I didn't even *know* until Philip's *niece* found out and—"

"Hey," Del interrupted, putting his hand on Ev's knee and giving it a squeeze. "It wasn't your fault."

"I'm a rotten friend."

"No—look at all you're doing—rescuing his stuff and making sure Sam has a place to stay."

Ev reached over to stroke Sam's flank, and Sam thumped his tail.

"Your friend," Ev said after a minute. "Is he...I mean, how does he feel about fairies like me or Asta?"

"He's like me. You don't have to worry. In fact, I have him to thank for meeting you that first time. I'd been upset because—" He stopped, not sure if he wanted to tell Ev about Lawrence.

"Because...?" Ev prompted.

"I'd been with somebody," he said slowly. "Lawrence, his name was. I thought we were...that he..." God, why was it still so hard to talk about this? "I thought he wanted to be with me. But he left me for a fellow who'd made money on the stock market. I think they went off to Florida together. I was feeling blue, but Glen said I had to get over him and told me about the Elephant's Ear. That's why I was there that night, when you walked in the door."

"I see." Ev drew his knees up and rested his arms on them. "Thank you for telling me. You haven't told me much about yourself, you know."

"I haven't?"

Ev shook his head.

"But..."

Ev tilted his head, looking at him.

Del cleared his throat. "There's not much to tell. That's all."

"I don't think that's true." Ev turned his gaze back to the street again. "And I want to know more about your life, about what you're feeling."

The anxious clench of his stomach worsened. If he had something worth telling Ev, he would. Of course he would. But talking about himself would only lead to trouble. And it wasn't just the bootlegging, although that was bad enough in and of itself. To tell Ev about his worries with his job, for example—to admit that he couldn't manage to type or file things correctly—no, no then Ev would think him stupid or worse.

After a few minutes, when it became obvious Del wasn't going to say anything more, Ev sighed and reached over to squeeze his hand. Del squeezed back and then returned to petting Sam, grateful Ev wasn't going to press the matter.

Glen arrived a few minutes later. As soon as he was parked by the curb, Del opened the backdoor of the car and whistled for Sam, who happily clambered onto the seat, stretching over it in an expanse of fur.

"Big fellow, aren't you?" Glen said, coming around the front of the car. "I'm Glen, by the way," he added, holding out his hand to Ev.

"I can't thank you enough," Ev said, shaking it. "This isn't how I wanted to meet Del's friends, asking for something like this. If you give me a few days, I'll be able to find someone to take Sam. And I'll pay for his food."

"Hey, there's no call for that. I can look after him while your friend's in the clink. It'll do Greta good to have some company while I'm at the office."

Ev repeated his thanks while Del put the box of Asta's possessions onto the floor in the back. By silent agreement, he and Ev squeezed into the front seat rather than try to budge Sam from his contented sprawl.

They stopped at Ev's to drop off the box of Asta's clothes and pick up the bones Camilo had bought. Camilo came out to fawn over Sam, who produced an impressive amount of slobber, eyes fixated on the bag of bones.

"Not yet, pal," Glen told him. "You share some of these with Greta, and I guarantee she'll warm up to you."

Greta, after the initial shock of having a strange dog waltz into her home, proceeded to ignore Sam while Glen divvied out the bones. After a decent interval of chewing, both dogs headed for the back door, each with a bone in their mouth, the same objective in mind. Glen let them out, then headed for one of the kitchen cabinets.

"You want a drink?" Glen asked Ev. "You kind of look like you could use it."

Ev hesitated. "I've already been so much trouble..."

Glen waved a hand. "No trouble for a friend."

"Friend?" Ev repeated, startled.

"Why, sure. Given that we'll be seeing each other pretty often."

"We will?"

Glen grinned, taking out a bottle of gin. "You realize how gone this fellow here is for you, don't you?"

Del flushed. Ev went rather red too.

"I—I—" Ev stammered.

Glen laughed and distributed their drinks. He clinked his glass against Ev's. "You can help me keep Del out of trouble."

Del expected Ev to laugh too or make a flippant comment, but Ev nodded, staring down into his glass and gripping it tightly.

Greta started scratching at the door, and Glen got up to let her and Sam inside. "By the way," he said as he sat down again, "I talked with Teddy, and he says he'd be happy to give Ev a tour of his darkroom and let him try out his camera."

"I'm sorry, what is this?" Ev asked, setting down his glass and frowning.

Del cleared his throat. "I remembered what you said to me that time—about how you'd always wanted to try photography, but never had the chance. So I thought, why, Glen knows photographers at the paper and maybe one of them could show you his equipment. If you wanted to take a look," he added uncertainly.

"Oh." Ev plucked at the fabric of his trousers, pinching one of the creases. "I never thought you'd remember a little thing like that."

"It wasn't a little thing. It was important to you, wasn't it?"

Ev didn't answer.

Glen glanced between them. "Well, Teddy's free most Tuesday evenings and Sundays, so..."

"We could just drop by," Del said. "I've never seen a darkroom either. It would be interesting, don't you think?"

Ev shrugged. "I guess."

He frowned, trying to find some clue to what Ev was thinking. He'd thought this was something Ev wanted, that it would make Ev pleased.

"If you'd rather not," Glen began, but Del interrupted.

"No, we want to. Right, Ev?"

Ev glanced at him and then shrugged again. "I suppose. As I've nothing else to do next Sunday."

"I'll tell Teddy you'll be by then. Let me grab some paper, and I'll write down his address," Glen said, clearly deciding not to get into whatever was going on between Del and Ev. Del wished he knew what was going on himself.

He tried to ask after Glen dropped them back at Ev's apartment, and they were shifting around to try and fit together comfortably in Ev's bed.

"If you aren't interested in the photography, we don't need to go. I only thought you might enjoy it. That was all."

"I know." Ev had his back to him, lying on his side.

"But if you wouldn't—"

"I said I would go, didn't I?"

Del fell silent, drawing away from the snap in Ev's voice.

A sigh from Ev, and the sheets rustled as he turned around. Ev's fingers touched his face. "Thank you—for remembering," Ev whispered.

He nodded, feeling for Ev's hand and pressing a kiss to his palm, then curling their hands against his chest. "You're not angry?"

"I'm not. I'm..." Ev stopped and sighed again, gripping Del's hand. "I'm tired. That's all."

He could understand that. It was only natural for Ev to be upset after all he'd dealt with that evening. Relieved, he kissed the top of Ev's head, keeping ahold of his hand as he drifted off to sleep.

Chapter Eleven

ON SUNDAY, DEL met Ev at a trolley stop close to Teddy's flat. When he swung off the streetcar, he almost walked right past the man standing by the window of a furniture shop before realizing it was Ev.

"Oh, hey," he said, halting.

"Hey, pal." Ev chucked the stub of the cigarette he had been smoking into the gutter. "I think the place is down this block, yeah?"

"Uh, I think so," Del stammered. Ev had never called him "pal" before. And Ev looked different somehow too. Was he wearing a new coat? Maybe so—it looked broader in the shoulders than the one he usually wore. And now that he thought about it, he'd never seen Ev wear such dark, plain colors, all browns and grays.

"I had a hell of a time reading Glen's handwriting," Ev said, waving the envelope Glen had written Teddy's address on.

"Oh, yeah, he's got awful handwriting."

"The Senators beat the White Sox last night, right?" Ev asked as they walked.

"Um, yeah. I heard the last inning on the radio." He paused. "I didn't know you cared about baseball."

"I don't," Ev said, which only confused Del further.

When they reached Teddy's flat, Ev went up the stairs first. "Looks like it's this door," he said, knocking.

A young man opened it a moment later, holding out his hand and smiling. "I'm Teddy Frasier. You must be Everett?"

"Yep, Everett Sharples," Ev replied, shaking Teddy's hand.

"Delbert Randolph," Del said, walking up beside Ev before shaking Teddy's hand too.

"It sure is swell of you to do this," Ev said as Teddy gestured for them to come inside.

"My pleasure. Glen told me you were real keen on learning photography. You can throw your hats and jackets over there." Teddy gestured to an armchair.

Ev took off his hat, running a hand over his slicked-back hair. He was wearing suspenders too under his jacket, Del noticed.

"I think photography is real fascinating," Ev was saying. "But I never had the chance to learn it myself."

"I have a couple cameras," Teddy said, going to the table where he had laid them out. The flat was attractively furnished, and the presence of several back issues of *McCall's* on an end table suggested Teddy was married, although his wife appeared to be out.

"This is the one I use for my job with the paper," Teddy continued, pointing to a large camera. "It's a reflex camera, which is what most press photographers use, although sometimes I take this old Speed Graphic with me. Of course, the latest news is about the Leica thirty-five millimeter. You've heard of it, I suppose?"

Ev hesitated, and so Del quickly said, "I haven't. What's that?"

"They're made in Germany, but we should be getting some here soon. They only came out this year. The first real handheld thirty-five millimeter. You can take a slew of pictures all at once. My other cameras are single plates. Not that I can imagine you get decent negatives from the Leica. It's so small."

"What about portrait work?" Ev asked.

"You'd want a longer lens. The Graflex is a nice model for studio work. Is that what you're interested in?"

"Yes—well, I'm not really sure."

"The best thing to do is get a simple camera and start taking pictures. You need to get a feel for what the light will do. Take photos of everything, especially pretty gals," Teddy added with a grin.

Ev laughed. "Sure, a great set of gams and a sweet smile—that'd make any picture look good, huh?"

"You bet."

They carried on, but Del wasn't listening anymore. He'd realized what was different about Ev—he was acting like a man. His clothing, mannerisms, language, all of it was masculine. Oh, Ev still had the same physique, slim and straight with delicate bones and small hands, but he wasn't...well, he wasn't *Ev* anymore. It was like being with a stranger who'd stolen Ev's body.

"I really admire Paul Strand's work," Teddy was saying when Del focused on the conversation again. "I imagine you must like Clarence White's photography, if you enjoy portraits."

"I don't know his work," Ev admitted, keeping his eyes on the cameras.

"Oh, well you should absolutely see some. It was tragic that he died recently—a heart attack, I believe—but he started a school for photography in New York around eleven years ago, and I imagine that will keep going."

Teddy reached over a stack of books and picked up a small circular piece of metal with a tiny black lens poking out. "Now this is a funny camera. It belonged to my granddad back in the eighties. You hid it in a buttonhole and could take pictures without anyone the wiser."

"I suppose detectives could use them," Del said, leaning closer to look at it.

"Maybe so, but you don't see them much these days. They were more of a novelty item than anything. But say, why don't we go into the darkroom now, Everett, and I'll show you how to develop a negative. Delbert, I'm afraid it's a bit cramped—do you mind waiting out here?"

Del did not, and he sat down in a chair, provided with a bottle of orangeade by Teddy and instructions to find a radio program that he enjoyed. Ev and Teddy went down the hallway to the darkroom, Teddy already talking about emulsions and various chemicals.

He was half-listening to a music show and dozing a little when Ev and Teddy reappeared. "How'd it go?" he asked.

"It was very interesting," Ev said. "I asked a lot of questions. Too many, probably. I can't take up any more of your time, Teddy."

"Not at all. It's always fun to talk about photography with someone else who enjoys it. Remember, get yourself a little camera and start snapping some pictures to develop. You'll learn the process in no time."

Del caught himself before he started helping Ev into his jacket and made sure he didn't hold the door, either, instead walking down to the sidewalk while Ev shook Teddy's hand and thanked him again.

It wasn't until they were sitting on the streetcar that Ev grew softer again and more like himself.

"How wonderful to see the picture emerge like that," he said, staring out the window. "Like magic."

"You'll be able to learn how."

"If I had the equipment."

"It's not an impossible wish, Ev. We could manage it somehow."

But Ev shook his head. "All that for me to what—take photos of ducks and flowers?"

Del paused, confused. "Don't you like ducks?"

Ev pressed his fingers into his temples. "I don't have any particular feelings about ducks. That's not the point. The reason I wanted a camera when I was younger wasn't to take silly photographs of birds or the family picnic. I wanted to be a real photographer, in a studio—a professional."

"But then why don't you want a camera? Like Teddy said, you need practice composing shots."

"I wanted it when I was younger," Ev said in a flat tone. "I know better now."

"What do you mean?"

"I mean that it was a stupid, impossible dream."

"But if you start practicing, then I think—"

Ev interrupted. "Let's not talk about it anymore. I want to go home—to my apartment."

Del fell silent, and Ev returned to staring out the window.

When they reached his apartment, Ev didn't tell Del he couldn't come up, so he followed Ev inside. Upon reaching his room, Ev tore off his hat and tie and kicked his heavy shoes into a corner. He sat down at his vanity, touching his things—the brush painted with a spray of forget-me-nots, the tins of face powder and blush, the green glass necklace Del gave him, always kept carefully in an old cocoa tin that served as a jewelry box. He dabbed some lilac water on his throat and unbuttoned his cuffs to do the same at his wrists.

Del sat on the bed, watching.

"I'm glad I got to talk to Teddy today and see his darkroom," Ev said, and it sounded as though he was trying not to cry. "I'm glad."

He didn't know if Ev was saying that for his benefit or if it was the truth.

"Goodness, I have to get to the barber soon or my hair will be falling in my eyes," Ev continued, looking at his reflection. "But I think you should keep your hair a little longer, as it is now. There's an attractive curl to it that goes away when it's shorter."

"Guess I will, then, if you like it."

A smile, even though it didn't quite reach Ev's eyes. He didn't know what questions he could ask without making Ev angry or hurt, so he settled for going over and enfolding him in a tight hug, Ev tensing for a moment before relaxing, the fabric of Del's jacket crumpling under his hands.

IT BOTHERED HIM that Ev should be so dismissive about his chances of becoming a photographer. Sure, maybe cameras were expensive, but that didn't mean it could never happen. Why, if someone had asked him a few years ago whether he'd ever get onto the motor patrol, Del would have laughed in their face, but now here he was, riding a motorcycle in his swell uniform. He resolved to talk to Ev about the photography again and encourage him to at least get a cheap camera.

On Wednesday night, Harrison talked him into going to a motorcycle race over at the flat-track across town. The track was theoretically used for club races, but that night there were professional riders and bets were secretly being placed on the race—all in violation of the city's anti-gambling ordinances.

"The word is that the Gray Wolf might be stoppin' by," Harrison said in a low voice as they worked their way through the crowd.

"You ever seen him before?"

"Got a glimpse of him in a hotel bar once. But we should keep our eyes open—might see somethin' useful. After all, we'll be makin' the move on his operation by this time next year."

"You really think so?" It was a bit hard to believe when Barrett hadn't even managed to open even one speakeasy yet.

"'Course I do. Now, let's go place our bets. You take my advice, pal, and put your money on number eight. I got a feelin' in my bones that he's a winner tonight."

Not without some misgivings, Del put a few dollars on number eight, then they found a place where they could see the track. The riders were still assembling, but Del looked with interest at their motorcycles, comparing them to this own.

You had to be a real daredevil to race on a flat-track, whipping around corners so fast your motorcycle skidded over the ground, sometimes going up on one wheel to make the turn. When the race began, his fingers kept twitching toward his pocket, ready to write up a traffic tag. Pulling any one of these stunts on the city streets would be a blatant violation of the law.

It sure was a thrill though and became even more so when number eight won. Even Harrison looked shocked for a few moments before he began bragging about how he'd pegged it and how you could always trust Jimmy Harrison's recommendations when it came to placing bets.

As they were going to collect their winnings, a hush fell over the crowd around them, and Harrison yanked Del to a halt.

"It's him," Harrison hissed, nodding at a group of men who had just gotten out of a Sports Phaeton parked at the edge of the field.

A tall man stood in the middle, dressed in a striped suit with a green bowtie and a Panama hat. Del could see a diamond ring flashing on his hand even from a distance.

"That's the Gray Wolf?"

"Yep—Charlie Crawford himself. All the fellows around him are sure to be carrying revolvers."

Crawford wasn't doing anything threatening or illegal, simply standing there talking with another man, maybe the organizer of the races. But an air of power rolled off him.

Del swallowed and took an involuntary step backward, seized by the irrational fear that Crawford would know about their plot to supplant him simply by laying eyes on them. He imagined Barrett standing there, bobbing up and down and talking excitedly about Egyptian tombs and experienced a sinking feeling in his stomach.

Harrison licked his lips. "'Course, we'll recruit some more muscle before we take on Crawford. Ain't no sense in putting our necks in a noose."

"That's right. And I reckon the Pharaoh will come up with a real smart plan too, right?"

"You bet, pal. Why, just hearin' the boss talk about them Egyptian pictures that mean words is enough to set your mind at ease. If a fellow can figure out that, he'll have no problems running rings around the City Hall Gang."

They edged away from Crawford's orbit and collected their winnings. A solid ten dollars for Del, which he tucked into his wallet. He'd be able to take Ev out on a whirl with this—no baptized booze and pretzels for them, no sirree.

BUT BEFORE HE could offer to take Ev for a night on the town, another chance presented itself. It was a few days later, and Del had gone 'round to Ev's for a visit. He wasn't so worried now that Ev would turn him away, and sure enough, Ev greeted him with a kiss, looking happy to see him.

"I had a letter from Asta today," Ev said as he pulled two bottles of Coca Cola from the icebox. "It sounds as though he's managing all right—says he got put in the wing with the other fairies and that he's found a few men who like him well enough to stop anyone from hurting him. He tries to put a good face on things, you know, joking that if he knew how easy it was to get a man in prison, he'd have been committed long ago. But he wants to know all the news, and he's worried about how Sam is getting along—asks after him twice. I know that he's awful homesick and lonely, no matter what he says."

"You'd like to go visit, huh?"

"Yes. I suppose I could manage to spring for a ticket, although I'd need a hotel room for at least one night too. I don't know anyone up in Oakland or San Francisco."

Del popped the top on one bottle and handed it to Ev, then opened his own. "They have motor coaches going there now, right? And the train, of course. We could see which one had the best prices before getting our tickets."

"Oh, you don't have to come," Ev protested. "I didn't mean it that way."

"I know. But I had some luck at the races the other night, and the money's just sitting in my pocket. And besides, I might be able to help out, if they don't want to let you see Asta for some reason."

Ev hesitated. "That would be nice then. I'd like the company," he finally admitted with a small, grateful smile.

"I think I could manage to take an extra day off work in a week or two. What about you?"

"Yes, I think so. And you're sure it won't be too expensive?"

The list of bills due at the end of the month unraveled in his mind—installment payments on the chairs and radio, rent and groceries, some debts that had yet to be paid off, and the money that needed to be sent to his father. But he pushed them aside.

"Of course not."

THEY ENDED UP taking the Southern Pacific's overnight Owl train up north. It left Los Angeles at six in the evening, due to arrive in Oakland around eight the next day. From there they could take another train to Richmond and then catch the ferry to San Quentin.

"You remembered everything you need?" Del asked Ev as they arrived at the station, suitcases in hand. "You have your toothbrush? And a change of socks?" His mother had impressed upon him that one should never travel without those two items.

"Yes, darling. I'm not completely scatterbrained."

Their berth in an open section sleeper car wasn't anything fancy, but it was comfortable enough. A porter passing by suggested they go to the dining car for supper before it became crowded.

"The first—only—time I ever took a train was when I left Texas for California," Ev said as they waited for their supper to arrive. He was looking out the window, observing the scenery rolling by at a steady pace. "Next I want to try an airplane."

"I remember you enjoyed that airplane ride at Venice Pier," Del said, with an inward shudder at the memory.

"I wonder what it's like, being that far up in the air. Or doing a loop-the-loop."

"I'd prefer not to imagine it, thanks." The thought alone made him queasy.

"That's right, you got sick on the rollercoaster, didn't you? Not your sort of ride, an airplane."

"I prefer my motorcycle. Wish they'd pick me for the department's motorcycle drill team. I'd get to be in parades and have a swell time of it."

"That does sound jolly." Ev turned toward him, a wicked glint in his eyes. "I might take you for a different sort of ride tonight, though."

Del flushed and jolted back in his chair when Ev reached across under the table and squeezed his thigh.

"Skittish," Ev teased, laughing.

"We're in public," he returned, wishing the waiter would hurry up with the meal. Now that Ev had mentioned sex, he wasn't going to be able to think about anything else.

Ev pouted. "I suppose you're right. I should behave myself—at least until later."

"We can't. There'll only be a curtain in between us and the corridor."

"If we're quiet we can. Wait until the other passengers have gone to bed, and then I'll slip down and join you."

"We can't," Del repeated without conviction, and Ev laughed again.

He didn't really expect Ev to carry through on his scandalous suggestion but around midnight, when he was almost asleep, lulled by the motion of the train, he heard the upper bunk creak as Ev climbed down. A moment later, Ev ducked under the curtain and slid into the bunk next to Del, who hastily moved over to try and make more room.

"*Ev,*" he hissed, nervous and delighted at once.

Ev giggled and pressed a clumsy kiss to his mouth in the dark. "You have to be quiet, Del." He started undoing the buttons on Del's pajama top.

Del reached for him, finding skin-warmed silk under his fingers. "Hell, are you wearing one of your camisoles?"

"I wouldn't travel in anything less than my best. Don't worry, I'll cover it with a shirt come morning. No one else will know." Ev slid a hand into Del's pajama bottoms. "Now hush."

Easier said than done with Ev stroking him like that. By now, Ev knew the best way to tease him erect quickly, and it wasn't long before he was finding it difficult to keep his hips still and not thrust into the touch. Ev swirled his thumb across the leaking tip, sucked it into his mouth, and then pulled his thumb out with a pop.

Del shut his eyes, swallowing down a moan. Then he felt Ev shifting and opened them again to see Ev straddling his hips and shoving his pajama bottoms further down his legs. Shit, was Ev going to...?

He had his answer a moment later as Ev gripped his cock and fit it into position. As Ev sank down onto him in an easy slide, he realized Ev must have fingered himself open in the top bunk. The thought chased away his concern over being heard for a moment, and he gripped Ev's hips, pulling him down faster, sending himself deeper inside. Ev gasped and choked off a groan. Recollecting himself, he patted Ev's thigh in apology. Ev chuckled, breathless, and rubbed a hand over Del's abdomen while relaxing his muscles and adjusting to the penetration.

The rhythm of the train vibrated through their bodies. Sometimes the car jolted to the side, and Ev swayed on top of him. Ev didn't try to move for a while, enjoying the sensations. Del closed his eyes again. The gentle movement wasn't enough to make him come, but it kept him aroused, pleasure coursing steadily through him.

Someone coughed in one of the other bunks. And then the car door slid open, footsteps sounding in the corridor. They both stilled, listening. Probably it was one of the porters.

Ev put his hand over Del's mouth and started to ride him.

Del wanted to protest—the porter was still there—but it was also intensely stimulating, knowing they might be heard. He dug his fingers into Ev's hips, helping him move up and down on his cock.

The footsteps moved closer and then passed by. The car door on the other end opened and shut.

Ev took his hand off his mouth. Del let out a shuddering breath, jerked up into Ev once, twice, and then came. A few moments later, when he was still caught in the receding waves of his orgasm, he felt the splatter of Ev's come on his stomach.

They didn't move for a few moments, recovering their breath and senses. Ev finally rolled off him and reached onto the shelf where Del had put his toiletries for a towel. He mopped the mess off Del's stomach and then leaned down, putting his mouth right by Del's ear to whisper, "Now, if I did that to you in an airplane, I bet your nerves would be the last thing on your mind." Then he slid off the bunk, Del reaching for him, his fingers trailing over Ev's leg and closing on the cool, empty air as Ev climbed the ladder back into the top bunk. It took Del a long time to fall asleep after that, and he wondered if he'd ever be able to ride a train again without blushing.

Ev was quite smug the next morning at breakfast and kept making comments about how tired Del looked and how something must have kept him up all night.

"When we're alone, I'm gonna kiss you quiet," Del threatened, hiding his smile with his coffee cup.

They arrived in Oakland to find a few low clouds still clinging to the hills above the city, the remnants of a fog bank that had retreated out to sea. A cool breeze blew too, and Del found he was glad of both his hat and jacket. They asked directions from a station agent and caught a streetcar up to Richmond, north of Oakland along the San Francisco Bay. At Richmond, they boarded a ferry for San Rafael, and once there found a cab to take them to San Quentin.

Ev's good mood diminished as they traveled. He grew quiet and solemn, worrying the lapel of his coat in between his fingers.

"I didn't write to Asta that I was coming to visit. In case anything came up, and we couldn't go or I can't see him, I didn't want him to be disappointed."

"You'll get to see him. Promise."

As they walked up to the walls of the prison, Ev drew closer. "I can't help thinking they'll take one look at me and *know* and lock me up here too."

"That won't happen. I wouldn't let that happen."

Ev nodded, taking a deep breath and following Del inside.

At first, the guard didn't want to let Ev see Asta, claiming it was too early in the day for visiting hours.

"We've come all the way from Los Angeles," Del said. "I'm an officer on the force down there—the motor patrol."

The guard's attitude thawed slightly. "Didn't think you fellows came and visited the convicts after they got locked up."

"Sure, usually I'm happy to turn them over to the Big House, but in this case, um—"

"It's a family matter," Ev interjected smoothly.

The guard hemmed and hawed a bit more but eventually agreed to allow it. They were taken to the public visitation room and left at a table while a guard went to get Asta, known in prison by his given name of Nicholas.

Asta looked confused when he emerged from the doorway a few minutes later, but then he saw Ev, and his eyes widened. The guards didn't bother cuffing Asta, and he hurried over to their table.

"What are you doing here?" he demanded.

Ev reached out and took his hands. "Visiting you, of course."

"But coming all this way—dammit, Ev, what did you have to sell to pay for that ticket?"

"I have a second job now. And Del helped a bit too."

Asta's mouth thinned as he looked at Del. "You're still around, huh?"

"Don't be like that," Ev chided. "You don't have to be suspicious."

Del broke Asta's gaze, feeling guilty. Hopefully he didn't look it.

Asta grimaced and disengaged his hands from Ev's. "Who you sleep with is your business, Ev. But let's not talk about it here. And you can't touch me like that, acting like we're girlfriends. What are you thinking? They already know about me, but you have to be more discreet."

Ev nodded, bowing his head.

Asta sighed. "It means the world to me to have you come here. You know that, don't you?"

"Are you okay? You make it sound in your letters like it isn't so terrible here, but I can't believe it."

Asta lifted one shoulder in a shrug. His prison suit hung loosely on his frame, and the collar flapped open a little. They both saw the bruise on his neck. Ev sucked in a breath.

"This?" Asta touched it. "That's nothing. One of the boys got a little too frisky is all. It's like I told you—as long as I'm willing to provide a few favors, no one's gonna hurt me too bad."

"But—"

"They stick us in a factory most of the day, making jute for grain sacks. I think I'll be deaf by the time six months is over, the machines are so loud."

Ev's face was full of distress. "Asta—"

"You wanted to know—that's how it is. But are you gonna be able to change anything? No. So there's no point in discussing it. Talk to me about something else, for God's sake."

Looking at them, Del remembered his first impression of Asta, that he was like Ev with all the softness stripped away, the hard, defensive shell locked into place permanently. But God, Del could see why. Shoved in places like this, living with skunks like that fellow Rex—of course it would turn you caustic and guarded, if it didn't kill you.

"How's Sam?" Asta asked.

"He's fine. I told you—he's staying with Del's friend, Glen."

Asta's eyes flicked to him again. "Guess I owe you thanks for that."

"It was no trouble. Glen likes dogs." Del shifted under Asta's stare and cleared his throat.

"Sam is real partial to cheese," Asta said. "For treats, I mean."

"I'll tell Glen," he promised.

"Did you get my little beaded purse from Rex when you went over there?" Asta asked Ev.

"I think so—the purple one, right?"

"Yes. There should be a couple dimes in there, so I want you to go get yourself a strawberry milkshake tomorrow. You can get the dime when you get back to Los Angeles, but your birthday will be over by then."

"Tomorrow's your birthday?" Del said to Ev, surprised.

"You didn't tell him?" Asta huffed. "You never want anyone to make a fuss over it."

Ev grimaced. "That's right—I don't want any big to-do."

Asta leaned forward. "Well this is our tradition. I can't go with you this year, but promise me you'll get that milkshake."

"I promise," Ev said after a moment, and his voice choked.

The guard didn't let them talk for much longer before he came over and said Asta had to go back.

"I'll keep writing. Every week. And it'll be February before you know it, and you'll be out of here," Ev told Asta, gripping the edge of the table as though to stop himself from dashing forward for a hug.

"Take care of yourself," Asta said, ignoring Del and following the guard through the door, which shut and locked behind them.

"Asta will warm up to you," Ev said to him when they were back outside.

"It's really your birthday tomorrow?" he asked, avoiding the topic of Asta. The fact that Asta's suspicions about him were in fact justified was not something Del wanted to dwell on today.

"Yep. Number twenty-three. When I first came to Los Angeles, it was right before my eighteenth birthday. I think I told you how Asta took me in, and on my birthday, he treated me to a strawberry milkshake. Every year since then, he's done the same."

"We'll make sure to go to a soda fountain. But I won't have any time to get you a present or anything."

"I told you, I don't want a fuss. Besides, this is a pretty fine present, I think—you travelling here with me and all."

Still, Del resolved to find the time to locate a present for Ev before tomorrow.

Back in Oakland they had lunch and then happened on a lake close to downtown—Lake Merritt someone told them it was called—and walked around its shoreline. On the southwestern edge, where tidal waters flowed in from the bay, a black sludge clogged stagnant pools, probably caused by sewage emptying into the water. It smelled awful, but once they walked farther north, the water grew clearer, reflecting the buildings along the shore. The hills rising above the flatlands were a mix of green trees and yellowed, dried grass, bright in the early September sunshine. Ev didn't talk much, walking quietly at Del's side. When they turned to find a hotel for the night. Del insisted on paying for the room, and once they were there, he enfolded Ev in a hug.

"What's this for?" Ev asked, even as he sank into it, relaxing against Del's chest.

"I know it was hard for you, going to the prison and seeing Asta like that."

Ev sighed, long and deep. "Sometimes I think I don't give a damn—that I'll dress as I want and act as I want even if it gets me arrested. But then other times I get so frightened. I don't want to go to prison. That time when I got picked up a few months ago, and you saw me—I was so scared, Del. I know I didn't act like it, but it was awful, stuck in a cell overnight and not knowing what was going to happen to me."

Del stroked the back of his head, trying to comfort with his touch.

When Ev stepped away, his eyes were tired but more relaxed. "I'm going to soak in the bath. Be a dear and go buy some cigarettes for me?"

He agreed, particularly as he had more than cigarettes to buy. At the desk, he asked if there was a place that sold cameras nearby. The clerk pointed him in the direction of one a few blocks over, adding that they'd probably be closing in twenty minutes or so. Del thanked him and dashed out the door, ignoring the looks of passers-by as he ran down the sidewalk. He was determined to get Ev a camera for his birthday. Nothing expensive, but one of the little Brownie cameras that sold for two dollars. Ev might think there was no point in taking pictures of ducks or picnics, but maybe once he tried, he would find he enjoyed it and would keep pursuing photography.

He was back with the wrapped package safely stowed in his suitcase by the time Ev emerged from the bathroom in a kimono, his hair damp. Del handed him the cigarettes, and Ev lit one, going to stand by the window and look down into the street while he smoked.

"Will you tell me about Lawrence?" Ev asked suddenly, and Del paused, his tie halfway unknotted.

"That was his name, right? Your last lover, who left you."

"Yeah." He took a deep breath. "What do you want to know?"

"What he was like. Why you loved him."

He undid the rest of the knot and pulled the tie off, draping it over the back of one of the chairs. "Lawrence was...flashy, I guess you could say. I met him at a nightclub Glen and I used to go to, and half the fellows there wanted him. Even the ones who'd only take women couldn't help looking at him. He was a chorus girl in a show and sometimes he'd come to the cabaret, still all dressed up, knowing how swell he looked and showing it off. I never thought I had a chance with him, but I'd always tell the bartender to send him a drink. One night he came over to me. I was so shocked, I could hardly manage two words."

The next part was harder to say. "I know Glen thinks he took advantage of me. And he did—I couldn't afford anything really fancy, of course, but clothes, liquor, cigarettes, records, jewelry—he only had to look at something, and I'd get it for him. He told me, when he left, that a week after starting to go with me, he was already sleeping with other men.

"But I don't think I was wrong to believe he liked me, even if it was only a little bit. Lawrence—he was always talking. No matter who he was with, he always said the most and said it the loudest. But sometimes, when we were alone, he'd get all quiet and let me put an arm around his shoulders."

Ev had continued looking out the window while he was talking, remaining silent. Now he said, "You like it when I act the same way too."

"But you don't talk anywhere near as much as Lawrence did," Del protested, confused.

"I mean when I'm vulnerable. You like that."

"I...well, I like it when you get all soft and sweet," he said, floundering for the words to explain.

"Vulnerable."

"Is that what it is?"

Ev huffed a mirthless laugh. "Yes."

"Am I doing something wrong?" Ev didn't answer, so he ventured, "Do you not want to be that way? I thought—"

"No," Ev said. "It's not that. But sometimes I get afraid, like I said, and it makes me angry."

"What should I do then?"

Ev glanced over at him and then back out the window. "Don't do anything different."

Del wasn't sure this helped him figure things out at all, but he nodded, and since it was almost time for supper, he went and bought some cheese and cold cuts to eat in their room, seeing as how they both felt pretty tired.

IT WAS FOGGY in the morning, and Ev burrowed closer when he awoke, dragging the blanket over both their heads.

"Happy birthday," Del told him.

Ev grunted into the pillow.

"If you get up, we can go out for waffles."

Another grunt.

"I have a present for you."

At that, Ev lifted his head, pushing his hair back and frowning. "When did you get a present? You didn't even know it was my birthday until yesterday."

"I dashed out when you were in the bath."

Ev kept frowning, still grumpy. "Does it have anything to do with coffee?"

Del admitted it did not, and Ev disappeared back under the blanket.

Finally he allowed himself to be coaxed from the bed and into his clothes. Suitcases in hand, they found a café, soon had hot cups of coffee at their elbows, and Ev descended upon the promised waffles with wolfish glee. When he was mopping up the last pool of syrup, Del handed him the little brown package.

Ev stared at it, his fork still in his mouth. Slowly he reached for it.

"If you don't want it, you don't have to keep it."

"A camera," Ev said, having torn aside the paper.

"Happy birthday," Del repeated, trying not to be disappointed that Ev didn't seem more excited. He'd known Ev might not like it straight away. "Later we'll go find that milkshake."

"Thank you—you're a peach to run out and get something for me. But," Ev hesitated. "What am I to take pictures of?"

"Why, anything you want. Remember how Teddy said it was important to learn how to frame shots? Even if it's a cheap camera, I thought you could practice with this."

Ev nodded, turning the camera over in his hands. "I suppose." He sounded reluctant.

Del wished he would come out and say plainly whatever was bothering him. "Like I said, if you don't want it—"

"No. No, I do." He forced a brighter smile onto his face.

Del dragged his fork through the remains of syrup on his plate. "I don't know what you want sometimes."

Ev bristled. "You're the one who got me the present. I didn't ask you to do it. I wasn't even going to tell you about my birthday."

"But why? I'd have wanted to know."

"Do I have to spell everything out for you?" Ev snapped and then scrubbed a hand over his face. "Look, I'm sorry."

He nodded, trying not to let his hurt show. He'd known the camera was a sensitive subject, for whatever reason, and maybe he shouldn't have bought one for Ev. But it didn't sit right with him, Ev giving up on his dreams. "Shall we go?" he finally asked after a long minute of silence.

"Yes." Ev tucked the camera into his coat pocket and rose to follow him to the door.

They took the ferry over to San Francisco and spent a few hours wandering around the city. Standing on the docks, watching the bustle at the ships, Ev slipped his hand into Del's for a second, squeezing it, and Del gave him a smile.

At the bottom of one of the long, steep hills, Ev took out the camera and snapped a hesitant picture. He took more as the day went on, and when they found a soda fountain, Del took a picture of him in front of it so they could prove to Asta that he'd taken Ev for the strawberry milkshake.

In the evening, they caught the Owl back to Los Angeles, rolling past the miles of farms and hills and dusty roads through the dark and emerging with the morning sunlight back onto the familiar streets of the city. Along with the well-known buildings and the streetcars trundling past came his guilt at lying to Ev about the legging. When they had been away, he'd almost been able to forget about it, to pretend it wasn't happening. But now they were back in the city. He'd be meeting with Barrett and Harrison again, and when Ev asked what he'd been doing, he'd have to evade the question or outright lie.

"Tired?" Ev asked, noticing his silence.

"Yeah. Just a bit."

"Go home and rest. I have to get over to the Western Chemical Company—my shift starts at nine."

"We should have come back earlier, if you have to work today."

"No, I wanted to spend a fun day with you. And it was—a lovely day. A lovely birthday."

Del smiled and touched his shoulder, hoping they'd be spending Ev's next birthday together too.

Chapter Twelve

SEPTEMBER TURNED INTO October, and Del spent as many days and nights together with Ev as he could. Ev still sometimes brushed him off or retreated behind his defensive, bitter barriers, but those moments seemed to come with less frequency.

One night, they were together in Ev's bedroom, the rungs of the bedstead digging into Del's back, the metal warmed by his skin and sweat. Ev straddled his lap, hands gripping Del's shoulders, breath slowing as he came down from his climax. Del was still inside him, and Ev's spasms drew a final shuddering spurt from his cock. He groaned, rubbing his hands up and down Ev's hips under his step-ins, which he had never gotten around to removing completely.

"Good?" Ev asked, leaning against his chest and combing his fingers through Del's hair.

Del kissed him in response.

After cleaning up a bit, they squeezed together in Ev's bed. Ev lit a cigarette and paged through an old magazine, while Del folded his arms under his head, gazing at the ceiling, drowsily contemplating a crack in the plaster that looked like a river with little tributaries branching to either side.

"Del, I want to show you something," Ev said suddenly. He sounded nervous.

Del sat up, concerned. "What is it?"

Ev didn't answer, getting out of bed and padding over to his dresser. He opened a drawer and took out some newspaper clippings. Then he got back in bed and, after a moment's hesitation, handed them to Del.

Del flipped through them. "Female 'Husband' Works as Doctor," read one headline. The story was about a woman who lived as a man. She—well, he—worked as a physician in a hospital and married one of the female nurses. The secret had been exposed when he was caught trying to pass fraudulent checks. "Man-Wife Found Innocent," said the next headline. This time it was a person named Bridger—probably an invert like Ev—who had been married to a man for fifteen years. Bridger was accused of murdering someone, and during the court trial, the judge upheld an objection by the State that Bridger's husband couldn't testify on his behalf. Why, that was as good as saying the marriage was legal.

He'd never heard of such a thing happening. It had never even occurred to him this was a possibility.

Ev had been kneeling next to him on the bed while he read, fingers knotted in the sheet. "I've saved these," Ev said as Del came to the end of the column, and then paused a moment.

"I used to dream about it," he finally continued. "I dreamed of finding someone who loved me and building a little nest together. I would even plan out my trousseau—oh, all these lovely hats and satin negligees and silk stockings. And I'd have a veil—yards and yards of lace—and a bouquet of white roses and purple violets. It wouldn't even have to be legal. After all, what do I care for a law that sees me as the worst sort of degenerate? But it would be more serious than a bull daggers ball. We would say our vows and mean them." Ev's breath caught, and he turned away. "Isn't that silly?"

Del smoothed a hand over the thin newsprint. "It's not silly."

"I'm not showing you these to make you propose to me. I'm sensible to the difficulties, God knows. I don't even know what I'd say if you did."

He reached over and freed one of Ev's hands from its tight grip on the sheet, holding it in his own instead.

Ev let him, although he remained hunched on his knees. "There's so little respect or dignity afforded to us by society. You can understand why I dreamed about being married, can't you?"

He nodded, looking at the clippings again. His own mind was in a turmoil, assaulted by this new possibility. He and Ev could be married. People did such things, even got them recognized in court.

There was no question that he would want to marry Ev. He'd get down on his knee this second. Except—

Except for the bootlegging. Except for the fact he was lying to Ev, if only by omission.

"You're awfully quiet," Ev said, breaking into his thoughts. "Are you upset with me?"

"Of course not. I was surprised is all," he choked out and then found himself unable to say any more.

"I wanted to share this with you." Ev withdrew his hand from Del's, smoothing his palms over his knees and the smooth silk of the step-ins. "I haven't shared it with anyone else, even Asta. She'd laugh at me and tell me to stop being naïve. And I know it's foolish—the idea of having a real marriage. After all, these people got caught out in the end, didn't they? God knows what their lives are like now. I should throw those clippings out, really."

"Don't do that. You deserve all those things—all the happiness in the world."

Ev's mouth twisted. "Most people deserve happiness. But that doesn't mean we get it." He held out his hand, and Del carefully handed back the newspapers.

I have something to tell you too.

That was all he needed to say. He watched Ev return the clippings to the tin, then come back to bed, lying down with a little sigh.

"Can you get the light?" Ev asked, and Del turned off the lamp.

I need to tell you something.

He lay down, staring at the dark ceiling, listening as Ev's breathing slowed with sleep, and the clock ticked steadily away toward midnight.

In the morning, Ev was prickly and cold, turning away when Del tried to kiss him and getting into an argument with Camilo over who was supposed to wait for the iceman. Del remembered what Ev had said to him in Oakland—*When I'm vulnerable...I get afraid and that makes me angry.*

So he didn't let Ev's brusqueness hurt him and made sure to tell Ev he loved him before he had to leave for work.

I love you—how easy it was to say those words, and yet he couldn't make himself tell Ev about his involvement with Barrett.

DEL RETURNED HOME with the growing conviction that he needed to respond in some way to Ev's confidences. Kisses and flowers were becoming dull. There had to be something else—something else he could give Ev to show him how much he loved him. Perhaps that was why, when he went to the Temple of Ra in the afternoon, his eyes lingered on Barrett's Studebaker Six, its red paint shining in the sun. With that car, he could take Ev somewhere in style. He was sure Ev would love to go for a drive in a swell machine like that.

There had been little action on the legging front in the past few weeks. Harrison was trying to track down a new liquor supplier but kept coming up dry. Del suspected that was partly due to the fact that he liked testing the goods and then got drunk and fleeced of whatever cash was on him. Harrison wouldn't admit this, of course, but his jacket and trousers were getting increasingly frayed on the edges.

Barret claimed he had been meeting with a studio executive concerning the film, yet they seemed to be spending most of their time debating on a location for the shoot, Barret adamant that only a real desert would serve while the executive thought a large parking lot filled with sand could serve the purpose. All Del knew was that he hadn't seen any money one way or the other.

He walked around to the alley entrance, thumping down the stairs and knocking on the door. After a few moments, the little metal plate in the door opened, and Jasper peered out at him.

"Let a fellow in?" Del asked.

Jasper grunted and opened the door, allowing him to step into the cool, dim interior.

The bar was in shadow, but one lamp shone over the table in the corner. Barrett, Hazel, Fletcher, and Harrison were all seated there, cards in their hands.

Fletcher was speaking in a tone of resigned disbelief to Harrison. "How could you forget that hearts were trump?"

"I didn't forget," Harrison protested, rocking uneasily in his chair. "It only slipped my mind for a second."

"So you played the king of clubs—*knowing* that I didn't have the ace—and that all they needed to do was play a heart to take the trick, anyway."

"Don't be too hard on him, Fletcher, honey," Hazel said, leaning over to pat his arm.

Fletcher groaned, tugging on his hair in frustration. "At this rate, it'll take weeks to get the basic rules down. We haven't even approached how to draw out trumps. Why can't you be his partner, Miss Hazel?"

Hazel fanned her cards. "Why it's fun watching you get so darned flustered, Fletcher."

Barret puffed up in his seat. "As it only took me half a year to learn ancient Akkadian, I had no doubt I would easily master a simple card game."

"Ancient what now?" Harrison blinked. "That's what all them pharaohs spoke?"

Barrett began expounding on the relation of Akkadian as a diplomatic language to something called "Coptic" and the differences between the Old and Middle Kingdoms while a glazed expression took over Harrison's face. Meanwhile, Hazel and Fletcher were still bantering, Fletcher's irritation replaced by a good-humored flush as he leaned close, pointing out some nuance in the cards Hazel held.

"Guess Fletcher finally got them all to play bridge with him," Del commented.

Jasper crossed his arms over his chest, peering at the table. "He's a slick talker. If the boss don't watch out, he'll be takin' more than tricks from him."

Del nodded, watching as Hazel laughed at something Fletcher had said, a flirtatious glint in her eye. Barrett chattered on, now onto the subject of what sounded like "Q-Nay Form." Del couldn't make heads or tails of it. Maybe it was some kind of advertisement, like the "Nix-O-Tine" mouthwash one of his uncles had used to try and cure his tobacco habit. He could still vividly recall the sound of his uncle cursing a blue streak in the bathroom after swishing a mouthful of the stuff.

Briefly, he entertained a vision of a pyramid with a billboard painted on the side. Then Harrison caught sight of him, and his eyes lit up at the prospect of a savior.

"Del!" he exclaimed, waving an arm.

Barrett halted mid-sentence and turned to them. "Ah, Delbert—I'd hoped you would stop by today."

Images of a big haul and thick stacks of money immediately filled his mind. "Are we bringing in a load of gin, sir?"

Barrett chuckled at his enthusiasm. "Mr. Harrison is still on the lookout for a new supplier. In the meantime, I wanted to enlist your help in another project." Jasper made a disgruntled noise behind Del's shoulder.

"I'm happy to help if I can, sir, although I do have a shift later tonight."

"A few hours will do splendidly. You see, now that we've added some fine artwork, I think that the walls need to be repainted. It is far too drab in here."

"Repaint the walls?" he repeated, disappointed.

"Harrison is going to bring in his cousin to do a mural—lotus flowers, water lilies, perhaps an ouroboros."

Del had never heard of an ouroboros and sincerely doubted Harrison's cousin had either.

"We'll do the lower half of the walls in light green, then a strip of yellow, and white on the top," Barrett concluded.

"I'll go out and fetch some sandwiches for you boys, as you'll be working so hard," Hazel said, standing up and looking around for her bag.

"Fletcher has begged off on account of not wanting to spill paint on his new oxfords," Barrett added. "So it will be you three undertaking this important renovation of the Temple."

Del could see Jasper giving Fletcher and his pristine white oxfords a glare out of the corner of his eye.

A short while later, Del found himself spreading a drop cloth on the floor and prying the lid off a can of paint. Jasper had claimed a far corner as his own, so Del stayed next to Harrison, even though Harrison had a very liberal policy when it came to how much paint he put on his brush. The excess dripped everywhere, and if they weren't careful, they'd track paint all over the floor.

"Any chance the boss has some cash on hand?" he asked Harrison, keeping his voice low. "I'm pretty short right now." After all, even if he wasn't hauling liquor, painting the walls still counted as work.

But Harrison shook his head. "Sunshine Mike came 'round earlier, looking to collect on the debt the boss owes him for buying this joint. The boss tried to put him off, but he took him for everything he had in his wallet. Say," Harrison added, "any chance you could put some heat on Sunshine? Maybe pay him a visit and flash your buzzer around."

Del didn't fancy that at all and said so. "I'm not going to shove my badge in that fellow's face. He's not gonna be scared off by one cop."

"Jasper and me would come with you."

"The last time I followed one of your plans, I got used as target practice. I'm not letting that happen again if I can help it."

At this abuse of his abilities, Harrison retreated into a sulking silence.

Del's thoughts wandered back to Barrett's Studebaker Six parked outside. "Hey, Harrison. You know the boss's car?"

"'Course I do," Harrison said, putting aside his sulk in favor of bragging. "Who's the one he trusts to take care of it? I washed it just yesterday and polished all the lights and fixings. Looks pretty swell, huh? Not like your run-of-the-mill tinsmith's delight."

"Any chance I could borrow it?"

"Borrow it? No offense, but she's a little high class for you, pal," Harrison said, chuckling.

"Yeah, but I have someone I want to impress."

Harrison leered. "That so?"

"Think you could help me borrow the Studebaker one day so I can take my baby for a spin?"

Harrison clapped him on the shoulder. "I never yet turned my back on a friend. Myself, I always take the girls out for champagne and bring them a box of chocolate-covered cherries. They don't turn me down after that." Harrison leaned closer. "We'll have to keep it quiet from the boss, of course, but I don't see any problem in you borrowing the Big Six for a day. I'll say I noticed some trouble with the engine and need to take it to a mechanic for a quick once over."

"And that'll work?"

"Sure. The boss may know heaps about them Egyptians, but he couldn't tell a carburetor from a magneto coil."

"Thanks, Harrison. I appreciate it." As he drew his brush down the wall, it occurred to Del that in avoiding one of Harrison's schemes, he had started another. But surely nothing would go wrong, and he would give Ev a real treat, getting to drive around in a fancy car for a few hours.

WHEN HE ARRIVED at the station that night for his shift, Kirkpatrick took one look at him and burst out laughing. "You trying to make yourself prettier, Randolph? 'Cause it sure isn't working."

Del frowned. "What are you on about?"

Kirkpatrick shoved him toward the john. "Take a look at yourself in the mirror."

He opened the door and stepped inside, pulling the chain to turn on the light. Oh. He had a big streak of green paint across his forehead. Flushing, he turned on the faucet and tried to scrub it off. In the process he got his collar and front of his jacket all wet and consequently showed up late to his briefing with Lieutenant Miller.

Miller gave him an unimpressed look. "Do I need to remind you, Randolph, that it's important to keep your uniform neat?"

"Sorry, sir."

"Remember that I'll be reviewing your performance in the next few weeks. There are lots of men who would like a promotion to your position."

"It won't happen again, sir."

"See that it doesn't. And mind your time, too. We're all busy men, Randolph."

Chapter Thirteen

DEL STOPPED BY Ev's place after lunch the next day to see if he wanted to go for a drive on Friday. Camilo answered the door, the ends of his hair curled in pins. He let Del in, explaining that Ev was out shopping with Nellie.

"That's all right, then," he said, relieved Ev wasn't with a rival for his affections.

Camilo laughed, holding up a pot of tea in a silent question and pouring him a cup when Del nodded. "You have no reason to be jealous. Ev is very in love with you, I think."

"Really?"

"That is how it seems to me." Camilo sipped his own tea, considering. "Ev talks a lot about silly things—gossip, gushing over handsome men. But the things that really matter to him, those he does not say as much about."

"So you're saying he doesn't talk about me at all?" Del asked, confused.

"That is it, yes." Camilo laughed again at Del's expression. "But he smiles more often since he met you, and I do not find him curled in his bed, trying to hide the fact he was crying."

"He did that a lot?"

"Yes. I do not know how much he has told you about his other lovers—"

"He told me all about them." He let his anger at those bastards color his voice, even as he forced down the guilt that he was doing something similar.

"See—there is your proof. He tells you everything, but he has never given me any details—I had to find out from Asta."

Del sighed. "I wish he'd say it plain, though. Sometimes I think for sure he's sweet on me, and then his mood changes, and I don't know."

"Do not give up on him. And do not tell him about this conversation," Camilo added. "The poor lamb would die of embarrassment to know we had talked like this."

Del nodded. "I came to see if he'd like to go for a ride on Friday."

"Oh, how divine! José takes me about in an old truck from time to time, but I would not call riding in it a pleasure."

"Ask Ev if he'd like to go with me? Say I'll pick him up at eleven, and to call if he can't do it."

Camilo agreed, and Del took his leave, thanking him for the tea.

Ev is very in love with you, I think.

Groaning, he rubbed his face. This couldn't go on. He needed to tell Ev the truth about the legging. Friday—that would be a good day. Taking Ev for a ride in Barrett's fancy car would show him the good things that would come from the bootlegging. One day, Del would be able to buy a car like that too.

HE WAS A little nervous that something would go wrong with picking up the car—it was Harrison, after all. But for once, everything seemed to go smoothly. Harrison arrived at the agreed upon spot at the appointed hour, driving the Studebaker, and handed the key over to Del, who promised to have it back by that evening.

"And if you're thinking of doing some heavy petting in the back seat, don't," Harrison added. "I just cleaned those leather seats last week."

"I'll keep it nice—the boss won't ever know I took it out."

You could have knocked Ev's eyes off with a barrel stave when he saw the Studebaker. "What—is that *yours*?" he stammered.

"I borrowed it from a friend."

"You have a friend who owns a car like *this*?" Ev said, incredulous.

"Happens I do," he replied, hoping Ev wouldn't ask too many questions. Thankfully, Ev was more interested in climbing inside and exclaiming over the comfortable seats and the gleaming wooden dashboard.

"Want to drive to Ventura and go to the seaside?" he asked as he got behind the wheel.

Ev nodded eagerly. "How fast does this go?"

"Over forty easy—you could probably push fifty. But we won't be going that fast."

"*Del.*"

"All it takes is one farmer driving a cart and horse, and you've got an accident in the making."

Ev groaned, slumping back in the seat. "What's the use of having motorcycles and swell cars, then? You are no fun, Del. No fun."

"You'll enjoy it plenty. Easier to see the scenery when you aren't tearing down the road anyway." He'd cave in to Ev's desires on most things, but he wasn't going to compromise on this.

Ev pouted awhile but soon brightened and slid over the seat to sit pressed against Del. "You haven't given me a kiss yet."

"You didn't give me a chance. You jumped straight into the car. And now I'm busy driving."

"Guess I'll have to take the initiative then," Ev said and kissed the side of his mouth.

Del knocked his head gently against Ev's. "You smell nice."

"You noticed?" Ev smiled, delighted. "It's Le Jade—Nellie swears by it and made me buy some the other day."

"Smells kind of exotic."

"We spent hours—absolutely hours—in Bullock's," Ev continued, curling one leg under himself on the seat so Del had more room to shift. "Nellie's cousin came along so it wasn't just the two of us in the ladies' department. She pretended to be Nellie's fiancée, and I pretended to be the bored friend and acted all embarrassed at the lingerie display. We played it marvelously, and no one suspected a thing."

"Be careful, though. You still staying away from the Crown Jewel?"

"You know I am," Ev said, sounding a little injured. "I've only been out to the places you've taken me."

"Sorry—I thought...maybe..."

"What, that I'd been going out on my own, looking for some quick fun?" Ev's tone was edging toward angry now.

"No, of course not." He squeezed Ev's fingers. "I'm sorry."

"You ought to have more faith in me, Del."

He took a deep breath. "Speaking of faith..." He should say it, tell Ev right now.

"Yes?"

But his courage faltered. Soon—he would tell Ev soon. "I just meant you're right, I should trust you. I do trust you."

Ev gave him another kiss, forgiving.

THEY STOPPED AT a hot dog kennel by the side of the road and ate while driving, Del slightly nervous about spilling food on the seat. A good crowd had gathered at Seaside Park by the time they arrived, but they found a spot to leave the car not too far from the beach. Del noticed a few men giving the Studebaker envious glances and made sure his hat was straight before getting out.

Both he and Ev took off their shoes and socks when they hit the sand, rolled up their cuffs, and walked closer to the water, each step taking twice the effort as usual. The damp sand provided firmer footing, but their steps grew slower as they tried to judge the reach of the waves, calculating the distance that would let the water wash over their ankles but not soak the legs of their pants. A woman a few meters away misjudged, the wave rushing faster up the beach than she could escape. Giving up, she followed it back into the sea, laughing and splashing.

"I should have brought my bathing suit," Ev said, watching her.

"I didn't think we'd have time for bathing today, as I have to get the car back to my friend by tonight," Del explained. "But next time we'll come for a whole day—promise."

Surely there would be another day, many days, with Ev, even after he told him the truth.

"Don't look so gloomy," Ev said. "I'm not that disappointed. Or maybe it's something else?"

He cast about for an excuse. He could tell Ev about being chastised by his lieutenant, about the worry always lurking in the back of his mind that he would be taken off the motor patrol for not being good enough. But that would mean admitting to his failings, and he didn't want Ev to think too much about how dumb he was, how inadequate, or no amount of fancy cars or jewelry would be enough to convince him to stay. So he said, "It's nothing," and gave Ev a smile. "How could I be gloomy getting to spend the day with you?"

"You could tell me, you know," Ev said, and he sighed a little, but then bent down to pick up a shell fragment, exclaiming over the smooth texture and butterscotch color.

THE TROUBLE STARTED on the way home when Ev discovered the box of single malt whisky under the front seat. He had been twisting around to take a last look at the beach when his foot caught on a little lever.

"What the—"

Del looked over in time to see him reach down and push the lever, which sent a spring-loaded box shooting out from under the seat. The whisky bottle rested inside, cushioned between cotton batting.

If Del had been quick witted, he could have passed it off, saying "Oh, my buddy likes to keep a little something around for emergencies." Instead, all he could think was that Ev was going to find out about the legging, and panic burned through him. Ev must have seen it in his face, for his eyes narrowed, and he shoved the whisky bottle in Del's direction.

"Who exactly owns this car?" Ev demanded.

Del couldn't drive like this—he pulled over to the side of the road, hands shaking on the wheel. "Just an old friend of mine," he said in a weak voice. "He...he likes to drink a couple shots now and then."

"Now and then, huh?" Ev looked around the car, his eyes sharp, and then he dropped the whisky bottle back in its container and scrambled over the seat to get in the back.

"Ev, what are you...?" He had been expecting a sustained interrogation, but Ev was poking at the seat cushions, prodding the corners, lifting—

It hit Del then. This wasn't just a Big Six, it was a *Whisky* Six. Barrett had outfitted the car to haul liquor. Of course he would like something flashy and extravagant, rigged with hidden compartments and tricks to get the Prohis off your tail. The spring-loaded box under the front seat was just the beginning.

"Don't—" he started, but it was too late. Ev had figured out how to flip up the seat, revealing a large compartment underneath it, filled with gin bottles. They were empty—Del was starting to wonder if Barrett's operation could ever manage a job successfully—but they were incriminating all the same.

"What the hell is going on here?" Ev asked in a flat, terrible voice.

Del hunched his shoulders. If he tried to come up with a story, he would dig himself into a deeper hole. "The car belongs to a fellow named Orville Barrett. I've been doing some...work...on the side for him."

"Work," Ev repeated.

"He's a...well, he's a legger, and I've been... helping."

He chanced a look at Ev's face and wished he hadn't.

"It's nothing big. Just waving through some liquor shipments, warning him about any raids I hear about, that sort of thing. Actually, I haven't really done much. They had me painting walls in their speak the other day."

A few beats of silence. He kept his gaze lowered, courage failing him.

Then—"You're a dirty cop. A legger. A damn *criminal.*"

Del swallowed, his voice trembling when he spoke. "The law is bunk. You know that. Hell, you break it often enough yourself."

"By drinking not—not running liquor and joining gangs. And that's not the point, anyway." Ev's voice cracked, sharp and vicious.

Del flinched but met his eyes. "Then what? You think I'm doing it just for kicks? I'm doing this 'cause I need the money."

"You have a decent job," Ev said, and now there was the sound of tears laced in with his words. "*You're* decent, or you're supposed to be, at least."

"And how am I supposed to afford treating you so swell and getting you the nice things you deserve on a patrolman's salary?" he demanded, voice rising even though he was making Ev cry.

Ev went still and when he spoke again, his voice was brittle. "You're breaking the law and taking up with criminals in order to buy me presents?"

"No—I mean yes, but—" He scrubbed a frustrated hand through his hair. "It's not like you're making it sound."

"So you think I'd fall in love over a pretty piece of jewelry or a fancy meal? I'd no idea what a high opinion you had of me, Del."

"Dammit, Ev, that's not it at all! I know there's no reason for you to love me unless I could give you that kind of life. And you liked it, didn't you? You've liked everything I've done for you. You've never turned any of it down."

"I would have if I'd known what you were doing! You asked me to trust you." Ev's face crumpled, eyes bright with tears. "And now I find out you've been lying to me and that you're no different from any of the bums I've been with. How could you do that? How could I be so stupid?" He scrubbed a hand over his cheek.

Del gripped the wheel so hard his fingers ached. "I didn't do it to hurt you."

Ev laughed, incredulous. "You lied to me—right to my face. I thought that for once in my life, I had something good. I let myself fall in love with you."

I let myself fall in love with you.

He'd been waiting to hear those words. To hear them now... "Ev...I'm sorry. Please—"

"Don't." Ev turned away, looking out the back window.

They sat silently. Del felt helpless, the same way he'd felt when Lawrence left him. He remembered standing there, listening as Lawrence told him he had found someone better, unable to think of any argument to make in his defense.

"Del," Ev said in a strange tone, and Del raised his head, heart pounding. Maybe Ev was going to say it was all right, that he forgave him.

Ev pointed out the back window. "Tell me the car that's pulling in behind us does *not* belong to the cops."

He shifted his attention from Ev to where he was pointing. A black car was drawing to a halt a few yards away. He could make out four men inside, all dressed in suits. The extra spotlight affixed to the hood also seemed an ominous sign.

"It might be the Prohis." A snappy car like Barrett's Studebaker Six on a road close to the shoreline where the cargoes of liquor from Mexico and Canada came ashore—it was enough to raise suspicions.

"Shit. Federal agents. Shit." Ev started pushing at Del's shoulders. "Get out of the driver's seat."

Del tried to grab his hands, confused. "Why—what—Ev—"

"We can't let them catch us!" Ev was breathing fast. "They'll throw us in jail. We have to get out of here, and there is no way in hell I am letting someone who *always goes the speed limit* drive this damn car. Now move!"

Del moved, although he couldn't help protesting that he wouldn't go the speed limit in a situation like this.

Ev ignored him, clambering back over the seat and sliding under the wheel as fast as he could, narrowly avoiding kicking Del in the head with his foot. Del shot a look behind them. Two of the Prohis—and yes, it was definitely them, he could see the holsters strapped under their jackets— were approaching the car. Of course, they could try to play it smooth, but the agents would probably grow more suspicious when they realized they weren't the types who could afford a car like this. Besides, he didn't want them scrutinizing Ev and interrogating him. Never mind the liquor, they could end up being held for sex perversion.

Ev was probably thinking the same things, for he pushed the hand throttle to full and slammed the accelerator pedal to the floor. The car screamed back onto the road, skidding on the loose dirt. The Prohis started yelling and raced back to their own car, leaping inside.

Ev was shaking, but his hands remained tight on the wheel. "Where should I go?"

"I don't know—head east and—shit, wait, those are railroad tracks!"

Ev hurtled right over them, the car rattling so hard Del jolted upwards in his seat and almost hit his head on the ceiling.

"A train could have smashed right into us!" he admonished Ev.

Ev swerved around a milk truck puttering along in front of them. "This—this right here—is why I didn't want you to drive."

"Ending up in an auto wreck isn't any better than letting them catch up to us."

"Then be quiet and let me concentrate, for God's sake!"

"Just watch out for livestock—cows, chickens—you never know what could come running out of the bushes."

"All *right*, Del. I'll look out for the damn chickens."

Del settled for rubbernecking between the back and front windows, jerking reflexively for the brake every time Ev took a curve too fast. The Prohis had cranked up a siren behind them, and it blared insistently.

"We can't go back to the city," Del said. "There's no way we can keep up this speed once the road gets crowded."

The short autumn dusk was fading into night, and Ev switched on the headlights. "Hold on," he said, and Del clutched the door handle as Ev took a sharp left onto a road headed in a north-easterly direction. The Prohis sped past the turn but quickly reversed and were soon in pursuit once more.

Then the first gunshot split the air.

"Dammit!" Ev swerved across the road at the sound. "Did we get hit?"

"I don't think so." Another loud bang followed this pronouncement and a spider web of cracks appeared in the rear window.

Del swallowed. "Guess the glass is bulletproof."

"Some of the tricks of this Whisky Six might come in handy."

Another shot sounded.

"They're going for the tires," Ev reported, hunching forward. He wove from side to side, going far too close to the ditch for Del's liking. The road was steadily decreasing in quality, filled with potholes and ruts. Del thought his teeth might shake right out of his head.

"What do you think that does?" Ev said suddenly, pointing at a lever on the dashboard.

He squinted at it. "Dunno."

Ev reached out and flipped it.

"Hey! That could be danger—" Del stopped at the clanking noise coming from under the hood, holding his breath.

"There's smoke pouring out of the exhaust." Ev coughed. "Smells like ammonia."

Sure enough, a cloud of smoke billowed behind them. Del's eyes watered at the stench. "Maybe that switch triggered something that dumped a mix of ammonia and oil on the manifold and made it start smoking."

"A smoke screen—it'll hide where we're going from the Prohis."

It might have worked if the wind hadn't been blowing in the wrong direction. A fact they discovered a few seconds later when smoke enveloped their own car instead.

Del pressed an arm against his nose, waving the other frantically to try and clear the air. Ev's eyes were watering, peering through the noxious haze to try and see where they were going.

"This is *useless*. Why didn't you tell me not to press that damn switch?" Ev demanded.

"I *tried*—ah, fuck! Ev—watch out!"

Ev jerked the wheel to the left, narrowly avoiding hitting a stop sign that loomed suddenly in front of them. They shot through the invisible intersection, Del saying a silent prayer, and continued on the other side. After a few more feet, the smoke had cleared, showing them an empty road ahead and the Prohis still hot on their tail.

"Don't press any buttons—don't touch anything else," Ev snapped.

"I wouldn't," he muttered, refraining from pointing out that it was Ev who had let curiosity get the better of him. He wanted Ev's focus on the road, not on arguing with him.

It was getting darker and darker. Sometimes they passed a farm, and once he spotted the lights of a little town off to their right. They couldn't keep going like this, though. If nothing else, they'd run out of gas at some point.

He pounded his fist on the seat, nervous energy boiling over. "We need a plan."

Ev accelerated a little more. "This is the plan—going fast until we lose them."

Whether that plan, such as it was, would have worked they never discovered because it turned out the Prohis behind them had friends with them and must have been radioing their relative positions—which was hardly fair, the police department didn't even have radios in its cars yet, but it figured that Mabel's Boys would be better equipped. They barreled around a curve and saw two more cars barring the road ahead. Officers stood in front of them, guns leveled.

"Hold on!" Ev shouted and slammed on the brake, skidding and turning the wheel sharply.

Del had heard about the bootlegger's slide, and he'd seen one in a movie once, but nothing could prepare him for the sheer adrenaline and terror of the actual thing. The patrol cars drew closer, visible right out his side window as the car began revolving to face back the way they had come. The guns drew closer. They were going to ram straight into the cars—they were going to—and then the car had wheeled completely around. One tire went off the side of the road. Ev wrenched the wheel straight and accelerated again.

Headlights burst into their vision. They came within two inches of running straight into the Prohis following them. And then they were past. Del looked back. The agents had run off into the ditch, the others scrambling for their cars.

He let out the breath that had clogged his throat in a long, shaky exhale. "Fuck, Ev, that was brilliant."

Ev gave him a manic grin, sweat shining on his brow. "Guess I didn't waste all those nickels at the movies after all. Where to now?"

"Remember that side road we passed a little ways back? Let's turn off there and hide the car. With a little luck, we'll be able to do it before they get their act together."

"Did you forget, we don't have any luck." Ev jerked his chin at the back window. Sure enough, two pairs of headlights had appeared behind them again.

Del cast about frantically for anything that might help them, eyes landing on the innocent little switch Ev had pressed earlier.

"We've got to try the smoke screen again," he said.

"What? No!"

"We're going the other direction now. So the wind should be blowing the other way."

"Del, we've been turning this way and that—God knows what direction we're going. It could be the same and with it this dark, I'll run right off the damn road."

The siren blared louder behind them.

"We don't have a choice!" he insisted.

Ev bit his lip, eyes flickering in the glare of the Prohis' headlights. "Shit. Fine—do it."

Del held his breath and flipped the switch again.

The terrible smell flooded the air again, and the smoke billowed out seconds later. But this time, it blew behind them.

"It worked!" he crowed. "They'll have to stop for a minute or two. This is our chance to get a lead on them."

Sure enough, when the smoke cleared the headlights had vanished. The Prohis wouldn't be far behind, but the side road they had passed earlier appeared again only a few seconds later. It was little more than a pair of wheel ruts. They had driven a few hundred yards down it when Del saw headlights back on the main road. "Stop for a minute and cut the lights," he told Ev.

They waited, holding their breaths, but the Prohis barreled past on the main road, missing them in the darkness.

"They'll return once they cotton on to the fact we aren't in front of them," Ev said.

"Drive ahead a little, and we'll look for some bushes or trees to hide the car."

They found a stand of scraggly bushes some distance further on, and Ev pulled off the road, bumping into the middle of them with much cracking of branches.

Ev gestured at the dirt as they climbed out of the car. "They'll see the wheel tracks."

Del paused, thinking. "We could cover them?"

"With what?"

"We could cut a branch and sort of...sweep it over the road." He made a brushing gesture with his arms.

Ev blinked. "We drove about half a mile, Del. It would take hours!"

"I guess that's so," he mumbled, embarrassed.

Ev heaved a sigh, looking out over the fields full of thistles and gopher holes, poison oak a distinct possibility. "We'll have to start walking and hope they don't find us."

Thankfully the autumn night was dry and not too cold. They didn't have a flashlight, but the moon provided enough light to get by on once their eyes had adjusted. Still, their walk had its own particular pleasures, such as the mosquitoes and the irrigation ditch they couldn't find a way around and had to wade through.

"So," Del began after they had clambered up the bank and were squashing along in wet shoes.

"No," Ev said. "The only thing I want to hear from you right now is 'there's a hotel up ahead.'"

He subsided, sensitive to the tension strung tight between them. It had vanished in the heat of the car chase, but now it had returned, and he had no idea how to break it.

They didn't find a hotel, of course, but an indeterminate amount of time later, an abandoned barn materialized out of the darkness, its roof sagging but still offering some protection. Ev grudgingly agreed to stop there and wait until morning.

"Otherwise one of us will break an ankle wandering around in the dark," Del pointed out, tossing his coat onto a musty pile of hay and dropping onto it. He took off his shoes and socks too, grimacing at the slimy mud coating them.

Ev settled several feet away from him. Del couldn't make out his expression in the dark.

"Would you like my coat?" he asked after a minute.

"No." The hay rustled as Ev curled up into a tight ball.

"Come on, Ev. It's kinda chilly."

"I said no!" Ev snapped.

He flinched, hovering there, groping for a word or gesture that might help. Finally he lay down too. He felt all to pieces and ached for Ev's touch. What would he do if the Prohis found the car and took it? How would he ever explain to Barrett what had happened or pay for the loss? But those concerns were secondary to the thought that Ev might never forgive him for this.

He could hear Ev choking back sobs. Del listened to him, blotting his own tears off his face with his shirt sleeve from time to time.

The full measure of his folly was becoming clear to him, there in the musty barn on the hard ground, Ev's muffled sobs piercing his heart. He had broken Ev's trust and for what? He was no richer, had nothing to show for his involvement with Barrett and Harrison. And he never would—he admitted that to himself now. All the failed jobs, the grandiose plans that had sounded so fine on the surface—thinking on them now he saw how silly they were in reality. Turning horses into camels with burlap sacks! Spending money on paintings and movie props instead of something useful! Dropping the bootleg rum into the sea! Barrett would never be able to challenge Crawford—he would probably never even manage to open the Temple or film his movie. He had been so stupid to join them. Why couldn't he ever manage to make the right decision?

THE NIGHT PASSED slowly. Del might have fallen asleep at some point, in between berating himself, but he was awake when the sky started to grow lighter, the indistinct shapes that surrounded them becoming clear—a wheelbarrow in a corner, a pile of rusted cans under a window, an old oil drum fallen on one side. He knew Ev was awake also, his body too tense to still be asleep, even though he remained curled on his side, his back to Del.

A hand on the shoulder would be rebuffed, and he couldn't think of any words that would make this better, so he stayed silent, getting to his feet and shuffling outside. A house stood about half a mile away, and he hoped the farmer who lived there didn't have any cause to visit his south fields that morning.

Ev joined him a minute later, keeping a careful distance between them. He looked as awful as Del felt—eyes red and puffy, listless from hunger, bits of hay stuck in his hair and jacket, shoes caked with mud.

"Did you get any sleep?" Del asked, his words cracking the brittle silence between them.

Ev's jaw trembled. "Not much."

"Me either." He drew a breath. "Look, Ev, I...I'm sorry."

"Sorry," Ev repeated, his tone bitter.

"Yes, and—"

"You know who else told me he was sorry?" Ev interrupted. "That old lover of mine, Michael. He said he was sorry the morning after he'd slapped me around and my face was all swollen."

"It's not the same," he protested feebly, the guilt sitting cold and heavy in his stomach.

Ev didn't reply, didn't look at him.

After an agonizing, awful minute, Del cleared his throat. "Better see if we can get back to where we hid the car."

"And if it isn't there?"

Please God, let it be there. "Hitchhike back to the city, I guess."

"I hate farms," Ev said. "I *hate* them."

He'd never heard Ev sound so vicious, and he shot sidelong looks at him as they started walking. Maybe being in that barn had brought back bad memories from when Ev was a kid. And now Ev would always think of this moment too—of discovering how Del had lied to him.

He would have fallen down on his knees in the dirt and begged forgiveness if he thought it would make any difference, but Ev was at his coldest and hardest, every defensive layer Del had broken through back in place and twice as strong.

Chapter Fourteen

BY SOME MIRACLE, the car was still there, hidden in the undergrowth on the side of the road. The return trip to the city was nerve-racking as hell, though, every car they passed possibly full of Federal agents or the Sheriff's deputies. But they made it to Ev's apartment in one piece with no signs of anyone following them. Del parked at the curb and turned off the engine.

"I can't see you again," Ev said, staring straight ahead out the window.

He had been expecting it, but the words still hurt terribly.

"I'm sorry." He choked out the apology again, knowing it wouldn't help but unable to think of anything else to do. His mind felt numb and slow. Part of him only wanted to get away from this, from the horrible tension in the air, from the guilt crushing his heart.

A patter of footsteps approached the car. "Ev?" It was Camilo, looking worried. "Is that you? I didn't know where you'd gone off to—you said you'd be back last night."

Ev opened the door, and Camilo sucked in a gasp. "Oh, darling!" he exclaimed, seizing Ev's arm. "You look awful. What happened?"

Ev shook his head, sagging against Camilo's shoulder.

Camilo's eyes landed on Del. "Did you get him in this state? Did you?"

Del stared at the dashboard.

Camilo made an outraged noise and started drawing Ev away. "Come inside, lamb, and I'll make you some *biko*, some sweet rice and a little coconut milk. That will help; that will make you feel better."

Camilo slammed the door behind them and led Ev up the steps. Ev didn't look back, only leaned into Camilo and hid his face in his hands.

DEL RETURNED THE car to Harrison at the shabby boarding house where Harrison lived with Jasper. Harrison almost had a conniption when he came out and saw all the mud splattered across the Studebaker.

"What the hell were you doin'?" Harrison demanded. "I gotta get this back to the boss before he gets suspicious, and you bring it to me looking like this?"

"Things went...badly," Del said, too exhausted to come up with some story.

Harrison took a better look at him. "Damn, what happened to you, pal?"

Del didn't mean to tell him, but the words started slipping out.

"The Prohis, huh?" Harrison shook his head. "That's some rotten luck." He cupped his hands around his mouth and yelled up at a second story window. "Jasper!"

Jasper stuck his head out. "What?"

"Get down here and wash the car."

"Fuck that. Why the hell should I?"

"If you do, I'll forget about the ten bucks you owe me."

Jasper narrowed his eyes.

"And I'll wash all those dirty socks in the laundry basket," Harrison added.

Jasper perked up. "Yeah?"

"Yep."

"And you won't drape 'em over the radiator to dry and get 'em scorched?" Jasper added with the caution of previous experience.

"Nope. I'll hang 'em out the window, all proper like."

"All right, then."

Jasper withdrew, and Harrison clapped his arm around Del's shoulders. "Come on, pal. I know just what you need."

Harrison took him to the butcher shop that was his blind—or in this case, dead—pig of choice.

"'Course it wasn't fair. You'd done nothing wrong," Harrison said as he topped up Del's glass of whisky. "If you hadn't run into the Prohis, your kid would have been none the wiser. Like I always tell Jessie when she asks where I was on a Saturday night: what you don't know won't hurt you."

Del sighed, leaning his elbow on the table and propping his head on his hand. "But I did hurt him. Real bad." He gulped some more whisky, already well on his way to being drunk.

"You didn't mean it. Give it a couple of days, and then give your baby some roses and an apology."

"You don't know how stubborn Ev is," Del slurred.

Harrison—also well on his way to being drunk, enough so that he apparently didn't realize Del wasn't talking about a woman—patted Del on the shoulder, although he missed his mark and clouted Del's ear as well. "There are other fish in the sea."

"I don't want them. I want Ev." Del slumped all the way onto the table, burying his head in his arms.

Past that point, things got hazy. He kind of thought they might have burst into a drunken rendition of "The Band Played On," to the horrified amazement of a lady buying a leg of lamb at the counter. Hopefully he was mistaken. When clarity returned, he was in his apartment, half-on and half-off the bed, still dressed and with a pounding headache. Stumbling into the other room, he discovered Harrison lying in the chintz armchair and snoring.

He sagged against the doorjamb. Instead of waking up next to Ev, he had a drunken Harrison on his armchair. He didn't think he'd ever felt so wretched.

THE REST OF the day passed slowly. He went to work, still too stunned to really comprehend what had happened. All he could think about was Ev's heartbroken expression.

When he finished his shift, he went home, locked the door behind him, slid down onto the floor, and put his head in his hands.

Ev had left him. All his grand plans had crumbled apart. He had no idea how to fix things either. Buying apology presents sure as hell wouldn't work.

It was all so stupid. Why couldn't Ev be reasonable? He'd never outright lied to him. He would have told him the truth when the time was right. It was Ev's fault in the first place for being so stubborn and reluctant to trust him.

The anger lasted a good ten minutes before guilt bled into it. The thought that he'd lost Ev forever hurt too much to contemplate. Surely he could get Ev back. Ev with his hopeful, tentative smiles—the real ones, not the come-hither ones he pasted on at cabarets. Del bet he was one of the few people Ev had ever trusted with one of those, and now he'd never get to see one again. He'd made things worse, not better.

He knew he'd never be able to sleep like this, and he couldn't sit in his apartment, listening to the clock tick and playing every awful moment over again in his mind. And so, although he knew it was probably a bad idea, he went to Ev's apartment.

Camilo answered the door and immediately tried to slam it shut when he saw Del. But Del put out his hand, stopping it from completely shutting. "Please," he begged. "Let me see him. I need to apologize. I need to—"

"The only thing you need to do is leave and never come back again," Camilo said, jerking the door open far enough to glare at him. "That poor boy cried his eyes out for half the night, and he only got to sleep a little bit ago. I am not going to wake him up to listen to rotten excuses. The best thing for him is to forget you ever existed."

He couldn't break down the door, and so he stepped back, defeated. But he couldn't bring himself to leave, and so he sat on the curb opposite the apartment building as the sun rose higher in the sky, eyes trained on their apartment window in case he got a glimpse of Ev.

Around nine, Camilo appeared and stalked over to where Del was sitting. He didn't say anything, just handed him a folded piece of paper and left. Del unfolded it.

I told you I didn't want to see you again. Please leave.

He crumpled the paper in his fist and slammed it against the sidewalk, scraping his knuckles on the coarse concrete.

Chapter Fifteen

"SO THAT'S THAT," Glen said, swirling the chips of ice in his glass. They were sitting in Glen's living room, Greta and Sam dozing on the rug between them. "I wish I could say I didn't see something like this coming."

Del swallowed past the miserable lump in his throat. "I only wanted Ev to be happy."

Glen sighed. "I know. But did you ever ask what would make him happy?"

"But that's obvious. Lawrence always—"

"Ev isn't Lawrence. Lawrence was a stuck-up bitch who didn't deserve you."

He flinched, startled by the anger in Glen's voice.

"I think Ev would have been happy with you just as you are," Glen continued in a calmer tone.

Del shook his head. "You're wrong."

"Why? 'Cause you can't figure out why someone might love you?"

He met Glen's eyes, saw the sadness there, and looked away again.

"Anyway," Glen continued after a moment, "What are you going to do about the bootlegging? You sticking with that Barrett fellow?"

The legging—God, what a miserable failure that had been too. He hadn't gotten more than thirty dollars, all told. All of Barrett's grand plans—Harrison's rosy vision of the future—it was all a mirage, all hopeless.

"No. I'm getting out. If I do..." He stared down at the melting ice cubes in the bottom of his glass. "If I do, maybe Ev will forgive me."

He knew Harrison would take it badly and would probably feel like Del was betraying him. Jasper too, who had only just started to warm up to him. But if it gave him a chance at earning Ev's forgiveness, he had to take it.

"That's probably for the best," Glen said carefully, sounding as though there was a lot more he would have liked to say but was holding back.

"About Sam—"

"He can keep staying here as long as necessary. Don't worry about that."

"Thanks. Asta's supposed to be out in February, I think, so it's only about four months more." Asta would probably take Del's head off when he heard what had happened. Del wasn't sure he'd try to stop him, either.

THE NEXT DAY, he went to the Temple of Ra.

He remembered the first time he came here, how scared he'd felt, and how he'd really believed he might get rich. God, how stupid he'd been.

Everyone was downstairs, of course. How secretive and important they'd all seemed when he first met them, crafting their plans in the shadows. It had been mysterious and thrilling. Now all he could see was the shabbiness of the place, juxtaposed with Barrett's ridiculous excesses, like the painting of him as a pharaoh. He realized now that all of them were sitting down here because they had nothing else to do. Well, Harrison would have found some scheme or other to occupy himself, but the others were only idling the day away and dreaming—of money in Hazel, Fletcher, and Jasper's case—and of grandiose plans for moving pictures and expeditions to the pyramids in Barrett's. Not much had been done to the room since Del had been enlisted in painting the walls. Paint cans were still scattered about and someone had started taking down the shelving behind the bar but stopped halfway through. He had no idea what had happened to the horses that were going to be camels.

Barrett was reading the *Times*, a half-eaten doughnut at his elbow. Fletcher and Hazel were conferring over a crossword puzzle, looking very chummy. Harrison had let Del in, but he and Jasper had been in the middle of playing a hand of cards. Jasper lifted his hand in a wave when he saw Del.

Jasper would hate him too after this. He wondered what Jasper would say to his uncle—probably how Del was a good-for-nothin' who left his buddies hanging in the lurch.

"Hey, pal," Harrison said, giving him a clap on the shoulder. "What brings you to this neck of the woods? Hope it's not news of a raid."

As if anyone would care about this place enough to raid it.

"No, I need to talk to Mr. Barrett—and all of you, I guess."

"Delbert," Barrett said, laying down the paper. "What's on your mind? Dare I hope that you are cultivating an interest in Egyptology and have come to ask me for my literature recommendations? Or do you have word of any likely camel suppliers for our film? We *will* need one or two to supplement the horses."

"Uh, no, sir." Del took off his hat, remaining standing while Harrison flopped back down in his chair. "The thing is...well, I'm afraid I'm going to have to part ways with you. The legging business isn't for me."

Harrison shot back to his feet. "Leaving us? Now whatever put such a fool notion in your head? You can't leave."

He met Harrison's wounded expression for a moment and then looked away. "I'm sorry. I do appreciate you taking me on and giving me a chance, but I need to go. Besides, I don't think I've been of much help to you anyway."

He hadn't been quite sure how Barrett would react, had imagined him getting angry, that maybe Fletcher might threaten him and try to force him to stay. But Barrett listened with his usual aplomb.

"Now, that's not true—you have been an asset to our organization. Wouldn't you agree, my dear?"

"Oh, absolutely." Hazel put her hand on Barrett's arm. "Why I feel awful at the thought of you leaving, Delbert. Positively awful."

Fletcher, on the other hand, looked pleased at the news, probably happy he'd have one less person to defend against in his place as Barrett's right-hand man.

"Thank you, sir, ma'am, but I can't stay," Del repeated.

"But—but, Del," Harrison stuttered. "You—I mean—we're partners in this."

Del shook his head, forcing the words out. "Not any longer."

Harrison slumped back in his chair, falling silent. Jasper stared at Del a minute and then grunted and looked back at his cards, his usual scowl affixed to his face.

"If you insist upon it, Delbert, I have no choice but to allow you to depart," Barret said. "But I do think you should reconsider. After all, we're planning an empire here—an empire!"

Del marveled that he had ever been taken in by this sort of talk, although if he was honest with himself, he'd had doubts along the way but had ignored them, determined to believe what he wanted to be true. "I wish you the best of luck, sir," he said aloud. "And of course, you needn't worry about me telling anyone about you or leading the Prohis here."

Barrett waved away the concern. "I hope you will still take part in my motion picture—costume provided, of course, although I cannot promise more than a cold lunch—the costs of feeding extras are quite astounding, according to my acquaintance at the studio. And do keep your ear out for word of any camels."

Del promised that he would, said his farewells to Hazel—who blew him an airy kiss—and Fletcher—who didn't even look up from the crossword puzzle.

He avoided looking at Harrison and made it into the areaway and halfway up the steps before the door banged open behind him. Reluctantly, he paused and turned around to face him. Jasper was there too, although he stopped at the bottom of the stairs while Harrison clattered up until he was level with Del.

"You can't just leave like this," Harrison said, jerking at the cuffs of his shirt, which stuck out from beneath the too-short sleeves of his jacket. "Why do you want to go?" He blinked, brow pinched in confusion. "This is a good thing, ain't it? We've been having a swell time—and sure, maybe we ain't seen much cabbage yet, but our pockets'll be lined with money soon enough, I promise."

Del sighed. "You gotta know that's not true. Barrett—he's not got the makings of a boss on the level of the Gray Wolf. He's going to spend any profits you make on his fool projects, like redesigning the Temple or making movies. He's more likely to go bankrupt than make millions."

"But lots of people make money in pictures," Harrison said, sounding lost.

Del put a hesitant hand on his shoulder. "You should leave too before you end up in jail for the legging or worse things. You won't gain anything, staying with him."

Harrison jerked away. "I don't run off and leave people. I thought we were pals, Del."

Jasper spat on the ground and stalked inside, slamming the door behind him.

"I'm sorry," Del said, looking away.

Harrison stared at him a moment longer and then shuffled down the stairs, shoulders hunched, absent his usual blithe spirit.

It hurt more than Del had expected. Whatever else Harrison was, he'd also been his friend, inviting him out on the town, even willing to wash socks in order to try and cheer Del up when he was down.

Even when he was trying to rectify a mistake, he still managed to hurt people along the way. As usual, he couldn't manage anything right.

HE STILL WENT to try and see Ev, though.

"What does it take to get you to stay away?" Camilo demanded. He had opened the door at Del's knock but now blocked it with his body. Del tried to crane his head to see if Ev was there, but Camilo pulled the door almost shut, squeezing into the narrow opening and glaring.

"Is Ev home?" Del asked. His hands were shaking, and so he shoved them in his pockets.

"None of your business."

"If I could see him for a moment—"

Camilo started to close the door.

"Wait!" Del put his hand out, holding it open. "Tell him that I've quit the bootlegging. Will you tell him that for me?"

Before Camilo could reply, a burst of footsteps sounded, and then the door was wrenched open. Ev stood there, breathing hard. Camilo glanced at him and then moved out of the way, going into the kitchen.

"You think I'm going to forgive you?" Ev demanded. His hair was a mess, and his eyes were red.

"I don't expect you to," Del mumbled. "But...but I stopped. I won't do it again. I—"

"You quit after I found out," Ev interrupted. "You quit *because* I found out. Not because you thought it was wrong or that you didn't want to do it anymore. Otherwise you would still be doing it. You'd still be lying to me."

Del hunched forward, crumpling in the face of Ev's scorn. "I was going to tell you."

Ev snorted.

"I was, Ev."

"You expect me to believe that? You expect me to forgive you?" Ev's voice cracked, and he put a hand to his face. "I thought you were different. I thought you loved me enough to get me away from all the— the *shame* and dirt, and instead you thought I'd want the money so much I wouldn't care."

"Ev, no. I—"

"That's enough," Camilo said, coming over and taking Ev's arm to draw him back. "Do you want him here, Ev, darling?"

Ev shook his head, turning into Camilo's hug and hiding his face.

"Leave," Camilo said to Del, tightening his arms around Ev. "If you try anything, I'll call for help."

That Camilo thought he might become violent and try to physically hurt Ev—did Ev think that too?

Feeling sick, Del stepped away, and Camilo shut the door.

He wandered slowly back down the street, an aching pain choking his throat and burning his eyes. He'd seen the houses and apartments and shops that surrounded him many times. But everything seemed different now that his mind no longer held the familiar and comforting idea that Ev was a part of his life. Up until that morning, he had still held onto the hope that Ev would forgive him. But that wasn't going to happen. For how long would he have to live in this disorienting, distressing world before he got used to it again? And that was a terrible thought too—getting used to Ev's absence.

His stumbling legs carried him at last to his apartment. He sat down at the kitchen table, staring blankly at the worn surface of the wood while the sun crept across the wall, narrowing into a sliver of light and then edging 'round the corner of the building, vanishing from Del's kitchen and casting its warmth on the tree-tops on the opposite side of the street.

Chapter Sixteen

NOVEMBER AND THE subsequent Christmas season passed in a dull blur. He went to visit his father in Kansas for a few days, and the snow and brown fields suited his mood better than the perpetual sunshine and orange trees of Southern California. His aunt asked if Del had found a young lady he wanted to marry yet, and he almost embarrassed himself by crying in the middle of cutting the Christmas ham.

He caught a train home on the twenty-eighth. It left Abilene at three in the afternoon and with the winter days so short, the sun was already casting long, cold shadows as the train rolled westward. He sat by a window, looking out at the scenery. He felt tired—tired of everything. The glass of the window was frigid against his cheek as he leaned his head against it, shutting his eyes.

Back in Los Angeles, he visited Glen and exchanged belated Christmas gifts—a new pair of waders from Glen and two new lures from him.

"Has Ev been round to see Sam?" he finally asked when they were listening to a concert on the radio.

"Yes," Glen said, sounding reluctant to discuss it.

"He's doing all right?"

"I guess. I didn't ask after his health, Del. It was awkward as hell." Glen rubbed the back of his neck.

"But did he—"

"He dropped off some bones for the dogs, petted Sam a bit, and we talked about the weather. He said Asta will be out the first week of February. And that was it."

"I was just asking," Del mumbled.

Glen sighed. "He looked tired to me. But I'd only met him the once before. I couldn't tell if he was blue or still angry with you."

A few minutes of silence passed.

"How are you planning to ring in 1926?" Glen finally asked. "I'd say we should go out, but the paper wants me to help cover all the celebrations downtown."

"I'm working that night. There's always a slew of accidents on New Year's Eve." He was relieved he'd be working. He'd hoped to be spending the new year with Ev, and at least this way Ev's absence wouldn't be so painfully striking.

THE OLD YEAR went out with a bang all right—five smashups and a dozen smaller accidents from drunk drivers running into telephone poles and the like. He was at the station long after his shift ended writing the reports and struggling with the typewriter. Then, just when he thought he was almost finished, he discovered that one of the clerks, Joe Logran, had spent the Christmas holidays rearranging the filing system, and now there was a new order for various forms, and some needed a special date stamp—you couldn't write the date, no, you had to use the little rubber stamp, and Del had done five before he remembered that it wasn't 1925 anymore.

He scratched out the five and wrote a six instead, knowing Joe would give him an annoyed glance the next time they crossed paths.

After all that, he went home and slept until late in the afternoon. When he got up and shuffled into the kitchen, he found the breadbox almost empty, and he needed more coffee too, so he dragged himself to Mr. and Mrs. Mantifel's P&W Grocery two blocks over. Del preferred shopping there because Mr. Mantifel always ran the till and liked discussing the latest sports news.

Mrs. Mantifel also always had an odd collection of used items in the back corner that she picked up at various rummage sales and resold. Del had acquired a very fine kettle once and always made sure to peruse the latest offerings. Today a typewriter sat there, sandwiched in between a waffle iron and a lamp.

Del looked at it. He pressed the "f" key. It stuck, but when he gave it another jab, it popped up again.

"That'll be eight dollars," Mr. Mantifel said when Del heaved the typewriter onto the counter.

"I could pay four now," he offered.

"Four now plus another six," Mr. Mantifel countered. "Within the month."

"All right," Del agreed. "Oh, and a pound of coffee, please."

Mr. Mantifel ground the coffee for him, and Del tucked the bag under one arm, then hefted the typewriter and backed out the door, which another customer held open for him. It wasn't until he was almost home that he realized he'd forgotten to buy bread, but by that point his arms were getting sore, and he wasn't about to lug the typewriter all the way back to the grocer's. He had some crackers in the cabinet anyway.

The only place for the typewriter was the kitchen table. Del set it down and went to fetch some stationery. He'd practice and practice until he could type as fast as Carl Hutton. That's what he'd told Ev about the photography, after all—that Ev needed to practice to get better. He would do the same.

A sense of determination suffused him as he cranked the paper into place. It was a relief, a distraction from his aching heart.

He hoped Ev was still taking photographs. It would be too hard if his thoughtlessness had ruined that for Ev too. But no—Ev was strong. He would make it without Del. And he would have to make it without Ev.

THE NEXT TIME Del saw Carl Hutton at the station, he asked him if he could borrow his latest copy of the *Police Journal*. Getting better at typing was only half of it—he would study up on all the modern methods of policing.

"Of course," Carl said, delighted. "It's in my locker. You'll have to tell me what you think about the article on the standardization of traffic laws. Personally, I think it's only common sense. The situation we're in now is ridiculous—different laws in every city, county, and state. How can we expect people to follow the law if they don't know what it is?"

Del considered this. "Making them all the same does sound easier," he ventured.

Carl nodded. "I'm planning to write a letter to the International Traffic Officers' Association in support of their campaign. You should write one as well. Having the endorsement of policemen will help the cause immeasurably."

Del wasn't at all sure about that plan—he had enough problems writing regular letters to his aunt and father, but he nodded. He had decided to set a goal for himself of making it into the motorcycle drill squad by the end of the year. Being able to say he was participating in an international campaign for better traffic laws sure would sound impressive to his lieutenants.

Kirkpatrick laughed when he saw Del holding the *Journal.* "Sure you can read all those big words, Mr. Minus?"

Del ignored him with as much dignity as he could muster.

"I HAD A letter from Sam's owner, Asta, today," Glen said, a touch hesitant, taking off his gloves and pulling out his handkerchief to wipe the sweat off his forehead. It was a pleasant afternoon, the January sunshine mild, and so Del was helping Glen take down the wooden stoop at the back of his house, to be replaced with a brick patio.

"Oh? What did Asta say?" He noted that Glen called Asta "Sam's owner" and not "Ev's friend."

"Says he'll be arriving in town on February 3rd and wants to come over to see Sam right away."

Del hooked his hammer's claw into a nail and started pulling it loose, rocking the hammer back and forth. "I'll stay away then. I'm sure Ev's told Asta what happened, and Asta never liked me in the first place."

"I figured. Still, I thought I might offer to keep Sam here, just until Asta's found a place."

"Asta would probably appreciate that. I think Greta might be lonely when Sam's gone, anyways."

Glen glanced over at where the two dogs were lying in a patch of sunshine, sleeping. "Might have to get her a puppy to make up for it." He cleared his throat and pulled his gloves back on, kneeling down beside Del again. "You seem to be doing all right. Better than I thought you'd be."

Del yanked hard, and the nail pulled loose. It wasn't too badly bent, so he tossed it onto the pile of ones they could straighten and use again. "I'm focusing on my job."

"That's good—takes your mind off of Ev, right?"

"I guess so." He took a deep breath so his voice didn't shake. "I can't be sad forever. And you?" he added quickly. "You with anyone? Didn't you start going with a new girl before Christmas?"

"Yes, but it didn't last long with Frieda. I've picked up a pansy for a night now and then, and there was a pretty thing over at my dry goods store that caught my eye, but it turned out he was with another fellow."

As usual, Glen didn't sound sad over his failed love affairs. Must have been nice, not to care, and Del couldn't help saying, a touch resentfully,

"Don't you ever want to be with someone for more than a couple of months?"

Glen didn't reply for a moment and then said slowly, "You think I don't care about them?"

"Well you don't seem sad about losing Frieda. Or that girl Lillian, or any of the others."

Glen sighed. "It's not that I don't get sad. I miss Frieda. She would go roller-skating with me, and she has a funny little laugh. And Lillian, she was a smart cookie, we'd end up arguing about politics all the time—kept me on my toes. But most girls, they want to get married. It doesn't do their reputation any good, to stay with a fellow for too long and not get hitched. But you know I'm not the marrying type. At least with pansies, I don't have to worry about that."

"They care about things like respectability too," Del muttered. "You shouldn't just...use them."

Glen lifted the loose board out, standing up to lean it against the wall with the others. "Hey, we both get something out of it. What, were you and Ev planning to tie the knot?" He laughed as he said it.

"It happens," Del shot back. "Ev showed me news stories."

"Maybe," Glen said, still skeptical.

"They don't have it so easy, you know. Someone like Ev deserves...commitment and—and a decent life." His voice caught, and he stopped, focusing on the board in front of him, which started splitting on one end when he tried to pull it free.

"Well, marriage doesn't guarantee any of that. Think of all the couples I see in divorce court—abuse, abandonment, adultery—what's respectable about that?"

"I know. I'm not *always* stupid. It's not marriage itself. I couldn't ever have married Ev in a church. But I could have respected him. And instead I..."

He fell silent. Greta, disturbed by their rising voices, trotted over and nudged his face with her wet nose.

"Ah, hell, let's not talk about it," Glen said. "That boxing match we want to listen to comes on at five, and if we don't finish this, we'll miss it."

TWO WEEKS LATER, Lieutenant Miller flipped through the stack of papers on his desk and then transferred his stern glare onto Del.

"Seven misfiled or lost reports this month, Randolph," he said. "And the problems don't stop there. You've recorded vehicle registration numbers wrong, mixed up people's names, or cited the incorrect traffic ordinance in half of this paperwork. You also need to keep the paper straight in the typewriter. Look at this one—I have to hold it at an angle to make the lines look even."

Del was holding his cap, and he pinched the edge tightly between his fingers, trying to contain his nerves. "I apologize, sir. I'll do better in future."

"There's also the amount of gasoline you're using in your motorcycle. I suppose young fellows like you enjoy tearing up and down the streets in an awful hurry, but unless you're responding to a crime, there's no reason for that. Our department is trying to stress efficiency and economy."

"Yes, sir."

"Police work isn't like it used to be. I know many in the department weren't too pleased when Chief Vollmer came down here from Berkeley last year, but personally I think he had many good ideas. Scientific crime detection, an organized system of records, and fingerprint files for identifying criminals—those are the foundation of excellent policing. And we need men of high caliber to undertake those duties. Now, I'm not suggesting that we recruit strictly from colleges or that men like yourself—what was your highest grade in school, Randolph? Seventh?"

"Yes, sir," Del admitted, heart sinking further and further.

"I'm not saying you can't make a good police officer, but you're going to have to put in some effort." He waved the stack of reports at Del. "This type of shoddy record keeping isn't going to cut it, Randolph."

"No, sir."

Miller cleared his throat, tapped the reports decisively on his desk, and dismissed him.

Del crept from his office. He did try to do his best with the reporting, but he'd never been good with letters. He'd make time to study the traffic ordinances and the California Vehicle Act again this week. He *did* know the laws, but it was easy to forget the right numbers and specifics. Carl and Lieutenant Miller must get along like a house on fire.

At home the next morning, he sat staring at the typewriter. Taking a deep breath, he poked at the keys. He'd purchased a ribbon and discovered the typewriter did work to a point. The paper always got stuck halfway through, and you had to go to a great deal of trouble to yank it out, crumpling it beyond saving in the process. The "o" and "c" keys also refused to fully depress. But he could practice on it. He *would* practice on it and get better.

He was mid-way through a paragraph when the phone rang. It was Glen.

"Hey, pal. I have a favor to ask."

"Sure, what is it?"

"Asta got into town last week, and I offered to let him stay here a few days. Well, I think he was kind of sickly after being in prison and now he's come down with smallpox. It's been going around the city—maybe you've seen the notices in the paper. The doctor's been by, but we're quarantined here for at least a week. Could you buy some food for us and leave it on the doorstep?"

"Of course. You're not sick, are you?"

"Nah—I had a mild case when I was a kid. Think I should be okay. Asta's doesn't seem too severe, but obviously he needs to rest."

"Right. Let me know what you need, and I'll bring it."

He had seen the reports in the paper, that there had been over four hundred smallpox cases in California since January, and he knew that they were vaccinating prisoners in the jails and forbidding relatives from visiting them. Asta must have caught it in San Quentin before being released. He wondered if Ev knew and hoped he wasn't too worried. Glen would take good care of Asta. Del had been vaccinated two years ago when there was another outbreak, and he figured he was still safe.

Over the next week, in between shuttling food and supplies to Glen's, he asked Joe to explain the filing system—again—to him too. Joe huffed irritably and spoke quickly, but when he saw Del taking diligent notes, he slowed down and repeated a few points, even asking if Del had any questions.

Of course, he also tried to perform his duties efficiently and effectively. He never failed to call in to the station once an hour unless he was involved in writing a traffic tag. He reviewed the list of traffic ordinances every other day so he remembered the correct numbers. One night, when a drunk driver crashed into a parked auto, he made sure to return to the scene after getting the driver booked at the station so he could supervise the mechanic who came to tow away the wrecks and ensure no debris remained in the road blocking traffic.

If Ev had been there, perhaps he would have said some encouraging words and wrapped an arm around him to show he thought Del was doing a good job and was proud of him. As it was, Del could only plod along through each day, telling himself that he could master the filing system and typing with enough practice.

He was glad that February was a short month, though. Even if it was only twenty-eight days instead of thirty, that was two less to cope with. Besides, now that spring was arriving, he and Glen might be able to venture up to the hills for some fishing soon. Glen had called the other day to let him know that Asta had recovered, and Del didn't need to keep bringing groceries. But as far as he knew, Asta was still staying at Glen's. He wasn't keen on meeting Asta again, but figured Asta couldn't be at Glen's all the time. Anyway, Asta could stay in the kitchen while he talked to Glen in the living room or vice versa.

He decided to try and visit on his next free evening to see if Glen was interested in a fishing trip. Glen's car was parked in the driveway when Del arrived, but no one answered his knocks.

"Glen?" he called out. "Glen, are you there?"

A minute passed in silence. Then he heard the sound of the doorknob turning, and Glen peered out at him. He was in his robe and barefoot. His face was flushed, and Del could see red marks on his neck. Embarrassed, Del looked down. Hell, Glen had been in bed with someone, and he'd dragged him away.

"Sorry," he mumbled, "I should have rung first." He hardly ever did so. Glen had told him once his door was always open to Del, and he was in the habit of popping 'round without notice. It had never mattered before.

"Can it wait?" Glen asked in a rough voice, casting a look back over his shoulder.

Del started to say that yes, it could, and then he saw who had stepped out into the hallway behind Glen.

"Asta?" he choked out.

Asta looked better than the last time Del had seen him. The ugly prison uniform was gone, his hair was curled, and he had on some makeup. Asta lit a cigarette, watching Del but remaining silent. He was wearing a silk kimono, like Ev—

Glen scratched the back of his neck. "It kind of just happened. I…I'd have told you."

Del's heart constricted. It was too much. Glen, who didn't care, who treated all his lovers casually, should have this when Del, who loved—*loved*—Ev more than anything—

"Del," Glen began as Del turned away.

"Don't," Del said, and he walked quickly down the sidewalk, heedless of where he was going, needing only to get away.

Chapter Seventeen

TWO DAYS PASSED before Glen called him.

"Look," Glen began, and then he stopped and sighed. Del leaned against the wall, holding the receiver to his ear.

"Do you want to go fishing this weekend?" Glen asked.

Del twisted his fingers in the telephone wire. "That's what I was going to ask you when I came over."

"I figured." Glen's sigh dissolved into static.

"I'd like to go fishing," he said after a moment. "The weather should be nice."

"Saturday, then?"

He shut his eyes and took a breath. "Yeah, Saturday."

When Glen arrived on Saturday morning, Greta and Sam were both crammed into the backseat of the flivver. Del paused, letting his knapsack sag onto the ground. Glen glanced at Sam.

"If it bothers you, I can—"

"No." He wrenched open the door. "It'd be silly to be upset by a dog. I like Sam."

They drove in silence for a while. "About Asta," Glen finally said. "It just happened, like I said. Spending all that time together while Asta was sick—we got kinda fond of each other. I wasn't trying to hurt you."

They were passing a fence painted with an advertisement for Dr. Pepper, white boards and red letters. "It doesn't matter," Del said. "That's what you always say, isn't it?"

Glen shrugged.

"Guess I should think that way too." The words came out of him in a tight, painful rush. "You never said it at the time, but I'm sure you wanted to tell me 'I told you so.' That I was stupid again. So stupid to get involved with a bunch of fool leggers. Stupid to hide it from Ev."

"Christ, Del." Glen blew out a hard breath.

"And now you'll have Asta for as long as you want, and you won't care when it ends, will you?"

"This relationship with Asta has nothing to do with you and Ev. So don't get angry—"

"It's not fair."

"And you're going to blame me for that?"

"I'm not blaming you," he said and fell silent. Glen shook his head, but didn't say anything more.

THEY DIDN'T SPEAK much on the rest of the drive, and as usual, they split up on the river, Glen going downstream with the dogs in tow, and Del wandering upstream along the bank. Plowing through a willow, the whippy branches stinging against his face and arms, he let himself cry, just for a minute, and blamed it on the wind and the brightness of the sun on the water. Then he scrubbed a hand over his eyes and set down his creel, preparing the lure and casting it into the stream. He'd chosen a spot where the hurrying water slowed, spreading into a wider pool. The air smelled of mud and wet grass. The lure bobbed along the surface, and he followed it with his eyes, watching the ripples, the endless motion of the water, letting it clear his mind and ease the frustration and guilt and regret that had been clinging to him.

When they rendezvoused back at the camp later, neither of them had caught any fish.

"That sort of day, I guess," Glen said with a rueful glance into his empty creel.

While lighting a fire and putting some bacon and beans in a frypan, he threw cautious glances Glen's way. Glen seemed his usual self again, smiling and throwing a ball for Greta and keeping an arm tight around Sam's neck so he didn't try to make a sneak attack on the bacon.

None of this was Glen's fault. It was his own actions that had led to Ev leaving him. If it had been anyone but Asta, he wouldn't have been nearly so upset. Besides, he couldn't begrudge Glen—or Asta—a chance at being happy.

"It's not steak tartare, but you can't beat a meal cooked over a campfire," Glen said, sniffing the air appreciatively.

"I'm sorry," Del blurted. "I got mad at you, and it wasn't your fault."

Glen shook his head. "I should have told you straight about me and Asta. I knew it might hurt you, seeing as how he's Ev's friend. But to be honest, I thought it would be a one-time fling, and there wouldn't be any need to tell you."

"Did he trip over Sam and into your bed or something?" Del asked, still not quite able to overcome the bitterness.

"No. We...hell, I don't know. We had a few drinks and were talking. And then I was helping him into his coat, and thinking about how pretty his mouth looked. Asta's tall—almost as tall as I am, and he put his arms around my neck and said as how he didn't really want to go sleep over at—" Glen stopped.

"At Ev's?" Del supplied, weary.

"Yeah. Said the bed is too small for two people, which makes me wonder how you managed."

There was an uncomfortable pause, and Glen cleared his throat.

"Anyway, I said he didn't have to leave just yet, and the sex was swell, and we had breakfast in the morning. I thought that'd be it, but, well...it hasn't been."

"I suppose Asta's glad I'm not with Ev anymore."

"He's not overly fond of you," Glen admitted.

Del dished out supper and settled back with his plate, holding it high enough so Sam, who had chosen Del as his target for begging that evening, didn't have easy access. He didn't take a bite right away, though, stirring the beans with his spoon. He was thinking of how Asta had looked in prison and that rotten Rex fellow.

"You gotta be careful, Glen," he said at last.

"Careful?" Glen repeated around a mouthful.

"With Asta. He's had a rough go of it. You should treat him right."

Glen frowned. "Don't I always? Christ, pal, I'm not going to hit him or nothing."

That wasn't what he'd meant, but he wasn't sure how to put it into words. And it wasn't as though he'd done any better with Ev, so he probably shouldn't be saying anything in the first place.

THE FOLLOWING WEEKEND, although the latest issue of the *Police Journal*, courtesy of Carl, sat next to the typewriter on his table, both silently accusing, he gave in to Glen's offer to accompany him and Asta to a cabaret.

"You don't have to invite me," Del said when Glen arrived at his apartment unexpectedly at seven o'clock, dressed in his evening suit and looking as though he had paid more attention to his appearance than usual. "Isn't Asta with you?"

"He's waiting in the car."

"I can't believe Asta agreed to spend time in my company."

Glen rubbed the back of his neck. "I wouldn't say he's thrilled. But I—well, I don't want you thinking we aren't pals anymore, okay? That I wouldn't spend time with you if he and I are together."

"Oh." He smiled, pleased. "If you don't mind waiting while I get changed—but," he hesitated again, another thought occurring, "What if we run into Ev?" The idea made him sick with longing and nerves, both wanting and dreading it.

"Asta says Ev was working a double shift at some factory and probably wouldn't be going out tonight."

"The Western Soap and Chemical Company," Del said absently, thinking of how tired Ev had been looking those last few weeks, working two jobs at once.

In the car, Asta gave him a frosty, "Good evening."

Del wedged himself in a corner of the backseat with a muttered greeting. But after a few blocks, he asked Asta hesitantly about how Ev was doing.

Asta's jaw tightened. "He's upset, of course. What did you expect? *His* feelings for you were genuine. He gave you his heart, and you treated it like—"

Glen reached over and put a hand on Asta's arm, and Asta cut off his angry words, huffing out a breath.

"It might be best if we didn't talk about Ev," Glen suggested in a dry voice.

"You're the one who insisted on bringing Del along. If he gets on my nerves, I'm finding someone else to spend the night with."

"If that's what you want," Glen replied with an easy shrug.

"If you didn't have such a swell cock, I'd be done with you right now," Asta snapped.

Glen glanced at him, raising his eyebrows. "Nice to know why you're keeping me around."

"That and Sam likes your backyard."

Glen laughed, and after a moment, Asta's mouth almost twitched into a smile.

Del had followed the exchange with concern and then confusion. Glen shouldn't be so flippant about the idea of Asta leaving him. Guess maybe they were being sarcastic. He'd never liked it when Ev was sarcastic—could never tell if it was a joke or not.

They didn't go to the Admiral's Blues, for which Del was grateful, but a flat that belonged to someone Asta knew. The balcony door on the second floor was open as they walked up, loud laughter and voices overwhelming the phonograph in the background.

Inside, a crowd of people pressed up against each other, crammed into the narrow rooms. On the hunt for a drink, Del squeezed past a large woman and found himself in a bedroom where a girl and man were grinding against each other in front of a small audience. One man was smoking marijuana, the scent cloying in the tiny space. He watched too for a minute, and then fumbled back into the hallway where he ran into Glen, who handed him a gin and tonic. Glen guided him upstairs and nudged his shoulder, nodding toward where Asta was talking with two other fairies. One was a kid, maybe seventeen, all rosy from the heat of the room, the other a bit older, with sharply drawn brows and a quiet smile.

"Let's get you someone for the night, huh?" Glen said. "They both look pretty damn nice, I'd say."

Del didn't feel anything beyond a vague interest, but he let Glen lead him over to the group.

The kid giggled and blushed and ran off to find some champagne. But the other one stayed, and Asta introduced him as Victor.

"Watch out for Del," Asta added to Victor. "He doesn't treat his lovers well, but I suppose he's good enough for a quick fuck."

"Come on, now," Glen interjected. "Del's heart got broken too. He's lonely."

"We're birds of a feather, then," Victor said and stepped forward, tucking his arm into Del's. "I'm lonely too. You want to comfort each other, sweetheart?"

Glen nudged him, and Del said, "Yes."

Victor patted his hand. "Let's find somewhere quieter. I can hardly think in here, it's so loud."

He followed Victor into the relative calm of the bathroom, where they perched on the edge of the bathtub, drinks in hand.

"So," Del began awkwardly after a minute, "I'm not sure if I'm really in the mood to show you a good time tonight."

"That's a shame." Victor's eyes lingered on him. "But I can't say I mind sitting and talking a bit either. Nice to be off my feet. I'm a counter-jumper at a dry goods store and never get a minute to rest."

"You said you were lonely."

"Oh, my sister got married last week and moved to Seattle." Victor's shoulders drooped. "We were playmates growing up and stayed chums even as we got older. I miss her something terrible."

"I'm sorry."

"At least she married someone decent." Victor held up a hand. "Although he *is* a mortician. How can you carry on a conversation over supper with a mortician? Asking about his work is impossible, and of course, I simply don't dare bring up politics or religion. You're left chatting about the weather and the stock market."

"I guess that would be pretty tough."

"But he'll never lack for work, so I suppose we have to look on the bright side." Victor tapped his fingers on the enamel tub. "What about you? What's your tragedy?"

"I don't especially want to talk about it," he admitted.

Victor laid a hand on his shoulder and didn't press for details.

They stayed there, sitting in a companionable, comforting silence, until someone started rapping on the door, needing to use the toilet and complaining about having to wait.

Emerging back into the noise and the crowd was jarring. Del stood still a moment, blinking and trying to get his bearings. He looked over at the window, and there, in his lamé coat, was Ev.

Del stopped breathing for a few seconds.

Ev's eyes passed over him, and then they flickered and snapped back, growing wide. Then he noticed Victor. For a second, the hurt was plain on his face. Then he stuffed it away, smoothing his expression, although his eyes stayed on Del.

Victor touched his elbow and murmured something about stepping outside for some air and a cigarette.

He hardly noticed, all of his attention consumed by Ev. His feet moved of their own accord, shoes like lead yet still carrying him forward. Ev too took a few stumbling steps closer before he stopped and went rigid, one hand closing his coat around his throat and holding it tightly.

Del came to a halt a few feet away.

Ev's face was tense, and his lips trembled.

What they would have said to each other, he never knew, for Glen and Asta descended a moment later.

"Ev, what are you doing here?" Asta exclaimed. "You told me you were working late."

"One of the machines broke, and they had to let the late shift out early," Ev said in a numb voice, still staring at Del until Asta shook him, breaking his gaze. Glen had a hand on Del, as though restraining him from rushing to Ev and damning the consequences.

"I didn't mean for you to run into each other," Asta was saying. "Glen and I were coming, and he wanted to invite Del."

Ev shook his head, dismissing the apology.

"But look at you," Asta continued. "You look exhausted, honey. What are you doing out? You should be home with your feet up and some hot tea. I don't like to see you not taking care of yourself."

"You know I can't bear to sit around and dwell on things," Ev said in a fast, low voice.

Del opened his mouth, but Glen's grip tightened, and he subsided. A strained silence fell for a few moments, all the more obvious for the revelry surrounding them.

Glen let go of Del's arm, clearing his throat. "I was going to ask Asta this, but since you're here—you still interested in photography, Ev?"

Ev looked startled at the change in subject, but slowly nodded. "I've been taking pictures, sometimes." He glanced at Del, then away again.

A tiny piece of the weight on his heart flaked away, a chip off a stone. He'd been worried Ev would throw the camera away, because it had been a gift from him.

"Why do you want to know?" Ev asked Glen.

"Teddy—you remember him—was wondering. He's been making inquiries for a friend of his, a fellow opening a portrait studio. He might need someone to help work the front and pitch in on the photography."

"And Teddy asked about me?"

"Yep. Since you're still interested, I'll let him know. Nothing might come of it, of course."

"Of course," Ev said quickly. He gathered his coat around himself, huddling into it. "I think...I think I'll be going. I..."

"Take a cab home," Asta said. "Do you have money?"

Ev nodded, but Asta frowned. "Actually, I think I should come with you. Glen, why don't you come by and pick me up at Ev's later?"

"I can make it home fine by myself," Ev began, but Asta hushed him and ushered him toward the stairs. Ev didn't look at Del again.

"Sorry about that," Glen said with a grimace. "Here I thought it would be good for you to get out—I'll go grab you a shot of whisky to settle the nerves. Stay put."

Del stayed put, thinking it would take a lot more than whisky to solve what was wrong with him.

"I'm guessing that was the reason you're lonely," a voice said next to him, and he turned to find Victor standing there.

"Oh. Yeah." He sighed.

"A lover's spat?"

"Something like that."

"Well, you need some comfort again, you come find me. I can tell you're a real sweet thing."

Del stammered and flushed at that. "Maybe so, but I sure make some awful mistakes."

"We all do, Del," Victor said and left after a parting kiss on the cheek.

Chapter Eighteen

ON THURSDAY DEL arrived at the station for his shift and received word the captain wanted to speak to him. He couldn't imagine why. If there was a problem, Lieutenant Miller would have berated him first. His heart started beating a little faster. Maybe the lieutenant had noticed an improvement in his work. Maybe he'd recommended him to the captain. Perhaps he was going to be invited to join the motorcycle drill squad after all.

"Randolph—please, take a seat," Captain Gardner said when Del knocked on his door. He gestured at the empty chair in front of his desk.

"Thank you, sir," he said, taking off his cap and sitting as directed.

Gardner pushed his glasses farther up his nose. "I've been looking over the latest report from Lieutenant Miller. Seems you need to work on your record keeping."

Del's heart sank. So he hadn't improved after all. "Yes, sir. I'm trying to do better."

"That's what I want to hear, Randolph." Gardner pushed the stack of papers in front of him aside. "But I've gotten some other reports about you. There have been rumors you've been getting involved in some funny business."

His heart sped up again, and he clenched the rim of his cap. "Sir?"

"To put it briefly, that you've been taking money from leggers."

"I haven't, sir." The protest sounded weak to his own ears. But it had been months since he had left Barrett and the bootlegging behind. Why would the captain be confronting him about it now, if he had known all along?

"Is that so?" Gardner adjusted his glasses again. "A word of advice, Delbert. You don't want to be the kind of cop who attracts rumors like this."

He shook his head, trying to keep his nerves steady. "No, sir."

"That being said, we're always looking for bright young lads to advance through the ranks. A man has to have good judgment and know when to exercise discretion."

"D-does he, sir?" Del was sweating now, wondering where this was leading.

"He does, Randolph. Now let's suppose for a moment that these rumors are true, and you wandered outside the bounds of the law a few times."

"But, sir—"

Gardner held up his hand, and Del fell silent. "Now in this case, you would have been in the wrong. But maybe, if the circumstances had been slightly different, you wouldn't have been. Do you understand what I'm saying?"

He shot a longing glance toward the door. "Not exactly, sir."

Gardner sighed and lifted his glasses to pinch the bridge of his nose. "I'm presenting you with an opportunity, son. I'm asking if you want to get a promotion and a raise. You just have to exercise discretion when and where I tell you."

Oh. Oh, hell. Gardner must be one of Heath's appointees. He must be trying to get Del to agree to being bought off by the City Hall Gang too.

"I d-don't know if I could do that, sir," he stuttered. "That's to say, I'll follow your orders, sir, but—but—"

"No call to be so nervous, Randolph." Gardner smiled. "Why don't you take a few days to think about it? You understand, opportunities like this don't come along too often. And I'm sure I don't have to tell you that refusing won't do your career any favors. Particularly given your lackluster record."

"Yes, sir," he managed.

Gardner smiled. "Well, I'm glad we have an understanding, Randolph. I'll speak to you again."

Del made it to the locker room, thankfully empty, and sagged against the wall. He didn't know how someone had cottoned on to what he'd been doing with Barrett. Maybe they never had, and Gardner was just saying that to put pressure on him. But if he said no to Gardner's offer, he'd be demoted back down to a beat cop—or worse, fired.

Being promoted to a motorcycle officer had been the first time in his life that he'd achieved a distinction like that. His father had been so proud—had paid the money to place a long-distance call to tell him congratulations.

But Crawford's gang...they wouldn't be like Barrett and Harrison, foolish and incompetent. If he messed up a job, there would be real consequences. What would they ask him to do? Intimidate people? Threaten them? Hurt them?

By the end of the day, he was so on edge that he jumped, startled, when Kirkpatrick suddenly loomed next to him in the locker room. Brooks appeared on his other side.

"Heard the captain's extended an offer to you," Kirkpatrick said.

"Never thought the day would come when Mr. Minus would get to join the big boys," Brooks added, grinning.

"Is it true you were trying to make a little profit for yourself on the side?" Kirkpatrick chuckled and put a rough hand on Del's hair, giving him a shake. "You gotta go about it in a smart way, kid. Striking out on your own ain't the thing."

Brooks jostled his shoulder. "God strike you dumb?"

"No, I, uh..." Del didn't know what to say and wished they would leave.

"Guess we don't have to worry about you squealin' to the wrong people, seeing as you can hardly say a word." Kirkpatrick laughed.

Brooks cracked his knuckles. "You remember to keep your mouth shut—no loose talk. You hear?"

He nodded, trying to sidle past Kirkpatrick, but he took a step to the right, blocking him.

"Where you going, huh? Shift's over. Why don't you come and have a drink with us. We'll introduce you to some fellas you should know."

He was searching desperately for an excuse, when the locker room door opened and Carl Hutton strolled inside.

"Hello, boys," he said.

"We were just headin' out," Kirkpatrick said, looping an arm around Del's shoulders.

"I have a...a...an appointment." Del ducked away. "Sorry, but I'll need a rain check."

"What's this?" Kirkpatrick started, frowning, but Carl interrupted.

"I actually need to speak to Delbert about a private matter," he said.

Kirkpatrick and Brooks didn't like Carl, but they respected him. He was the best shot at the East Side station, and of course, everyone knew the story of how Carl had apprehended a burglar who was about a hundred pounds heavier than him, disarming him and bringing him in safely.

"We'll catch you later then," Kirkpatrick said to Del, and he and Brooks left, tossing their jackets over their shoulders.

"I didn't actually have anything important to talk to you about," Carl said apologetically when the door had closed. "But it seemed like you didn't want to spend any more time in their company."

He was simultaneously grateful to Carl for the rescue and ashamed he had needed rescuing. "Thanks, I appreciate it," he said, trying not to sound grudging.

Carl smiled. "I'll take the opportunity to ask how you liked the latest issue of the *Journal*?"

"Oh, I forgot to bring it back," he said, realizing he'd left it on the kitchen table. "I'll return it to you tomorrow."

Carl waved a hand. "No matter. But you read it, didn't you?"

Del said yes, he had, relieved that it was the truth.

"They profiled some fine departments, didn't they? So efficient and professional." Carl lowered his voice. "If this department were run like that, we'd have no use for louts like Kirkpatrick and Brooks. They beat up another prisoner yesterday, you know. Some pitiful petty thief who'd robbed the till at a drugstore because he hadn't had anything to eat for three days."

Del knew how fond Kirkpatrick was of his brass knuckles and had seen him wield them against a variety of persons, including suspected Bolsheviks, strikers, and your run-of-the-mill crooks.

"They frequent a brothel on the west side too. I confronted them about it one day," Carl continued, a determined blaze in his eyes. "Kirkpatrick said to me there was no harm in a few cat houses—that if we got rid of them, we'd just have more rapes on our hands. I was stunned speechless, let me tell you. The public health issues alone—the imperative of stopping the spread of social diseases—is enough of a reason to shut down brothels, let alone saving those poor girls."

The prostitutes Del had known hadn't struck him as being particularly interested in being saved. One girl had told him she preferred it to boring factory work and could make more money besides. Of course, not all of them did it by choice. Some of the Oriental girls, in particular, got sold into it, no better than slaves. So he couldn't say Carl was wrong exactly.

"And that's not to mention the degenerates one can find in those places," Carl was saying. "Men dressing as women and the like."

Del nodded vaguely.

"Anyway, if we're to put a stop to crime, we need to prevent it before it can occur, not try and beat the law into men with fists and rubber hoses. But I'm sorry to go on like this." He gave Del an apologetic smile. "Our reform coalition in the department rather went to ground after Chief Vollmer left. I'm that happy to find a like-minded fellow. Sometimes I think it's only myself and Lieutenant Miller stemming the tide."

"It's no trouble," Del said and finally made his escape, hurrying to catch his streetcar before anyone else could stop him and expound on their philosophy.

He could never pin down exactly how he felt on these matters. He didn't think that extracting confessions from criminals through the third degree was a good thing, necessarily, although he wasn't sure how else they were supposed to get them. Some men didn't respond to anything except strength and violence. You had to show them who was boss or they'd run roughshod over you. There were also plenty of people like Harrison who did what they did not out of any malice but because of circumstance. He imagined Carl wouldn't have any sympathy for a fellow like Harrison.

On the other hand, if people like Carl were in charge, a captain of the police wouldn't be trying to force Del to join a criminal outfit. The police wouldn't be accepting bribes or protection money from Crawford's gang. But then again, Del would never have been promoted to motorcycle officer in the first place, because he couldn't score high enough on all those intelligence and psychological tests. So when it came down to it, he didn't know which side to support. He just wished they'd let him alone to do his job and not bother him about typing or filing or bootlegging or any of it.

MRS. MANTIFEL AT the P&W Grocery bagged the onion, three potatoes, and four Baby Ruth candy bars that Del had bought while he searched his pockets for the final necessary nickel.

"You still owe us four dollars for that typewriter," Mrs. Mantifel reminded him.

"Can I bring it to you next time?" he asked, nudging the nickel across the counter. He'd clean forgotten about owing that money.

Mrs. Mantifel allowed that would be fine, as she knew Del was good for it. He thanked her and left the store, gripping the bag tightly as he walked home, wondering how he would manage if he said no to the captain and lost his job. Even getting demoted would be a sore blow, the difference of ten or fifteen dollars a month meaning he would get even more behind on all his bills.

Back home, he dropped the bag on the kitchen table and then turned on the radio, recollecting that he'd missed his last installment payment on that and the kitchen chairs too. Sighing, he sat down in the armchair. The words—some news program—washed over him, unheard. If Ev had still been here, he would have wanted Del to refuse the captain. Ev had thought Del was above graft and crime—had thought so until he found out it wasn't true.

That was right—he'd already proved himself willing to join a gang for money. And Ev wasn't here—would never be here with him again. So what did it matter if he agreed? It wasn't fair that he should lose his position.

The next evening, he went over to Glen's to tie flies. Glen had declared them ready to move on to this next step in "conquering the wild rivers." When Del arrived, he already had tools, thread, and feathers scattered all over his kitchen table. Greta bounded over to greet him, Sam lumbering behind.

"Hey, you two," Del said, bestowing pats and behind-the-ears scratches.

Glen looked up from his study of a fly pattern in *Outdoor Life*. "That Sam—you'd never think it to look at him, but he's a sly old fox. Yesterday I made myself a sandwich, set it on the table, turned my back for no more than three seconds, and when I turned around, he was chomping down the last crust. I could have sworn he was out in the backyard with Greta or I'd never have put it in such easy reach."

"I warned you about that." Asta's voice floated out of the living room, and Del paused halfway to taking a seat.

"Asta's here," Glen said unnecessarily, fiddling with a pair of scissors.

"Hello," Del called out, resigned.

A long pause and then a grudging "hello" in return.

A half hour later, Del finished his first fly and looked over to where Glen was sweating over his own attempt.

"Blamed thing," Glen muttered, trying to get a better grip on his hook. "These pieces of feather keep shifting—how the hell did you get them to stay put?"

"Maybe if you try starting them a bit farther down on the hook?"

"Then I have to undo all this damn thread…" Glen cursed quietly for a few more seconds before laying down the fly and rubbing his eyes. "Maybe I should go to the doctor and have my eyes checked."

"You need glasses?" he asked, concerned.

"I meant it more as an expression, pal. Still," Glen picked up his hook again, freshly determined, "this is only my first attempt. One or two of these and I'll be ticking along, full speed. You go on and make another one too."

Del found it soothing, wrapping the thread around the hook and the feather fibers. He thought about telling Glen about Captain Gardner's demand. But Asta would hear. He was sure Asta would have a few choice words on the subject.

"Better pick up the pace there, Del," Glen was saying. "We need a bunch of these to get us through a weekend."

"We could always buy more, like we usually do."

Glen clucked his tongue. "Del, there'll be no more talk of *buying* flies. That's for amateurs, and we are on our way to becoming experts."

Asta appeared in the doorway and came over, standing behind Glen's shoulder and observing what they were doing.

"Is this sad, twisted little thing yours, Glen?" he asked, picking up the one Glen had managed to complete.

"Yes, it is mine. You might laugh, but I'm proud of that, for a first attempt."

Asta put the fly back on the table. "Maybe the fish will take pity on you."

Del watched out of the corner of his eye as Asta went to the sink and plucked a cup out of the mess of dirty dishes. He sniffed the inside, grimaced, and reluctantly grabbed the dishrag.

"Did Ev get back home all right the other night?" Del ventured to ask.

"What's it to you?" Asta demanded, drying the cup and then lighting the range to heat some coffee left over from the morning.

"Asta," Glen said.

Asta heaved a sigh. "Yes. Tumbled right into bed, he was so exhausted."

"He shouldn't work so hard."

"Oh, *now* you're concerned."

"I was always concerned," Del shot back, not willing to take that blow lying down.

"Funny way of showing it."

He grit his teeth and snapped his thread off too short.

"Look, you two," Glen said. "You need to be able to have a civil conversation."

"Oh, do we?" Asta said, cool.

"Yeah. Seeing as how Del's my friend and all. Go easy on a fellow's nerves."

"I can just walk out of this kitchen—this house—if I don't like the company you keep."

"Do it then."

"Glen," Del said. "Don't—"

"No." Glen held up a hand. "We need to get this straight. I'm not giving up Del as a friend."

"You're not such a good fuck that I have any reason to stay," Asta began, heated, but Glen kept talking, quieter now.

"I'd like you to stay, though, Asta."

Asta fell silent. Del looked at Glen, surprised. He'd expected Glen to say something flippant, to suggest that it wouldn't matter to him whether Asta stayed or left.

Taking a careful breath, Del ventured to say that it would be swell if Ev could get a job with Teddy's friend and get the chance to improve his photography.

"Maybe leave off the subject of Ev," Glen hissed at him.

But Asta didn't flare up. Instead he said quietly, "The photography isn't all of it, though, is it?"

"What do you mean?" Del asked.

Asta gave him a look, somehow both pitying and scornful all at once. "Greeting customers, working with clients and his boss—he'd have to be the respectable young man, wouldn't he? No curls in his hair, no pretty scarves, no dainty hats. Of course we've all done it—played at being masculine—but there's always a chance you slip-up. Sometimes people don't care and other times they do, and then you're back on the street or sporting a split lip for your troubles."

He remembered how Ev had been when they went to visit Teddy. He remembered how upset Ev had been afterward.

"It's all right if you're one of those bohemian sorts," Asta continued. He wasn't looking at Del anymore, his gaze turned inward. "Then you can write your little books or paint and talk about philosophy and people expect you to be funny and queer. Or if you have a voice or can dance—well then you're part of the theater crowd and everyone knows they're outrageous. But if you can't do those things—if you've never had much of an education and are always trying to find a bit of work, well then you'd better watch out. If you decide to hell with it and that you can't bear fighting against your nature, then you'll never amount to much in this world. No chance at a good job or saving to buy a house, no sirree. It's—"

Glen stood up, his chair screeching over the linoleum, and went over to Asta. He bent close and said something in a low voice that Del couldn't hear. But Asta barked a startled laugh and put a hand on Glen's chest, shoving him backward.

"As if I'd ever want *that*," Asta said.

Glen chuckled and crowded Asta against the counter, snatching a kiss.

Feeling embarrassed at witnessing such an intimate moment, Del turned back to the table and gathered together another little bunch of feather fibers. He had never thought about how difficult it might be for Ev to work as a photographer.

Asta laughed again, Glen's voice a quiet undercurrent in the background, and Del pinched the feathers tighter, focusing on winding the thread around the hook.

CAPTAIN GARDNER'S OFFER—demand—hovered uneasily in the background, although he didn't hear anything more about it the rest of the week. That Saturday he faced a different trial, though to his mind they were related, as both involved Carl, who had invited Del to watch the Trojans play the Stanford Cardinals.

Carl's younger brother, Charles, attended the University of Southern California and was one of the team's top batters. Del had accepted the offer, pleased that Carl should want to include him, yet nervous as well. He could only hope most of the conversation would revolve around baseball and not the latest advancements in criminology. Another of the motorcycle officers, Oscar Irgens, was joining them as well. Oscar belonged to the motorcycle drill squad and had merited one of the new motorcycles the department had purchased that year, which came with a mobile jail attached as a sidecar.

Del met them at the field at two in the afternoon, almost missing Carl and Oscar in the crowd as they looked so different out of their uniforms. His heart sank a bit when Carl handed him two journals—another back issue of the *Police Journal* and one called *The American City.*

"I started subscribing to *The American City* in December," Carl said, snatching it back almost immediately to flip to an article. "They have some excellent commentary on law enforcement and traffic problems. This one, see, is all about pavement markings and highway safety. The American Engineering Standards Committee recommends uniform colors for signage, such as a purple background with white letters for any crossroads. Oh, and this article too, about speed limits. It's an interesting debate between those who think motorists simply cannot be trusted to judge safe speeds for themselves and limits should be posted in all cases versus those who think setting any safe limit is impossible and will only encourage contempt for the law, constant violations, and subsequent accidents. What do you think, Del?"

"Uh, well," he stammered, overwhelmed, but Oscar threw an arm around his shoulders.

"Gosh, Carl, leave off for a day," Oscar said, laughing. "We want to watch baseball, not debate traffic laws, right Del?"

"I'll read them later," he promised at Carl's slightly dejected look.

Carl laughed too, his face clearing. "All right. And I'm sorry. I know I get carried away."

"It's awful important, though," Del said. "Traffic laws and signals, I mean. What I think we need is a better paint that doesn't fade so quickly. The city painted all those signals on the roads last year, and already you can't read them in places."

"I read about a paint and varnish works in Rochester that's making a special brand just for that. It should be—"

"Stop, stop," Oscar interjected again, ushering them toward the bleachers. "Del, don't encourage him, for pity's sake."

They got popcorn and found seats behind the first base line, with a view of the Trojans' bench. "That's Charles," Carl said, pointing out a heavy-set kid practicing his swing. "It sure gave him a thrill when I told him some of my buddies were coming to see his game too."

"The Trojans are a pretty swell team," Oscar said. "They got that new coach two years ago, right?"

"Yep. They're on a five-game winning streak right now. But Charles tells me the pitcher for the Cardinals has a doozy of a curveball. You ever play much baseball, Del?"

"Only for fun when I was a kid. Nothing serious."

"I played in high school—fancied myself a bit of a swell batter. Then Charles came along and boy, he knocked me right out of the water." Carl stood and cupped his hands in front of his mouth, yelling toward the bench. "Hey kid! Hit on all sixes today!"

Charles squinted at them, then waved back, smiling when he recognized his brother.

The game started off fast, with the Cardinals getting three runs off the Trojans at the top of the first, and in the bottom, the Cardinals' pitcher only sacrificed one hit.

Del was enjoying the game and the mild weather, but sometimes he couldn't help glancing over at Carl, thinking of how appalled and disappointed he would be when he found out Del was going to become part of the Gray Wolf's gang. Carl would never invite him to another baseball game or share his favorite articles on traffic laws again.

If he said no, instead...

He forced his attention back to the game, regretting all that popcorn he'd eaten as his stomach cramped with nerves.

Charles had a few hits but didn't score until the eighth when he slid into home, bringing the score to 7-6 with the Trojans in the lead. Carl yelled his head off, and Del found himself joining in, cheering and raising his hat. The Trojans held the Cardinals off in the ninth and earned another win.

Carl was jubilant, crowing about his brother's runs, and they stopped at a café by the campus, toasting the win with bottles of ginger ale, and eating hamburgers for supper.

"See you tomorrow, pal," Carl said when they parted, and Oscar raised a hand in farewell.

Del returned to his quiet apartment, and the silence engulfed him. The radio didn't hold any appeal—he wanted to be with people, friends. So he went and changed into his evening suit, combed and slicked his hair, and took the streetcar downtown.

It wasn't so much that he was looking for a date, only that a night surrounded by people and music and noise seemed better than the alternative. Better than remembering Ev.

There was the usual business of figuring out which cabarets had paid their protection money that week and weren't getting hassled by the Prohis. He finally settled on the Caterpillar, which had an energetic, if not necessarily in tune, jazz band and a big crowd. Two dolled-up girls appeared willing to let Del buy them cheap giggle water and in return sat with him and chattered about the latest Hollywood gossip and whether they could afford to buy stocks because everyone *was* and it was absolutely *the* way to make it rich these days.

Del shared his cigarettes around the table, sipped his drink, and listened to the band career its way through "Brown Eyes, Why Are You Blue?"

"You in a funk, honey?" the girl on his left—Adeline—asked.

"Oh." Del looked into the dregs of his glass. "I was missing someone, that's all."

Lulu, on his right, cooed sympathetically. "How long?"

"A few months, but I can't seem to forget about it."

More sympathy, agreement on how it was the sweetest thing that he should be pining for a lost love.

"You want to forget about it for the night, sweetie?" Lulu asked, fingers warm on his hand. "You get two for the price of one with us."

"Don't be so vulgar, Lulu," Adeline protested. "We should have a late supper first, maybe find a place with some decent wine, and get to know each other a little better."

He knew they were only angling for him to treat them to more food and booze before agreeing to sex. But maybe it would help, let him move past the feeling of Ev's lips on his, of silk clinging to Ev's hips and shifting under his hands.

"We can get some supper," he said, even though his wallet really wasn't in good enough shape to offer it. "You got some place to go afterward?"

"We've a lovely little place," Adeline assured him. "We don't usually take gentlemen home on first acquaintance, but for you, I guess we can make an exception."

So they went and had supper, and the wine couldn't be called decent, but no one complained. Adeline and Lulu had a flat above a laundry, and they took Del there afterward, coaxing some more cigarettes out of him on the way.

Del had never had two girls at once, and he wasn't expecting Lulu to kiss Adeline for a minute first before turning to him. Lulu explained that Adeline didn't like getting fucked, but *she* did. Then Adeline worked his trousers open and started stroking him, giggling breathily, while Lulu laid on the bed and fingered herself.

Lulu wanted him from behind, and Adeline crawled in on the other side, and they kissed and groped each other while Del thrust. He didn't last long, pulling out and coming into his hand with a groan. He listened to Lulu and Adeline work themselves to an orgasm.

"We met a fellow the other day who wants to film us together for a naughty picture," Lulu told him as they lay there. She was stroking her fingers across his chest. Adeline had fallen asleep, curled into a ball. Lulu laughed. "Isn't that a scream?"

Del didn't know why it would be funny. He stared at the cheap prints on the walls, the wallpaper pattern faded and unrecognizable. There was a lingering smell of boiled cabbage in the air.

"I'd better get on home," he said after a bit.

Lulu pouted but didn't try to dissuade him. "Did it help, hon? You feel better?"

"Yes," he lied.

Sitting in the streetcar on the way home, he imagined Ev's hand in his, their fingers wrapped together, the weight of Ev's head resting on his shoulder and felt sick.

Chapter Nineteen

EVERY TIME HE went to the station, Del expected Captain Gardner to summon him to his office and demand to know his decision. But the days passed and nothing happened.

He was going to say yes, of course. He didn't have a choice, not really.

"Hey, Randolph," Kirkpatrick said, passing him in the hallway.

Del braced himself.

"A couple of us have a betting pool going on Dempsey's next fight. You want in?"

"Uh, sure," he said, blinking.

"Swell. By the way, kid," Kirkpatrick added, taking a step closer and lowering his voice, "once everything's been straightened out, I can cut you in on a side deal Brooks and I have going with a lottery. Nothin' big or the bosses wouldn't like it, but it's somethin' at any rate. Word is there's been some heat on at headquarters, and we're all playing it low for a bit. That's why the captain hasn't talked to you again."

"Right," Del managed. Kirkpatrick hadn't called him "Mr. Minus" once.

He supposed there wasn't really any point to practicing his typing anymore. If he said yes to the captain's offer, then it wouldn't matter if he could type well or not. And yet he continued sitting at his kitchen table most afternoons, pecking stubbornly at the keys. When he practiced his typing, he couldn't have the radio on, as it distracted him too much. There was only the occasional alligator bark or passing car to break the silence on long afternoons before his shift started.

He was sure that he was improving, though. Not rapidly, not as fast as he wished, but he didn't make as many mistakes anymore.

He hadn't gone out for an evening since the night with Lulu and Adeline, unsure if it had made things better or worse. But when Glen called, inviting him to attend a pansy ball that fell on a night Del wasn't working, he accepted immediately. If Glen was there, he'd have a friend and wouldn't feel compelled to search for a partner for the evening.

"The thing is," Glen began, and then paused.

"Yes?"

"The ball is at the Admiral's Blues. Ev will probably be there."

"Oh."

"But there'll be lots of people. It's not as though you'll have to talk to each other."

"Right." Del took a deep breath. "That's okay. I can handle it. But what about Asta?"

"He didn't outright protest."

"Guess that's the best I can hope for, huh?"

"Sorry, pal." Glen hesitated again. "I wouldn't...if it had been anyone else, I..." He sighed, and Del could picture him scrubbing a hand through his hair.

"I get it. Asta's important to you, right? And I deserved some of what he's accused me of anyway. I don't mind the two of you being together."

Glen made a few more embarrassed mutterings and then hung up after telling Del to be ready at eight on Saturday.

IT DIDN'T OCCUR to him until he was making his way through the press of people in the Admiral's Blues on Saturday that Asta wasn't the only one he should be worried about. All of Ev's other friends—Nellie, Phillip, Camilo—might be here as well. He couldn't imagine they'd be too pleased to see him.

"Is Ev going to be in the ball?" he asked Asta, who was on Glen's other side, arm looped through Glen's elbow. Asta was not taking part, claiming that neither his figure nor complexion had recovered sufficiently from his time in prison. His makeup and hair were done very carefully, however, and Glen had given him a corsage to wear.

"No—Ev can be so shy sometimes. He'd die of embarrassment up there on the stage." Asta fanned his hand in front of his face. "Lord, it's sweltering in here already. I did see Nellie's dress—she went completely wild with feathers this year."

It was awful crowded—Del took an accidental elbow in the ribs and a lady's heel stabbed down on his toe as they made their way to a table. The Admiral's Blues generally tried to avoid drawing notice but made an exception for pansy balls.

"I see the normal ones are all here today," Asta commented. "Here to gawk at the spectacle. No surprise, considering it was advertised in all the papers."

"Enjoy it. No worries about the morals squad arresting anyone for gender-fraud," Glen said as they sat down. "And hey, Del, maybe you'll find someone who catches your eye."

"Maybe," Del said. But as he scanned the crowd, he admitted to himself that he was really looking for Ev.

He finally spotted Ev in a far corner, sitting with Camilo and a man who was probably Camilo's José. Ev had curled his hair in tight waves and wore an evening suit that emphasized his slim build. A lavender scarf floated around his neck.

"I see who you're staring at," Asta said in a dry voice, and Del flinched, hastily looking away, but not before Glen had seen Ev too.

"Ah, hell, Del."

"I'm all right." He pointed at the stage. "Look—here's the first contestants."

He tried to keep his attention on the dazzling parade of silk, beads, feathers, and lace on the stage, but they blurred in front of his eyes.

"Oh for heaven's sake," Asta muttered. "That fool boy keeps staring over here too."

Del couldn't help looking. He met Ev's eyes over the crowd. Ev blinked, startled, and then broke their gaze, cheeks flushing.

"Absolutely impossible," Asta said and got up, dragging his chair so that he could block their view of each other. "I'm not going to sit here and watch the two of you do...do whatever it is you're doing all night."

Del sighed, slumping a little. It was probably for the best.

They all cheered loudly for Nellie when she appeared, and Nellie blew everyone kisses.

Del was of half a mind to leave when the competition segment of the evening ended, not sure if he could handle seeing Ev dancing with someone else, despite what he had said. But as the crowd swirled around their table, Ev suddenly appeared, pushing past a man and catching himself on Asta's shoulder.

"Ev," Asta said, surprised, casting an uneasy glancc at Del. "I thought you were staying with Camilo and José tonight."

Ev was looking directly at him. Del swallowed and sat up straight.

"This is getting silly," Ev said. "Avoiding each other at all costs. We're adults, aren't we? We can manage being around each other without causing a scene."

"Yes." Del cleared his throat. "Yes, of course."

"Good." Ev turned his attention to Asta. "What did you think of the dresses? That yellow one with the beaded fringe was a peach, wasn't it?"

Asta still seemed a bit taken aback by Ev's presence, but soon they were chatting about the ball and the outfits. Del couldn't stop staring at Ev, who was now ignoring him. Ev smiled once, and a pain, sweet and sharp, lanced his heart. Then the scarf around Ev's neck slipped down a little as he moved his arm, and Del caught a glimpse of the green necklace he had given to him, fastened at Ev's throat.

Ev adjusted the scarf immediately, eyes flickering to Del and then skittering away.

"I was going to ask you this the next time you dropped by the house, Ev," Glen said when Asta and Ev had both paused to take a breath, "but since you're here—you remember that fellow who's opening a portrait studio? Well, Teddy mentioned you to him—his name is Leon Kee—and he's interested in interviewing you for the position of his assistant."

Ev gaped at Glen a moment before finding his voice. "He wants to speak to me?"

"Yep. What do you say? Interested?"

"That's so wonderful, honey," Asta said, squeezing Ev's hand.

"Yes," Ev said slowly. "I...I suppose it is."

Del remembered what Asta had said to him—about the strain Ev would face, having to watch his actions and words all the time. And yet it was a tremendous opportunity. A chance for Ev to become a real photographer and to get a job that paid well and offered the promise of advancement.

"You should give it a try," he said quietly.

Ev's fingers were twisted in his scarf. "You think so?"

"Yes."

"I'll give Asta the address for Kee's shop, and you can ring him up," Glen said.

A pause, and then Ev nodded. "All right. Thank you. I appreciate it."

Glen waved away his thanks. "Now, if you'll excuse us, I need to persuade Asta onto the dance floor."

"I've told you I have two left feet," Asta said, remaining seated even though Glen stood and offered his hand. "And you're no better. The last time you stomped on my toes three times. Like hell I'm dancing with you."

"Ah, come on, love. You look so beautiful tonight—can't let it go to waste."

Asta actually blushed, shot Ev a quelling look, and grabbed Glen's hand, yanking him onto the dancefloor and positioning Glen's hands to his satisfaction.

And then it was just him and Ev.

"I...I should go say hello to Nellie," Ev stammered, and fled.

Later that night when they were driving home, Del couldn't help but ask Glen a question plaguing him. "Does Ev come over to your place a lot?"

"A few times a week, I guess, since Asta's living with me now. I didn't want to say anything because, well..."

"We make voodoo dolls of you, Del, and stick them with pins," Asta said.

"You do?" he said, distressed.

"Of course not! It was a joke. As though Ev would ever—*I* might, but never Ev."

"I guess forewarned is forearmed," Glen said, chuckling. "Better get myself some sort of magic charm."

Asta didn't reply, his jaw tensing.

"Not that I'm saying you'd leave," Glen said hastily. "Or that I'd leave. That is, nothing's certain, is it?"

Asta made no reply, and the rest of the ride passed in an uncomfortable silence. Del was relieved when they dropped him off at his apartment.

He went inside and sat on his bed to remove shoes. Loosening his tie, he pulled it off, and ran it between his fingers, wondering what it meant that Ev was still wearing the necklace Del had given him.

THE BLINKING YELLOW light pulsed across the ground and then the steady red took its place before switching to green. All the lights glowed under their round cover, like jewels excavated from the ground. The city had installed traffic lights downtown the year before, but this was the first one for the East Side. Instead of the ones that hung over the intersection, this was one of the mushroom traffic lights, embedded in the pavement in the middle of the street crossing, its sturdy cover able to stand the weight in case an automobile accidentally drove over it.

Del idled his motorcycle, watching the changing lights as they cycled through the pattern, over and over. He still remembered when his family moved to Los Angeles from Kansas and for the first time had an electric light in the house. And now they had lights in the middle of the street, running on a timed pattern.

His thoughts seemed to be cycling on an endless loop too, from Captain Gardner's offer, to Ev, to several bills coming due next week that he would only be able to pay if he was late on the rent. He'd had a letter from his father too, mentioning he'd had to go to the doctor several times recently. His father didn't ask for money outright, but Del knew it would help if he could send him some. He lingered on that thought awhile, then returned to Gardner's demand.

If Ev knew about what the captain had told him, Ev would want him to refuse. But it wasn't Ev's job on the line.

The yellow light pulsed again, and he squeezed his eyes shut for a moment, acknowledging that guilt and hurt weren't the only emotions lodged in his heart from when Ev had discovered his extralegal activities and left him. There was resentment too. He resented that Ev hadn't tried to understand why he had done it. Ev should have understood how hard it was for someone like Del to get ahead in the world. If he refused Captain Gardner and didn't join the Gray Wolf's gang, then he would end up right back where he had started with even fewer prospects of ever advancing.

The light was green when he opened his eyes again. He revved his motorcycle and moved on down the street, no less conflicted than before.

He was changing out of his uniform at the station, stifling yawns and looking forward to getting some sleep, when Carl came into the locker room.

"Hey, buddy, you have a minute?" Carl asked.

"Sure—hey, how did your brother's team do last weekend?"

"They lost. The pitchers gave away too many runs."

"Too bad. I thought their starter's fastball was the Darb."

Carl waved a hand. "Charles said he was having a bad day. But say, Del, let's not get distracted with baseball. I have an important matter to discuss with you."

Carl straightened his shoulders, and Del did the same, somewhat alarmed at the intensity in Carl's expression.

"You know the city council will be developing the new city budget in April," Carl began. Del had not known, in fact, but Carl breezed along, taking Del's knowledge for granted. "Many of us in the department feel it is essential that the council agree to raise the salary for all policemen. What they pay us now can hardly be called a living wage, and it is impossible to attract good men—the best men—to enter the department when the pay is so low. So we're planning to circulate a petition to put the question on the ballot for a special election at the end of April. The firemen are going to join with us. If we collect enough signatures and build enough public support, the council will have no choice but to acquiesce to the election."

"How much are we talking about?"

"Thirty dollars more a month for the lower grades and twenty-five a month for the higher ones."

"That much? I'd be able to pay off some loans then, and send some more money to my dad." The anxious tightness in his chest eased a little just at the thought.

Carl opened the case he was carrying and took out a sheaf of papers. "This explains our petition, and then all these pages are for signatures."

"You want me to try and collect some?"

"That's right, Del. I'm counting on your help. If you would canvass your neighborhood, and of course ask all your friends to sign—the more we get the better."

"I suppose I could try." He took the pages, frowning at the text.

"Hey!"

They both startled as Kirkpatrick came into the room, and Del reflexively clutched the papers against his chest.

"That the petition I heard some of the boys talkin' about?" Kirkpatrick asked, and when Carl nodded, he held out his hand. "Give me one. I'll get some signatures. About time those cheap bastards on the council gave us a raise."

"Ah, yes, thank you," Carl said, sounding surprised but pleased and giving Kirkpatrick one of the petitions. Apparently even Kirkpatrick and Carl could come together on some matters.

Del smoothed out the papers he had crumpled, wishing this had happened a year ago. What a better way to get more money than joining a bunch of fool leggers, like he had. He glanced at Carl, wondering how he knew that things like this were possible. Perhaps it just came to one when you were intelligent and had a good education.

HE EASILY COLLECTED Mrs. Johnson's signature and those of Mr. and Mrs. Mantifel at the market. Before taking the more drastic step of knocking on doors and attempting to explain the petition to strangers, Del went to Glen's to get his signature, and Asta's if he was in a sympathetic mood. He couldn't deny that after hearing how Ev was often at Glen's place visiting Asta, he was also hoping they might run into each other. It hurt to see Ev, but at the same time it was better than when Ev had simply vanished from his life.

Luck was with him because as he came up the walk, Ev and Asta stepped out the door. All three of them stopped.

"Is Glen in?" he asked.

"No," Asta said, taking Ev's arm and beginning to walk around him. Ev was looking at him, but Del couldn't read his expression. He noticed that Ev was in the same suit he'd worn when they went to visit Teddy, with the heavy brown shoes, and that his hair was all slicked down.

"Wait," Del blurted, fumbling for his petition.

Asta huffed and tried to keep walking, but Ev halted.

"The policemen are trying to get a salary raise," Del explained, smoothing out the paper with trembling hands. "We're circulating a petition to get signatures."

"I suppose you deserve it—keeping the city safe and all," Asta said. "You sure did a fine job of arresting me last year. So efficient. You had me before the judge in no time at all."

"Asta," Ev murmured, putting a hand on Asta's arm. "Don't."

"Sorry," Asta said, sounding a bit chagrined. "I'll sign it anyway."

Ev nodded. "Me too."

"I, um, don't have a pen," he realized. "Could we, er, go inside?"

Asta made an exasperated noise, but motioned for Del to follow as they trooped back in the house.

Greta and Sam looked surprised at their sudden reappearance, but Greta treated them all to some barking and tail waving, while Sam looked on from his sprawl in a patch of sun. Asta found a pen, signed, and handed it to Ev, who put his own name on the paper.

Then Ev paused, head down. "Would you give us a few minutes, Asta?"

"Ev…"

"Please?"

Asta sighed and gave Del a hard glare. "I'll meet you at the car, then."

Seconds later, the door shut behind Asta, leaving him and Ev truly alone for the first time since that awful morning in the car so many months before.

Ev didn't say anything at first, and it was silent except for Sam panting. Del fidgeted, his heart beating fast.

"Where are you going, dressed like that?" he asked Ev, unable to stand the quiet any longer.

"To meet Mr. Kee at his photographic studio and see if he'll offer me the job."

"Yeah?" He smiled. "I'm glad you decided to try for it."

Ev jerked his head in a sort of nod, pawing at his tie and then picking up the pen instead, twirling it in his fingers. "Asta's driving me there and providing moral support."

"I wish—" He bit down on the words before he could say "I wish I could go with you too."

Ev faced him, his eyes nervous and hesitant. "Look, I haven't got much time now. But if you're free tomorrow or the next day, perhaps we could meet somewhere to talk."

His heart leapt back into his throat. "All right. I'd like that, Ev."

Ev took a deep breath, then released it and gave Del a tiny but so very welcome smile. "We could meet at that café down the block from my apartment."

"I can't do tomorrow. But Thursday, say at four?"

"Yes. I could do that."

"You should go then, before you're late. Good luck. You go on—I'll lock up here."

He watched from the front window as Ev walked to the car, holding a black bowler hat that he finally jammed onto his head. He pulled his shoulders straight, but Del saw his hands curl into fists before Ev stuffed them into his pockets.

THE DAY BEFORE, Lieutenant Miller had informed Del that his shift on Wednesday was being switched from night to the afternoon. This happened occasionally, so Del didn't think anything of it. Besides, now his thoughts were consumed by his meeting with Ev, wondering what Ev would say, and trying to suppress any hopeful, excited suppositions that perhaps Ev was going to give him a second chance.

Carl cornered him in the garage when he arrived for his patrol on Wednesday, eager to know how many signatures Del had collected.

"Only five," he admitted, hastening to add that he hadn't had a chance to visit any of his neighbors yet.

"You mustn't worry about knocking on people's doors," Carl said. "Everyone I've tackled so far has been swell about it." He clapped Del on the shoulder. "I've faith in you, Del."

"I'll get them," he promised, holding back a sigh.

"Oh, by the way, Captain Gardner asked that you see him in his office."

Del dropped his gloves. "Now?"

"Yes, I believe so. You all right?" Carl added.

He controlled his expression with difficulty. "Yeah. Just a little warm in here."

Pausing in the john a moment on his way to the captain's office, he splashed some water on his face. There was no call to be anxious. He'd say yes—he'd decided to say yes. There was no choice really.

The captain waved him inside when he knocked and greeted him with a genial smile. "Close the door, Randolph, and have a seat. You remember our conversation from a few weeks ago?"

"Yes, sir."

"Well, you've had time to think about it, and I'm sure you've made a wise choice."

Del tried to work some moisture into his dry mouth. For some reason he was thinking of Ev yesterday, how he had fiddled with his drab tie and resolutely stuck the bowler hat on his head.

Gardner waited a moment. "Let me remind you this is an important decision for your career."

He nodded, unable to meet the captain's eyes, fingering the soft leather of his gloves instead. Beat cops didn't get to wear such fine gloves or the special jackets the motor patrol received.

"So what do you say?"

He opened his mouth and found himself blurting out, "I can't, sir."

There was a short silence.

Gardner frowned. "Don't be foolish now, Randolph. I know you have no qualms about exercising discretion when it comes to the best way to uphold the laws."

He cringed in his chair. "I'm sorry, sir."

"If this is your decision, then I'm not sure I'll be able to recommend that you keep your current position."

"I've been typing, sir," he managed to get out.

"Typing?"

"Yes, sir. To practice so I get better at my reports."

Gardner raised his eyebrows. "You realize that this year we're opening a Police Training School. Numerous qualified candidates will be joining the department, not to mention ones already here. Officer Hutton, for example, is being wasted as a beat cop. I've received many recommendations for his promotion."

His efforts—all the hours typing—were crushed with a few words. He clung to his resolve, thinking of Ev wearing the heavy brown shoes he hated.

"This is your last chance to reconsider, Randolph."

His every nerve wanted to capitulate, to say yes so he could escape this confrontation, so he could keep the job he loved, so he could avoid the disgrace and disappointment that would follow if he refused.

"I can't accept, sir."

Gardner tapped his pen on the table, annoyed, and then dismissed him with a shrug at what he considered Del's folly.

In the hallway, Del stood in the middle of the floor until two passing officers chivvied him aside, and he shuffled into a corner, wondering why he had done that and amazed too that he had stood firm, refusing to capitulate to the captain's threats.

Well it was done now. Perhaps he should feel proud, but he didn't, only shaken and confused.

Somehow he managed to collect himself, get his motorcycle, and go on patrol. He knew it might be the last time that he did, and the day passed in a haze, filled with half-formed regrets and sharpening worries.

NO ONE CAME to tell him he had been fired when he returned to the station. But he spent a long time polishing the fenders and headlight on his motorcycle, brushing the leather seat and cleaning the dirt off the metal plate affixed to the front fender which read "Los Angeles Police Department."

He remembered how on his first night on the motor patrol he hadn't been able to eat supper because he was so excited. He had spent two minutes in front of the mirror simply adjusting his cap and the cuffs and lapels on his freshly pressed coat. He'd issued three traffic tags that night and almost ran over a cat that darted out of an alley. On his way home in the morning, he'd stopped at the diner that served the best coconut cream pie in the city and ate a piece for breakfast.

Numbness had settled over him by the time he got home, and he slept surprisingly well. When he woke in the morning, he remembered that he would be meeting Ev that afternoon, and emotion jolted through him. His eyes grew damp, and he had to find a handkerchief to blow his nose.

After breakfast, he gathered the petition and went to knock on his neighbors' doors. Even if he was demoted or fired, that didn't mean he'd leave the others hanging. He'd promised Carl he'd collect more signatures, and he wanted to come through on it.

It went better than he expected, although he thought most of the housewives took pity on his blushing, fumbling attempts to explain rather than a deep commitment to the issue when they signed.

He spent a careful hour shaving and dressing that afternoon and arrived at the café thirty minutes early. The waitress brought him coffee, and he asked her to sign the petition—he'd remembered to bring a pen this time.

"Sure, hon. You're a cop, huh?"

"Yes," Del said, wondering for how long he'd be able to say that was true.

With the petition out of the way, he was left to sit there, clasping and unclasping his fingers around his cup, continually looking out the window to watch for Ev.

Ev arrived a few minutes late, hurrying through the door, and glanced around the room, looking for him. He raised his hand in a greeting when he spotted Del, and Del half-rose in his seat, crouching anxiously, his instinctual reaction to go and touch Ev. He suppressed it, sinking back down when Ev sat across from him. Ev wasn't wearing the heavy brown shoes or broad-shouldered coat, but his more usual attire of a trim, light-gray jacket and vest, a green handkerchief tucked in the pocket, and a cap at a slight angle on his head.

"Hello, Del," Ev said, shy.

"Hey, Ev," he replied. How different this meeting was from their first. Ev had been the complete opposite of shy then, brusque and on the edge of bitter. He was so grateful that Ev wasn't holding up those shields around him now. Ev was still willing to show him his gentle, vulnerable nature.

"How did it go the other day at the photography studio?" he asked after the waitress had brought Ev some coffee too.

Ev smiled, his eyes bright. "Mr. Kee hired me. I'm starting next week."

"Congratulations—that's swell." He smiled back. "You excited?"

"Yes. And nervous. A little worried too." Ev's smile faded.

"You'll be fine."

"I hope so. There are so many things that could go wrong."

"Nah. You deserve a break, and I think this is it. You're gonna become a swell photographer."

"Thanks," Ev said softly, stirring some sugar into his coffee.

Del watched him, studying his features, the memory of how Ev had felt in his arms pressing against his heart.

"God, Ev. I've missed you," he said thickly.

"I know." Ev pressed a hand to his eyes, hiding the shine of his own tears.

"Why did you want to talk to me?" he asked, desperate to have this question answered.

Ev took a deep breath, then put his hand down, meeting Del's eyes. "The thing of it is that I'm not angry at you anymore, Del. Once I had time to think about it—I understand why you hid the truth. Why you thought you had to join those leggers."

"It was a mistake. But I only wanted...I only wanted you, and I didn't know how else to get you."

"But you know that it wasn't the treating or the presents that made me love you, don't you? It was because you were sweet and kind and thought I was a beautiful person. That's why. I'd never had that before, Del."

"You could have it again, Ev." His voice shook, and he tried to keep it steady. "If you say the word—I still love you. I'd give anything if—"

"Del," Ev broke in gently, and he stopped, his rising hope sinking back to earth.

"Part of me wants that," Ev continued. "But I don't know if we should be together again. I was with a lot of men who hurt me, Del. You remember how I told you about them. I stayed with those fellows longer than I should have. I know you don't mean to hurt me again, and I want to trust you, but I'm afraid that's the kind of thinking that always got me into trouble."

Ev sighed, his voice smaller and softer as he went on, "But I miss you too. I suppose it isn't fair of me to ask this, but could we be friends at least? I'd...I'd like to talk to you from time to time. To see you."

It was both a gift and a disappointment. But he couldn't say no. "Of course. I'd like that too."

"I'm so glad," Ev said, real relief in his voice, and he reached across and touched Del's hand.

For a minute they sat there, now unsure what to say. "How are you?" Ev finally asked. "Glen said you'd been working hard to try and get on the motorcycle drill squad."

This proof that Ev had been asking about him, thinking of him when they were apart, would have been so welcome if not for the events of the previous day. Here was Ev, getting a new job, pursuing his own dream, and Del was facing being demoted to a traffic cop at best and losing his job at the worst. And he knew—*knew* Ev wouldn't hold it against him, that Ev would be sympathetic and understanding, but there was still a part of him that could only feel ashamed, that wanted to hide what had happened from everyone.

So he said, "Yes, I've been working hard," and then drank some of his coffee to avoid looking at Ev.

"And the petition?" Ev asked, a touch hesitant now. "Are you getting signatures?"

This was easier to discuss. He could tell Ev about the adventures of the morning—getting yapped at by small dogs, accidentally knocking over a pot of petunias on a porch, and how nice it had been to meet so many people who agreed that their policemen should get paid more for their service. "One woman asked me how the city would pay for it, though, and I didn't know."

"I suppose there'd have to be a tax or something."

"People wouldn't like that. If we do get it on the ballot, maybe it won't pass."

"Getting the petitions signed is the first step, at any rate." Ev sipped his coffee, then tipped the cup from side to side, swirling the liquid inside. "Asta seems awfully happy with Glen."

"Yeah. I didn't expect that—the two of them getting together. It hurt me a lot at first," he confessed. "Because Asta is your friend, and it seemed like Glen had what I'd lost."

"I was a little upset too," Ev admitted. "Actually, Asta and I had a fight about it. But I came to my senses the next day and apologized."

"Glen and I went fishing."

Ev smiled. "Is that how you resolve your differences?"

"I guess so."

"Asta and I do each other's hair and go see a picture." Ev rubbed his thumb along the edge of the table. "Do you think Glen is...I mean, I don't want to see Asta hurt."

"Glen can be awful casual about love—never seems to get too attached. But," Del paused, considering. "He seems to be pretty interested in Asta. Maybe he won't bail the first time things get rough."

"I hope so. It's a relief to know Asta is with a decent fellow and living somewhere nice, for once. I know Asta hasn't been very friendly to you, Del, but don't hold it against him, please. It's only because he cares about me."

"I know. Anyway, I think Asta's warming up to me a little. He signed my petition, at least."

"Yes." Ev smiled again, looking at him. "This has been real lovely, Del—talking like this, I mean. We didn't do enough of it, before."

It was true, and he almost reconsidered and told Ev what was happening at the department and how he'd refused Gardner's offer. But no—he'd rather sit here and enjoy Ev's smiles and not think on the whole mess for a while.

"There was something else I wanted to ask," Ev said slowly, and Del nodded for him to continue. "At that party a few weeks ago, when I ran into you—who was that fairy you were with?"

It took him a moment to remember. "Oh, just someone I met that night. I think his name was Victor. Glen and Asta introduced us, but all we did was talk for a bit. He was feeling kind of down at the mouth too. I haven't seen him since. I...well, I could never manage to forget you, Ev, and I didn't want anyone else."

"That was how it was for me too. I tried, a few times, but..." Ev laughed a little. "I know I had no right to feel jealous, but when I saw the two of you that night, I couldn't help it."

"I'd have been the same, seeing you with someone." He had spent more than a few early mornings lying awake, even after a long night shift, tormented by the idea of some other man getting to put his arms around Ev, to kiss him, to see him in his lacy underthings. It had been awful to contemplate.

"Maybe we can meet again soon, then," Ev said when they parted outside the door of the café.

"Sure thing," he agreed, even though he wondered if he'd be able to withstand the longing for Ev's touch, for a kiss. Receiving Ev's forgiveness—he knew he was greedy to want more than that, but he couldn't help it. If he could still support Ev as his friend, he would do it, but it hurt, to still have a separation between them that he couldn't cross.

THAT EVENING, WHEN he arrived at the station, Lieutenant Miller called Del into his office and told him that based on his performance, he was being removed from the motor patrol and reassigned to traffic duty at the Central station, where he would be given the task of standing at busy intersections to conduct the flow of pedestrians, automobiles, streetcars, and the odd horse.

Del had expected it, but still, it was hard.

Leaving the station, he started walking in the direction of the streetcar stop that would take him to Ev's apartment before recollecting himself and turning toward his own instead.

Chapter Twenty

"IT'S ROTTEN STUFF," Glen said, sucking moodily on the stem of his pipe. As soon as Del had told him the news, he'd brought Greta to Del's apartment for some "therapeutic tail wagging," leaving Sam behind with Asta.

"At least I wasn't fired," Del replied around an armful of dog. He'd sat down on the floor to better contain Greta's exuberant greeting.

"No, only demoted for doing the right thing and refusing that crook of a captain. Hell, it makes me boil! And why in tarnation didn't you tell me about it, huh?"

"Sorry," he said, voice muffled in Greta's fur. "Guess I didn't want to even think about it. Besides, there wasn't anything you could have done."

Glen grunted, displeased.

A wet tongue tickled his ear, as Greta began giving him an enthusiastic bath. "That's enough, Greta," he told her, finding he could still manage a laugh. He looked up at Glen. "What's with the pipe?"

"I think the pipe lends me a certain sportsmanlike air, don't you?" Glen removed the article in question from his mouth and held it up to catch the light.

"It does?"

"Of course. Think of all those paintings of hunters gathered by a cozy fire in their deerstalker caps, hounds lying on the rug, a mounted deer head on the wall, and pipes in their mouths."

Del thought but couldn't remember ever seeing such a thing. "I suppose."

"Asta doesn't mind the smell of the tobacco, either."

"Asta." Del tugged gently on one of Greta's silky ears. "So Asta's still living with you, huh?"

Glen cleared his throat. "Well, he was having a hard time finding an apartment, what with Sam and all. And Ev's place is really too small. So he's staying with me for the time being. I've given out to the neighbors that I'm renting the room."

"First time that's happened—you wanting to live with someone."

"Like I said, it's temporary."

"Is that what you want? For Asta to leave?"

"No—I don't want Asta to leave. But he will eventually."

"What if he doesn't?"

Glen huffed, annoyed. "Then—then I suppose he'll be there with me, won't he? That's obvious."

"Would it make you happy?"

"I don't know." Glen frowned. "We're happy now, and that's enough. There's no point in looking ahead to some hypothetical tomorrow."

There Glen went again, never willing to take his loves seriously. "I saw Ev yesterday. We talked and kind of patched things up."

Glen brightened. "That's swell—he forgave you?"

"Yeah. But he doesn't trust me. Not completely."

"I see. Well, give it some time, pal."

Time—the next time he saw Ev, he'd have to tell him about his demotion. It would be so humiliating. Sighing, he buried his face back in Greta's fur.

THE FOLLOWING DAY, he had to return to the station to sign some papers. He passed Kirkpatrick and Brooks in the hallway. They didn't say anything, but Kirkpatrick shoved his shoulder into Del, knocking him against the wall.

But Carl did speak to him.

"This is a hell of a thing, Del." The distress was plain in his voice. "You get transferred, and I get promoted to take your place on the motor patrol."

So Carl had gotten the job. It had been a forgone conclusion, really, but he still experienced a spike of jealousy.

"This doesn't sit right with me," Carl continued. "You're a good officer, so there's no reason for a demotion except politics. Is that what's going on here?"

"I wasn't so good as all that," Del said because he knew breathing a word about Gardner's offer to someone like Carl would be a sure ticket off the force and out of a job. Carl would raise a fuss—might even go to the papers.

"That's nonsense, Del. You're a committed officer, with excellent ideas on improving traffic control. I can't see why they'd get rid of you like this."

"You deserve the promotion," he said, touched by Carl's outrage on his behalf. "You should have gotten the place anyway, all those months ago."

Carl gnawed on his lip, still troubled. Then he leaned closer, lowering his voice. "There are rumors that the police commissioners are going to ask for Heath's resignation."

"Heath? But he's Parrot and Crawford's man. You're not pulling my leg?"

"Nope. I was surprised too, but it's what I hear. Word is that Jim Davis will take his place. That'd be swell, wouldn't it?"

Del knew Davis by reputation only. He had made a name for himself when he seized a gun from a crazy Mexican after running out of ammunition himself. It was said that Davis always got his man. Now he was with the vice squad and was known for his professionalism and strict adherence to the law.

"There'll be no more coddling of bootleggers and gamblers if Davis is in charge," Carl concluded. "And it means that maybe you can get your place back. He'll be sure to look favorably on anyone so dedicated to the law as you."

For a moment, hope flared—maybe he really would have a chance to return to the motor patrol. But then it dwindled as he remembered that Davis was also likely to favor men with intelligence and education who represented the best in the department. The plum positions would go to officers who graduated from the Police Training School.

Biting back a sigh, he held out his hand.

Carl shook it reluctantly. "Del..."

"It's all right, Carl."

"I hope you'll come to some more of Charlie's games. Maybe play a pick-up game or two ourselves sometime."

"I'd like that." It helped that Carl wanted to remain friends, and he felt guilty over being jealous. Carl really was a stand-up fellow.

"And don't think I'm letting you get out of obtaining those signatures," Carl added, half-joking. "I'll come 'round to Central to collect them and keep you apprised of the situation. The council has been threatening to reinstate the occupational license tax if the measure passes, but that's baloney—there's plenty of other ways to get the money. God knows how much of the city's budget is going to line Parrot's pockets, for starters."

The next morning, Del reported to the Central station and his new lieutenant, who dealt with him in a brisk and officious manner. The other patrolmen he met as he changed into his uniform nodded politely at his greeting but didn't make any move to include him in their conversations.

Word had clearly got 'round of both the official and the unofficial reasons for his transfer. He spared a wistful glance at the motorcycles parked in the garage before trudging to his post on foot. Two hours into his shift, and his feet and back hurt from standing on the pavement, and his throat was dry from blowing his whistle and shouting. Bracing himself to endure until noon when he could have a break for a bite of lunch and some coffee, he gestured for a cluster of pedestrians to venture into the street and flung up his hand to stop a delivery truck from making a reckless dash across the intersection.

By the following week, he had already come to loathe the sight of one particular streetcar conductor who seemed to delight in speeding up as he went past Del, practically blowing him off his feet. He also became acquainted with a newsboy who frequented one of the street corners where he directed traffic. The kid's name was Jurgis, and Del sometimes bought him bubble gum in exchange for keeping an eye on the man selling tamales from a cart down the street, who Jurgis was convinced was really a gangster hiding bootleg gin under the cornhusks. At the station, he kept his head down, listened to the familiar chastisements of his new lieutenant about his terrible handwriting and made a few attempts at getting friendly with the other men, who at least responded politely.

Glen had relayed a message from Ev that Del should send him a note or come 'round so they could grab lunch together or maybe catch the latest picture, but Del hadn't responded.

So when he spotted Ev in the crowd waiting to cross the street one afternoon, for the first time his heart sank at the sight of him. Ev was wearing a suit and a tie and carrying a package under one arm. The heavy brown shoes encased his feet. Del turned his face away, even as he blew his whistle and beckoned for the crowd to cross the street. Perhaps Ev would only see the uniform and not look past to the one wearing it.

But no—there was Ev's voice, saying his name. He turned, resigned.

"Asta said I'd find you here."

He shouldn't have told Glen where he'd been posted.

Someone jostled Ev, and a driver beeped his horn. Ev hesitated, but when Del didn't reply, he reluctantly moved to the sidewalk. But he stopped there, standing under the awning of a store.

Del grew increasingly nervous and sweaty under his gaze. Why was Ev standing there, watching? Humiliated, he tried his best to ignore him and keep his voice steady as he yelled directions.

His shift lasted another forty minutes, and Ev stood there the whole time. When Del's relief arrived, he walked slowly over to Ev.

"You haven't called me," Ev said, reproachful. Then his tone became more tentative. "Did you not want to see me again?"

"That wasn't it," he blurted. "I...I didn't want you to see me *here*. Like this. To tell you that I've been demoted," he finished in a mumble.

"Asta told me you had," Ev said, and Del could see only sympathy in his face, not pity or derision. "I couldn't understand why, though."

The honest confusion in Ev's voice as he said that lifted Del's spirits a little. "It's a long story."

Ev shifted the package in his arms. "Want to get a bite to eat and tell me about it? Unless you have somewhere to be."

"No. But what about you—shouldn't you be at work?"

"I'm done for the day. I have to post this package, but that can wait."

So they went to a café nearby, and Del ordered a piece of apple pie, and Ev a piece of lemon meringue.

"Tell me what happened," Ev said to him. "Please."

He did, the words coming with surprising ease under Ev's sympathetic gaze. "I suppose people would say that I should feel proud, like I did the right thing. But I only wish I could have gone on as I was and never had to choose," he finished.

"I can see why you'd feel that way. But Del, I *am* proud of you."

He crumpled the napkin in his lap, heartbeat loud in his ears. "You are?"

"Of course. You were brave, to refuse."

"I thought of you, and it helped."

Ev tilted his head to the side. "Of me?"

"'Cause you're always so brave."

Ev's hand trembled, sending coffee spilling down the side of his cup to drip onto the table.

"I'm sorry, though," Ev said, flushing a little and reaching for a napkin. "I know you loved your motorcycle."

"Getting onto the motor patrol—it was the one time I'd ever been promoted."

"Maybe you will again, though. Cryer and Heath—the whole City Hall Gang—can't stay in power forever, can they? Once a new police chief gets appointed, you'll have a chance again."

"Guess that's so." Privately, he still thought it as unlikely as when Carl had voiced a similar opinion, but he could tell Ev was trying his best to cheer him. "Anyway, I'm sorry I didn't call you. I was...ashamed."

"You shouldn't be. And you should feel like you can tell me anything, Del. I'd never cut you down."

"Thanks." He mustered a smile for Ev. "What about you? How is the photography?"

"We don't have to talk about that. If you—"

"No," he interrupted. "I want to know how you're doing."

"It's...I don't know, really," Ev confessed after a moment. "I get anxious about making mistakes. Mr. Kee is very patient and encouraging, though."

"That's good. He doesn't treat you funny or nothing?"

"No, but I'm trying hard not to give him reason to."

"But you're liking the photography, aren't you?"

"Yes. It's so interesting. A heap better than any job I ever had before." Ev poked at the remaining pie crust on his plate, the crumbs soggy from the lemon filling. "I quit working at the Western Soap and Chemical factory and dishwashing at the hotel, so I can only hope this one lasts."

Del finished his own slice of pie and then laid down his fork and propped his chin on his hand, looking out the window at the people walking past. He shouldn't have been so afraid of talking with Ev about his weaknesses—should never have been afraid, not when he knew firsthand what a sweet and gentle soul Ev possessed.

Chapter Twenty-One

THE SOROPTOMIST CLUB of Los Angeles held their monthly meeting at the Women's Athletic Club on Flower Street. Entering the attractive lobby gave Del a feeling akin to when he had tried to take Ev for supper at the Barrenburg and gotten snubbed. His nerves intensified as he took his seat at the front of the meeting room itself, facing the rows of women who had come to hear Carl speak on the proposed measure for increasing the policemen's and firemen's salaries. Del wasn't sure why *he* was here—thankfully Carl hadn't asked him to actually give remarks. But when he had presented his petition, with every page full of signatures, Carl had asked him to come.

"Mrs. Gilbert—she's heading the women's division of the Police and Firemen's Salary Adjustment Committee—secured an invitation from the Soroptomist Club to have us speak at their next meeting. You'll attend too, won't you, Del? I'll be giving an address, but a few more uniformed men to answer questions and drum up support can't hurt."

Del, flushed with the success of his signature-gathering efforts, had rashly agreed and now found himself sweating on a too-small chair while Carl spoke about budgets and made affecting appeals to the dedication of the police and fire departments in protecting the lives of the citizens and questioned how anyone could then deny them a living wage to provide for their own families.

Del had drawn his pay this week, and the twenty-dollar cut thanks to his demotion meant he'd missed another payment on his radio and kitchen chairs, as well as on the loan he'd taken out from an industrial bank to pay the dentist when he'd suffered a bad tooth back in January. The thirty-dollar raise they were asking for would bring him back to where he'd been before, and even give him ten dollars extra.

The audience gave Carl a vigorous round of applause after his speech. There were a few more remarks from the club president, and then the meeting moved into a dining room where the wait staff served luncheon. Del found himself at a table with three older women and a younger girl around his age. They all introduced themselves, but he promptly forgot their names as a waiter placed a plate of the jellied tongue salad in front of him. His mother used to make a similar dish, but he hadn't tasted it in years, and for a moment he was back in his parents' kitchen, listening to his father read the latest news about the war while his mother made supper and nagged Del to straighten his collar and sit straight in his chair instead of slouching.

Thankfully, his table companions didn't seem to expect much of him in terms of keeping up the conversation, and he could say "yes, ma'am" and "no, ma'am," at suitable intervals until Carl rescued him after the raspberry mousse cakes, saying they needed to return to the station.

"The president promised Mrs. Gilbert that they'll endorse us," Carl said as they walked to where his car was parked. "We've already gotten the endorsements of the Business Men's Association, the Metropolitan Club, and the Afro-American Civic League. Not to mention that we collected over 200,000 signatures on our original petition."

"So you wager we've a chance, then?"

"Absolutely. I wouldn't be surprised if the proposition passes two to one."

Still, his feet dragged as he walked down to the butchers to buy some chops for supper. He was frying them when there was a knock on the door. Probably it was Mrs. Johnson needing help with her leaking kitchen faucet again. Del wasn't sure what had ever given her the idea that he was handy with plumbing, but he could give it another go, especially as he might get a plate of fudge squares in exchange.

When he opened the door and found himself face-to-face with Ev instead, he took a step backward in shock, too stunned for the moment to speak. It had been a little over a week since he'd last seen Ev, and he'd never expected him to show up at his apartment.

Ev offered a hesitant smile. "Is this a bad time?"

"No—no, come in," he said, finding his voice and hastily opening the door wider. Ev was dressed for work, and he took off his hat as he stepped through the door, smoothing a hand over his slicked-back hair. Del took the hat from him and hung it on the coatrack.

"Are you—"

"Is it—"

They stopped, and Ev gestured for Del to go first. He took a deep breath. "I was just cooking some chops, and I have an extra one, if you'd like to stay for supper." Why Ev was here, he didn't know, but he was going to make it clear Ev was welcome.

"I'd like that. I'm awfully hungry." Ev adjusted one of his cufflinks. "It's rotten of me to turn up so suddenly, I know."

"Ev, I'm always glad to see you," he told him softly, and Ev flushed.

"Soda pop?" Del asked, walking toward the kitchen. "Coffee? Or something stronger?"

"I'll make some coffee. You still keep the pot in the same place?"

For a moment, they both paused at this reminder of the past, of how close they had been, and of how far apart they still remained.

Del cleared his throat and took out the frying pan. "Yep, it's still in the cabinet over the sink."

They worked silently, side by side, bumping against each other now and then. When he'd poured the coffee, Ev took his cup over to the table and sat down, waiting for Del to finish cooking. The silence began to wear on Del's nerves, and so he started telling Ev about the luncheon that day.

"I'd have been terrified to speak publicly too," Ev said when Del mentioned how glad he was it had been Carl giving the speech and not him.

"If it had been about traffic laws, I might have been able to manage it. But I'm over my head with politics and budgets."

"Well, you have one certain vote in me."

"Carl reckons it has a good chance of passing. I hope it does." He fiddled with his fork. "Everything still all right at the studio?"

"Yes," Ev said, but there was a catch in his voice, and he didn't look at Del.

It wasn't until they were almost done with supper, though, that Ev returned to the subject.

"A woman came into the studio today," he said. He'd loosened his tie and unbuttoned the top of his shirt and now propped his head on one hand with a sigh. Del had been trying not to stare at the dip in his collarbone or remember carding his fingers through Ev's hair.

"She was an aspiring actress who wanted her portrait done. We get about ten of those a week, I think. But this one had a genuine charm about her. I helped her touch up her makeup and convinced her she should pin her hair in the new fashion. She was wearing a honey of a dress too, with the sweetest collar and little fake pearl buttons."

"That sounds pretty," he said cautiously, unsure where Ev was going with this.

"It was lovely. And there I was standing off to the side, adjusting the lighting while Mr. Kee took the photos, and I looked down at myself. I saw these awful brown shoes, and my hands—I haven't been able to do my nails in weeks, and they're getting so ragged and rough, and I—I—"

Ev hid his face in his hands.

Del gripped his fork, pinned in his chair by his desire to offer physical comfort and the knowledge that he shouldn't. But then a tremor shook Ev's body, and he knew Ev was trying not to cry, and it became too much. He went to Ev's side and hesitantly put a hand on his shoulder.

After a moment, Ev clutched it. Then, abruptly, he stood and pressed against Del's body, the movement so sudden Del staggered back a step before his arms went around Ev, holding him close.

"Tell me you think I'm beautiful," Ev whispered. "Please."

"Oh, Ev." He smoothed a hand over Ev's hair, wishing, as he was sure Ev did as well, that it was arranged in soft curls instead of slicked and straightened. "Of course you're beautiful. I've never met anyone as gorgeous as you. Ever. Don't cry, Ev. Come on, don't cry."

"Why does it have to be so difficult?" Ev dug his fingers into the front of Del's shirt. "I couldn't face it by myself tonight. And I know it's cruel of me to come here, when I don't even know my own mind when it comes to us. But I wanted you so badly, Del."

"It's all right. Don't worry about any of that."

He kept petting Ev's hair, holding him until his sobs quieted and he drew back, wiping at his eyes.

Del let him go, but said, "I know what will make you feel better. Wait a tick." He went into his bedroom and returned carrying his robe.

"It's not pretty like your kimono, but..." He cleared his throat and held it out to Ev.

Ev's eyes widened, and he grasped it, the silk spilling over his hands. "I can...stay, then?"

"I want you here," he said, honest, and Ev shuddered a little, but took a breath and nodded.

"I'll just..." He waved toward the bathroom.

"Sure. I'll clean up out here."

Ev disappeared into the bathroom, mopping at his eyes. Del cleared the table, listening to the sound of running water. He left the dishes in the sink for later and made some more coffee, putting out a tin of shortbread cookies too.

When Ev emerged, he had the robe wrapped around his body, his clothes and shoes discarded. He'd washed the pomade out of his hair, which curled damply around his ears.

"There you are," Del said, smiling, and Ev came to him, seemingly wanting to be held again.

Ev was so warm and sweet in his arms that Del couldn't suppress the impulse to do what he'd been yearning to this whole time. He bent to kiss Ev, a soft, gentle brush against his mouth. Ev didn't turn away, only sighed and closed his eyes, resting his head on Del's chest.

"Would you like some dessert?" he asked after a bit, still petting Ev's hair. "I rustled up some cookies."

Ev's arms tightened around him. "I'd rather have you," he said in a low voice.

Del sucked in a breath, heart thumping. "You mean that?"

"Yes." Ev sought out Del's mouth this time. "Please," he whispered as they broke apart, breathless.

It had gotten dark, and Ev closed the curtain on the window when they entered the bedroom before returning to Del. Ev cupped his cheek, caressing his face.

"Can I turn on the lamp?" he asked, leaning into Ev's touch, starved for it after so long. He wanted to see every expression, every arch and bend of Ev's body.

"Yes," Ev allowed and relaxed on the bed, watching as Del shed his clothes except for his shorts and came to lie next to him. It seemed almost a dream, the night taking on a quality of unreality in Ev's presence.

"I thought this would never happen again," he murmured. "It about killed me, Ev—wanting you so bad."

"Don't talk about it—or about anything else," Ev pleaded. "Let's have this—just this—for now."

Was this a one-time thing, then? But what did it matter if it was? He could no more turn away from Ev now then stop breathing.

"What do you want?" he asked.

"Let me watch you," Ev murmured, trailing his fingers along Del's thigh and making him shiver.

He'd never exhibited himself in such a way, and he flushed a little as he unbuttoned his shorts and shoved them down his legs. When he wrapped a hand around his half-hard cock and started moving it in a slow rhythm, he almost closed his eyes to try and escape from the exposed and vulnerable nature of it. But this was Ev, and it was all right. Ev wanted this—wanted him.

Ev scooted a little farther up his body and took Del's free hand in one of his, twining their fingers together. His eyes roamed over Del, lingering on his cock, the spread of his shoulders, lighting with the hint of a smile when they reached his face.

His peak wasn't far away, building as he quickened his pace. Ev reached over and brushed his fingers through Del's hair, smoothing it away from his forehead. Del kept his eyes on Ev's until the last moment, finally squeezing them shut as he came.

"That was lovely, darling," Ev praised and swung a leg over Del's hips, settling on his thighs. The robe hung open from his shoulders, revealing the small peaks of his nipples. He dipped his fingers in the sticky mess on Del's stomach and rubbed it over himself, mingling it with his own wet arousal.

"Will you—with your fingers?" Ev asked after a few moments of rocking back and forth.

He nodded, unable to manage words at this point, and they resettled on their sides, Ev's one leg crooked up and over Del's. Del wet his fingers in his mouth, slowly pushed one into Ev and moved it in circles until he loosened enough for him to add another. He fucked him like that until Ev came with a shudder and a gasp that he muffled against Del's shoulder.

He didn't know what could be said and thought he might cry if he tried to speak.

"Turn off the light," Ev said, rolling off him and hiding his face in the pillow. "Let's...let's sleep."

The night wasn't particularly chilly, but they drew the blanket around themselves, creating a quiet, sheltered space. For his part, sleep did not come quickly, and he suspected Ev remained awake a long time too. His last conscious thought was that he didn't have any butter for their toast in the morning, followed by the comforting realization that there was an unopened jar of strawberry jam in the pantry.

WHEN HE WOKE in the morning, he kept his eyes closed. Ev was a warm presence next to him, but he was afraid what Ev's expression would show. It was nice to pretend Ev would be here with him every morning after, but he didn't know what Ev would say to him or where they would go from here.

A moment later, his stomach growled, announcing it wanted breakfast and soon. Sighing, Del opened his eyes. Ev was lying on his back, staring up at the ceiling, tears slipping from the corners of his eyes. He sniffed and scrubbed at his face when he realized Del was awake and watching him.

"Ev," he began, heart breaking, but Ev hushed him.

"I'm fine. Let's have breakfast and then...and then we can talk," Ev finished, his voice hoarse from sleep and his tears.

"All right," he said, touching Ev's shoulder.

"What will become of me if I don't make something of myself now?" Ev said later when they were at the table and he was staring down at the sausages Del had cooked, congealing in grease on his plate.

Del's own appetite had faltered after a piece of toast and jam. Ev's tears could only mean one thing, really—that Ev thought last night had been a mistake.

"Make something of yourself?" he forced himself to say.

"With my new job. This is my chance, and maybe one day I can have my own studio or—or sell my photographs to magazines." He glanced at Del, as though nervous Del would find this notion laughable.

"That would be swell, I think." He cleared his throat. "But does that mean that we...can't?"

"It's risky, you *know* that." Ev sounded irritated now, and Del hunched his shoulders. "Maybe it's time for me to leave my way of living behind. Lots of fairies do, you know. After a few years of it, they stop."

"You mean you wouldn't wear your pretty step-ins again or curl your hair?"

"Yes," Ev said and repeated in a firmer voice, "Yes, that's what I mean."

"Ev, no," he protested, distressed. "How could you change your nature? And how could we be together if you did?"

"We couldn't. That's what I'm saying. You wouldn't want to be with me if I was a man." Ev lifted his chin. "And I could change."

"No, Ev." It would destroy something precious to lose Ev's gentleness. "I know you have to act that way at the studio, but with me—at home—if we had a home, together...?"

"A home," Ev said in a choked voice.

"Yes. But..." He made himself go on because he couldn't deny the truth in what Ev was saying. "I don't want to be the reason you lose your job."

They sat in silence awhile, neither of them touching their breakfast.

"And yet," Ev said, his voice shaking a little. "I can't seem to bring myself to say goodbye to you. It would be better for both of us if I could make a clean break of it. It's not fair to you, especially."

"I don't think it would be better," he protested, miserable.

"I know, Del. But maybe you should think about what's best for you too."

"Having you with me is what's best."

Ev's expression crumbled, and he put a hand over his eyes.

"What do we do then?" Del asked at last. His jaw ached, he was clenching it so hard to keep from sobbing or shouting or whatever outlet this pain in his chest demanded.

"I don't know." Ev sighed, his head drooping. "I'm sorry."

In the end, they left it at that. They both had to get to work, and neither of them could—or wanted to—deal the final blow to the fragile renewal of trust and love between them.

TWO DAYS LATER and Del's mind was still three-quarters occupied with Ev and their night together as he walked home. The other quarter dwelt on his sore feet and the absolute necessity of getting new shoes, price be damned.

It seemed almost...well, sacrilegious to mix thoughts of Ev with those of footwear, but he couldn't help it, and besides, that had been one of the most wonderful things about Ev, how he had started to fit into all the aspects of Del's life from breakfast and supper to shopping for groceries to riding the streetcars.

If he could have that again... But he didn't want it if it meant sacrificing Ev's chances of building a successful life for himself. After all, he couldn't make any guarantees about his own ability to support Ev.

He was so consumed by these thoughts, that he didn't register the presence of Asta waiting outside his door until they were almost face-to-face.

"Hello, Del," Asta said. A pale-yellow scarf wound about his throat and rouge darkened his cheeks. "We need to talk."

"We do?" he stuttered, not relishing the prospect of being alone in the same room as Asta. Where the devil was Glen?

Asta didn't reply, just stared pointedly at the door until Del unlocked it and held it open while Asta walked inside.

"This business with Ev," Asta said before Del had even finished unbuttoning his coat. "I want to know what you think you're doing."

Del gaped at him. "What do you mean?"

"I mean that Ev came to see me last night, all in a dither, and talked my ear off for half an hour straight."

"He did?"

"Yes, he did!" Asta's voice was a sharp snap. "And I'll tell you this—"

"What did he say?" Del interrupted. "Was he happy? Or sad?"

"He said a bushel of nonsense—crying half the time. Ev always behaves like a fool when it comes to men, I declare. But I'll tell you this— I'm not going to let him have his heart broken again."

"I wouldn't do that."

Asta gave a disgusted snort and sat down in the chintz armchair, crossing his legs and drumming his fingers against the armrests. "The hell of it is that I believe you. Glen must be rubbing off on me. He's always saying you don't mean any harm. Besides, I know that no matter what I say, Ev will do exactly as he pleases."

Del perched warily on one of the kitchen chairs. "Ev told me he didn't know what we should do," he ventured, and when Asta merely looked at him, waiting, he added, "I don't know either."

"Seems like you've already done something," Asta pointed out. "Involving a bed."

He cleared his throat, knowing his ears were turning red. "Yes, but Ev said he might give it all up—stop living as a fairy and loving men, I mean. Because of his new job."

Surprise flashed across Asta's face, and then he frowned, troubled. "Silly thing. As if that would make things all better. Although maybe...well, I suppose I can't say for certain that he's wrong."

"I don't want him to do it. I think it would be awful."

"'Cause you couldn't fuck him again?" Asta said, spite returning.

Del winced, mumbling, "That's not why."

Asta heaved a sigh. "I know. Lord, you really do love him that much, don't you?"

He nodded. Of course he loved Ev—that had never been in question.

Asta plucked at a loose fiber in the chair cushion. "He's worth loving. Ev's been my dearest friend, you know. But he looks up to me too, for advice and protection. And I've been lousy at it. I'm sure he told you about Michael. I swear to God, I never knew he'd get violent with Ev when I first introduced them. But I should have—Lord knows, I've been with enough fellows who roughed me up. And then when Ev wouldn't leave him..." Asta drew a shaky breath. "I was frantic, half out of my mind—sure he was going to get hurt so bad it might kill him. Christ." He put a hand over his face. "You have any whisky on hand? Or a cigarette?"

Del had cigarettes and a bottle of cheap wine. He got both for Asta and lit a smoke for himself too.

"Do you think it's better for him, if he isn't with me?" Del asked after they had each made their way through half a glass. Although it seemed a touch surreal to be discussing this with Asta of all people, it was also a relief to talk about it. "I can't offer him much, you see. I don't have a lot of money, and I'm not likely to ever make a good deal more. And if coming back to me cost him his chance at becoming a photographer..."

"That's Ev's choice to make. But you shouldn't trouble over money. Just keep loving Ev like you do." Asta glanced over at him. "Besides, isn't trying to make it rich what landed you in this pickle in the first place?"

Del grimaced. "I suppose Ev told you all about it."

"Oh, yes. Gotta say, though, I'd have paid good money to see Ev tearing down the road ahead of the Prohis, just like a gangster in the movies." Asta chuckled and sipped his wine, pursing his lips at the taste. "By the way, this chair has the most fantastic pattern on the fabric. I adore the colors."

"You do?"

"If Glen has one fault, it's that bland decorating style in his house. All wood paneling and plaids. Says he wants it to be rustic. As though we were out in the forest and not the middle of Los Angeles."

"Glen likes the outdoors."

"Oh, I know. Promise me you'll keep going on fishing and camping trips with him so I never have to go myself. He keeps trying to convince me to accompany him. Claims the stargazing will be so romantic it will make up for the mosquitoes and lack of a bathtub. I've told him plain I'm not going any more primitive than an auto camp."

Del laughed.

Asta smiled, a quick, bright flash that made him look much younger. Then it faded, and he said quietly, "Although I suppose I'd do it, if it meant he'd stay with me."

"Is Glen giving you reason to doubt that?" It wouldn't surprise him if Glen had been treating Asta too casually and not telling him how he really felt.

Asta lifted one shoulder in a shrug.

"'Cause I can tell he cares about you. He's not so good at showing it sometimes, that's all."

"He's been flirting with the girl who sometimes sings in Philip's band at the Admiral's Blues. Making love to her with his eyes."

"Right in front of you?" He frowned, not having expected Glen to ever stoop that low.

"Keeps asking me if I don't think she's a looker too. Which I suppose she *is*, but I don't exactly appreciate having him point it out to me."

"I'll talk to him about it. Knock some sense into him."

Asta looked startled. "Thanks," he said at last and then grimaced. "Damn, I suppose I shouldn't have come here, yelling at you like I did. It's only that I love Ev, you see, and it's difficult to see him unhappy."

"I know. I'm glad he has friends looking out for him even if...even if I can't."

Asta left a short while later, leaving Del to wonder if he could consider Asta a friend now. Given that Asta must be the only other soul on the planet who liked the chintz armchair besides Del, he felt at the very least a cordial acquaintance between them could not be long in coming.

HE WASN'T WORKING the next day, and in the morning, he pottered around his apartment, doing the odds and ends left for his days off, like putting away his laundry.

In the afternoon, he put on his hat and took the streetcar downtown. He walked along until he found the jewelry store he always passed on his way to and from the police department. The thought had been in the back of his mind ever since Ev showed him that article about the inverts who got married. Now that it seemed he might have a chance again, he wondered if proposing to Ev would show him he was willing to be in this for the rest of their lives. Maybe it might deter Ev from the drastic choice of trying to be a "man" and turning his back on Del and all the rest of it.

"Let me show you some of our special items," the sales clerk said when Del came in the door and asked to look at some rings. "This diamond ring is modest, perfect for a young lady of refined taste, and reasonably priced."

Del allowed it was quite pretty.

"We offer an installment plan. You'd only pay ten dollars down."

"I'm only looking today," Del said. His eye caught on a gold ring with a peridot surrounded by a circle of seed pearls. It would look perfect on Ev's finger.

"What's the name of your intended?" the clerk asked, seeing the direction of Del's gaze and bringing the ring onto the counter.

"Ev," he said without thinking.

"Is that short for Evelyn? How charming."

"I want to get Ev the perfect ring. But I don't even know if I should propose."

The clerk smiled, sympathetic. "Afraid she'll turn you down?"

He nodded, although it went beyond simply worrying that Ev would refuse. However much he might wish it wasn't the case, he couldn't say for sure that Ev's life would be better with him.

"If I can give you a bit of advice, Mr...?"

"Randolph."

"A bit of advice, Mr. Randolph, from my own experience." The clerk leaned closer. "There's nothing more important than showing the lady your true feelings. If you propose with a simple silver band, that hardly expresses the depth of your affection. A diamond, or a lovely ring like this, will chase away any doubts the lady might have. Countless men have come through our shop and walked down the aisle a few weeks later."

Del looked at the ring again. It really was beautiful.

"Remember," the clerk chirped, "only ten dollars down."

He said he'd think about it and stuffed his hands into his pockets as he left the store, feeling the thin leather of his wallet. He didn't have the money to buy that ring for Ev or give him the sort of home he deserved anyway. He could hardly be a good husband to Ev under these circumstances.

Why, he would want Ev to be proud of him, to feel comfortable and secure with a husband who had ample wages and a fine job. He thought of his sparsely furnished apartment. If they were married, they would need a bedroom suite at the very least. He remembered how his father had bought the furniture for his parents' home back in Kansas on an installment plan and couldn't make the payments. The furniture store repossessed almost all of it, and his mother had been furious, demanding to know how his father expected her to manage the housekeeping under such circumstances.

And yet, there was the chance he'd be getting a raise soon if the proposition passed. Was it wrong to believe they could have a life together? A life where Ev didn't have to give up his photography, but also wouldn't have to destroy his gentle, delicate beauty. A life where Del might make his way back onto the motor patrol through dedicated work. A life where they wouldn't have to abandon the things that mattered most to them, including each other.

"MARRIAGE?" GLEN CHOKED on his coffee and went into a coughing fit. "I didn't even know you were together again."

He had gone over to Glen's after his visit to the jewelry store. Asta wasn't there—apparently he'd managed to find some work as a waiter at a cabaret. "The place has a tough reputation," Glen had said. "Lots of dope peddlers and pimps among the clientele. Don't like the thought of him working there exactly, but I guess Asta can take care of himself."

Now Del reached over and mopped up Glen's spilled coffee with a napkin. "Ev and I aren't together yet, and I don't know if we can be. But Ev deserves to be treated with respect. I want him to know for sure how I feel about him."

"But... I mean..."

"We wouldn't try and do it in a church or nothing. Ev said we could exchange vows just the same. He showed me some stories where people had done it—really gotten married, not just calling each other 'husband' and 'wife' like you'll see with some of the fairies and their trade."

"Well, that's..." Glen searched for the words. "It's a big decision. You sure about it?"

"No. That is, I'm sure about wanting to marry him. But Ev's thinking maybe he should act like a man, now he's got this new job. And I...I don't want to lose him, Glen. But maybe it's selfish of me, and I'm thinking of my own happiness more than his."

Glen sat silently for a minute or two. "Hell, pal, I don't know what to tell you," he finally said. "If it was me—seems as though bringing up the subject of marriage would only make a complicated situation worse."

Of course Glen would say that, and it reminded him of his conversation with Asta. "Hey, what is all this about you trying to get friendly with another girl, by the way? She sings sometimes at the Admiral's Blues, Asta said."

"*Asta* said?" Glen repeated. "What the hell were you doing talking with Asta?"

"He stopped by my apartment—wanted to talk to me about Ev, and he mentioned it."

"Guess I should be grateful the two of you managed a civil conversation alone," Glen muttered. "What's there to say? Katey is real pretty and friendly."

"But Asta—don't you get that it hurts him?"

"It doesn't change how I feel about Asta. I'm not trying to hurt him, but I can't stop noticing other people that I find attractive."

"Asta's worried it means you don't want to be with him anymore."

Glen groaned. "Dammit—this always happens." When Del opened his mouth again, Glen raised his hand. "I'll talk to him about it."

"Don't give up on him," Del urged.

"I don't give up, but usually it isn't worth fighting." He caught sight of Del's expression and sighed. "We can't all subscribe to your brand of optimism and infatuation when it comes to love. But I'll try my best. If Asta left, Sam would go too, and that would break Greta's heart, after all."

Del let it go, hearing in the words what Glen couldn't bring himself to admit openly.

IT WAS A good thing directing traffic at a busy downtown intersection required so much attention, as whenever his mind wasn't occupied it wandered straight to Ev. He desperately wanted to see Ev again, but up to this point, Ev had been the one initiating all of their interactions. Maybe it was best to let Ev set the pace.

There was the upcoming election on April 30th to think about too. In addition to the proposed salary raise for policemen and firemen, there was also a measure to allow dancing at Venice Pier on Sundays. Since Venice had been annexed to Los Angeles earlier that year, it had been subject to the city's laws against such practice, to the consternation of the amusement men at the Pier. A few naysayers who thought allowing dancing on Sundays in any location would be intemperate faced off against those who thought the populace should be free to spend its Sundays as it wanted. Councilman Hall stated that if fountains and theatres were open on Sundays, why single out dancing? Del thought that sounded fair and imagined taking Ev there again and swirling across the dance floor together with the ocean breeze tousling Ev's curls.

On the subject of their own proposition, Carl was jubilant over the support it was garnering. He'd had Del out several evenings in a row, handing people automobile stickers to people urging a "yes" vote.

Del had managed to get rid of his stack that evening, and after a late supper, he put on his robe and settled in front of the radio. He was dozing in the chair when a series of knocks sounded on the door, startling him.

"Del!" Ev's voice called. "Please tell me you're still awake."

"I'm coming," he said, leaping up from the chair and hoping Ev hadn't woken Mrs. Johnson or any of the other neighbors.

When he opened the door, Ev tumbled inside, giggling. He was boiled as an owl—Del could smell the liquor along with a quantity of cheap drugstore perfume. He wasn't wearing a jacket, and his shirt gaped open at the neck to show off a pale purple scarf with beaded embroidery on the edges. He'd rouged his cheeks and curled his hair too.

Ev landed a kiss in the general vicinity of his mouth and then tottered over to the armchair, collapsing into it. "I was out with Camilo— we found a speak with a band that was the berries and a bartender who could make divine brandy flips and gin daisies. But when we got back to the apartment, the cops were there. Mr. and Mrs. Miraglia were *going at it* again. It's been awful the past few nights—they're two doors down, and we can hear *everything*. Him yelling, and her screaming and then crying when he beats her. And God, Camilo and I want to help, but if we tried, he'd turn on us. I'm already nervous he'll come break down our door one night when he's drunk and yelling about fags. But someone must have called the cops tonight, and so we couldn't stroll into our apartment. Not looking like *this*. So Camilo went to José's, and I came here."

"I think you need a big glass of water."

"Mmmm, you're right. I'll have an awful headache in the morning, won't I? I'm so zozzled." Ev laughed again.

Del got him the water, standing over him as Ev drank. "I guess you didn't mean it, huh?"

Ev blinked, confused.

"Giving that up." He gestured at Ev's attire, feeling unaccountably angry that Ev should have been out, dressed like this, having a swell old time while he was tying himself in knots.

Ev's mouth trembled. "I can do as I like."

"Then why did you do it?"

"Because." Tears overflowed Ev's eyes. "I think I'll go crazy if I don't, Del. It's too hard. I can't stand it." His breathing sped up, hiccupping between sobs.

"Ev—shit, I'm sorry. God." He took the glass and set it aside, then hauled Ev into his arms.

"It's too hard," Ev repeated, burying his face in the crook of Del's neck. "Don't be angry with me."

"I'm not. I'm sorry." He rubbed Ev's back. "It's just...it's hard for me too."

Ev's sobs slowed, and he moaned. "I feel sick."

"You gonna throw up?"

Ev moaned again, and Del figured it was prudent to lead him to the bathroom. Then he went to light the water heater while Ev sat on the toilet lid, pale and miserable.

"Why don't you take a bath?" he said when he got back, brushing Ev's hair off his face. "That'd make you feel better."

"Will you take one with me?" Ev asked, his voice small. "Not to make love—I'm too tired and drunk for that. But it would be nice with you there."

Del wasn't sure they would fit into the tub, but they managed somehow, Ev crammed in between his legs. Taking a cloth, Ev dipped it in the water, wrung it out, and then drew it over his face, washing away the makeup and the tear tracks. Del soaped his hands and rubbed them up and down Ev's arms and over his chest.

"Shampoo my hair too?" Ev asked.

"It'll take out your curls."

"Yes." Ev shut his eyes, lashes clinging to his wet skin. "They need to be gone."

He cupped his hands and poured the water over Ev's hair, then worked up a lather and started massaging his scalp. Ev was silent through the process, head lowered.

"So sorry," Del whispered.

Ev patted his leg. "It's all right."

It wasn't, and it made his heart hurt, but he finished rinsing all the soap away. Ev sighed and leaned back against him.

The pipes made a few creaking noises, and the water swished against the sides of the tub whenever they shifted, but otherwise it was quiet. Del traced idle, wandering lines on Ev's chest. It was clear to him that they couldn't go on like this. It was going to tear him apart, to keep having Ev come to him, distressed and hurting.

Later, lying together in his bed, he watched Ev's sleeping form, able to dimly make out his features in the darkness. Leaving Ev to fend for himself couldn't be the right answer. Ev needed him, and he needed Ev.

"I'm going to ask you to marry me," he whispered. "Maybe you'll say yes. It would be the best thing that ever happened to me if you did."

Ev slept on, unaware, and he moved a little closer so he could touch Ev's hand, curled loosely in the sheet.

ON APRIL 30TH, Del rose early so he could go to the polls and cast his vote in the special election. As he filled in his ballot, he thought of how exciting it would be if the proposition passed, and they received such a large salary raise. He'd be able to afford that lovely ring for Ev. They could save for a bungalow with a backyard—an automobile as well.

Of course, there was no guarantee that Ev would say yes to his proposal. After their last night together, Ev hadn't said anything about whether he wanted to keep seeing Del or not. They'd eaten a quiet breakfast, and Ev had borrowed one of Del's coats so he wouldn't have to take the streetcar in his evening attire. They had both been subdued, although Del's emotions bubbled insistently just below the surface, and he was pretty sure Ev was feeling the same way. But they hadn't exchanged any words on the matter of their relationship and its future.

He reminded himself of this, but it was difficult to rein in his excitement. Carl had invited him and Oscar to a restaurant after work so they could wait for the evening editions and the initial speculation about the election results. Del arrived around seven and found the other two already at a table, newspapers spread over the surface.

"It's almost certain that we'll win," Carl said, shifting a page so he could reach his knife. He sawed at his steak. "Of course, then there'll be the usual political nonsense, and the council will have to vote on the budget, so it will be a while before we'll actually enjoy the results."

Del paused, his own knife and fork hovering over his plate. "How long is a while?" He hadn't expected having to wait.

"Oh, a few months perhaps."

A few months—but his loans were due now and what about Ev's ring? He slowly cut a piece off his own steak. "I didn't realize it would take so long."

"There's also no telling what Cryer will try to pull," Oscar said. "I think he'll probably use it as an excuse to raise taxes—thereby giving him and his cronies more money to throw into their illegal activities. That's where a good percentage of our tax dollars go now."

Carl dug his knife in with excessive force, screeching it along the plate. "It's a travesty, and it doesn't stop at allowing the legging and gambling. There's the condition of our city streets for one—the pavement is in shocking condition. But Cryer gives the paving contracts to the companies who pay him kickbacks, with no concern for whether they do an adequate job or not. Then we're left having to repave the streets in a year or two."

"Very inefficient," Oscar agreed.

"At least we have Davis in charge of the police now," Carl added. "He's supported the proposition and won't take any funny business from the council."

Del poked at his own meal. These were all factors he hadn't considered before. He'd vaguely known there might be some issues with paying for the salary raise, but this was all more complicated than anything he had imagined. He went home unsettled, but in the morning, he hurried to the drugstore to buy the morning edition, scanning the headlines for the election results.

The proposition had passed by a two to one margin. He sagged against the wall in relief, his earlier excitement returning. Maybe there would be a few hurdles still to cross, but the first and largest had been cleared. Surely with men like Chief Davis and Carl in command, they would be able to overcome whatever political problems might arise with the council.

Taking the paper home, he made breakfast and then sat down to eat and peruse the classified advertisements for the section on the companies and individuals offering loans. Many of them offered cash in return for stocks, bonds, or mortgages. Del didn't have any of those, but then he spotted an ad for the Western Adjustment Company, which offered quick money to people with steady employment. You didn't even need an endorsement. He circled the advertisement and folded the newspaper, setting it aside.

He had to work that day, but on the following afternoon he got off early enough that he could go over to Seventh and Broadway and the nondescript brick building that housed the Western Adjustment Company. A secretary greeted him inside, and he told her his name and asked to see someone about a loan.

"Of course, sir," she said and led him to an office down the corridor. "Mr. Taylor? A gentleman to see you about a loan. His name is Mr. Delbert Randolph."

Mr. Taylor rose to greet Del and shook his hand. Then Del sat down, tugging the wrinkles out of his jacket and taking off his hat, which he propped on his knee.

"Need some cash, do you?" Mr. Taylor said, giving Del a quick smile and uncapping his pen. "Creditors breathing down your neck, are they?"

"Actually, I'm thinking of getting married," he said, flushing a little at the thought and hoping Mr. Taylor couldn't see how nervous he was. "I want to buy a ring, but I need some cash for the down payment and—"

"Marriage? And who's the lucky girl may I ask?" Mr. Taylor chuckled, reaching over to shake Del's hand again.

"Uh, well," Del stuttered.

"A gentleman doesn't kiss and tell, is that it?" Mr. Taylor laughed again. "Let's see what we can do for you, sir. How much do you need? Don't want to buy anything too cheap, now do we?"

"Er, no. I was thinking maybe about twenty dollars. That'd give me enough for the first two payments."

"Oh, that's fine, that's fine. Twenty dollars—why that's no problem at all, is it?"

"Is it?" he repeated, somewhat overwhelmed by Mr. Taylor's habit of ending his sentences in a question.

"Got a job, have you? What do you make a month, sir? Can't just give a loan to anyone, can we? Sure you understand."

He straightened in his chair. "I'm a policeman. You probably saw the news about the election, and how we've had our pay raised. I won't have any trouble repaying a loan."

"That's swell—yes, sirree." Mr. Taylor whipped out a form and began filling it in. "Why, we'd be happy to lend to a person of your caliber, Mr. Randolph. Couldn't turn down one of our brave protectors of the peace, could we? We offer very low interest rates. Couldn't find any lower in the business, no sir."

Fifteen minutes later, Del walked out of the office with twenty dollars in his pocket and headed for the jewelry store and the ring with Ev's name on it.

Chapter Twenty-Two

OBTAINING THE RING—now nestled in a box and buried under his handkerchiefs in the bureau drawer—was of course only the first step. Actually proposing to Ev presented a whole new dilemma.

He couldn't propose in public. If he was proposing to Glen, he'd take him fishing and tie the ring to the end of his fishing pole, but Ev wouldn't appreciate that at all. Perhaps he'd try his hand at cooking a fancy supper, invite Ev over, and ask the question over glasses of champagne and chocolates during dessert. Or maybe he could bake a pie and put the ring in the center. Then he recollected that he had never baked a pie before and probably shouldn't try for the first time on such an important occasion.

Chocolates it was, then, and he would do his best to manage a fine supper. Nothing with a sauce. He still remembered his mother despairing over a white sauce that wouldn't thicken before a party. Maybe he'd try a baked liver and onions with bacon and tomatoes. That had been one of his father's favorite meals, requested on his birthdays and the Fourth of July.

Before getting carried away with menu planning, he needed to ask Ev over for the supper in the first place. So the next evening, after a visit to the barber for a haircut so he didn't look so scruffy, he took the streetcars to Ev's neighborhood. Somehow it seemed an age since he had last seen Ev's apartment building, with its peeling paint and the gutters falling away from the roof, even though it had only been a few months.

When he knocked, Camilo answered the door.

"Good evening, Del," Camilo said in a neutral tone.

"Hey, Camilo. Is Ev here?" He figured Ev had probably been telling Camilo about his visits with Del—hopefully or else this would be an even more awkward conversation.

Camilo did not immediately answer his question nor open the door any wider. "Two weeks," Camilo said. "That is how long Ev cried over you the last time. Every night for two weeks I made him warm milk and gave him my handkerchiefs when his ran out."

He hung his head, contrite, hating to hear how shattered Ev had been.

"I do not want to go through that again. I do not want *Ev* to go through that again. But now he is sleeping with you once more—as lovesick as the last time."

"I'm not going to hurt him again."

Camilo huffed and opened the door farther. "I suppose we are all fools when it comes to love. Ev should be home soon. I was having some tea, and you are welcome to some if you like."

"Thanks," he said, adding, "And thanks for looking after him."

"You were heartbroken too, yes?"

"Yes," he allowed, silently thinking that he might be again soon.

Camilo went into the kitchen, Del following and taking a seat at the kitchen table. "Since Ev has his new job at the studio, we managed to pay our rent on time for once, and so I can offer you cream and sugar with your tea," Camilo said, taking out another cup.

"I'll take some sugar, then, please."

"Ah, and see this," Camilo said after handing him his cup. He shuffled through some papers on the counter and then brought Del a stack of photographs. "Ev did these."

Del flipped through them. They were all portraits of Ev's friends. There was Philip, leaning his head on his hand, a few kiss curls dropping onto his forehead. Nellie sat by a bouquet of flowers, lips and cheeks painted, a mink stole wrapped around her neck. In the third picture, Camilo leaned against a brick wall next to a rose bush, smiling, a paper fan in his hand. And finally there was Asta, with one arm around Sam, who was staring avidly at the camera. Del wondered if Glen had been standing in the background, holding a piece of steak.

"I never had a portrait done before," Camilo said. "Ev's going to do another one that I can send to my family."

"I knew Ev would be a swell photographer." He handed back the photos, wishing there had been one of him and Ev together. Maybe soon there would be.

Ev arrived around half an hour later. He paused in the doorway on seeing Del, who stood up so fast the chair fell over, clattering on the floor.

"I wasn't expecting you tonight," Ev said, removing his hat and coat.

"I know. Sorry to drop by so sudden."

"Tea, Ev, dear?" Camilo asked and after pouring Ev a cup, he tactfully removed himself to his bedroom, leaving them to talk.

"Camilo showed me those portraits you did," Del said after a minute, when they had both sat down at the table. "They're awful good."

"Thank you." Ev sipped his tea. "What brings you by?"

He took a deep breath. "I wanted to invite you over for supper."

"Supper?"

"I'm not much of a cook, I know. But I wanted to see you and…and talk."

"Supper would be nice," Ev said carefully. "When did you have in mind?"

"Saturday night?"

"I've actually promised Nellie I'd come to a party she's hosting on Saturday."

"Friday then?"

"All right." Ev hesitated. "Though I'm only promising supper. I know the last two times we've ended up falling into bed, but—"

"I'm only asking for supper," he said hastily. "For your company."

Ev nodded. "Then yes. I'd like that."

He smiled, relieved.

Ev caught his smile and gave him a small echo of it, his expression softening. "I guess congratulations are in order on your pay raise."

"That was swell, huh? It wasn't even a close call."

"And how are things with the new chief? Davis, right? Any chance you might be able to get back on the motor patrol?"

"I don't know. Davis—he's a big supporter of professionalism—wants officers who are educated and smart. And I'm not any of those things."

"Don't say that," Ev said, his voice sharp. "I think you're a fine officer."

"Thanks," he mumbled, choking up a little at Ev's words.

"Besides, any fellow who remains concerned about traffic laws even as he's being chased by the Prohis sure as heck deserves to be a motor patrol officer." Ev's tone was teasing, but he reached across the table and squeezed Del's hand.

"Guess that's so," he allowed, laughing a little.

"Sure it's so." Ev sat back again, letting go of his hand, to Del's disappointment.

He cleared his throat. "Well, I'd better be off. I'm sure you're tired, and I have to run some errands before the stores close."

Ev stood with him and opened the door as he put on his hat. "I'll look forward to Friday," Ev said, and then gave him a quick kiss on the cheek before darting back inside.

Those words and the kiss buoyed his confidence for two whole days, but by Thursday he was beset with nerves, anxious and unable to sleep a wink.

He woke at four in the morning on Friday. He lay there staring at the dark ceiling, repeating the proposal he had spent hours scratching out on ink-stained sheets of paper.

Life would be bogus without you.

No, that wasn't right. He frowned for a moment. *Life would be barren without you.* Was that it? Yes, "barren" sounded right. He had looked it up in a dictionary at the library. He was going to say that just after "You are everything to me." And then there was the tricky bit with the poetry. He couldn't remember the name of the poet, but the librarian had pointed it out to him as a particularly romantic verse, and he'd memorized two lines, although he kept mixing up the ending.

He'd done the shopping yesterday and gotten all the ingredients for supper, as well as the box of chocolates. With regret, he'd forgone the champagne, as it was expensive, and he needed to save all he could manage until they got their pay raised.

He was able to keep his mind on directing traffic that day, but at the station, he misfiled several reports and then typed his account of an altercation between two motorists on the wrong form and had to retype the entire thing when he realized his mistake. Running late, he changed out of his uniform as fast as he could and ran down to the streetcar stop. No time to get flowers for the table now.

By the time he made it home, his watch gave him half an hour before Ev arrived, and he quickly began chopping an onion and some celery, then remembered he should start the liver cooking first. He lit the oven and then took the liver out of the icebox. Checking over the recipe—written out for him by Mrs. Johnson, who had also bestowed a good deal of unsolicited advice on liver's nutritional benefits and a cousin of hers who insisted eating it twice weekly had cured his chronic indigestion—he saw he needed to dredge it in flour first. That done, he put it in the pan with some bacon slices arranged on top and slid it into the oven.

Ev rang just as he was paring the potatoes. Pushing back his hair, he dashed over to the door and answered it.

"Hello," Ev said, smiling. "I know I'm a bit early, but I thought perhaps you could use some help."

They both looked at the general chaos in the kitchen.

"Help would be good," Del admitted.

"You have flour in your hair." Ev reached up to brush it away, and Del's heart thumped at the casual intimacy of the gesture. Then Ev lifted the satchel in his hand. "I thought, just in case I ended up staying the night..." He glanced away, a blush coloring his cheeks.

"I'll stick it in the bedroom," Del said, taking the satchel and using the few moments away from Ev to try and regain his equilibrium.

"You didn't have to go to all this trouble," Ev protested as they reconvened in the kitchen. He found a spoon and poked into the can of stewed tomatoes sitting by the pile of celery.

Unable to explain why it *was* necessary, Del mumbled an incoherent reply and turned back to the stove.

The meal turned out better than he had expected—nothing burned or overdone. There was a concert playing on the radio that provided pleasant background music. Ev was talking about developing prints, sounding cheerful and pleased to be there with Del.

For his part, he concentrated on not dropping his utensils and praying Ev didn't notice the way his hands were trembling. As the moment drew nearer, his heart seemed to beat louder and louder, and every word of his carefully written proposal flew clean out of his head.

Ev wanted seconds, a fact that would have pleased him at any other time, but now seemed only to prolong his anxiety.

At last Ev laid down his fork. "Should we see if there's a mystery program on the radio?"

"Actually, there's something else I—wait here," he stuttered, getting up and going into the bedroom to fetch the chocolates. Earlier he had removed one of the caramels and put the ring in its place before tying the ribbon back around the box.

"Are those chocolates?" Ev asked when he returned. "You shouldn't have gone to the trouble," he added as Del handed him the box, and he looked up at Del a bit helplessly.

"Just try one or two," he said.

Ev bit his lower lip, brow creasing. "This isn't going to be like before, is it? Buying me presents, thinking that's going to buy *me* too."

"No," he exclaimed, horrified. "No—it's—it's not that."

"I *hope* not." Ev frowned at him a second longer and then began opening the box. "I do love vanilla creams, but we're sharing these. I'm not eating the whole box myself."

Del found he couldn't quite breathe or look away from Ev's face as he lifted the lid.

"Oh, look, it's like a Cracker Jack box with a toy," Ev said, catching sight of the ring. He picked it up. "Although this seems..." His voice faltered. "It's not paste jewel, is it?" he whispered, his eyes wide.

Del shook his head.

"Is this really...?"

He swallowed, nodded.

Ev's eyes filled with tears, and they overflowed, spilling down his face. "Del... I... *oh.*"

"I know you're worried," he said, voice cracking with emotion. "I know you think maybe it would be better if we didn't try to stay together. But I think we can manage it, Ev."

"I never—*never* expected..." Ev scrubbed the back of his hand over his cheeks, sniffing. "To think that—when I'd *dreamed* and..."

He reached out and carefully took Ev's left hand, wrapping his fingers around it. All the flowery words he'd intended to say were gone, and he could only ask quietly, "What do you say, then?"

Ev was still for a long moment. "You truly believe this could work?"

"Yes. Or maybe..."

"Maybe?"

"Maybe I just can't bear the alternative," he admitted.

Ev met his eyes. "I don't think I can either," he whispered.

He couldn't stop his voice from shaking as he asked, "Are you saying yes, then?"

Ev squeezed his eyes shut for a second.

"Ev?"

His eyes opened again. He looked scared, but thrilled—happy. "Yes."

Del sucked in a breath, dizzy with relief.

"But—"

"But?"

"I can't put on the ring with you holding my hand in a vise, darling," Ev told him, breaking into a smile.

"Oh!" He released his hand and watched as Ev slipped the ring onto his finger.

Then Ev held his arms open, and Del crushed him against his chest, kissing his hair.

"But, oh—" A fresh wave of tears appeared in Ev's eyes as he drew back. "The ring is *beautiful*, Del, but I—I could never wear it. You know I couldn't. It's a woman's ring, and if I did, people would—"

"You can wear it here, when it's just us."

"Yes, but—"

"It will be enough, won't it?" He gripped Ev's hand again. "As long as we're together."

"Together," Ev repeated. "I feel—I can't put it into words."

"I know. I reckon I've never felt happier. Except for the first time I saw you smile for me—really smile, you know, all sweet like you do."

Ev flushed, twisting the ring around on his finger.

Del touched his cheek, a soft brush.

"It seems too good to be true—that I should get to have all these things I've wanted for so long. I had stopped myself from hoping, you know. And then you showed up and suddenly I felt—oh, darling."

Ev embraced him again, and Del clutched back, reeling with another dizzy wave of happiness.

"Make love to me," Ev whispered. "Hold me and love me and never, ever stop."

"IT'S FUNNY," EV said later, his voice hushed in the dark. The open window let in a few noises—a passing car, voices from another apartment, the occasional bark of an alligator—but it all sounded distant and far away from their tangled limbs and breaths.

"What is?" Del asked, on the verge of sleep.

"I always thought getting close to someone meant giving more and more of yourself. And I found out it's easy to get hurt when you do that, and it made me afraid. But that's not the only thing—maybe not even the most important thing one needs to do, is it?"

Ev was rubbing his thumb in circles on Del's chest, and Del concentrated on that soft pressure, working through what Ev was saying.

"I think you also need to draw out the other person," Ev continued. "It's like wandering in an unfamiliar city—you stumble on beautiful, unexpected delights—a bakery that makes delicious cakes or a little park with a bench in the shade or a house with red geraniums in its window boxes."

"Or you get sore feet and lose the way back to your hotel," Del said, remembering a long-ago trip to Kansas City with his parents.

Ev laughed. "That too. Nothing is ever perfect, is it? But you have to explore nonetheless or else you'll stay locked in the same old room forever."

"You're talking about us, aren't you?"

"Yes. See, I thought opening the door to that old room would be enough. I forgot I needed to walk outside it."

Del mulled this over, trying to grasp Ev's point. "I like finding good bakeries," he said at last.

Ev kissed his cheek. "Then let's hope there are lots of those along the way."

THEY MADE PLANS for a wedding in the first week of June. "A June wedding just sounds so romantic," Ev said, holding his hand at arm's length so he could admire his ring.

Ev also paraded Del around the Admiral's Blues to announce their engagement.

"I still can't believe a sweet boy like you took up with leggers, and I want you to promise all that nonsense is over," Nellie told Del. When he promised he would only have Ev's best interests at heart from now on, Nellie melted into a smile and cooed over Ev's ring. "The ring is a real peach—to think our little lamb is getting married!"

Camilo was there and related all the details of the proposal, which Ev had already confessed to him.

"Did you really think it was a paste ring?" Philip asked, laughing and squeezing Ev's shoulders. Then he insisted on having the band play "The Love Nest," and Nellie and Camilo ushered Ev and Del into the center of the floor. Del put his arm around Ev's waist, and they stumbled through a dance. Ev blushed furiously at a few of the comments Nellie and Philip shouted their way, to the whoops of the gathered crowd. But he also leaned close and whispered in Del's ear, "It's true, though. We'll build a cozy little nest, the two of us."

Del didn't get to see Asta's initial reaction when Ev told him, but a week later, all four of them—Del, Ev, Asta, and Glen—went out for drinks.

Asta knew of a place that served decent cocktails, tucked in the back rooms of a barbershop, and had told Ev the correct sequence of knocks to gain entrance. Glen and Asta were going to meet them there.

"At least it was there last week. You never know with these little hiccough hideaways. A flying squad of Prohis might have dropped in unannounced," Ev said as they walked down the street.

"Haven't heard word of any crackdowns." Del tugged on his collar. "You sure Asta isn't going to try to pop me one?"

"I'm sure. Besides, didn't you say the two of you were getting along better?"

"Yeah, but now you and me are getting hitched."

"I told you—Asta was happy for us."

By this point they had reached the back door of the barbershop. Curtains were drawn over the windows, but lights shone inside. Ev rapped on the door—two short knocks, followed by a pause and then three slower ones. A teenage boy opened it a few seconds later, peering at them and then jerking his head for them to come inside.

"Two more, ma!" he shouted.

A woman carrying a tray of drinks paused. "Evenin', fellas," she said to Ev and Del. "You're in luck. We got some real good booze from a gin jogger earlier today. Have a seat, and I'll have my husband mix you some drinks."

"There they are," Del said, touching Ev's shoulder and pointing to their right, where Glen and Asta were sitting at a table in the corner.

Glen hauled Del into a back-slapping hug as soon as he approached. He'd told Glen about his engagement to Ev over the phone, but hadn't seen him in person since it had happened.

"So you're gonna be a married man, huh? I know you're over the moon about it too, pal."

"Just about," Del agreed, grinning.

"Ev, congratulations," Glen said, turning to Ev and giving him a hug too.

That left Asta and Del facing each other. Asta stared at him a second and then sighed and shook his head, a hint of a smile twitching the corner of his mouth. "Ev could have picked someone worse than you, I suppose."

"Asta," Ev chided. "Tell him what you told me."

Asta's smile faded, and he looked at the wall. "I'm glad Ev has you," he muttered.

A knot of tension uncoiled in him at Asta's words. He knew how much Asta's friendship meant to Ev, and he would have hated to be a point of contention between them.

"Honestly," Ev grumbled, nudging Del into a chair, but he was smiling and reached over to squeeze Asta's hand.

After their drinks arrived, Glen proposed a toast to Ev and Del. When he set down his glass, he added, "And if you're looking for a place to have your wedding, it can be at my house."

"Gee, thanks, pal. Ev, what do you say?"

"That would be lovely. I won't be inviting many people, only our closest friends. Philip's already offered to read the vows. He does know how to play some hymns on the piano, so I suppose he's the closest we can get to a minister."

"Is Nellie still insisting on baking the cake?" Asta asked, and Ev laughed.

"Yes. Of course, I can't refuse, although I can't help remembering the disaster with the coconut cake two Christmases ago and be a little nervous." Ev cleared his throat, looking down at the table. "But thank you—both of you. I can't quite believe the four of us are together like this. I'd never have imagined Asta would end up with Glen." He hesitated, then added, "Maybe there'll be another wedding."

"Ev, stop," Asta said, a warning note in his voice.

Del looked between them, then at Glen, who sighed and shook his head.

Asta put his hand over Glen's. "We talked about it, Glen and me. Even if he loves other women or men, that doesn't mean he's stopped loving me. Why, I'm getting kind of fond of the girl he's sweet on now myself."

"How modern of you," Ev muttered.

Asta's lips thinned. "I'm not having this argument with you again."

"It's not that I don't respect Asta or care about her," Glen added in a low voice.

"And it doesn't mean I'm not happy about your wedding, Ev," Asta said. "You know that."

Ev blinked, taking a deep breath. "I'm sorry. I guess I can't wrap my head around it. If Del—I could never—"

"I wouldn't," Del said, touching Ev's shoulder. "But I trust Glen. He'd never throw Asta and Sam out on the street."

"I know that." Ev threw an apologetic glance at Glen. "I only... worry."

"We'll both get wrinkles, with all the worrying about each other that we do," Asta said in a light voice, and Ev laughed, relaxing.

"DID YOU AND Asta really have a fight about him and Glen?" Del asked later when they were back in his apartment. He was sitting on the bed, watching while Ev applied cold cream to his face in the bathroom mirror.

Ev paused, fingers resting on his cheek. "Yes. When Asta told me that Glen was flirting with that singer, I told him to leave. I don't understand how he can be all right with it. And it's not because I think Glen would abandon him. I *like* Glen, and he's your friend. But if it came down to Asta or...or a normal girl..."

He frowned and stood, walking over and meeting Ev's eyes in the mirror. "Are *you* worried about that? When it comes to us, I mean?"

Ev's jaw worked, and he swallowed, breaking Del's gaze.

"I love *you*," Del said. "You're more beautiful to me than any girl."

Ev looked up again, his eyes bright. "I know. I—I try not to worry over nothing."

"Glen and Asta—I don't quite understand either, but that's them. This is us."

"You're right. I'll let them alone." Ev returned to applying his cream. "It's swell of Glen to let us have the wedding in his home. And isn't it wonderful that I'll be able to take pictures of us? Imagine if we tried to go to some studio—we'd have to pretend it was a stunt, and I wouldn't want to do that. I'd never cheapen us in that way."

"We can get one of the pictures framed and put it on the wall."

"We'll be paying off this wedding for months, but I don't care," Ev continued. "After all, I don't plan on having another one."

"That's good to hear," Del said, and he bent over to cover him in kisses while Ev laughed and pretended to push him away.

A SHARP PIN punctured the bubble of Del's happiness the next day. He was collecting his paycheck from one of the clerks at the station, noticing that there was still no sign of their promised raise, when the clerk said in an offhand way, "Think you'll manage to keep your job?"

"What?" Del said, shocked.

"Haven't you seen the papers? Or heard the rumors? The city council is refusing to enact an occupational tax and so the only option is to let a bunch of employees go in order to pay the salary raise. I've heard anywhere between three hundred to four hundred policemen are going to get the ax."

Del numbly took the check the clerk handed to him, too stunned to answer the clerk's "have a good afternoon."

They were going to fire three or four hundred policemen? But winning the election had been supposed to make things better.

He couldn't lose his job. Not now. He and Ev were getting married. If he lost his job...

He had planned to take his laundry to Mrs. Huang after work, but now he went to try and track down Carl at the East Side station instead. He didn't like going there, as it meant seeing everyone he used to work with, including the possibility of running into Brooks or Kirkpatrick. But he needed to know what was going on.

Luckily, Carl was at the station when Del arrived. He grimaced when he saw Del's face.

"You've heard, then?"

"So it's true? Lots of us are going to get fired?"

"Hopefully not. We knew it was a risk, of course."

He hadn't known. It had never occurred to him, all that time he was working so hard to get signatures for their petition.

"Chief Davis is doing his best to fight this with the council," Carl continued. "We have support in the papers too."

"But why? If there wasn't the money to give us a raise, then why did we ask for it?"

Carl's face softened at his plaintive tone, and he put a hand on Del's shoulder. "It's politics. The money is there, but people have different opinions on how it should be spent. It doesn't help that Cryer's administration is corrupt. Money gets wasted on bribery and funneled into Parrot and Crawford's illegal schemes. It's a tough nut to crack, that's for certain. But the first step bwas forcing the council to agree to a raise—nothing else can be accomplished without that. Now we've made them sit at the bargaining table."

Carl made it all sound so logical. He swallowed down his instinctive protest that he didn't want to lose his job over this—that a lower salary was better than no job at all.

His first impulse as he said goodbye to Carl and left was to go find Ev. But no—he couldn't tell Ev about this. Ev was so excited for the wedding. He couldn't darken that with such troubling news. And what if…what if he told Ev, and Ev changed his mind about marrying him?

For a second, panic seized him. All he could think was that Ev could never know.

Then he took a breath, and remembered Ev saying, *you should feel like you can tell me anything, Del.*

Yes, that was right. This was exactly what he should be telling Ev.

So instead of creeping home, he went to Ev's and knocked on the door, waiting in the hallway and hoping that Ev would be there.

EV HAD ONLY arrived a few minutes ago and was still dressed for work when he answered the door, still in the brown shoes and a stiff collar with his hair slicked down.

"Del, I didn't expect you," he said, hands straying to pluck at his clothes.

"Could I…come in?"

Ev opened the door wider, nodding, and shut it after Del had stepped through. They stood there, suddenly awkward and hesitant. He wanted to embrace Ev, needing the comfort of Ev's warmth, but didn't know if Ev would appreciate it, when he was still in his work attire, still caught halfway between the world outside and their own private one. Except for that one time, when Ev came to see him, he was never in his suit when they were together. But this would be how it would be once they were married. Ev would come home like this every day.

"Sorry, I don't have much to offer," Ev said, moving to the kitchen. "We haven't been to the market. Camilo's been spending more time over with Nellie, anyway. He'll probably move in with her after I come to live with you."

"After we're married."

"Yes." Ev reached to touch his ring, but of course, it wasn't there, and he rubbed his hands instead.

"If you're tired or…or busy, I can leave. I only…" Del paused, nervous again, his earlier doubts returning.

But Ev looked at him and then stepped nearer, returning, and put a hand on Del's arm. He grew softer, gentle now, the clothes and hairstyle immaterial. "No, it's no trouble, darling. What's happened?"

"I..." He couldn't say it.

Ev frowned a little, concerned, and he drew Del into his room where they could sit side-by-side on the bed.

Del took his hand, squeezing it for courage. "I...I might lose my job," he whispered and then waited for the annoyance, the recriminations.

Instead, Ev wrapped an arm around his shoulders and kissed his temple. "Why?" he asked.

"Because of that fool petition." Tears had started in his eyes, from his frustration but also in reaction to Ev's kindness. He scrubbed at them, trying not to go completely to pieces in front of Ev.

"The salary raise?"

"Yeah. The council is saying they don't have enough money, I guess, and so some of us will have to be fired, so they can pay the bigger salary to the fellows who stay."

"And you think you'll be one of the ones who's fired?"

He nodded. Of course he would—probably first on the list.

"Maybe not. You're a good cop, Del. Maybe you don't think it, but I know it's true."

"They say three or four hundred of us will have to go, though."

"So many? That's a rotten job, then. It's not fair to approve a raise only to let people go because of it."

"Yeah." He swallowed back more tears until he could speak again. "I'd understand, if I do get fired, if...if you...if you don't want—"

"No," Ev broke in, fierce, drawing him closer and tipping his forehead against Del's. "I love you. It doesn't matter—we'll get by—together. I want to be together."

"Thank you," he choked out, turning fully into Ev's arms.

"You know what? I'm going to go down to the corner store and get us a can of pineapple. That was my mother's cure for the blues. She always said eating some pineapple cheered her right up—made her feel she was on some tropical beach far away from all her troubles. How does that sound?"

"That'd be swell," he managed, pulling back and wiping his eyes.

The pineapple did taste good, sweet and such a bright, happy yellow too. In the coming days, he tried to hold onto that cheer and not worry about the chances of losing his job. He wanted Ev to enjoy their wedding—*he* wanted to enjoy their wedding, and he couldn't let the specter of unemployment ruin it.

TWO WEEKS LATER, Del was walking past the drunk tank on his way out the door, tugging on his cap and making sure all his buttons were fastened, when someone called his name. He turned and there was Harrison, waving cheerfully from behind the bars.

"Harrison?" Del walked over to him. Although he could think of many reasons why Harrison might be here, he couldn't figure why Harrison wanted to talk to him. The last time they'd met, Harrison had called him a traitor and swore he'd never have anything to do with Del again.

"Hey, Del. Wouldn't happen to have a smoke on you?"

"Uh, no, sorry."

"There was a bit of a dust up at Porter's Café last night." Harrison probed the side of his jaw, which was red and swollen. "Some bloke clobbered me and stunned me long enough for the cops to catch me."

"What were you doing at Porter's Café?" He'd have thought Harrison would be with Barrett's gang at the Temple.

"I know, I know—not up to my usual standards, is it? But I had a lead on a guy looking for someone to help him shift some, er, expensive items of dubious origin."

"Trying a new line of work, huh? Never took you for a fence though."

"I have a variety of talents," Harrison replied with an astounding measure of dignity for someone who was unshaved, collar flapping open around his neck, and stinking of beer.

"Isn't your work with Barrett keeping you busy?"

"Ah, that." Harrison scratched his neck, looking embarrassed. "Turns out you, uh, may have been right about the boss. We never did manage to fix up the Temple, but he kept spending money like it was water. He'd borrowed heaps from some pretty shady characters and finally they got impatient. Last I saw, the Pharaoh was on a steamer headed out of port for parts unknown."

"And Hazel and Fletcher?"

"That dame knew which way the wind was blowing. About a week before the enforcers came for the boss, she and Fletcher cleaned out his mansion of anything worth more than ten bucks and hightailed it for Nevada, looking to set up their own legging business in a town where the competition ain't so fierce. I figure she'll hold her own, but I'm glad I won't be workin' for her."

"I guess I can't say I'm surprised." Even he'd noticed how close Hazel and Fletcher had been.

Harrison sucked moodily on his teeth. "Yeah, well." Then he brightened up. "But hey, I know of a fella looking for someone like you for an easy job."

For a second, he was tempted. If he did get fired then maybe this would cushion the blow. Then he came to his senses. "No. Just no." God strike him dead if he ever got involved in something with Harrison again.

"As you say, as you say. But if you ever need some extra cash, you know Jimmy Harrison is your man."

He hesitated, then asked, "What makes you offer a job to me? When I left Barrett's gang, you seemed pretty upset. I didn't think you'd give me the time of day if we met again."

Harrison reached out and patted his arm through the bars. "Why, sure I was hopping mad at the time, but I've never yet held a grudge. It's not Christian."

It surprised him how relieved it made him feel. "That's decent of you, Harrison."

Harrison waved it off. "Can't change your mind about the job, can I? You walking the straight and narrow from here on out?"

"That's right." Whatever happened, accepting Harrison's offer of help would only make this worse.

"Hopefully not so straight you can't stop in for a drink with a friend once in a while."

He couldn't turn him down flat, not knowing how much it would hurt Harrison if he did. "I suppose I can take a little detour now and then," he agreed. "But just for a drink. Nothing else. And hey, say hello to Jasper for me."

"You bet. He ain't so mad with you anymore neither."

Del had to go, then, but he waved goodbye as he walked down the hallway. He was glad he'd run into Harrison. Not only because he'd learned that Harrison had forgiven him, but also because it had been a test of his resolve, and he'd passed.

THREE DAYS BEFORE the wedding, they moved all of Ev's things over to Del's apartment, with Camilo and Asta's help. Ev flew about his room, harried, boxes and an old trunk scattered across the floor.

"I found a few old bits and bobs I'd forgotten I even had, rattling around in the back of my bureau drawers. I finally found that pair of gloves I thought I'd lost too. They were wrapped in my turban hat. I've no idea how they got there." He was a bit breathless, trying to stuff a pillow into the top of the trunk.

"I cleared more space for you in my dresser. It'll be nice, having all your things there next to mine," Del said, coming over to help wrestle the pillow into submission.

"Darling, I'm going to simply take over your dresser, you know. I might leave you a drawer or two if you're good to me."

Moving Ev's possessions turned into a bit of an adventure, as the vanity only fit in Glen's car if they kept one of the back doors open. Ev and Camilo sat crammed in the back seat, hanging on to it, while Del drove slowly down the streets, and Asta yelled out the window at any motorist who dared pass too close to them.

Mrs. Johnson emerged from her apartment to see what all the fuss was about and watched with wide eyes as Del and Asta heaved the vanity down the hallway, while Ev and Camilo followed, arms laden with bundles. Everyone paused for a moment outside of Del's door while he fished out his key.

"You remember my friend Ev, right?" he said to Mrs. Johnson.

"Oh, yes—from the theater," she said.

Asta made some sort of exclamation and turned it into a cough.

"Right, well, he's moving in with me," Del continued. "We're splitting the rent. Our wallets are both a little too empty these days."

Mrs. Johnson nodded. "You're wise to economize, Delbert. Too many young folks think money grows on trees these days. I'll have to make a batch of my special fudge squares for you, Mr..."

"Sharples," Ev said. "That would be lovely."

They escaped into Del's apartment and soon all was chaos, boxes half unpacked and cluttering the floor. Del glanced in the bedroom where various frilly articles were strewn over the bed and decided he'd best stick to the kitchen for the time being.

"Don't worry, we're planning to go back to my old place to get dressed for tonight," Ev said to him later. "I won't start off living here by traipsing down the street with the other girls in our evening best." Ev's friends were holding a bridal shower for him that evening—Del and Glen were not invited, of course.

"I know. I'm sorry, though, that you can't."

"The reliable hot water and electricity make up for it. And you're not a bad addition, either," Ev teased with a smile. "After I've been here a few weeks, I figure I can sneak about in my curls and rouge—after all, I'm a member of the *theatre*."

Del managed a smile back, although he couldn't help wondering if they'd be able to keep living here, should he lose his job and income.

Chapter Twenty-Three

THE ORANGES ON the tree in Glen's neighbor's backyard hung round and ripe amid the leaves. Del could see the top of a trimmed shrub too and what looked like a rose bush, climbing its way up the fence. In comparison, Glen's yard was in a sorry state, mostly due to the large number of holes spotting its expanse, some of them quite deep.

"What have you been doing, trying to dig to China?" he asked Sam and Greta, who had been banished with him to the backyard.

Greta whined and scratched at the porch door.

"Come here, girl." Del patted the stoop next to where he was sitting. "We can't go inside until Ev's ready. It's mostly your fault," he added to Sam. "If you hadn't started chewing on one of Nellie's shoes, they might have let us stay."

Sam blinked at him and placed a heavy paw on his knee. "All right, I guess we played our part too," Del allowed, removing Sam's paw and scratching his chest as requested. Greta had become overexcited by the arrival of the entire wedding party and run around, barking and refusing to be quiet. Ev, Nellie, and Asta had vanished into Glen's bedroom to get dressed. Del, who had been growing increasingly nervous since he woke that morning, paced the kitchen, getting in Glen and Camilo's way, and when he tried to help Philip choose a selection of phonograph records, he ended up dropping two of them. Then Sam was discovered in the pantry with one of Nellie's French heels in his mouth.

"You three, out," Glen decided and shooed Del and the dogs into the backyard.

Del looked back in the direction of the orange tree, but he wasn't really seeing it. He saw Ev in his mind's eye, on the night they met. To think that with all the people in the world, thousands in Los Angeles alone, their paths had crossed. Del would have said he had used his lifetime's supply of luck in that moment, except that Ev had given him a second chance after he messed up so horribly. Not only that, but now Ev was marrying him and would be with him always.

"I'm the luckiest fellow in the world," he said to Glen when he came to fetch Del with the news they were ready for the ceremony to start.

Glen laughed and pushed him gently inside.

They had shoved the chairs to one side in the living room to make an aisle leading from the door to a side table, usually supporting a lamp but now moved under the window and covered with a tablecloth. Philip stood behind it, holding the piece of paper he'd written the vows on and looking unusually serious. Camilo waited by the phonograph, ready to start playing a recording of the wedding march. Glen walked Del to the makeshift altar and then stepped to one side. Del took a deep breath and turned around to face the door. Camilo started the music.

Asta and Nellie came in first. Del had a dim impression of satin and flowers before all his attention was claimed by Ev.

Nellie's skill with a needle had altered the white dress to fit Ev perfectly, its hem ending at Ev's knees to show a pair of white stockings. A net veil floated from the silk cap perched amid his soft curls. Ev wasn't smiling, but his cheeks were flushed with emotion, and as he drew closer, Del realized he was shaking, his hands clenched around the stem of his bouquet.

Del held out his own hand, meeting Ev's eyes.

Ev pried one hand off the flowers and clutched Del's. They kept holding hands through the ceremony, repeating the vows as Philip read them.

When they had done so, Philip cleared his throat. "I'm not a minister or a judge, but that sure as hell isn't gonna stop me from pronouncing you husband and wife or wishing you all the happiness in the world."

The next second, Ev had thrown his arms around Del's neck to kiss him.

"Ev, you're supposed to wait until Philip tells you to kiss," Nellie exclaimed in the background, and everyone laughed.

Del chased Ev's mouth as Ev started to pull away. Ev was smiling now, radiant, and for his own part, Del thought he might lift right off his feet and float away from happiness.

Ev called for his camera, and they spent a long time posing in different attitudes and lighting, Ev calling out instructions to the person behind the lens whenever he was included in the photo.

"I'll be able to develop the pictures myself, so there'll be no trouble," Ev said.

He heard Asta ask Ev if he could have one of the photographs when they were done, and then Glen was calling for him to come carve the ham so they could make sandwiches. Philip put a new record on the phonograph, and Camilo started mixing drinks.

The cake, baked by Nellie and transported with great care and apprehension in the backseat of Glen's car, came out later, when most of the sandwiches and potato salad were gone. Del remembered Ev had been worried about how the cake would turn out, but the piece he ate tasted delicious, although on such a day, he'd be liable to pronounce even moldy cheese heavenly.

They played a game of Hokum and then charades. As it grew later, though, Philip and Camilo took their leave, then Nellie.

"Maybe we should take off too," Del said to Ev both because Glen probably wanted his house back soon and because he and Ev still had their wedding night to enjoy.

Ev's happiness dimmed a little. "I don't want to take off my dress and veil," he admitted after a moment.

"You can put them on again when you get home," Asta said, reaching over to tuck one of Ev's curls back behind his ear.

"It won't be the same, though."

"I know." Asta gave him a sympathetic smile. "But you'll have the pictures to remember."

Ev lingered in the hallway a few minutes longer, the veil falling around his shoulders, his thoughts turned inward. But finally he disappeared into Glen's bedroom, and when he emerged, he was back in his trousers and shirt. Glen was going to drive them home, and as they walked out onto the driveway, Asta flung two handfuls of rice over their heads, laughing at Ev's yell and ducking back into the house with a wave.

"No petting parties in the backseat, now," Glen joked. "The honeymoon doesn't start until you're out of the car."

After Glen dropped them off, they went upstairs, quiet, neither of them talking, but a sense of anticipation building between them. Once in their apartment, Del put the leftover cake in the icebox while Ev arranged his bouquet in a vase. Del walked over to him as he stood there, tugging a rose into position, and slipped his arms around Ev's waist.

"Did you want to wear your dress again?"

"No. That's all right. Besides, Nellie gave me a lovely nightgown for a wedding present at my shower. I'm dying to wear it." Ev tilted his head back, smiling. "You'd like that too, wouldn't you?"

He nodded. He always loved Ev draped in silk and lace, soft and feminine.

The nightgown was a pale blue chiffon with long lace sleeves. Ev put it on while Del undressed and then sauntered over, pushing Del onto the bed.

"I think we should try something a little different tonight," Ev said, looking down at him. He leaned over and grabbed Del's tie from where Del had draped it over the bedstead, then drew it back and forth between his hands. "Will you put your arms behind your back for me, husband darling?"

Hearing Ev call him that, not to mention the request itself, sure was a thrill. He put his arms behind his back, and Ev looped the tie around his wrists, knotting it.

"Now you're going to sit here and be good, and I'm going to play with you until you come," Ev said, straddling Del's thighs, the nightgown pooling around him, cool and smooth where it brushed Del's skin.

Ev started by sucking his fingers into his mouth, getting them wet, and then curling his hand around Del's cock, stroking it a few times. But then he let go, ignoring Del's groan of disappointment, in favor of peppering Del's shoulders with kisses and teasing Del's nipples with his fingertips. He licked one nipple and blew on it lightly. Del shivered, forgetting that his hands were tied and trying to reach for Ev to pull him down and get him to do it again.

"Did that feel good?" Ev whispered, noticing. He cupped Del's face in his hands. "I love you, so much," he said, and then smothered Del's mouth in a long kiss before Del could reply. All he could taste and breathe was Ev.

When Ev drew away, he was wearing the gentle smile that he only gifted to Del. Ev studied his face, tracing his brow with his fingers, smoothing back his hair, and giving a little tug on his earlobe before sitting back. This, Del realized, was how it felt to be treasured.

His eyes burned with sudden tears. He had never expected—never imagined—that anyone would ever feel so deeply about him.

"Are you all right?" Ev asked. "I can untie you if—"

"No." He cleared his throat and shook his head. "It's fine. It was only...knowing that you love me and...and how much I love you."

Ev smiled again, understanding. Then he shifted a little, squeezing Del's thighs and changing the mood. "I think I'm neglecting a part of you that's absolutely begging for attention."

Del looked down at his cock, hopeful.

Ev fondled his balls this time before stroking his cock again until the tip was wet and leaking his arousal. Then Ev lifted up the lacy hem of his nightgown and draped it over Del's cock, pulling it down so the lace dragged over the sensitive head.

"Fuck." Del sucked in a hard breath, not quite sure if it had hurt or been one of the best things he'd ever felt.

Ev did it again. And again.

Then he took Del's cock in a firm grip and milked his orgasm out of him.

Ev untied his hands while Del was still recovering. Del watched, dazed, as Ev stretched out next to him on the bed. He could see the outline of Ev's cock through the silk. It looked almost unbearably erotic, and if he hadn't just come so hard that his limbs felt lax and heavy, he'd have rolled Ev onto his back and rutted against him, the silk easing the slide of their cocks against each other.

"Well?" Ev asked, looking smug. "How was it?"

He gathered the strength to heave himself up and kiss the smirk off Ev's face. "I'm going to repay the favor now."

Ev's eyes lighted in anticipation, and he parted his legs, inviting Del between them.

He wasn't going to rush it, though, and he wanted to enjoy the soft, pale skin of Ev's thighs. He spent several minutes kissing there, drawing close to Ev's cock but never touching. Bunching the chiffon higher, he kissed Ev's stomach too and tickled his ribs, making Ev twist away and laugh.

Satisfied, he sat up and reached for the bottle of lotion they kept on the bedside table. He unscrewed the top and dipped his fingers in while Ev tracked his movements and rolled his bottom lip in between his teeth, restless.

"I want to fuck you open with my fingers," Del said, and Ev nodded.

"Please." His voice was husky.

When Del had two fingers in him, he found the right angle to rub the spot that made Ev moan with pleasure and push into the touch. He kept a steady, relentless pace. Ev tilted his head back, eyes shut, kneading his hands in the nightgown.

"So beautiful," Del told him and reached to stroke Ev's cock with his other hand.

Ev came with a little cry, a spasm shivering through his legs and jerking his hips. Del kept Ev's cock covered in a loose, warm grip and removed his fingers, waiting until Ev relaxed and opened his eyes. He stayed kneeling in between Ev's thighs. Ev eyed Del's cock, half-hard again.

"Do I get that too?"

"Soon, I promise."

He wasn't fifteen anymore, but it didn't take long. He fucked Ev slowly at first, resting on his elbows over Ev's chest so they could kiss. Ev's cock started to stiffen again too from the stimulation. They changed their position, Ev turning onto his knees and gripping the bedstead, the muscles in his arms flexing under the lace sleeves. Del pushed into him and gave it to him harder, chasing his climax with a few deep thrusts. Then he finished Ev off with his fingers again, working them through his own come, messy and wet, until Ev tightened around them as he came.

Del could hardly keep his eyes open after that, and he surrendered to sleep, conscious of Ev's warmth beside him.

He woke in the middle of the night. It took him a minute to realize Ev wasn't in the bed. A sliver of light shone under the door, though. Groggy, he got up and went to the door, opening it and looking into the living room. Ev was sitting in the armchair, his veil and dress draped over his lap in a spill of lace and silk. He glanced at Del, then back down, running his fingers over the veil.

"You all right?" Del asked.

A nod. Ev's eyes drooped shut. "It was like a dream."

Del went to him and carded his fingers through his hair, Ev tilting his head into the caress. "Let's go to bed. You're falling asleep."

Gently, he took the veil and dress from Ev who let them go with a forlorn sigh. But he let Del help him up and guide him to bed, cuddling into Del's chest once they were under the blanket.

THEY WERE STRANGELY shy around each other the next morning, blushing when they each reached for the salt at the same time during breakfast.

Ev kept his ring on until the last possible moment, putting it in an empty coffee tin and tucking it inside the breadbox when he had to leave.

"Have a good day," Del told him, giving him a kiss.

Ev stepped back, turning his hat over in his hands. "I haven't asked because of the wedding, and I didn't want to spoil things, but is there any more news about the mess with the council and the salary raise? Are...are you going to lose your job?"

"The chief is still fighting it, but it doesn't look so good. I don't know what will happen," he admitted.

Ev nodded and then gave him a quick hug. "We'll worry about it only if we need to, right? I'll see you tonight, Del."

He nodded, watching Ev move away, thinking of the pile of unpaid bills in his bureau, including the payments on Ev's ring. But maybe there was still a chance that it wouldn't matter, and he would keep his job and get a raise, and everything would be all right.

TWO DAYS LATER, when he got home, he found a notice from the furniture store where he had bought his radio and kitchen chairs in the pile of mail that Ev had put by the door. Ev wasn't in the room, though, so he ripped it open and scanned the contents. It was a form letter, notifying him that his items would be repossessed if he missed another payment.

The sound of glass shattering against porcelain drew him away from this gloomy news. "Ev?" he called out, shoving the letter into his pocket.

There was no answer, and he hurried to the bathroom where he found Ev standing at the sink, staring at the broken glass littering the basin. The last drops of whisky trickled down the drain.

"Are you okay?" Del asked, alarmed. "What happened?"

"I dropped the glass. Isn't it fucking obvious?" Ev said in a blank voice and pushed past him into the kitchen to fetch a dustpan.

Ev had seemed in good spirits that morning, discussing plans for blocking the light in the bathroom so it could be used as a darkroom. But now—

"Did something happen at the studio?" he asked tentatively as Ev crouched down and swept the bits of glass into the dustpan.

Ev didn't reply.

"You seem upset," he tried again.

Ev dropped the dustpan with a clatter and stood up, leaning over the sink and gripping the edge. "I ruined a set of prints," he said in a low, tight voice.

"Was Mr. Kee angry?"

"Not really. He said I was still learning and that now I knew what not to do next time."

"Then—"

"It's that it matters so much!" The words burst out of Ev, and he turned to face Del, an angry yet almost helpless expression on his face. "Washing dishes, making soap, all of the other rotten jobs I've done in my life didn't mean anything. I didn't care about them, except for getting paid. But this—it *matters* to me, Del. I want to do well at it. If I make a mistake—if I fail—then..."

Ev stopped for a moment, breathing hard before he continued, "It's the same with you, with us. If I ever did something to break us, I—I—" He stopped and turned away, shoulders sagging.

Del stepped closer and put his arms around him, gently until he was sure Ev would allow it, and then holding tighter. He tried to think of words to say that would make Ev feel better.

"I'll clean this up," he said at last. "Why don't you go down to the grocery store and get us a can of pineapple?"

Ev's shoulders shook in a half-laugh, half-sob. "I thought we'd make it through a week of our married life at least before needing that."

"You don't have to, then—you can lie down a bit or have another drink."

"No, I'll go get the pineapple. It'll take my mind off things."

By the time Ev returned, Del was heating some soup for supper. He talked while they ate, telling Ev about his day.

After the dishes were washed, Ev opened the pineapple and served it. They sat back at the table, and Del gathered his thoughts, wanting to say this right.

"I understand why you feel that way," he said at last. "How caring about things makes it harder."

"And if I lose the job?" Ev asked, staring down into his bowl.

"Then you find something else. The same...the same with me."

Ev prodded his pineapple with his fork. "How do things look at the department?"

"It's hard to say. Every day it seems there's different rumors." He could feel the letter from the furniture store crinkling in his pocket, and he cleared his throat, shifting in his chair. "But it's not all bad. Did I tell you that my intersection has one of the best traffic safety records in the department? Only three accidents last month when I was on duty."

"I'm not surprised. You're very conscientious about the traffic laws."

"They're important," he said, slightly defensive at Ev's teasing tone. "I think we should try this new scheme where you paint lines on the road to show people where to turn left at an intersection. We've got a line down the middle, but everyone is still dodging about, like marbles a kid poured out of a jar."

"You're so adorable when you talk about road signage," Ev said and came over and plopped in his lap, kissing Del thoroughly before he could protest that there was nothing adorable about basic safety measures.

SOMETIMES, THOUGH, IT didn't matter how well you did or how hard you tried. Sometimes, you got swept up in larger forces that buffeted you and tossed you about, heedless of your own private hopes and needs.

On Friday, Captain Thompson summoned Del and explained that regretfully, they couldn't keep him employed, given the current political situation. Chief Davis had managed to talk the council down from reducing the force by three hundred, but at least seventy positions needed to be eliminated.

"Given your record—a demotion and your low scores on the Army Alpha test—we're no longer able to keep you on, Randolph," the captain explained.

Del took it quietly—what was there to say?

But oh, it was hard to tell Ev that night. Even though Ev hugged him and kissed him and told him it would be all right and that he didn't mind it. Even then, it didn't stop the anxiety gnawing at his mind. He'd said to Ev that if he lost his job, he would find another, but how long would it take? All the payments on loans and bills he owed were coming due at the end of the month. He started combing the help wanted notices in the paper and went to see about a few delivery jobs, but arrived to find they'd already hired someone else.

"WHAT ABOUT A job as a chauffeur?"

Del blinked at Asta, who had made the suggestion. Glen and Asta had come over that Saturday afternoon to play a game of Lost Heir. Del hardly ever managed to take tricks and always seemed to end up with the

Wrong Boy, but Glen and Ev had discovered a mutual fondness for the game, so he was willing to suffer through a few rounds.

The conversation had turned to his search for a job—it had been a week now, and he'd had no luck.

"A chauffeur?" he repeated, hesitating with his card in hand.

"Yes. Ev says you always follow traffic laws to the letter. I imagine there's some rich old lady who would love to have you driving her around town."

"That's quite a smart idea," Ev said, turning to Del with a smile. "What do you think, darling?"

He considered the notion. It didn't sound half-bad. "But where do I find the rich old lady?"

"Advertise in the paper," Glen suggested.

"You think I should?"

"Couldn't hurt. I agree with Asta—you'd be good at it."

"You'd get to wear a uniform again," Ev added, sounding a bit dreamy.

Del was about to reply that he wasn't sure a chauffeur's uniform could match that of a motor patrol officer when a knock sounded on the door. He frowned, laying down his cards.

"You expecting anyone?" he asked Ev, who shook his head.

Rising, he went over to open the door and found himself facing two men in overalls and caps.

"We're here from Brookins Furniture, Mr..." The man consulted a piece of paper, "Randolph. I have an order to repossess a radio and four oak chairs as you have defaulted on the payments."

"Repossess them?" he repeated, painfully aware of the others in the background. He'd known this was coming but had held onto hope that he might yet scrape together the money.

"Yes, sir."

"But...but I'd only need another week or two and then I'll pay off the loan." It wasn't true, of course, but what else could he say?

"Sorry, pal, those are my orders," the man said. "I don't have the authority to give you more time. You'll have to come into the store and take it up with the manager."

A hand touched his back, and Del realized Ev had come to stand next to him. He hadn't told Ev how behind he was on the installment payments. What a horrible way for him to discover it. But Ev kept his hand on Del and said steadily, "If you have to take the furniture, can't it wait until Monday? We have guests."

"Can't do it—we've gotta haul it out today. Come on, Henry," he called to another man waiting behind him in the hallway. "Let's get this stuff moved out."

There wasn't anything to be done, short of physically blocking the door with his body. If he did that, though, the men would only call the cops, and the already humiliating situation would become even worse. So Del stood aside, drawing Ev with him.

"Guess we'll have to break up the party," he said to Glen and Asta, trying to smile. "Sorry about all this."

"No call to apologize, pal," Glen said, standing and sticking his hands in his pockets. Asta leveled a glare at the men.

So all of them stood there, in an awkward silence, while the two men tromped into his apartment, hefted the radio and took it out and down the stairs to their truck, then returned twice more for all the kitchen chairs. Several of his neighbors, including Mrs. Johnson, peeked out of their doors to see what the commotion was about. He could feel Ev's eyes watching him.

Finally it was over. Del shut the door, but remained facing it.

Then Ev's arms slipped around his waist. "Guess we'll have to eat supper on the floor. It'll be like a picnic."

"Not a very nice one," he said in a choked voice, trying to get control of himself.

Ev tightened his arms briefly and then let go. "Asta, Glen, I think we'll skip going out to supper tonight. You understand?"

"Of course. We'll head out now—that would probably be best." Glen cleared his throat. "Del, write an ad for the paper and send it along to me, okay? I'll make sure it gets in. We'll have you behind the wheel of a Rolls in a jiffy."

He turned around to face them, managing a smile. "Right—I will. Thanks, pal."

Asta gave Ev a hug and kiss on the cheek and even patted Del's shoulder as they left.

And then he and Ev were standing there, alone.

Feeling unbearably tired, Del sank down into the chintz armchair, now the only place to sit left in the room. "I'm sorry," he mumbled.

"It's not your fault." Ev crouched down next to him and pulled Del's hand into his. "I have more money now. I can help."

"Hell, Ev, you shouldn't have to! I should be able to do it. To look after you, and instead—"

"Look, we'll get through this. All right?"

He started to nod, but then his gaze landed on Ev's ring, the circlet of pearls and peridot perched on Ev's finger. "Your ring... I'm still paying that off too," he admitted because Ev needed to know. "If... If I can't..."

Ev was quiet for a long moment. "Then we'll return it," he said, lifting his chin and meeting Del's eyes.

"What—no! No, I won't have it, Ev. Not that."

Ev twisted the ring where it sat on his finger and then tugged it off. "I love the ring, but it's just a ring, Del. I love you more, you know."

He swallowed, throat tight. "Ev..."

"Don't do what you did before, thinking that giving me pretty things was the only way to keep me."

Is that what this was? Repeating the same mistakes?

"And you should have told me about the debts, Del," Ev continued, gentle but firm. "We're in this together. This is *our* life, isn't it? All the decisions and troubles, the ups and downs, don't I have a right to be included in them?"

He nodded, abashed. "I'm sorry. We'll...we'll take the ring back. And I won't do this again. Won't keep things from you, I mean." He sighed. "Hell, you'd think I'd have learned by now. But I keep doing the same thing, over and over."

Ev leaned up to kiss him on the cheek. "It's because we're afraid of losing the things we love. But you listened to me, and you're respecting my choice. Thank you, darling."

He couldn't find words and settled for hugging Ev tightly.

They didn't talk about it anymore that day, and for supper they made sandwiches and took them down to the nearby park to eat at a picnic table, which seemed more comfortable than sitting on the floor. When they went to bed, Ev fell asleep quickly, but Del remained awake a while longer, lying next to him, smelling the sweet scent of the lilac water Ev had splashed on after his bath. The raw, achy feeling in his chest started to ease a little, the humiliations of the day diminishing.

It wasn't until he woke the next morning, though, that the full realization hit him.

All the things that he had feared had happened. He had lost his position and then his job and had more debts than he could manage. Hell, he didn't even have kitchen chairs anymore. Ev had discovered his lies about the bootlegging and knew he wasn't smart or successful or wealthy. He'd even done the same thing again, not telling Ev about the debts until they'd had their furniture whisked away from under them.

And yet, Ev was here, sleeping beside him. Ev was willing to give up his ring to help clear the debts and make things work.

He sat up, heart pounding. Ev was still here—was going to stay—loved him despite it all.

A last, tiny sliver of doubt and fear that had remained in him since—well, for a long time—disappeared.

He turned, lying back down facing Ev, who was still asleep. Carefully, he cupped Ev's face, but it wasn't enough, not with this feeling overflowing inside him. He kissed Ev once, then again, petting back his hair.

Ev woke, scrunching his nose in confusion, then smiling when Del kissed him once more. "What is this?" he asked, rubbing his eyes before opening them.

"You're here. You're here with me."

"Of course—we *did* just get married, in case you forgot."

"Yes, but you stayed. Despite...despite everything."

Understanding lit Ev's eyes, and his expression grew softer, sadder. "Oh, Del. Still? You were still worried?"

He nodded, then shook his head. "Not anymore."

Ev studied him, judging the truth of his words. "Good," he said at last. "Because you don't need to worry."

He nodded again and lay back on his pillow, smiling. After a moment, Ev scooted closer and put his head on Del's shoulder.

"I think," Del began after a few minutes, and then stopped, not wanting to sound foolish.

But Ev rubbed a hand up and down his arm. "What do you think?"

"I think it's a pretty grand thing when a fellow can be forgiven for the mistakes he's made. When you can get a second chance."

"I reckon that's true."

He put an arm around Ev. "The world can be a kind place, sometimes."

"Sometimes," Ev agreed. "And when it isn't—it helps, having each other."

"And canned pineapple," he added after a moment, and Ev laughed and agreed.

Epilogue

MRS. BASENBOCK PUT a shaky hand on the seat of the sedan, the other clutching her stole around her throat. She inched inside, her frail body almost swallowed by the leather cushions.

"All settled, ma'am?" Del asked.

"Yes, Delbert. I'm quite ready, thank you."

He shut the door and went 'round to the driver's seat, tipping his hat at Mrs. Basenbock's housekeeper, who was watching the proceedings from the front steps of the house.

"Where are we off to today, ma'am?" he asked as he started the engine.

"To my sister's for luncheon, and then to the bank."

"Yes, ma'am." He drove them down the street, turning right at the corner, and then stopping at the next crossroads while a horse-drawn garbage wagon made its way across the street.

"Don't see too many of those nowadays," he commented.

Mrs. Basenbock nodded, straightening a bit so she could peer over the seat and see the horse as it passed. "I never liked horses—skittish things. Of course, you remember my Uncle Rufus was killed when his horse spooked and the carriage overturned. But I wasn't sure automobiles were any better. Noisy, dusty, and terribly fast. But I always feel so safe when you're driving, Delbert."

"Thank you, ma'am. I only follow the laws. It's the folks as don't that make a mess of it."

"Very true, Delbert. Now tell me, how is your lovely wife doing?"

He grinned. "She's grand, thanks for asking. I was proud as a peach for her the other day. She'd submitted one of her photographs to a magazine contest, and she came in second place. Got twenty-five dollars as a prize."

"How marvelous. You must tell her congratulations from me."

"Sure will, ma'am. Guess I shouldn't brag about it, but I can't help it."

"Don't apologize, Delbert. There's nothing more admirable in the world than being proud of the ones you love."

Ev was over the moon about it, of course. They were planning a little celebration tonight, using some of the money to splurge on a nice cut of steak.

"And be sure to keep your uniform on when you get home," Ev had told him that morning, tugging one of Del's buttons, a heated look in his eye.

"Like it even without my old boots, huh?"

"You know I do, darling," Ev purred.

Del had kissed him quiet before he could keep going and end up making them both late for work.

Laughing, Ev had finally extricated himself and fetched his hat. "I'm posting a letter about it to Asta and Glen at their hotel in Yellowstone. I hope it gets there before they leave."

Glen and Asta were on vacation for two weeks, Asta grudgingly agreeing to brave the wilds of Wyoming on the condition they stay at the Lake Hotel and not an auto camp. Del suspected Asta was spending the days on the veranda sunbathing, while Glen tramped around geysers and along rivers, fishing pole in hand.

"They'll be thrilled for you too," he'd told Ev and snuck in a last kiss as they locked the door behind them.

"I can tell by that smile on your face that you're still thinking of her," Mrs. Basenbock said from the backseat, sounding amused. "But do keep your attention on the road."

"Of course, ma'am. Don't you worry. I've got my eye out for cats, children, and streetcars."

After all, that was always how he drove—his attention on the road, and his heart with Ev.

About the Author

R.A. Thorn lives in Northern California, although her heart remains in the Colorado mountains. She holds a PhD in history and enlivened her academic research by always being alert for historical facts she could use in her fiction writing. In addition to learning about past eras, she enjoys hiking and lazy weekend mornings watching anime.

Facebook: www.facebook.com/romanceofthepast

Website: www.romanceofthepast.com

Also Available from NineStar Press

Connect with NineStar Press

Website: NineStarPress.com

Facebook: NineStarPress

Facebook Reader Group: NineStarNiche

Twitter: @ninestarpress

Tumblr: NineStarPress